DEATH OF A WRITER

By the same author

The Man Who Dreamt of Lobsters
The Keepers of Truth
The Resurrectionists
Lost Souls

DEATH OF A WRITER

A NOVEL

MICHAEL COLLINS

BLOOMSBURY

Published by Bloomsbury USA, New York
Distributed to the trade by Holtzbrinck Publishers

All papers used by Bloomsbury Publishing are natural, recyclable products made from wood grown in well-managed forests. The manufacturing processes conform to the environmental regulations of the country of origin.

Seven lines from "Poem for a Birthday: II. Dark House" (copyright © by Ted Hughes) from *The Collected Poems of Sylvia Plath*, edited by Ted Hughes. Copyright © 1960, 1965, 1971, 1981 by the Estate of Sylvia Plath. Editorial material copyright © 1981 by Ted Hughes. Reprinted by permission of HarperCollins Publishers.

"The Red Wheelbarrow" and "This Is Just to Say" by William Carlos Williams, from *Collected Poems: 1909–1939, Volume I*, copyright ©1938 by New Directions Publishing Corp. Reprinted by permission of New Directions Publishing Corp.

"Asphodel, That Greeney Flower" (excerpt) by William Carlos Williams, from *Collected Poems 1939–1962, Volume II*, copyright ©1944 by William Carlos Williams. Reprinted by permission of New Directions Publishing Corp.

Library of Congress Cataloging-in-Publication Data

Collins, Michael, 1964–
Death of a writer : a novel / Michael Collins.—1st U.S. ed.
p. cm.
ISBN-13: 978-1-59691-229-8 (hardcover)
ISBN-10: 1-59691-229-4 (hardcover)
1. College teachers—Fiction. 2. Women graduate students—Fiction. 3. Novelists—Fiction. I. Title.

PR6053.O4263D43 2006
823'.914—dc22   2006001950

First U.S. Edition 2006

1 3 5 7 9 10 8 6 4 2

Typeset by Westchester Book Group
Printed in the United States of America by Quebecor World Fairfield

Dedicated to my parents, wife,
and children,
Nora, Eoin, and Tess

You know what kind of man I think you are? You're the kind of man who would stand there and smile at his torturers while they were tearing out his guts—if only he could find faith or a god.

—Fyodor Dostoevsky, *Crime and Punishment*

PART 1

DESPAIR

ONE

IN THE FRIDAY AFTERNOON lull within the English Department of Bannockburn College, E. Robert Pendleton sat listening to the sound of life outside his window. He had been trying to distract himself by grading papers. It hadn't worked. He took off his glasses and rubbed each lens in the ponderous way he had perfected years earlier to create a pause while teaching.

He looked at the clock again, something he had sworn he wouldn't do. There was a half hour yet to wait before leaving for the airport to pick up fellow novelist Allen Horowitz, whose latest work, an autobiography, had occupied the number one spot on the *New York Times* Best Seller List for most of 1985. Horowitz was in to lecture as part of the Bannockburn College Distinguished Lecture Series, and if it hadn't been that Pendleton was now being watched by the department over the fiasco surrounding Horowitz's visit, he would have taken a drink. But for now he remained sober, at least until the party he would be hosting at his house that night.

Outside his office window, Bannockburn's quad of ivy-covered buildings was again an armada of painted, billowing sheets—Homecoming Weekend, students spurring on a rivalry with Quaker-founded Carleton College, an annual game billed as Non-Believers vs. True-Believers. Traditionally, Bannockburn students held up past scores during the game, while Quakers held up numbered scripture references.

But in this, the twenty-second Homecoming Weekend of his tenure track at Bannockburn, things were different, and even he, tired and troubled as he was, would miss this spectacle, this myth of Bannockburn College, self-described venerable cradle of learning. In reality, the college was a "venerable cradle of mediocrity," accredited academic redemption sold at exorbitant prices to talentless drones of despairing, wealthy parents.

That the myth of Bannockburn could still be foisted on people amazed Pendleton. To an extent, he had been lured by this myth, a brochure with images of honey-lit fall, the season of change, from one shot of a student sitting akimbo against a tree reading a book, to another of a long-haired coed caught in stride, her books cradled to her breasts, to intimate class-room seminar settings, students encircling a professor theatrically reading aloud from a book held at arm's length. Who wouldn't have wanted that?

Pendleton took a deep breath and felt he was watching everything for the last time. He was facing a review by the faculty board regarding his tenure.

The frenetic atmosphere below had reached its climax with the mass ar-rival of parents after lunch, the new cars gleaming against the low-slung sun, pyres of burnt leaves scenting the air in an almost pagan ritual, meat sizzling in oil-drum barbecues as fraternities hosted welcoming parties.

Voices carried across the quad as he rose and stood at the window. An in-tramural flag football game was being contested under the watchful eye of the founding father of the college, an industrialist Russian émigré, Iosif Zhvanetsky, who had turned philanthropist as industrialists like Carnegie did in the early twentieth century. To Pendleton's way of thinking, there were so many demigods in this country, so many men who had clawed their way to the top, then had given it all away, men who wanted monu-ments built to themselves. That was the essential irony of these Bannock-burns, colleges founded by intuitive, illiterate geniuses, men who had come from nothing and gained everything without ever having opened a book.

A liberal arts education was something Pendleton had never fully rec-onciled as truly benefiting anybody.

Indeed, Bannockburn College's history was founded on such an arc of rapaciousness and contrition. Pendleton knew the fifty-cent version by heart. Bannockburn was built on the ruins of a clothing factory along what had once been a half-mile meandering bend on the St. Joe River. The bend had officially become an island when the illiterate Russian émi-gré factory founder had the slim margin of connective land dug away to create a feudal mote. Before an infamous fire in 1911 destroyed the factory and took the lives of eighteen women locked inside, the Russian had amassed a fortune. Although cleared of charges of criminal negligence, the unmarried Russian died a few years later, bequeathing his fortune to the establishment of a women's college on the ruins of the factory site. The name Bannockburn, it turned out, had been chosen by the Russian for an unrequited love he had held for a married woman, Lucy Bannockburn, who had rejected his advances and died in the fire.

The facts had surfaced as a historian collated and gathered the Russian's letters for a permanent library exhibit. The rumor of ghosts haunting the campus led to a dramatic decrease in enrollment, though it was more probably the reality of the Great Depression. The college was similarly fated when the school's library began to tilt and sink into the ground. Seemingly, architects had forgotten to take into account the weight of the books when designing the foundation. Some insisted it had been done maliciously, in response to the growing suffrage movement.

The abandoned college served as a dormitory for the National Guard through World War II and on through the beginning of the cold war, reestablished itself in 1952 as a liberal arts college catering to ex-military granted educational stipends under the GI Bill, and then morphed again in the Vietnam era as a refuge for rich white males seeking to avoid being drafted. The raising of a makeshift drawbridge during the height of the Vietnam draft struggle, cutting off the landmass of Bannockburn from the outside world, remains a quintessential image of Bannockburn's liberalism.

Pendleton knew that history by rote now. He felt a strange melancholy in the pit of his stomach that so many years had passed, that the rave reviews for *Winterland* had been eventually traded for this place. That was how he liked to remember leaving New York, trading it for the seductive lure of tempered academia with its sabbaticals.

The truth of his arrival at Bannockburn was far starker, although even now he was loath to admit the reality. He had lost his publisher at the time, his back against the wall careerwise. His latest work had been rejected by every major house in New York. Three years for naught on a work he had poured his heart into. He had lied to his interviewers and, like so many other struggling job candidates, euphemistically called it "a work-in-progress," though his crisis was different. The book was done. It was a good book, in fact, a breakthrough book, but nobody would let him break through.

The waiting had become a sickness. And then, suddenly, Bannockburn had granted him an interview. Oh, Bannockburn, out there on the plains, an institution blithely unaware of his despair or failure as he interviewed in a downtown Chicago hotel during the annual Association of Writers & Writing Programs hiring convention. Hadn't they seen through him? But they hadn't! He'd ended up getting the job on his past record, on a slew of past reviews, a job gained against no fewer than sixty other desperate applicants, a job offer he wept at getting when the letter arrived confirming his appointment.

These were the facts.

That Pendleton could look back on his history like this served only to make him feel old, useless, and confused. It was hard being honest with himself anymore, to understand the real circumstances of his life. These silent interrogations had gone on too long.

The truth was, all was not as it seemed here, the subterfuge so great, the camouflage of desperation so complete, failure bestowed with a title, with a bronzed nameplate on a polished oak door. It was that nightmare where you tried to run but your legs wouldn't carry you, tried to scream but nothing came out. That was the sort of silence that belied the long corridors of academic ease.

How often had he wanted to confide in someone, to speak the truth, to arrive at least at a semblance of honesty with those around him, or, in his more heightened moments of anxiety, to shout out to passing parents, to warn them off as they came through the college on Open House for Prospective Students. But of course he hadn't shouted, instead posing as one of those glad fellows of learning in the nook of the creative writing offices, reading manuscripts, grading papers, one of those professors hemmed in by bookshelves of leather-bound editions of the ancients and Enlightenment figures with sophisticated names like Rousseau, Descartes, and Voltaire, among tomes of literary criticism and slim volumes of their own published poetry that one could be forgiven for assuming held essential truths.

Poetry was the de facto genre for those who still wrote here, onetime novelists who had philosophically abandoned the novel's bourgeois demand for narrative structure for the whittled creative five-minute exercises of despair, chrysalides of dysfunction, impenetrable, hopelessly self-referential, or concerned with ancient civilizations. Such works were published through a subworld of lesser presses established as so-called legitimate outlets for tenure-track faculty desperately needing publication. It went without saying, though Pendleton had said it on more than one occasion, most notably during an uproarious outburst at a faculty party after a week of rejection letters from such presses, that the editors at these subworld presses were ultimately colleagues, each publishing in what amounted to an inner sanctum of mutual gratification, where the goal of these works had become not so much to be read as to be interpreted, creating a subspecies of literary bottom-feeder, generating a perpetual and self-sustaining machinery of critical analysis.

Achieving mental illness was the highest accolade in this so-called literature.

Pendleton looked up and listened to the faint din of students' shouts muffled by the inlay of stylized Victorian lead-paned stained glass.

A kid with a backpack had his arm slung on the shoulder of a girl in a hunter's-orange jacket and tight jeans. She was casually kissing the kid's hand. How did one become disconnected from that youth, from that ease, from the languid sexuality of hanging out in dorm rooms, of eating and sleeping with someone, of staying up all night studying in the company of someone you loved?

These were the questions spiraling in his head. Was there a definitive day when things changed, when you found yourself on the other side of life? Pendleton took a shallow breath, feeling light-headed, the stream of questions running their course, staring out the latticed window of his office, the crisscross of shadows like a mask, watching life below him, feeling the loss. Wasn't this the muse of poets, lost love, lost time?

So why hadn't he written anything in a decade?

The greenhouse effect of the window made Pendleton hot. He knew he shouldn't have worn the twill wool jacket to work, but today he was confronting his longtime nemesis and fellow Columbia graduate, Allen Horowitz. He needed to hide behind the façade of a professor given to the profession of teaching. If the cocoon of isolation was complete at Bannockburn, or at least if self-delusion could be maintained for months at a time, it was broken in these encounters, in this infiltration by outside life. Unlike others within his department who could publish in small academic journals, novel writing was in the public domain. There was an expectation of notoriety.

You were either famous or not famous.

Allen Horowitz was Pendleton's particular nightmare, a guy perennially atop the best-seller lists, author of eight novels, and a guy whom he had initially toed the line with, way back in grad school, when both had works-in-progress appear in major anthologies. They had shared the same editor and publisher at first, two rising stars, at least during the initial years, then the divergence, the meteoric rise of Horowitz as Pendleton slipped into oblivion.

Horowitz's most recent work was an autobiography titled *I'm Sick of Following My Dreams: I'm Just Going to Ask Them Where They're Going & Hook Up with Them Later*, a work that had purportedly captured the glibness of the modern age in what a *New York Times* reviewer called "a free-spirited journey of soaring individuality and genius, irreverent, iconoclastic, funny, and peculiarly American," the back cover given completely to a shot of a beachcomber Horowitz in an unbuttoned Hawaiian shirt, a string of blanched coral beads around his neck, his hair tousled, his face windburned like that of a castaway. The pièce de résistance was a tropical drink with a paper umbrella Horowitz held toward the camera.

The book was as much about the picture as anything else, or so Pendleton concluded, because he had not brought himself to read the book.

These days he read just the reviews. In fact, he assiduously kept a tally of them with a spreadsheet of who had reviewed whom, charting the incestuous nature of literary reviewing, convinced that the rise and fall of writers had all to do with this tight interconnectedness. That this preoccupation with reviews had sidelined his own work, that it had become a psychosis, was something he knew in his heart but not his head. Having not published any major fiction in ten years, he felt at times like a priest turned atheist who continues to preach from the pulpit because there is no place else to go. He stood up before students day in and day out, discussing the writing process, dabbling in the formula of genres, deciphering how genre worked, deconstructing structure and character, plot elements, tearing apart the seams of fiction until sentences unraveled into words and words into squiggly lines. There were times he would repeat a word over and over again until the word became disconnected from what it represented, when it became merely a sound, rendering the word meaningless, something he practiced, obliterating the world of representation, the world of his so-called craft.

Horowitz's impending arrival had become a flashpoint in Pendleton's life. He had been on leave for mental problems in the past and had been able to take a leave of absence without prejudice. He was safe with tenure. But what he did to Horowitz was something different entirely. It changed the stability that had for so long held him shackled.

The college's Humanities School had agreed to fork out over three-quarters of its yearly budget from the Distinguished Lecture Series for Horowitz's appearance, and Pendleton had been asked to arrange the details with Horowitz, given they were onetime classmates, not that he ever got to speak with Horowitz. Everything went through Horowitz's agent.

Horowitz was getting nearly half the yearly salary of tenured faculty for his appearance, a fact that made Pendleton physically sick, given Horowitz was already pulling down seven figures for his novels. He kept thinking that at one point they had been equals. That was an indisputable fact! Even Horowitz would have had to admit that. It wasn't all in his head, this rivalry. Hadn't Horowitz found out through the Columbia alumni magazine that Pendleton had suffered a medical setback and sent him a sardonic "get well" cartoon card of a raven sitting on a windowsill looking at Edgar Allan Poe? The cartoon bubble over Poe read, "Hello, Birdy," the caption beneath, "What if there had been Prozac in the nineteenth century?" It was signed, "As always, Allen!"

If Pendleton had been fixated on Horowitz, so, too, Horowitz had been watching him.

It galled Pendleton that Bannockburn thought so highly of Horowitz as to front him that sort of money. In the years he had suffered to read on campus, Pendleton had read exclusively to students, either those taking his class or those wanting to endear themselves to him before taking his class. No faculty had ever showed to his readings.

It was the fixation that eventually led him to take his revenge on the school as much as on Horowitz, to choose Homecoming Weekend, the worst weekend in the academic year, to schedule an academic event. Nobody had voiced concern regarding the date of Horowitz's appearance—well, not until the date was set and posters had been printed. It was only then that Pendleton was confronted, but it was too late to reschedule the event.

Despite his feigned air of distress when confronted by the Chair of the English Department regarding the date, it was obvious the event had been a setup. That's the word the Chair used, "setup," as though Pendleton had put out a professional hit on Horowitz.

It was an outburst even Pendleton hadn't figured on, the Chair outlining the scenario, shouting it at the top of his voice. There would be no way the library auditorium could be filled on Homecoming Weekend. No amount of extra-credit seeding or quasi threats by teachers would get students to attend the event. What Horowitz was going to find on arrival was a campus gone riot, painted-faced drunks roaming the quads, a send-up of college life. And though that might have had its charm, in keeping with Horowitz's devil-may-care autobiography, not so Horowitz's eventual humiliation, reading to a press-gang faculty of English professors with a supporting cast of spouses in an annex of the library not big enough to swing a cat. Horowitz was a man who would get his own back in print, or, as the Chair shouted, "This goes beyond some personal vendetta, beyond your own sickness. Do you know what Allen Horowitz could do to the reputation of Bannockburn College?"

It had pained him to suffer this outburst from a guy fifteen years his junior, but particularly from a guy with whom he had held philosophical disputes before. Charles Camden, PhD, was an Anglophile, New Historicist, Edwardian scholar with a phony British accent who specialized in the sexual dynamics of male cross-dressing in English theater. Camden was a homosexual who had only recently come out of the closet, a guy who had been seen in drag in Chicago on more than one occasion, but such was the lamentable way of life at the Bannockburns of the world. Guys like Camden had for a decade been at the vanguard of the humanities, having abandoned the study of the novel and poetic form for the so-called legitimate contention that all societal text was of equal importance. Camden didn't trust intentionality. Ergo, he didn't trust writers or art. Even before this heated exchange, the fault line between Pendleton and Camden had shifted.

In the end, Camden redefined Horowitz's appearance not as a public reading, but as a symposium for faculty. Pendleton was to contact Horowitz's agent concerning the change in focus, while Camden sent out a memo requiring faculty to remain in town over what had unofficially always been a long weekend, where tradition had long been to cancel Friday classes. A dinner party was to be hosted by Pendleton at his house to welcome Horowitz.

Pendleton had faxed a letter to Horowitz's agent outlining the change of focus, underlining the word "symposium." He thought the word would have appealed to Horowitz's ego.

A pall had settled over him. He was avoided by colleagues in the lead-up to Homecoming Weekend. His two prior breakdowns, or "sabbaticals," as the department administration had previously and prudently defined them, were brought to bear again, in light of what he had done. He was asked to advise the medical office on campus of the prescription medicines he was taking. A formal letter arrived in his departmental in-box, voicing concern regarding his mental health. On another day, he was asked to list his recent publications and appearances.

On yet another day, the in-box was stuffed with printouts of enrollment figures for his Intro to Creative Writing and Advanced Fiction Writing classes, the enrollment cap circled along with actual enrollment. His Advanced Fiction Writing class was just above half-full and though his Intro to Creative Writing was necessarily full since it was a core requirement, student evaluations rated him as unmotivated and ill prepared. As one student put it, "Pendleton sucks!"

More forms arrived, with student evaluation scores over the years, charting a steady decline in performance that frightened him. What had he become?

In the end, he just retrieved the material from the in-box and emptied it all into the garbage without even looking at it. If he was going to challenge any board review regarding his tenure, the best policy was to act erratic, not to cooperate, and to fall back on a claim of manic depression. If he was lucky, a sabbatical might be suggested, though he knew this endgame of personal destruction was coming to a close.

Time had slipped by. Pendleton looked up at the clock and left his office. He crossed the quad against the throng of students, going toward the dining hall, where he was meeting up with Henry James Wright, an ex-military, laid-off ex-county newspaper reporter who now worked quasi-full-time for the college, taking pictures of student life as part of *The Heritage Project— Bannockburn Through the Ages*. Wright was the last person in the world Pendleton wanted to accompany him out to meet Horowitz, but the Chair had insisted Wright go along to capture Horowitz's arrival at the airport.

Pendleton saw Wright moving behind the spider of his tripod, catching the Brothers Grimm allegory of the homecoming festival, the yearly spectacle of Little Red Riding Hood—bodiced women with sausage legs, setting up tables with an autumnal harvest of misshapen gourds, squash, and rutabaga around the glazed heads of slow-smoked pigs.

Wright barely acknowledged Pendleton when he saw him, merely gathered his equipment, and both men walked toward the parking lot without uttering a word, though thank God there was a final member in the Horowitz greeting party—Adi Wiltshire.

Adi was waiting by Pendleton's car, dressed prudishly in a librarian skirt and matching hound's-tooth jacket with a ruffled white shirt buttoned to her neck, as was her MO.

Handpicked by the Chair, Adi was, at second glance, an amorous, big-breasted, longtime grad student, a true lover of literature who was known to have tit-fucked no fewer than two Pulitzer Prize recipients.

Just seeing her standing there, Pendleton felt more at ease that this weekend could be navigated. Adi Wiltshire inspired recklessness in men of his age. He was thankful that Horowitz might thus be occupied over the weekend with Wiltshire, that events might pass without incident, and that he might as yet keep his job.

For where was a man like E. Robert Pendleton to go if he ever left Bannockburn College? What would become of him on the outside?

Yes, he was thankful that someone as unlikely as Adi Wiltshire might be his savior. But just to be on the safe side, as he pulled into the regional airport, he turned and said quietly to Adi, "Don't spread this around, but rumor has it Horowitz is being considered for the Pulitzer."

TWO

ALMOST AN HOUR CREPT by as the usual gray-suited fat regional sales reps for food and pharmaceutical companies from places like Battle Creek and Kalamazoo emerged from twin-engine planes, but no Horowitz.

Pendleton was at pains to keep from Wright the fact that he had left the information regarding Horowitz's flight back at his office. Wright paced in the background, his tripod set up for the shot. Pendleton was scared of him at a deep, personal level, Wright with his chain smoker's thinness and edginess and his bristled military haircut. He had reminded Pendleton of a Swiss Army knife the first time he had encountered him at the college, everything about him all sharp edges and angles, the small beady eyes set unnaturally far apart, giving him a predatory, atavistic look of a man more desperate than he was, at least on the outside.

Wright was on his fifth cigarette since getting to the airport. He kept checking his watch. Homecoming was one of the major events he had been commissioned to photograph by the college.

For security reasons, the agent working the counter wouldn't confirm Horowitz's schedule. Wright overheard the conversation and, turning toward Adi, said sardonically, "You hear this? We don't even have the right airline! You want to leave now? I'll take you back to the college."

Adi shook her head.

Wright glared at her. "Why?"

Adi said defiantly, "I don't have to have a reason."

"You think you're better than me, right? I can see it in your eyes, Miss Perpetual Grad Student. Let me tell you, I know all about your reputation on campus."

Adi looked toward Pendleton, who heard what was going on but didn't turn around.

Wright followed her gaze. He started talking louder. "What the hell do either of you produce? What do you add to society? Just tell me that. You know, the professor hasn't published a book in years? He's washed up, a goddamn joke. You name any other profession where you can live out your life doing nothing and get paid for it!"

Pendleton kept staring at the ticket agent.

Wright shouted, "I know you hear me, *Professor*! Let me tell you something. I work for a goddamn living! I can't *afford* a mental breakdown! I got bills to pay." Then he wheeled around, gathered his equipment, and left.

Adi stayed sitting, though her face had reddened.

Pendleton watched Wright leave out of the periphery of his vision, not daring to turn his head. The confrontation with him had been imminent. In the convoluted history of his tenure, he had rubbed so many people the wrong way.

In the fall of 1976, Henry James Wright had audited a course Pendleton had offered under the creative writing emphasis titled The Art of the Novel, a course description vague in its definition, ultimately designed so he didn't have to read student works. It was all theory. It had been, again, during one of those crisis times in his life, another incident in the long litany of provocations into which Pendleton had entered out of a personal sense of despair.

But so, too, it had been a watershed for Wright, age twenty-eight and going nowhere fast, a guy who had worked for an auto-trader magazine before taking a freelancing job with the county newspaper as a photographer/writer covering high school sports and the crime blotter.

Wright had come to the course with a sense that there was nothing else in life for him save writing something great. The military was paying for the course. It was his last chance. He told that to Pendleton. He used that word, "great." He had been candid in his sense of despair. But what had constituted "great" for Henry James Wright held no literary aspirations to his nineteenth-century namesake.

Rather, Wright had been inspired by Stephen King's *Christine*, the story of a 1958 Plymouth Fury that first seduced a teenager, then went on a killing rampage, and by King's *Cujo*, featuring a rabid dog stalking a woman stranded in Ford's infamously fireball-prone Pinto.

Wearing jeans and a plaid hunting jacket that first day in class, Wright had announced, without any sense of irony, simply, that he knew a hell of a lot more about cars than Stephen King.

Anybody in their right mind would have let him sail through their course, and if it had been at any other time in his life, Pendleton might have seen the humor—or, equally, the pathetic—in things and might have played along, but it had been the worst time of his life, and it was to get worse when Wright brought King novels to class, novels with italicized raised letters on their covers announcing things like *Now a Major Motion Picture*, or *Seven Million in Print*, something Pendleton ridiculed as "a marketing strategy as interchangeable as selling burgers, akin to McDonald's signs advertising '_____ Million Served,'" but it tipped Pendleton toward the edge.

Wright, though, had been up to the task and had instinctively captured the exchanges, writing op ed pieces in his defense, not always eloquently, but nevertheless getting to the kernel of what was not merely a philosophical debate, but his very survival, his right to be in the class.

The crème de la crème of his and Pendleton's classroom spats was eventually to gain national notoriety, if an aside in a September 1978 *Reader's Digest* counted. It had concerned an argument between him and Wright over the definition of the word "manifold." Wright associated "manifold" with the automobile, with all the component labyrinthine fittings of the internal combustion engine. Pendleton had literally pushed Wright out of the class during the heated argument as the seminar had somehow ranged from seventeenth-century pastoral Christian-inspired poetry to Wright's detailed drawing of an internal combustion engine. Pendleton, when challenged by the Chair of the English Department, had called Wright disruptive, though some students had glibly commented on campus that it had been the only day they had actually learned something tangible in the Humanities School—how a car worked.

Wright had made his defense in an op ed piece in the paper, though in response, a farmer had countered that "manifold" was "the third stomach of a ruminant animal." At least Wright had the wherewithal, equanimity, and nascent journalistic instinct to include the farmer's response, hence the exchange eventually making its way into *Reader's Digest*, where what was tacitly agreed upon was that nobody used the word "manifold" as "many in number" anymore, except old-time Baptist preachers and, seemingly, academics.

That so much controversy could be compressed into a life seemed to suggest the hand of ill fate, or the opposite of providence, whatever *that* word was, but there were such people, such lightning rods of discontent, people who didn't know when to shut up, when to quit, when to back off.

For Bannockburn, Pendleton had long since become such a lightning rod.

Pendleton hadn't backed off, and in response to Wright's constant undermining of his authority throughout the course and demand that his novel-in-progress be critiqued, he had written bluntly at the end of the fall session, "Life constitutes more than the verisimilitude of mere cataloging of facts. Your characters lack dimension and humanity, the essential underpinning of the art of fiction," sentences he had culled from a letter he had received from an editor at a publishing house. He knew how much something like that would hurt.

Wright had retaliated with a curt comment in his weekly op ed pieces, naming Pendleton directly and quoting the writer's adage "Those who can, write. Those who can't, teach," but he wanted more than simple revenge in print and hinted he was seeking legal advice with a view to suing the college. Thus *The Heritage Project—Bannockburn Through the Ages* had been conceived, in a moment of administrative genius by the English Department Chair, summarily approved by the board of trustees, and offered to Wright. He pragmatically accepted. As the Chair had put it to Pendleton at the end of the incident, "This was just a guy trying to get by in life, that's all he was doing."

But the story ran deeper.

For months after the incident with Wright, Pendleton had received a chilling series of anonymous expletive notes in his in-box telling him he was going to die a slow and agonizing death. He'd assumed Wright had written them, with individual letters, ransomlike, each letter cut and pasted from newspapers and magazines, Wright mimicking Pendleton's latest novel, *Word Salad*, published the previous year.

Word Salad was a slim, postmodern jumble of cut-and-paste lettering that revolved around a man receiving death threats. The protagonist had been mailing the letters to himself all along, or so it seemed, until the protagonist, finally institutionalized, continued to receive the death threats. It had served as a testament to the deep sense of mental instability that had begun to characterize Pendleton's existence at Bannockburn. By 1975, he had taken a so-called sabbatical through the fall. The novel had been rejected by even the smaller presses, though not for the usual reasons. The fact was, Pendleton had become anathema with small presses, since after his tenure he had railed against the farce of what he called "those circle jerk, quasi vanity presses of the foppish and washed up" at every writing conference he attended. In the end, he had published the book himself under the guise of a literary press, shanghaiing some fellow literary outcasts to legitimize the press by becoming board members.

Wright, using Pendleton's own work against him in this bizarre "art imitates life" intimidation, had deeply affected Pendleton. He had kept the letters at his home office, filing them away, showing them to nobody. Who would have believed him? Even he had begun to doubt his own sanity, and after the fallout of his altercation with Wright, he had suffered his second breakdown at Bannockburn, entering another so-called sabbatical of utter isolation spent in his house through the following spring.

Against such a storied background, against years of despair, Pendleton fought the urge to just walk away. The Chair had, of course, sent Wright along to further rattle him.

Using a pay phone to contact the English Department office, Pendleton got the answering machine. He didn't leave a message. He thought if he called enough times, somebody would pick up. The itinerary was on his desk. He was on his fifth try to the department when Wright stormed back into the airport, shouting, "Where is that incompetent son of a bitch?"

Wright had forgotten that he hadn't driven his own car. He kept shouting, "I was due back on campus over an hour ago!"

Pendleton stayed by the pay phone until Wright left in a taxi.

It was already 5:40 p.m. and dark. The airport, a former National Guard building, had the look of a Greyhound bus station, squat and dilapidated. The light had the brilliant starkness of an operating room, tubes of fluorescence charging the air.

Adi sat alone on a plastic seat, like a specimen.

Pendleton called one last time to the English Department. He had his eyes closed. He could see the office in his mind's eye. There was no answer. There were less than two hours before Horowitz was to talk.

In retrospect, he knew he should have scheduled Horowitz's arrival a day ahead of his event, but these were the fatal errors of a man preoccupied with his own troubles. Why had he lolled around his office all afternoon pretending to grade papers when he should have been home setting up for the party? Why had he not taken the flight information with him?

There were no good answers.

At the United desk, there was no listing under Horowitz either, but the agent was friendlier than the agent at American, suggesting the booking might have been made under a different name. She seemed willing to help, but Pendleton didn't get into it. He would just await the 6:00 p.m. flight.

Adi looked up and said, "Any luck?"

"There's nobody answering at the department."

Adi looked toward the arrivals board. "Maybe Horowitz will be on the six o'clock flight on United?"

Pendleton said, "Maybe. . . . Look, I'm sorry about this . . . about Wright. We have a history together. I had him in a class. He said he suffers from post-traumatic stress disorder."

Adi shrugged. "Don't worry. . . ."

Pendleton just nodded. He had run out of things to say. He looked toward the small car rentals desk. A woman was smoking and reading a magazine.

Adi raised her voice. "Anyway, I was busy reading a very interesting book." She was holding up an out-of-print edition of Pendleton's first collection, *Winterland.*

Pendleton's face flushed. It took him a moment to regain his composure as he just looked at the book, his throat tightening. He said eventually, "I haven't opened that in almost two decades."

"Well, I think you should read it again."

Was that a compliment? Pendleton felt his heart racing, though he tried to look calm. He said quietly, "Where did you get it?"

"I checked it out at the library." Adi handed the book to Pendleton, who took it and stared at it as an amputee might stare at a severed limb. He whispered the word *"Winterland"* just to hear the sound of it, a work that had consumed two years of his graduate life. Just holding it brought back a rush of memory, the slur of Manhattan outside his window, the rush of traffic and blare of horns, the babel of different languages outside.

Once upon a time, he had lived only for writing, crawling from his typewriter to his bed, sleeping at all hours, waking in the deep of night to begin again, the sense of competition fierce among his fellow students writing against their phantoms, against Horowitz, writing with that sense of what it takes to make a fellow writer, even a sworn enemy, concede to the genius on the page. All art, Pendleton understood, was written in defiance or against something. It was a line Pendleton had begun his lectures with a long time ago.

The question was, where had that feeling of old gone, that sense of being alive? It was a question that sent a chill through him.

Pendleton closed the book.

Adi was staring at him when he looked up. She had her hand out. "I want to finish it."

Deep within him, he wanted to ask her what she thought of his writing, those old butterflies in his stomach again, but instead of asking her, he said stiffly, "So why the sudden interest in my work?"

Adi shrugged. "I saw that you and Horowitz were at grad school together. I just wanted to—"

Pendleton cut her off. "Compare the difference between success and failure? So did you find your answer?"

Adi said quietly, "Why did you stop writing?"

"Look, I don't need someone feeling sorry for me. Is that what you're doing?"

Adi said again, "Why did you stop writing?"

"Who says I *stopped* writing?"

"Are you writing?"

It took him a moment. "No, I'm not writing."

"Why?"

Pendleton shook his head. "I don't know. . . ." It was a long time since anybody had asked him a direct question about what he was supposed to be, a writer. He looked at her, and she just stared back at him, struggling to answer the question, saying finally, "The fundamental problem with my work was it didn't make people laugh or cry."

"And is that who you were writing for?"

"The reality is the other kinds of people don't necessarily buy books. They get them from the library. At a certain point I asked myself, 'Why write more stuff for people not to read?'" Pendleton's eyes got big. "There you have it."

Adi looked at him. "I don't get it."

"Okay, let me put it this way. The people who need to laugh and cry silenced me. They didn't buy my books. It was that simple, a matter of taste, not politics, an absolute totalitarianism of the marketplace that no ministry of censorship can ever hope to achieve."

Pendleton stopped. He glared at Adi. "You see how degrading an explanation that is? Does that satisfy your curiosity? People didn't want to read me. Tell me, how do you fight that reality?"

Adi answered, "Hasn't great art always been like that? Anyone who cannot come to terms with his life while he is alive needs one hand to ward off despair and the other hand to write down what he sees among the ruins."

Pendleton laughed in a ridiculing way. "You think I haven't heard this before, this kind of romantic claptrap we are paid to tell students, the struggling artist crap? Writing was my existence, my so-called career, once upon a time. It's all I knew, and look at me now!" His voice trailed off for a few moments, then he said with a cold edge, "What's it to you, anyway?

You see an obscure PhD thesis possibility in me? You've been at Bannock-burn how long? You want my notes, my half-finished novels?"

Adi looked away, and Pendleton knew he had gone too far. He moved toward the darkness. A tract of runway lighting burned against the dark. He could see his reflection in the glass. He felt as removed from this reflection as he was from the book he had held. Who was this staring back at him? Why had he lost this opportunity with her? She had seen something in his work, even all these years later, it was still apparent, what he had once been, the disembodied ghost of his former self, his soul. Wasn't this why he had started writing, for that magical transmutation of the flatness of words into something more, for immortality?

If he could have explained that time to her, or even to himself, maybe he could have found a way back. In those days, he had used his own poverty to his advantage, that sense of desperation, disappearing into the swell of city blocks, into a tide of human flesh, seeking it out— anonymity, the thing he feared most. In winter months, he had gone underground into the lurid gelled light of the subway, life flitting through stations, letting fleeting glimpses of faces of beauty or sadness seep into his head, inventing lives for this flotsam of refugees. It had been how *Winterland* had been created, in the labyrinthine tunnels of New York, following the literal thread of metaphor tunneling through darkness. If he could only verbalize this, could he recover, could he find a way back into writing?

A warbled voice came over the intercom announcing a flight from Chicago, breaking Pendleton's thoughts. He opened his eyes, came out of the depths of New York. It was still there in his head, a world abandoned.

Adi said just loudly enough to break Pendleton's thoughts, "I'm going to admit something to you."

Pendleton still had his back to her.

"I want to apologize, if you'll let me. I underestimated who you are as a writer. I took two classes in theory with you over the years, and I never took the time to read your work. I should have. That's all I wanted to say." She said nothing more.

The heat of the exchange had dissipated. Adi Wiltshire was not the problem. He knew that, and standing there in the airport, he was reminded of a line in *A Hundred Years of Solitude*, that maybe men lived for one moment and then spent the rest trying to end it. It was the dying lament of a colonel in the book, a survivor of thirty-two wars, fourteen attempts on his life, seventy-three ambushes, and a firing squad, a man who ended up dying of old age while urinating.

Maybe there was a time to concede to posterity, to be discovered posthumously by a PhD with the insight to explain one's life and work. And for the first time in a long time, E. Robert Pendleton smiled and said quietly, "I bet you are one of those people who carry a library card?" Adi, too, smiled, and in those briefest of moments, Pendleton decided he would do what he had been thinking about for a long time.

He would take his own life.

THREE

Horowitz walked through the arrival gate in the same Hawaiian shirt he wore on the back of his book jacket, right down to the shark's-tooth pendant and coral-shell necklace. An overpowering smell of Panama Jack preceded him, a coconut tropical smell that until then Pendleton had forever associated with spring break, with the riotous lust of adolescence.

Horowitz had no bags except for a drawstring sack slung over his shoulder that could romantically be imagined to hold a hunk of cheese, a bottle of red wine, and one's favorite book. He wore khaki pants cinched with a belt above his hips, the pant legs coming down to his hairless shins. On his sockless feet, he wore shiny penny loafers.

Horowitz stopped and shook hands with two businessmen who Pendleton could tell were going to rush out and buy Horowitz's autobiography.

Pendleton kept staring at Horowitz, at so-called white middle-aged success, at the Hawaiian shirt that belied the frog shape of Horowitz's body, the paunch of stomach, the skinny legs. Horowitz was an approximation of the two businessmen he was talking to, physically, anyway, yet different from them in his Hawaiian shirt and tanned skin. He looked like a guy on permanent vacation, a guy with the answer to the riddle to the mystery of life. There were no exercise routines, no stomach crunches, in his world. This was whom he was appealing to, those harried business types, dreamers of beachfront vacations. Horowitz reminded Pendleton, at that moment, of the bittersweet melancholia of Jimmy Buffett's male menopausal laments from Key Largo, "Cheeseburger in Paradise" and "Margaritaville," and conceded that maybe the essence of Horowitz's message was ironically existential after all. This was, after all, his last night on earth, but the first words out of Horowitz's mouth were sardonic. "So what now, Bob? Another two days upriver by canoe?"

Pendleton stiffened but played along. "The natives have been restless, Allen. It's good you're late. We'll travel better now under cover of dark."

Horowitz licked the tip of his finger and held it in the air. "Touché, Bob, score one for the manic-depressives. You've still got a sense of humor after everything. I admire that, Bob, that *tenacity*. They say genius is born of suffering, of being misunderstood."

Pendleton was against the ropes when Adi stepped forward and without introduction pointed at Horowitz's coral necklace. "Good thing you dressed like a primitive. We can trade your beads and shark's tooth with the natives to appease the river gods."

Horowitz's eyes locked on Adi as she took Pendleton's hand, as though they were a couple, and before Horowitz could respond, Adi said with fawning obsequiousness, "If Robert won't do the honors, I will. Adi Wiltshire, your most devoted fan."

Adi held two of Horowitz's books to her breasts. "You will sign these, Allen, won't you?"

There was a sense of disbelief on Horowitz's face. With her long straight black hair combed to either side of her wide-open face, Adi reminded Horowitz of the coy, innocent devotion of Ali MacGraw in *Love Story*.

All Pendleton could do was act the part of a staid professor at a venerable college where, lore had it, bookish women like Adi Wiltshire, true lovers of literature, were there for the taking; for such were the thoughts Pendleton knew were racing through Horowitz's head.

For his part, Horowitz wished he were dressed in anything other than what he was.

Walking across the cold night toward the airport parking lot, Adi kept hold of Pendleton's hand.

Bannockburn College glowed against the dark of night, an oasis set apart from the small, dying town. A smell of ethanol hung in the air from the plant upwind of the college, giving the air a smell of stale beer.

Pendleton drove alongside the riverbank, heading toward the college, explaining again delicately to Horowitz that the nature of his visit was a pedagogical symposium, that the event had been timed to coincide with Homecoming Weekend, thus avoiding hordes of students milling for Horowitz's autograph. He kept his eyes on the road while he talked.

Adi turned toward the dark outline of Horowitz's head. "This is Robert's gift to you. He wanted to give you a reprieve from fame, to assess who you are and why you write."

Horowitz said frankly, "I think contemplation is overrated."

Adi smiled. "You know, I think you're right. My mother was studying for a doctorate in animal behavioral psychology at Ohio State, and after years of research, she summed up the burden of human consciousness by first asking an audience, 'What if a dog had to think about what all the other dogs in the world were thinking about?'"

Horowitz said, "Interesting, but can you ask a creature that lives one-seventh as long as we do the hard questions? I think age is the key to meta-physics, to the deeper issues of transcendence."

"My mother's emphasis wasn't on transcendence, but on the burden of sociopolitical awareness in a media-saturated world. Imagine if a dog had to know about starvation in Africa, genocide in Cambodia, nuclear prolif-eration, interest rates . . ."

Horowitz made a whistling noise. "Those must have been *some* research dogs." He reached forward and touched Pendleton's shoulder. "You got a live one here, Bob! I'll give you that. Let me go out on a limb here, Adi.

Your mother ate lots of tofu, believed in free love, wore Birkenstock sandals, and advocated communal living? I say she's divorced . . . *twice* . . . but is in a committed Christian union now!" He smiled. "I'm right. Tell me I'm right!"

Adi didn't answer him.

"I know I'm right. You see, I used to sleep with women like your mother in the sixties, dreamy idealists with flowers in their hair. Thing is, they are the ones that fall the hardest, change the most over time, or not really change, exactly, more like they show the flipside of their idealism, which is a conservatism at its core. A fanatic is a fanatic."

Adi looked at Horowitz. "I think you're full of shit! And for point of clarification, my mother's focus was on primates, not dogs. Specifically, her research was on primate signing, on acquired linguistic expression with the intent on trans-species communication."

Horowitz raised his hands. "A noble endeavor, no doubt, wanting to speak to the animals. For a rational, agnostic humanist, I see that as a perfectly legitimate line of inquiry, seeking a sense of universal understanding through a dialogue with apes. If we are all of the same order, why not speak to the apes, right? I'm not knocking your mother at all. What I admire is the exquisite rationality. . . . You know, this quest for a true language has historical precedence. It goes back to the Middle Ages, when there was a belief that newborn children knew the language of angels, but with the corrupting influence of human language, they lost that first language. So some sects carried out experiments where they isolated children from humanity, usually in dark spaces underground, feeding them but never letting them hear human language. The belief was, if left alone, these children would grow up speaking the language of heaven, and so, too, humanity could learn this language. I think that an ironic application of the scientific method carried out by religious fundamentalists, don't you, but a logical deduction from the premise that heaven existed and that all human souls were really spirits made incarnate. . . . So, you see, your mother and the ancients were alike, each seeking a secret language of universal understanding . . . a quest born out of a misplaced nostalgia for the past."

It took Pendleton a moment to realize that Horowitz was tapping him on the shoulder.

"Well, what do you think, Bob? Hypothetically, is it an option for twentieth-century man to hide from the historical reality of where we are now as a civilization?"

Pendleton felt the flush of the insinuation. "If you're talking about Bannockburn—"

But Horowitz cut him off with an unmistakable air of condescension. "I was talking hypothetically. It's not all about you. That's always been your biggest problem, Bob."

Horowitz leaned toward Adi. "I think the philosophers of old got it wrong. The big question in life is not how much pain and suffering can we endure, but how much happiness can we bear. That's the real existential question for post-industrial, agnostic man. Things are going to get better for us. How many cruises can you take in retirement? How many all-you-can-eat buffets can you visit? These are the real issues facing us!"

Adi stared back at Horowitz. "You're joking!"

Horowitz shook his head. "I'm talking about the Garden of Eden, about eternal, mind-numbing happiness. We gave it all up. Isn't that what Adam and Eve categorically rejected, happiness? We know how to cope with suffering, but eternal happiness? Where's the free will in that?"

Adi pushed her hair behind her ear, showing the smooth profile of her face. "I'm not sure . . . I . . ." She hesitated. "I've never thought about things like that before."

Horowitz said softly, "Why would you, you are too young and beautiful." And with a masterful sense of timing, he stopped talking, leaned back in his seat, and began fumbling with papers, as if he were beginning to review his speech notes, while Adi, for her part, turned and sat facing forward, not least because Horowitz had ceased talking. He had left her hanging.

Pendleton kept driving, though he had lost any sense of his earlier victory. Adi didn't look at him. She stared out the window. Horowitz had done what Pendleton had been unable to do, captivate her as an intellectual and, more important, as a man. Pendleton caught Adi turn and look at Horowitz, then turn again when Horowitz didn't look up.

It was a stinging moment of personal failure, and for a split second, Pendleton felt like taking them all to their deaths. How easy it would have been to turn the car into the dark flow of the river running beside them, to wend his destiny to Horowitz, to see him struggle and die, and Adi, too, for only he would have braced for the impact of the car as it hit the water. What would it be like to leave a public always wondering what exactly happened?

He felt they all deserved such an end, all three of them.

They were already late as Pendleton edged toward the crescent-shaped drop-off area of the college library. The area was riot with a gathering of horse-drawn carts piled with hay readied for the midnight barn dance at the gymnasium. It was like going back two centuries. The drivers were dressed in Pilgrim outfits, feeding the horses. For five Homecoming Weekend celebrations, to secure tenure, he had submitted to dressing as a troll during this spectacle, collecting tickets at the gymnasium for admission to the dance.

Pendleton hit his horn, and a horse stomped nervously backward in that high horse canter, its eyes in blinders. The Chair saw the car and ran toward it, as did Pendleton's ad hoc murder of graduate students, a so-called greeting committee of pasty, greasy-haired, black-clad doctoral candidates.

Wright was there, too, camera flashing away. He had, of course, told the Chair about the fiasco at the airport.

True to form, Horowitz was laughing at the spectacle. He tapped Pendleton on the shoulder blade. "Is this a college or a circus, Bob?"

Pendleton turned and, staring through Horowitz, said, "How will *you* be remembered in a hundred years, Allen? What about immortality?"

It set Horowitz off balance for a moment, before he flashed a smile. "I believe in the here and now, Bob." Then he got out and opened the passenger door for Adi with a theatrical flourish.

She was stepping from the car when, in a seeming afterthought, she turned and said, "You're joining us, right, Professor?"

Pendleton said coldly, "Let me try to find a parking space."

FOUR

Pendleton circled the library lot once as Adi watched him. He drove away, his mind already made up as to what he would do. Adi Wiltshire had made it easier for him. He passed along the water again, then turned up a slope toward his neighborhood of old colonial homes.

It was a final insult, how she had switched sides. He took a deep breath. She had merely discussed his book to pass time.

How could he have let down his guard like that, to have answered her questions? He imagined her getting drunk, telling Horowitz, telling everyone who would listen. Would she do that to him?

Why wouldn't she?

Pendleton wound back toward the campus again, past the library.

Adi Wiltshire had gone inside. She had not waited, but he had wanted to see it for himself. If he could have taken solace in the mere fact that he was too old for her, that would have been something, a subterfuge he might have lived with; but he couldn't. Horowitz was the same age.

It was something else, something that had been lacking in him all his life. It was hard facing that truth, or even saying what it was that was lacking, but whatever it was, it had ruined his life. Maybe Horowitz had been right about him. It had always been about himself, about his writing, his problems, his fears. His life had been eclipsed by a sense of failure and want, by a crippling self-consciousness. That was simply it. He had become self-consumed.

Pendleton drove on. As yet his mind was not given to how he would die, just that he would. His foot eased off the gas. It was not as easy as he had thought, even now, with the pain of rejection.

Around campus, the night was alive with shouts, groups of fathers and sons already lit on shots, heading across the baseball fields for the off-campus bars to slum it for a few hours on cheap beer and pickup pool with townie losers. Such were the moments of privileged intimacy, the bigness of America that fathers could reconcile with sons out here in the dim nightmare of how the other half lived.

Tonight there was poignancy to it all. These occasions of Homecoming Weekend and fall break formed a literary genre unto themselves at college writing programs, a sort of mock heroic, stories set against a Hemingway backdrop of shaky alcoholic pronouncements, at hunting cabins or run-down bars, where male vulnerability was laid bare.

Each culture found its rites of passage, so why not here as well? Was it that bad here? There was time to stop this decline. Why didn't he just park and go on in and listen to Horowitz? There was nothing to stop him, but he didn't get out of the car. This was beyond Horowitz now, beyond Adi Wiltshire.

Alongside the quad of women's dorms, he drove slowly, seeing the clusters of daughters and mothers caught in the amber glow of marshmallow roasts and hot cider parties. Pyres of oil-drum fires threw shapes against the dorms. An effigy of a Carleton College player was set atop a bonfire. The mothers were in the perfunctory uniform of school spirit—plaid pants, saddle shoes, oversize sweatshirts with turtlenecks; the daughters were dressed likewise, younger versions of their mothers. So much for enlightened education: Paradoxically, the more you learned, the more you retreated, or, if not immediately, inevitably it turned out that way. Pendleton had been around enough to see it all, from bra burning to the pantsuit, to the linebacker-inspired shoulder pads of feminine power dressing, to this demure nostalgia of fifties soda parlors, mothers and daughters discussing recipes for homemade cookies and ice cream.

Even now he could not stop himself from deconstructing everything around him, yet to be outside all of it hurt deeply. The simple reality was that Bannockburn was a place where fathers and sons, mothers and daughters, were allowed to reclaim those years of rebellious and alienating adolescence, all admitting to mistakes, healing old wounds, beginning again as families.

* * *

Pendleton drove away slowly toward home. There was no escaping what he had given up, and even early on he had recognized the need to find someone, the need for companionship after moving away from New York. He had understood the disease of loneliness, had tried to forestall this inevitability.

In the years of precipitous mental decline at Bannockburn, he had staved off despair with a series of disastrous relationships, the longest a relationship of passionless convenience with a poet within the department who eventually took another teaching position and later published a coming-out lesbian book of award-winning poetry titled *The Oral Tradition*, which figured him as the central antagonist, though he had been mercifully referred to as the rhetorical *YOU* of poetry.

On the rebound that same year, he had begun a semester-long affair with a junior writing major, an upper-middle-class wannabe poet looking for a hurt equal to how she felt inside, a hurt she eventually found in a series of encounters at cheap motels with Pendleton that ended in an inevitable abortion, though she went on to win the college poetry award.

He had been deeply troubled throughout the affair. It had gone on while he had been going through tenure review and lacked a recent major publication. In an eleventh-hour stay, he had secured publication of a dubious work titled *The Collected Writings of E. Robert Pendleton*, merely a fragmented collection of unfinished stories, through a small press, where the editor, a fellow professor at another college, had tacitly made it clear he had expected his own collection of poetry to come out with Bannockburn Press. It was a deal Pendleton had eventually reneged on and the real reason his novel *Word Salad* was wholly rejected by all such presses and had seen him scurrying to vanity publish his own work.

He had shot his own reputation.

Ironically, the only relationship that might have saved him had been with a widowed woman from the Human Resources Department, a woman outside the milieu of writing, a woman who had announced on their first date that she was the kind of person who would go see the movie that was based on a book but wouldn't read the book.

She had been exactly the kind of person he had been looking for all his life. The problem had been that she had come with a past, more exactly a fourteen-year-old problem who turned out to be Pendleton's paperboy.

Evidently, when the kid saw his mother's car at Pendleton's one morning when delivering newspapers, he went off the deep end. The kid showed up on his bike later that night, tanked on cooking sherry, shouting that he wanted to fight Pendleton. His mother's car was in Pendleton's driveway again, his mother in Pendleton's bed. It was that obvious. The kid was fourteen and with the noblest of intentions. He was carrying a baseball bat his father had given him. His father was dead just over a year. That's how long his mother had waited, a year.

Pendleton knew the story. They had been a family. Divorce had never been on the cards. It seemed as though Meredith Spears had done the right thing, but here she was hiding upstairs in another man's house, peering through his curtains, a sheet drawn around her body. Her kid had ended up swinging at Pendleton's mailbox with the baseball bat, then turned it on his mother's car, smashing the headlights and taillights first, then onto the windshield, then the body paneling, before his mother could get down the stairs and out the door to him, until she caught him from behind.

Pendleton had watched it all, seen how the kid had become rigid, then just slumped and begun crying in his mother's arms, and how she, too, had cried. In the end, she had asked Pendleton to throw down her shoes and purse. The car keys were in her purse. Pendleton had been standing at the window. He threw down the keys and the purse and, when he turned, saw her panties still in a pool of silk where she had stepped out of them by the bed.

It was the last time he had been with a woman.

In a twist of fate, the incident with the widowed woman had come back to haunt Pendleton eventually, for in canceling his subscription to the local newspaper in the aftermath of the kid showing up, he had unwittingly irked Henry James Wright, who, along with being photographer/writer for the paper, had managed subscriptions during the paper's precarious flirt with going under. It was something Wright had brought up in a one-on-one meeting with Pendleton when he took the writing course later on, when he was struggling to find a new career. Wright wanted to know why Pendleton had stopped his subscription, why he, of all people, would forsake the written word.

Pulling into the drive, Pendleton saw the dark façade of the house. Inside, he knew his rabbit had again eaten through another electrical cord and tripped the fuse box. That was the sullen reality of his life now, a shared existence with another creature with a death wish. He used the flashlight inside the front door, scanned the dark, a cone of light finding the rabbit compact and trembling beside its eternal beloved, an aged pink slipper Pendleton's mother had worn during her convalescence after a stroke, before she went into a long-term-care facility. It was another story of quiet desperation, the hours a rabbit spent humping its silent mistress. The rabbit was still in shock, its eyes showing red in the beam of light. It gave him the creeps, the air smelling of damp alfalfa, as if the house were one giant cage.

In the pantry, Pendleton lit a candle. He didn't want to go down to the basement. There was no point. A shifting flame licked the darkness in the small pantry. He said the name "Adi" as he found a bottle of vodka along with his sleeping pills next to an unopened bottle of vitamins in the cupboard. It was her rejection that hurt most. He wanted to deny it, but it was there, at the edge of consciousness, that sense of hurt.

Still, he kept his promise, got a pen from the living room, passed the rabbit again, and went back into the kitchen. Adi Wiltshire would get a thesis yet from his work and notes. His hand was shaking as he made his last will and testament by candlelight, bequeathing everything to her. He signed his name one last time in the looping script he had perfected so long ago in the hope of signing autographs.

He stood up and opened the refrigerator, suddenly caught in the brilliant cleanness of its light. The refrigerator was on a different circuit. It struck him as strangely spiritual, like that light people talked about on the other side. He got out a sweating carton of orange juice, then shut the refrigerator, his shadow amplified and distorted in the candlelight behind him.

He tasted salt in his mouth. Evidently he was crying, but without sound, as he tipped the pill bottle into the cup of his hand and began eating the pills, washing them down with alternate swigs of vodka and gulps of orange juice.

At times he coughed and spluttered. He had to stop and catch his breath, then pour more pills into his hand, fisting them and bringing them to his mouth. His throat tightened.

He drank more vodka, washing down the pills, a vague warmth at the back of his throat, then he drank straight from the sweating carton of juice until it was empty.

As yet he felt nothing, or not that he could tell, though he was aware of his heart in his chest. It was done, nearly over, this indeterminacy, this failure, so he waited.

Time passed. He felt a sudden coldness and shivered, closed his eyes, then surfaced again. Through a small window in the pantry, the moon dimmed, brightened, dimmed, then was lost to darkness for a few moments. He was becoming weightless, without limbs, everything becoming dreamlike, a slow slippage out of consciousness. He felt his head tip, caught it. There was a dull pressure at the base of his skull, but not pain, a slight vertigo of tumbling through space. He tried to reach for the bottle of pills again, but his hand didn't move.

He felt tired now, his breath shallow, but he wasn't scared. It's how he had imagined it, a sense of peace, like those final lines at the end of writing a novel, when the hard work had been done, as the head began to rise and look elsewhere, to another life, to a different story.

It was passing with that lightness, with that sense of closure, and for E. Robert Pendleton the question simply, Why he had waited so long to end it?

FIVE

IT WAS DURING HOROWITZ'S loquacious banter in the faculty alcove, as he was flitting from the familiar to the erudite, that Pendleton slowly started to fade in the flickering darkness of his kitchen, and if there were such a phenomenon as clairvoyance, then Adi Wiltshire experienced it at that moment, an intuitive sense that Pendleton was doing something terrible to himself. It's what drew her away from the hall.

As she went to phone Pendleton, the Chair, suitably satisfied that his damage control had worked in hoodwinking Horowitz, caught sight of her. He asked her to head out to Pendleton's to make sure everything was ready for the party. It was the last hurdle in managing Horowitz.

Wright, standing off to the side, smoking as always, came forward and offered to drive Adi, something she couldn't necessarily refuse, since Wright made a comment about drinking and driving. He was a reformed alcoholic.

The Chair, oblivious to the tension in Adi's face, simply concurred and walked them to Wright's car, saying enigmatically to Adi, "Keep Bob happy, no matter how you have to do it."

Even Wright caught the inference and smiled. Men, even the most avowed poets and writers, were braggarts at their heart. Her reputation had been sealed in acts of kindness, in acts of mercy.

A quiet prevailed in the journey to the house, the college receding in the side-view mirror as Adi consciously tried to ignore Wright, who, it seemed, lived out of his car: The front was littered with fast-food wrappings and condiments along with camera equipment and rolls of film.

The car was old, one of those late sixties models of Detroit's glory years, the proverbial living room on wheels, a fortress of the highway. A forty-eight-ounce jumbo cup from 7-Eleven set in a plastic holder added to the enormity of scale.

Adi drove a Honda Civic.

Wright was the first to break the stalemate. "So, how much do you think Horowitz is worth?"

Adi shifted. "I don't know." She felt uncomfortable, her hands demurely in her lap, as if this were some bad blind date.

"Come on, I figure maybe five . . . ten million? What do you think?"

Wright took a drink from the jumbo cup, a flat cherry-flavored Dr Pepper, his all-time favorite drink. "Come on, guess."

"I really wouldn't know. I couldn't guess."

"That stuff doesn't interest you?"

Adi shook her head.

"So what does interest you?"

Adi didn't answer.

Wright said bluntly, "Do I interest you? I write, and I'm a great lover of literature. See . . . we have that in common. Do you like Stephen King?"

"I've never read him."

Wright drummed his hands on the steering wheel. "How come everyone's so prejudiced against King when they've never read him? You know, I think he's the most important figure in American culture. He's the new gothic. Gothic is good, right? You should read him. I really think you should."

Adi tried to change the subject. "You sure you know where we're going?"

Wright kept talking. "For me, King is Emily Dickinson with balls, Emily Dickinson if she got the hell out of her house and lived in the real world."

When Wright turned and smiled and breathed on Adi, she smelled the sickly sweet taste of the Dr Pepper on his breath.

Adi rushed out of the car as soon as it came to a stop, leaving Wright in her wake. The house was in total darkness, though Pendleton's car was in the drive, a simple fact that registered with Adi. Where was he?

Adi rang the bell. No answer. She turned the door handle, and the front door opened slowly. Tentatively she called out, "Are you there, Professor?"

Standing in the doorway, she waited, called out again, scanning the lower floor, her attention drawn to the cavernous dimension of the living room, a gleam of streetlight catching a silver tray of plastic-wrapped sandwiches, and then another tray, and another, a gray banquet of catered and crackers and pastries and bowls of dip.

Adi moved farther into the hallway, stopped at the wooden post of the staircase, and called out again, "Professor!"

Still no answer.

Then, turning, she became aware of a seam of light under a doorway at the end of the long dark hallway leading to the back of the house.

Slowly, Adi moved toward it. There was a scraping noise on the other side of the door when she got to it.

"Professor . . . ," Adi whispered, her hands shaky with hesitation before she opened the door slowly on a small grotto of candles burning a soft orange hole in the dark.

It took her eyes time to adjust, to see a bottle of vodka on the table along with the carton of orange juice, to make out the small vial of pills, to process everything, until finally her eyes found the slumped figure of Pendleton facedown on the ground beside the table.

It was at the exact moment Adi screamed that Wright took his first of many rapid shots, the camera flash charging the room with a storm of lightning brilliance as he caught her just so, frozen, standing over Pendleton, her face turned, taut with anguish and fright, her hand toward the camera, shunning the light, a series of shots capturing her every move.

Hours later, when developing the shots in his darkroom, Wright saw a pair of eyes emerge, burning in the extreme upper corner of the photographs, red eyes of something unearthly, some enigmatic crouching incubus—some spirit.

Under closer inspection, the glowing red eyes were just barely recognizable, if one knew what one was looking for, as the compact form of Pendleton's rabbit atop the refrigerator, although Wright, as he developed the shot, darkened the image of the rabbit to the point of obscurity so only the eyes showed.

It became one of the most haunting of images that captured the tragic despair, captioned by Wright, who had simply titled the shot "Death of a Writer."

SIX

PENDLETON SURVIVED THE SUICIDE attempt, kept alive for three months in a limbo of modern medicine, a nightmare one wouldn't inflict on murderers. It was after Christmas break, amid the beginning of a blizzard, when Adi got the call she had been dreading.

Pendleton's eyes were open.

Adi hugged herself, standing in the gray oblong hallway, still holding the telephone in her hand, Pendleton's forlorn rabbit watching her, the security of the past months over. Her secret wish since he had gone comatose had been that he die quickly, but he had lingered.

But now Pendleton was awake.

Adi had moved into Pendleton's house at the beginning of Christmas break, becoming a spectral ghost, a silent figure inhabiting his former world, caretaker to his life, to his house, to his work.

Somehow, Wright's shot of her standing over Pendleton had imbued her with a sense of guardianship over his life, and emboldened by his letter bequeathing his work to her, she had moved in, started work on her thesis. She felt she had gained a measure of atonement. What was strange was that after seven years of floundering through grad school, she had found a sense of dual purpose in his attempted suicide: honoring Pendleton while achieving what had previously been so elusive, the completion of her thesis.

But what now? In the latticed windows of the old houses, she stared out into the world that had become so familiar to her. This was real life, suburbia, the stolidity of these homes, the canopy of trees, the raking of leaves, the burden of lawns, of house repairs, the changing of summer screens for storm windows, fathers on ladders in flannel shirts.

It was something she had missed out on, her childhood ruined in a social experiment of liberal idealism, her parents, nomadic academics, pseudocultural anthropologists ranging in studies from clinical human psychology to animal behavior, grad school hangers-on at Ohio State who never did get their doctorates.

In a way, the trajectory of her life up to that point had been hauntingly similar: She was in her seventh year at Bannockburn, a graduate student going nowhere, though her fixation had been in literature, not science, in the permanence of great books, hers a story of an intellectual fascination with writers gone awry that had become caricature and lore on campus. Through her twenties at Bannockburn, in the stalling sense of never arriving at a specific thesis, a real focus, she had instead become a generalist, an avid reader. She had become infamous in the ghetto of literary fiction to a horde of underpaid, underappreciated writers of substance who had gone under the ludicrous, euphemistic umbrella of so-called Great Young Voices. They were all forty-somethings, vagabond intellectuals giving lectures, writers who had forgone teaching to write, the chasm of bankruptcy looming for most, the carrot of the Pulitzer and National Book Award there, sadly, for one writer alone each year. In her, writers had found solace in a campus muse, in the fact she had read their work. They had shadowed her at departmental parties hosted in their honor and ended up with her at the campus hotel, encounters that had found their way into more than a novel or two, mostly postcoital reflections on aging, one such encounter ending up in a novel that went on to win a Pulitzer.

It was strange that this feeling of renewed life she had yearned for had been bestowed by a man who had tried to kill himself.

In her mind, during the months of Pendleton's coma, she had thought of the house as her own, seen herself as a widow inhabiting the silence of a life once shared. The stark memory of finding Pendleton unconscious had become less troubling each time she had entered the house, replaced with a sense of the familiar.

But now it was ending. She kept coming back to that reality.

Adi stared along the hallway at Pendleton's *New Yorker* cartoon poster, "A New Yorker's View of the World!" Beyond the cartoon rise of New York's skyline, there was nothing but horizon. It defined him. His dream sat here, in the no-man's-land of the hallway by the coatrack.

Her thesis would have contained these images, glimpses into Pendleton's ironic and bittersweet betrayal, along with reference to his poster, in a closet-size toilet off the pantry of the paranoid character played by Robert De Niro in *Taxi Driver*. There had been something elegiac for her in the gathering of his material, in capturing his long decline at Bannockburn. There had been an arc to her thesis, the pathos of initial genius, from the splendor of *Winterland*, to the fragmented sham of *The*

Collected Writings of E. Robert Pendleton, to the postmodern surrealism and metaphysical crisis at the heart of *A Hole Without a Middle*, to the mental crisis at the heart of *Word Salad*.

She had uncovered in his office the haunting, starkly psychotic, death threat, ransomlike cutout letters he had obviously mailed to himself while writing *Word Salad*. It had been a chilling discovery, a view into the self-delusion or method acting he had adopted to continue writing, and indeed, Adi had cross-referenced the publication of *Word Salad* to Pendleton's so-called sabbatical in 1975, seeing the emotional strain he had been under. It was a book that had augured his eventual decline, his flagging desire as an artist, until his attempted suicide, until his *death*.

That's what she had really needed to complete the thesis—his death.

But what now that he had awakened? What now, when he discovered it had been Adi who had foiled his death?

Adi went back up into the rounded enclosed turret of Pendleton's office atop his house. She could see Bannockburn in the distance. She felt shaky. Snow had reduced the world to a two-dimensional flatness. A scar of black river cut through the white world, demarcating the perimeter of Bannockburn. The small AM radio was issuing a storm advisory. The historic district had already taken on an alpine, gingerbread appearance in a series of storms over the break, the fire hydrants having long disappeared under drifting snow.

The escape and fantasy of living in Pendleton's house was passing. Adi felt that in her heart. She had to move on from here this year, get her thesis submitted. She was in a race against time. Another year of failure would see her drop out of the program. She was already marked by the undergrads as a failure. In a way, too, her association with Pendleton had marked the end, the unspoken rumors: Why had Pendleton bequeathed his work to her?

It was as she was sorting through Pendleton's notes in the living room, her mind made up on leaving and moving back into her apartment, that the electricity went out in one of those snowstorms defining winter's presence, making summer such a remote and distant memory.

She stopped in the darkness, kneeling over the various piles, and felt truly alone. She stood up. The lights were off everywhere. Even Bannock-burn was invisible.

The room was freezing. She had deliberately kept the heat low over the last few months to save money and had taken to wearing shapeless, heavy sweaters, but now her breath showed in the cold.

Adi listened as the giant mouth of the fireplace whistled in the pull of wind, in the coming storm, a backdraft of snow forced downward, charging the air with a faint hoary crystalline luminescence. She hugged herself, went to turn up the thermostat in the hallway, and found it wasn't working.

In the kitchen drawer, she removed a plastic bag of votive candles, turned on the gas stove, and lit the candles from the blue crown of gas flame. The heat felt good against her hands and face, made her aware of just how cold the house had become.

The votive light threw shadows into the recesses of an unfinished base-ment as the stairs creaked under the pressure of her tentative steps, the place filled with sundry items. A ghostly table and chairs were draped with a cloth. A drift of snow swirled and eddied where a window had broken, a whistling sound that came and went.

The furnace was set next to the brick chimney that served the four fire-places in the house. A series of insulated ducts ran upward, following the line of the chimney before snaking off toward the various levels of the house.

Adi flicked a red reset switch, and a click reignited the pilot light. A moment later the furnace shuddered in a subterranean *woof* of combus-tion. At a vague level, she felt proud of coming down here alone and ac-complishing this task.

It was a short-lived feeling. The flame went out again. It didn't catch a second time.

It was as she was going back upstairs that the candlelight passed over a box of books tucked under the staircase. Lowering the light into the recess under the stairs, she squatted, then brought the light closer still.

It was a box from a publishing house. Inside the box was an invoice from a printing press, and underneath, wrapped in plastic, were hard-bound books, the title of the books all the same, *Scream*, and below the title the name E. Robert Pendleton.

It was a book she had never known Pendleton had written.

SEVEN

A GAINST A WORLD OF falling snow, in the quiet of the kitchen, Adi stood in the whispered bluish glow of a lit stove burner. In her immediacy to Pendleton's work, she had never even checked on Pendleton in the card catalog at the library, assuming all she had needed was here in his office. All his publications had been set on a shelf over his desk.

The books had obviously been hidden away, or so it seemed. On Pendleton's CV, updated not four months before his attempted suicide, there was no mention of the novel. It had been mysteriously omitted.

Adi retrieved a book. It was thick, over four hundred pages. She checked the title page. The novel had been published by a small academic press in 1977. The cover depicted the shadowy figure of a man in a professorial tweed jacket, staring from a window toward a dome in the distance, toward what was unmistakably Bannockburn College, and at second glance, the shadow figure, undoubtedly, was Pendleton.

Under the title was a brief extract from the book and an accompanying blurb:

> "I did not want to hurt the girl. She was an innocent. I thought so up to the moment I slit her throat."

> E. Robert Pendleton delivers a virtuoso, existential nightmare of chilling genius.
>
> —Malcolm Hintz

The quote gave Adi goose bumps.

Early on, in sorting through Pendleton's notes, she had come across a large manila envelope of clippings and photocopies of articles related to the gruesome discovery of the body of a local thirteen-year-old girl, Amber Jewel. Was this a book he had written about the case? If so, if he had written something of this depth, some four hundred pages, and published it, why omit the book from his CV?

In macabre fashion, sitting within a circle of votive candles with the fire ablaze, Adi began reading *Scream*, while the world was held in the limbo of the storm. Through the night, as she read, *Scream* proved to be a marked dark departure from Pendleton's previous work.

She saw why Pendleton had hidden the book.

The novel marked the turning point in his mental deterioration, his movement toward true insanity. Unlike *A Hole Without a Middle* or *Word Salad*, *Scream* was an autobiographical, existentialist nightmare, wholly personal. In a way, it was the piece of the thesis she needed, the self-reflective sense of personal crisis. It was a novel about professorial failure, an aging novelist living out existence in obscurity at a small college, while an archrival went on to fame and fortune. There was no doubt as to what and whom Pendleton was writing about—his own specific crisis at Bannockburn.

The protagonist introduced himself as, simply, *Professor*, initially italicized for effect, and Adi thought of how she had called Pendleton "Professor" as she got out of the car with Horowitz.

It chilled her, the sense of vitriolic self-hatred that characterized the first third of the book, rendered in a simple, declarative style that caught a lucid sense of failure, the simple accretion of disasters both professional and personal. She had heard about some of the episodes over the years, especially the rows with the Chair, Pendleton detailing in the book a succession of uproarious arguments with faculty, often without even the foil and legal protection of changing names, speaking with a sense of desperation and professional suicide.

Adi had come to understand this was a man who had truly wanted to die for a long time. The bitter irony that he had failed to end his life echoed against the words within *Scream*. At times, she looked up from the shifting light of the fire and candles as they flickered and eventually faded out.

Standing in the dark between the hallway and the pantry, she listened to a grandfather clock ticking off time, wanted to feel a sense of cold, to surface from the pages of Pendleton's nightmare.

Then she put another log on the fire so the room came up in shadows, lit another circle of candles, and kept reading—the room a glowing eye amid the storm.

Scream's introspective chronicle of personal disintegration took a turn, in a strange sequence of events first hinted at on the cover, as Pendleton's Professor moved from the abstract idea of challenging the notion of God philosophically to a planned "chance" encounter and senseless murder of a random young girl.

The notion of a random killing aligned again with material Adi had discovered in Pendleton's office, in a book entitled *The Crime of the Century: The Leopold and Loeb Case*, a book she had initially assumed had been used in Pendleton's research for *Word Salad*.

The book had centered around the infamous 1924 case of two teenage Jews, Leopold and Loeb, who had committed a brutal and senseless murder after reading Friedrich Nietzsche's theory on the "Superman," believing that they, as Supermen, had the moral freedom and right to violate the rules and laws governing ordinary man. To that end, to prove their moral superiority, they had planned the random selection and murder of a victim, a crime that would leave no clues, what the perpetrators called "the perfect murder."

Now, Adi understood, *The Leopold and Loeb Case* fitted more exactly with *Scream*. The murder of such an innocent, someone of such vulnerable age, the perfect metaphor, a random act charged with an arbitrariness challenging the existence or nonexistence of God. Pendleton had taken real life and transmuted it into literature.

As the narrator put it:

> In deep winter, with the light of the world eclipsed in darkness, I set about my God test, as assuredly and sanely as God tested the biblical Abraham. I sought out a yellow school bus in the afternoon after class. I drove at a

distance behind it. Girls got off at different stops. For various reasons, I let them go. I was waiting for someone special. She was riding in the back of the bus. She had a sweet face. She gave me the finger at one stage.

Adi sat up and kept reading as Pendleton's thinly veiled alter ego drove alongside the girl, trying to coax her into the car, before he simply ran her down, though he hit only her left leg. The girl struggled to her feet, already in shock, limping toward the cornfields like a wounded animal, the car following. The Professor stopped and got out.

What unfolded was a shocking, slow, and detailed description of the girl's death. The sheer clarity of the scene chilled Adi. At a certain point, the girl, knowing she was going to die, took out a pen from her school bag, her sole weapon, and used it as a literal weapon against her attacker, fought off the Professor with her pen, before he slit her throat.

What Pendleton had done was take a missing thirteen-year-old as his muse, borrowing from the newspaper accounts, projecting the horrors to which the child had been subjected by her abductor onto his own issues. It was a shocking indictment against his sense of propriety to have used the real-life case of a pubescent thirteen-year-old, but in a way, it reminded Adi of Nabokov's *Lolita*, the willingness to use such a taboo figure.

But of course, that had been the point.

EIGHT

TWO WEEKS LATER, PENDLETON sat in a chair for the first time, but there was no sense of recognition of where he was, or who he was, or what had happened to him. He had regained the ability to look at people as they entered the room, though it seemed a reflexive reaction, and he simply turned away each time to stare again out of the window he was set in front of each day.

It was established he had suffered a massive stroke during his attempted suicide. The prognosis was pessimistic and summed up by a neurologist who described him as neurologically lobotomized. Adi noted the deficits, Pendleton's unfocused gaze, how the right side of his face was more affected, pulled down by gravity. His right eyelid had begun to droop. His mouth turned downward, and a perpetual trail of drool glazed his chin, making it red and irritated. His sentences, when he spoke, were mere words concerned with primitive needs, slurred words like "eat," "cold," "drink."

Each day, Adi faced the fact that she had, at some level, done this to Pendleton, betrayed him on the evening he had been driven to attempting suicide by going over to Horowitz's side, and when she went home, she recalled the photograph Wright had taken of her standing over Pendleton, her arms outstretched toward the camera.

Somehow, Wright, in a single instant, had caught the sheer anguish and guilt she had felt deep down that night, the feeling that had drawn her from the auditorium to seek him out.

Pendleton suffered a bout of pneumonia in late January, and for a time it seemed as though he would die; but he survived, pumped full of antibiotics, and the nightmare of modern medicine prevailed.

The coldness of winter persisted, the campus walks becoming labyrinthine mazes. Everybody wore masks or scarves, faceless, hunched entities moving between buildings. A ceramic blue sky augured a subzero cold.

It went down to minus twenty in mid-February.

Adi was left to herself in this deep freeze and, despite everything, reached a new contentment. In the afternoons, she took to watching the cool wintry light settle against the carriage house out back of Pendleton's garden. She ate within her budget, mostly scrambled eggs or noodles. This had become her house again, her world. Even Pendleton's forlorn rabbit, with his pink slipper, had come to trust her, to count on her for his survival.

Two weeks after Pendleton's awakening, Adi had arrived at the hospital to find Wright sitting beside Pendleton, Wright talking earnestly with a pained expression on his face. Atonement was something she hadn't figured existed in the heart of a guy like Wright, but there he was holding Pendleton's hand, leaning toward him.

As Adi went into the room, Wright simply stood up. He had the negatives from the photos back at his house. He said he wanted the professor to have them. He talked between Pendleton and Adi as though he weren't sure what Pendleton did and did not understand.

Later that week, true to his word, Wright arrived with the negatives, along with a copy of *Carrie*, King's novel about a tormented adolescent who had her first period in a shower during gym class and who eventually harnessed supernatural powers of telekinesis—the ability to move objects—to kill those who had ridiculed her all her life.

Ironically, Adi had seen the movie but not read the book—the opposite of Wright, who had just read the book and not seen the movie. It made for a momentary icebreaker between them, though the permafrost of social distance remained and was underscored when Wright said, as the joke subsided, "I think I see a lot of Carrie in you, Adi . . . I bet your childhood sucked!"

Whether it was a question or a statement, Adi hadn't decided. A rush of blood had filled her head, Wright in Pendleton's living room, the two of them alone together. It had been evening, just before dark. Wright had asked her out to eat, or words to that effect. It had ended up a blur in her mind. She had turned and pointed at her work, at the pile of student papers set beside her electronic typewriter on the dining room table, making up the excuse that she had to keep working.

That night she read *Carrie*, a slim book that captured so well the sense of adolescent isolation, of being different, a feeling she had lived with for so many years. She had been scared as hell about the arrival of her period all through the twelfth year of her life, with it finally coming late in Ohio's long winter, so that the pillowy down of her winter coat absorbed its jam slickness. She found it strange that a man could capture that fear of menstruation so exactly.

She looked at the picture of King and saw in it the face of an outsider, of a voyeur, saw the vestiges of a boy who had been stood up at junior high graduation, now a grown, bearded man whom she did not think she would have felt comfortable being alone with.

*   *   *

One day, later on during her hibernation, Adi had been dressing facing Lee Porterfield's house, Pendleton's history professor neighbor, when she had seen, in the reflection of a mirrored dresser, Porterfield watching her, his arm moving in a masturbatory way.

There was, of course, nothing that could have been said. It was part of the confines of neighborhood living, of how lives and relationships were forged, the errant words of domestic squabbles overheard through a screen door in summer, lovers' quarrels, money problems, children fighting, children getting punished . . . or that was how Adi rationalized it.

She was as much to blame, walking around naked.

She had begun to dress with the curtains drawn, although behind every passing neighborly wave she always thought in her mind that Porterfield saw her naked.

Curiously, it was a combination of the two incidents, the phantasmagoria of King's *Carrie* and what Adi had dubbed, in Porterfield's case, *The Secret Life of Men*, that helped Adi move past the horror of the crime in *Scream*, or at least understand the latent luridness of men at some base level. After all, here was a like-minded academic and neighbor of Pendleton's who occupied so many roles—father, husband, lover, neighbor, teacher, scholar—and who lived so many distinct, compartmentalized existences.

She had been wrong to associate author and protagonist in *Scream*. There was the autobiographical dimension to the work—that was undeniable—but the protagonist in *Scream* was different, a literary and existential creation. Thematically, the book was a playing out of the arbitrariness of the universe. Through the latter part of the novel, the Professor had moved closer to insanity, phoning the police from phone booths and taunting them, leading them ever closer to where his victim lay buried. He had wanted to be found, and then, in the last chapter, amid a blizzard, as the Professor returned to college after a Thanksgiving break, he lost control of his car. It slid off an overpass and down an embankment, end over end, before settling upended in a drift of snow. The Professor died instantly, his spine snapped at the base of his skull, and the novel ended with the perpetual turning of wheels on the upended car amid the whiteout.

In rereading the end, Adi came to see the upended car with its perpetual spinning wheels as a metaphor for the arbitrary universe. There was something profound in the exactness of the image, in the integrity of the novel, in its symmetry, this death in a whiteout, an inversion of light as Enlightenment. There was no peace, no sense of closure, the crime unsolved.

It was how Adi finally separated herself from the initial horror of what she had read earlier and came to understand that part of Pendleton's genius had been in borrowing the verisimilitude of the real crime for his novel, imparting the novel with a chilling quality of authenticity that, no matter how many times she read it, always made her feel she was reading the confessional of the true murderer; but of course, that was the essence of great fiction.

It was in late February, in the quiet of night in Pendleton's office atop the house, that she arrived at the irrefutable fact that Pendleton had charged her with his papers and notes, but also with *Scream*. Pendleton, she rationalized, had shied away from the work, not because of the morbid nature of the crime, but because of the personal and litigious attacks he had launched on his fellow professors at the college. If the book had ever been read, he would have been liable and most assuredly would have lost his job. It was the reason the book had been hidden away.

To protect him now, she felt all she had to do was put in an enigmatic underline where the names of his colleagues were mentioned, as in "Professor _____." In a way, it would only add to the disdain, heighten the megalomania of the protagonist. It didn't compromise the work in the least. In fact, it made it better.

In a sad way, Adi knew she was using Pendleton, though she tried to see it as him commending his life and work into her hands. For hadn't so many great writers died in oblivion, only to be resurrected by critics? In attempting suicide, he had liberated his work, given it life, for now there was no definitive authorial voice, no author to question.

Wasn't that the hallmark of great literature, that the author be first and foremost dead?

However, the reality was far starker in the end, for there was no turning back, the decision made the same week the first foreclosure notice arrived regarding Pendleton's house. His funds had run out. Medical bills had been piling up as well, long-term care not fully covered by insurance. The bills and mortgage notices had been coming to his in-box at the college. The security of the house Adi had come to call her own would soon be lost.

Adi went to see Pendleton and explained what was happening. She had the foreclosure notices in her hands, though he only swallowed and blinked as she spoke. He looked at her from time to time, but mostly his eyes were set on the purgatory of Bannockburn in the distance.

Adi said, "I want to help you. I want to try to get *Scream* republished."

Pendleton's head turned slowly, but all he said was, "Water," his voice raspy, the word barely audible. He brought his frail hand to his parched lips, said the word "water" again.

Adi held a glass of water to his lips as he drank. She said softly, "Do you understand me?"

Pendleton seemed to let his weight rest against the glass, stopping between sips, the tremulous effort of breathing making his body rise and fall. He coughed and took another drink, swallowed and breathed shallowly, then his hand reached for her, the bony fingers curling around her arm. His head turned slightly, and he looked into her eyes with a sense of recognition, with a sense of understanding. It lasted just an instant before his grip eased and his eyes closed again. He had understood nothing.

Later that evening, perched in a night sky of stars, with the glow of Bannockburn across the river, Adi began writing her thesis again, borrowing the caption under Wright's photograph—*Death of a Writer*.

NINE

IT WAS 9:30 IN the morning, eastern standard time, when Adi called Horowitz, who had just returned to Key West after his successful book tour. He was supposed to be organizing his thoughts on Pendleton for a chapter Adi was writing for her thesis called "The Early Years."

Horowitz was already drinking tequila from a shot glass with a salted lime wedge. He was at a loose end. He said he was glad to hear Adi's voice.

Adi heard the way Horowitz smacked his lips between sips.

Horowitz said, "We're expecting a storm here this evening, damaging winds and hail. It is seventy-six degrees and humid already, water all choppy and dark, wind kicking up strong. Here, listen to this!"

Adi heard the buffeted wind, a sucking sound as though her ear were against a seashell. She was sitting at her small office on the eighth floor of Bannockburn, behind an embankment of books. The campus was in the middle of a mid-March thaw, a world blanched of color, sun melting away the dirty snow to reveal matted clumps of grass, a soggy, grayish marshland. Wind blew rain against the window as the reflecting pool below threw back the jagged monolithic shape of the library.

Horowitz was out on his deck, overlooking a long beach. He almost tripped over a piece of balcony furniture, a plastic chair. He barely caught himself. "Have you ever felt the unbearable insubstantiality of goddamn plastic furniture? Jesus Christ, it's like everything has become unmoored, like living on the moon. . . ."

Horowitz took another drink. He gave a running commentary on what he was staring at. He said loudly into the phone, "A woman in a halter top and sweats is running along the beach. Her hair is like a sea anemone, all tossed in the wind. I'm in a pair of boxers. I've a shot glass in my hand. I'm waving at the woman running. She's waving back at me. That's the kind of neighbors I have. I feel like Dudley Moore in *10*."

Horowitz's voice was pulled by the wind. "That's what this life is like, a reel of film played outside my window, something inaccessible. Life is like a big TV screen down here." He pulled a sliding door behind him, sealing himself from the wind, and in the sudden vacuum of silence said, "Do you know the sand inside every hourglass comes from this beach here? That's a fact. You can check with the Realtor who sold me the house. . . . What the general population thinks is writers need time on their hands. It's the opposite. We have too much time on our hands."

Adi smiled and breathed into the phone.

Horowitz took another drink. "I've come to a decision. If they want to evacuate us, I'm not leaving."

It wasn't hurricane season, but Adi said anyway, "Is that a good idea?"

"It's settled. I discussed it with my editor. It's a done deal. He thinks there's a coffee table book on storms in it, a two-hundred-thousand print-run guarantee, a big glossy book. We're going to stick Hemingway into the title somewhere. That's a guaranteed seller."

"Well, then stay."

Horowitz made a huffing noise. "I was hoping someone would come save me."

"I'm afraid I'm out of the saving business, for obvious reasons."

Horowitz breathed a storm down the line. He was over by his mirrored wet bar, topping up his drink and adding ice cubes with a pair of silver tongs. "I'm sorry. . . . It's all about me, right, is that what you're thinking?"

"You're the star."

"Shit . . . that's right . . . I'm the star." He said it sarcastically. "You know something, I don't think one-twentieth of the people who bought my book have read it or are ever going to read it. It was all in the title; a catchy title can vault you to the top of the best-seller list. We judge a book by the cover, that's the simple truth, no matter what anyone says. Believe me! The book was an ideal corporate gift, a stocking stuffer, something inoffensive, a safe gift for Father's Day."

He drank some more. "That's how it was marketed, G-rated, accessible to the general public. They just put it out into the public arena like it was detergent soap. Slash a book by thirty percent and stick enough of them in the public eye, at points of sale, and you've a sure best-seller. It's as simple as that. It's just getting a publishing house to make that commitment, that's all."

"Well, you got that commitment, that respect, Allen. I don't think success cheapens a person or the quality of the work."

"The way you're talking, I *know* you didn't read it. I wouldn't even ask you to answer me honestly. We're talking about a coffee table book this time around. I'm in the league with those *Mothers and Daughters* books, toilet reading. You know something, it's a great pity the right to free speech and freedom of the press isn't based on the obligation to say something goddamn meaningful. A fucking coffee table book on storms, that's what my editor wants, *The I of the Storm!* a book peppered with literary quotes from American maritime heavyweights, Melville, Crane, Hemingway. Here's a Hemingway quote for you: 'Ernest Hemingway, when asked what was the most frightening thing he ever encountered, said, "A blank sheet of paper." ' That's the kind of banal shit I'm facing. That's a fucking page in the book, a photo and the quote. I don't even think Hemingway said that, either, but who the hell is going to say he didn't!"

Horowitz let out a sigh. "Here's another Hemingway one: 'Unlike all other forms of combat, the conditions are that the winner shall take nothing; neither his ease, nor his pleasure, nor any notions of glory; nor, if he wins far enough, shall there be any reward within himself.' Now that's a suicide note to die for! They won't publish that, I can guarantee you that! What I'd like to get is a shot of Hemingway's brains splattered against a wall with a subtitle, 'Inside the writer's mind!' "

Adi watched the rain fall in sheets across Bannockburn. The campus never looked more depressing and isolated than at this time of year, the doldrums of academic life, courses midway through, the flare of classroom crushes long gone. She said quietly, "We all reach a crossroads in life, that's a simple reality. For what's it worth, I think you are a genius."

"Geniuses don't live on beachfront property. That's an indisputable fact!"

"In my world they would. . . . What do you want, Allen?"

"I don't know. I ask myself that question all the time. Self-reflection is like trying to bite your own teeth." Horowitz stood staring at himself in a full-length mirror, his face discolored by the heat, as if it had been poached in warm water. He turned, moving toward the jigsaw of sectional couches. The huge glass window in his living room framed the world outside, a crescent of beach, to either side the glass façade of modern beachfront houses on stilts. They looked extraterrestrial.

"Hey," Horowitz shouted. "The runner is coming back again. You know something strange that scares me?"

"What?"

"I feel like Bob's character in *Scream*. What if I just went down on the beach and dragged that runner up to my house?"

Adi tensed. It was the first reference he had made to the fact that he had read *Scream* since she'd sent it to him weeks ago. She said quietly, betraying nothing, "You thought the book was good?"

Horowitz snorted, "Shit, *good*? Let me put it this way, what do you say you pull the plug on Bob, and I publish the book under my name? We can go seventy-thirty on the profit." He took another drink. "It's nine-thirty in the morning, and I'm drunk, and I feel alone!"

"We all do."

"No, this is existential aloneness, and it's because of you! Jesus, you know, you got me into a real funk. Why the hell did you send me that goddamn book?"

"Because I know you."

"Know me how?"

"You know talent."

"Yeah! Well, to tell the truth, my first inclination was to kill Bob, and you along with him. That's how I react to talent, with a vengeance!"

"I think Bob would take that as a compliment."

"Jesus, do you ever stop?"

"Stop what?"

"What the hell do you see in him, anyway, that I don't have?"

Adi didn't answer him. "I was thinking you could take the book to your publisher on Bob's behalf. I checked on the publishing company that put the book out. It was a vanity press founded by Robert. He owns the rights."

Horowitz's voice took on a sharp quality. "That's what this is about? It's all business? You and Bob! That's why you called, right?"

"No, I just wanted to talk to somebody."

"Why *me*?"

"Why *not* you?"

"What is this, emotional blackmail? You think I give a shit Bob tried to commit suicide the night I arrived? Well, I don't. Bob was a tormented fuck all his life! Quote me on that for your thesis. You wanted a quote. Well, there you have it!"

"Allen, they're going to foreclose on Bob's house. Right now I'm trying to find a way to cash in his portfolio. He's got nothing. The horror is, he's going to go on living. . . ." Adi sniffled and wiped her nose with her sleeve. "You know, I feel guilty for saving him. God, I didn't understand what was going on inside him."

Horowitz's voice came down a notch. "Calm down . . . take it easy."

Adi sniffled again. "I'm sorry . . . I shouldn't have called you . . . I just couldn't think of anybody else to turn to. I just thought that you could help. You know people."

"Look, the thing is, I don't want to jeopardize the coffee table book. . . ." Horowitz waited a moment. "That's a joke. Laugh!"

Adi cleared her throat. "I am . . . as much as I can laugh. I want you to know, I knew in my heart you were a good person. I know what Bob said about you in the book must have hurt, but if you help him—"

Horowitz cut her off. "I'm not helping him. I'm helping *you*. Look, what I want you to do is figure out how much you need right now to cover things, the mortgage, the medical bills, all of it. Then call me back. I'm going to wire money to you."

TEN

EITHER HE WAS A consummate actor or a genuine apostle, but something undeniable had happened to Allen Horowitz. Gone were the coral beads and the Hawaiian shirt. Over the course of almost two years, Horowitz championed *Scream*, sent it first to his publisher, who rejected it, then worked down the line, calling in favors, until a respectable literary imprint of a major New York house agreed to publish the novel.

Pendleton was again at home, by then under Adi's care.

Horowitz had been true to his word, bailing Pendleton out of financial problems. He had intimated to her that the money had been only a fraction of the unseemly high advance he had been given for the coffee table book, which incidentally he had written over three long weekends, merely culling quotes.

The affability and support from Horowitz was almost eerie. Adi had never expected such a transformation, though she had sent Horowitz a most abject Polaroid of Pendleton staring out toward Bannockburn. She had written the word "Immortality" beneath the photograph, Pendleton's last word to Horowitz before he had driven away to attempt suicide.

In a way, that seemed to have been a defining moment, when she looked back on things. She described it as "Horowitz's guilt." He had referred to a work of his own he was picking up again, a work from his college days before he had, as he put it, "gone astray."

Horowitz wrote a foreword to *Scream*, titled "Notes from Bannockburn," a piece he had submitted to Adi as part of her thesis. The foreword ran in the *New York Times Book Review*, in conjunction with the rerelease of *Scream*, on the morbidly appropriate second anniversary of Pendleton's attempted suicide.

Horowitz called *Scream* a bellwether work tapping into the loss of an omniscient God. *Scream*, Horowitz asserted, offered up a parable of modern absurdist nihilism, with an antihero who stared down God, who openly defied God to do what He had done in biblical times, to show Himself unto Man.

Commenting specifically on the spiritual searching at the heart of the novel, Horowitz likened the raised eyes of the murdered girl as she was forced to perform fellatio as reminiscent of a stare not rendered with such fearful awe and saintly supplication since the glory days of Christian Renaissance art, most notably in images of Mary Magdalene before the Cross, so too in the kneeling Bernadette of Lourdes and the little rose, St. Theresa. All these women were rendered looking heavenward. Horowitz asserted that Pendleton's iconoclastic genius was in his co-opting and transfiguring of an archetypal Christian representation of female awe with the sublimated forced act of fellatio.

It was this that created the maelstrom of fury over *Scream* and took it beyond the aesthete pages of the *New York Times Book Review*. In the October 18 issue of *Time* magazine, Pendleton, a shadow of his former self and now officially a professor emeritus at Bannockburn, was featured on the Bannockburn campus in a wheelchair with a blanket wrapped around him, the picture set in contrast with an inset of Wright's suicide shot, Adi standing over the prostrate Pendleton, the burning effigy of the rabbit eyes glowing in the upper corner. Horowitz had insisted the shot be used, paying Wright the biggest check of his life, $3,500.

Scream improbably cracked the top hundred on the best-seller lists for a week at least, owing in no small measure to the furor surrounding Horowitz's article. The subheading under a *Newsweek* piece picked up the crisis of faith, asking, "In a war with a so-called absurd universe, in opting for suicide, was E. Robert Pendleton denied death in an ironic and cosmic stalemate? Did God make the last move? So argues the Christian Right."

Bannockburn College, too, played its part in advancing the mystique of E. Robert Pendleton in the fall of 1987, as it was yet another Homecoming Weekend. Pendleton arrived on campus for the game in his only public appearance. He looked like FDR in those rare shots FDR allowed, showing his infirmity, bound to his wheelchair. He was wrapped in the same tartan blanket in which he had been photographed for *Time*, Adi at his side, captured just so, her enigmatic beauty adding to the allure of the story.

She was described as "a longtime grad student and devotee of literature." The reporter went on to credit her with rediscovering *Scream*, hidden away in Pendleton's basement. It had been her faith in the work that had led to Pendleton's literary rebirth.

Ablaze in autumnal color that weekend, Bannockburn had been the picture of a pastoral enclave, a citadel of learning, the central faux English quad with its ivy dorms again a fleet of sheets, a campus tacking against the winds of change, contrasting so with the eighties era of conspicuous consumption, when education was all about the MBA, and a high-flying stock market that had ended that same fall on Black Monday.

Somehow, *Scream* seemed to catch the moment. People were looking for something that transcended the rapacious immorality of businesses chasing quarterly profit margins. Retirement funds had evaporated, years of real work gone in speculative markets. Billions had disappeared in single keystrokes, economies crippled. It was difficult coming to terms with the devastation. There was no single event, place, epicenter, or carnage to cover.

Scream straddled the age of letters and psychopaths, one journalist putting it, "This is Nietzsche meets Charles Manson."

* * *

Yet there were those, namely the publishing house publicity people, who felt the success of *Scream* could have gone meteoric if Adi Wiltshire had been more open to speaking with the press. She had been obstinate in granting no personal interviews. She had seemed overly protective of Pendleton's privacy.

On occasion, she had voiced concerns over his health. She kept herself and Pendleton as enigmatic as possible, and while suffering her single public engagement, at Bannockburn's Homecoming Weekend, she had not answered questions, her hand on Pendleton's shoulder while he stared straight ahead.

Still, there was something almost spiritual, transcendent, about both of them, given what they had been through together, or so argued Horowitz, who called it reverse psychology, defending Adi's right to privacy. In a world of cheap publicity tricks, her demure deflection of praise elevated her.

There was, however, another reason Adi had wanted *Scream* to fall from critical scrutiny, to fade so it didn't reach the broader reading public, a far more complex reason than anybody could have guessed.

Two months prior to the republication of *Scream*, as she had begun getting callbacks from various colleges regarding potential jobs, as review copies had already gone out, and as the first glowing trade reviews for *Scream* had already appeared, she had been at the library working on her thesis, gathering and collating the entire sequence of local newspaper articles concerning the murder of Amber Jewel.

She had coveted the connection to Amber Jewel, kept her work hidden from Horowitz, and been vague in what she had given her thesis committee, keeping all reference to Amber Jewel to herself. She had not wanted Horowitz or anybody else stealing her sources, to reference any of the material she had uncovered.

This was *her* thesis.

It was petty, but then survival often centered on such pettiness. In mid-August heat, alone on campus with a handful of grad students, and with just weeks to hand in her thesis, she had begun to weave in a chapter related to Amber Jewel's murder to substantiate the artistic sleight of hand Pendleton had pulled, using the clippings from the local newspapers for his own work, interweaving a local tragedy with his own existential novel.

Something troubling struck Adi as she scanned the microfiche rolls.

At first Adi felt confused. She read through the articles again. Amber Jewel had disappeared on November 6, 1976, and her body was discovered five months later, on April 8, 1977. Adi felt certain that, according to the invoice she had seen inside the publisher's box, the novel had been published *earlier* than April. The dates didn't make sense, disbelief her first gut reaction, then denial. She had to have been mistaken about the invoice date. A thesis, the burden of work, could confuse a person, skew facts and dates.

Rushing home, she opened the box of books, and there, on top, sat the print-run invoice, dated February 14, 1977, enigmatically adorned with a glossy sticker of cupid shooting an arrow. Standing there in the vapid humidity of late Summer, with the novel already out for review, in the hushed quiet of Pendleton's house, as he slept in the shade of the screened porch, Adi came to understand *Scream* was not just a novel, but the autobiographical *confession* of a child killer.

For a long time Adi stared at Pendleton, her body trembling. Was she really standing before a man who had not only murdered, but butchered a thirteen-year-old girl? She kept looking at him, the perpetual dribble of spit shining on his chin, this, the same man who had appealed to her at the airport, baring his soul, a man so lost and abject, looking for a kind word, for something to salvage who he was as an artist.

How could he have lived in the intervening years? How could the pettiness of his own artistic failing have led him to such a desperate and savage act?

But the reality was, it had. His sense of failure had become a mania directed heavenward, toward the infuriating silence that characterized the New Testament, an age when God had stopped revealing Himself as He had to men like Abraham.

But a child, a young girl?

Adi shivered again as she continued to look at Pendleton. The passage of years and his attempted suicide had reduced him to a skeletal figure, and though she wanted to call the police, her rage that great, her mind settled that nothing could be done now. It was a once-off murder, a desperate and heinous act, but there was no danger it would ever happen again. Pendleton was a vegetable. Bringing the case to light meant nothing. It would not bring back the victim, and what of Pendleton, beyond the law, his story a spectacle that would serve only the interests of an insatiable media?

Adi slowly came to realize she would be cast into the center of the maelstrom, her life destroyed by association with him, and as she continued to stare at Pendleton, she began to rationalize that his life sentence had already begun. He had been denied death by the very God he didn't believe in, her thoughts foreshadowing what the Christian Right would eventually assert, that God had made the last move in an ironic and cosmic stalemate, that Pendleton was suffering an eternal limbo, in this, the only world in which he believed.

In the hours of indecision, as the afternoon waned toward evening, slowly an instinct for her own survival surfaced. For who would believe she had discovered the material in this eleventh hour? It seemed too convoluted a story to tell, at least now. If she had discovered the connection six months previously, she would have acted, called the police, but she didn't, or *couldn't*, now.

Adi simply lit the invoice on the gas range, let it curl and burn.

Her fingerprints on the microfiche were the sole remaining evidence that she had actively pursued the connection with Amber Jewel. She could not risk leaving the microfiche at the library. She was unsure of how to wipe down such a long reel of tape inconspicuously, or even if merely wiping the tape would remove the prints.

Taking the microfiche, she went out to the campus again and, in a daze, wandered aimlessly, ending up eventually along the banks of the river, where she let the microfiche slip from her fingers into the water and kept on walking.

Back in her small office, she tried to convince herself nobody would ever make the connection, the murder coming deep into a novel over four hundred pages long, the dumping of the body a mere two paragraphs. It had taken her a side-by-side comparison to establish the similarities—*she*, who was intimate with the novel.

Who read books that closely? *Scream* was an arcane novel of personal crisis. Its readership would be solely academics, a novel that would in all likelihood go nowhere.

For a moment back then, she ashamedly felt relieved that the victim had come from a white trash background, a people who didn't read books, or not books like *Scream*, anyway.

ELEVEN

ALMOST TWO MONTHS had passed since Adi had discovered what Pendleton had done, and despite her revulsion toward him, a more pressing self-preservation had taken hold of her, and, eerily, she had made an effort to be *nicer* to Pendleton, more attentive to his needs, to talk and pass the time with him, though he understood little, or pretended so, Adi could not tell now, her own paranoia always alive within her.

Was he hiding within? Was he watching her? Ludicrously, her sole goal had become to convince him she knew nothing, as though she were the guilty party, not Pendleton.

As the weeks progressed, as the reviews and the publicity increased, the single fact that she had thrown away the microfiche pressed on her. Who would have thought anybody would have cared about *Scream*? But then, Horowitz had been unstoppable, vaunting the genius of the work.

With each review, with each dogged call for insights into the historical Pendleton, Adi dreaded that the connection between *Scream* and Amber Jewel was going to be made, that some reporter, in angling for a new perspective, would figure it out, somehow, some way. It didn't matter how. It just spiraled in Adi's head so that, in some nightmares, there was someone shouting, "She took it! She knew all along!" In other nightmares, she saw the microfiche hadn't actually reached the water, that it was stuck in the muddy embankment. She had visions of it unwound and catching the daylight, so much so that on her lunch breaks she had gone down seven times, twice in the rain, scanning the bank surreptitiously.

It was how she had ended up with the flu, after having gotten soaked the last and final time she had gone there. It had been the onset of the flu that first led her to take Pendleton's medicine, a leftover antibiotic, but then she moved on to Pendleton's antianxiety prescription for her insomnia and for her guilt. It had been against this increasing paranoia that her cycle of addiction had taken hold.

During this paranoia-induced exhaustion, while in conference with a student in the small cubicle of her grad office on the eighth floor of the library, Adi noticed a man in a long coat standing in the book aisles. He had his back turned to her. At first she didn't pay him notice, but when she looked up twenty minutes later, the man was still lurking in the aisles, still facing away from her.

She thought he might be some dogged reporter waiting to speak to her or some pervert waiting to expose himself to women. It was something that happened a few times a year at the library, men unzipping their flies and holding their cocks in the gray light of these book aisles, most always up on the top floors amid the ancient manuscripts, usually sick grad students. The bathroom stalls on each floor were scrawled with pornographic images along with phone numbers and meeting times, defining the desperation of loners seeking others in this pathetic and abject perversion. Sometimes it was disturbed faculty, and Adi experienced a sense of déjà vu, reminded of what Pendleton had done.

Adi had a hard time concentrating on the student sitting across from her. The kid was a biology major, arrogant in the way those outside the arts were about having to take humanities core requirements. She hated him in his Letterman jacket. He had been aggressively sexual toward her, leaned too close to her. If circumstances had been otherwise, she would have ended the conversation and called the dean, but she didn't want to draw attention to herself.

The kid had been arguing vehemently over the C– she had given him for his three-thousand-word essay on William Carlos Williams's "The Red Wheelbarrow," a deceptively simple poem the kid argued meant nothing at all.

Adi's question had been unnecessarily complicated for undergraduates: "In twentieth-century verse, an enjambment can occur without interest in shock or abruptness as a mimetic effect by itself . . . so argues John Hollander of how one should interpret 'The Red Wheelbarrow.' Discuss what Hollander means. So much of *what* depends on a red wheelbarrow?"

It was the fifth argument she had engaged in already that morning with students. This particular one had been going on for a half hour and was going nowhere, but against the background of publicity surrounding *Scream*, as it gained relative fame, she had felt she needed to maintain more academic rigor and focus than she had done at any point in her past.

Almost a minute of silence had passed when the kid said, "Miss Wiltshire?" He said it loudly enough for Adi to realize that she had zoned. She responded immediately, asking him to close his eyes and feel the words as she recited the poem aloud.

so much depends
upon

a red wheel
barrow

glazed with rain
water

beside the white
chickens.

With the kid's eyes closed, Adi stared out into the book aisles. The man was at the end of the aisle, staring directly at her. Adi hesitated, then let out a cry loud enough for the kid to open his eyes, see the look in Adi's eyes, and turn.

There was nobody in the aisle.

Adi recovered. She couldn't afford to break down. The conference ended a few minutes later. The kid was to redo the assignment. Adi said it coldly as she looked askance at the aisles.

The kid got up to leave in a huff, his bag slung over his broad shoulder, and despite the awkwardness of the situation, Adi accompanied him to the elevator and waited, scanning the aisles for the stranger.

In the library basement vending area, Adi bought a soda. Her blood sugars were low. She felt dizzy. Sitting next to the hum of the vending machines, she ate a bag of chips, remained there for a half hour, and tried to set aside her paranoia. Maybe the man had simply been looking for a book?

At some level, Adi knew she was losing it. Her addiction had taken her so quickly, but then there was a history of it in her family. Her mother's fits of manic depression had for years been treated, or mistreated, with prescription medications that eventually put her in drug rehab.

Adi kept telling herself over and over again that she would kick the need once she felt safe again. *Scream* had stubbornly stayed in the top hundred for over a month, but she felt the next week or two would indicate which way the novel would go, whether it would break out or go adrift.

What hurt her was her sense of entrapment, the fact that she was going to be spending another disconsolate year at Bannockburn. After she threw away the microfiche, she had to ask for a six-month extension on submitting her thesis. She was initially unable to articulate any real reason for this delay when challenged by the committee that reviewed her ongoing work. It had been a demeaning, heated exchange, and it was only her personal association with Pendleton that had kept her from being summarily dismissed from the program. She was granted the extension as the first rave reviews came out, arguing during a second committee meeting the necessity of including critical reaction to the novel.

As Adi was getting up to leave, she spotted Wright studying. Seemingly, he had not noticed her.

Wright was in the 200-level poetry seminar she was teaching, the same class as the biology student with whom she had argued in her office.

Strangely, Wright was one of the standouts in the class, with a nascent gift for poetics and nuance. He was studying part-time toward his degree in English.

Adi looked at him, retreating from her own fear.

Wright was leaning over a book, taking notes, a cigarette smoldering in a foil ashtray along with his Dr Pepper. He had on a T-shirt with the sleeves rolled up so his faded tattoos showed along his forearms, his hair grown out and combed back in a fifties greaser way. He looked like the Fonz, not in that slick, comedic *Happy Days* way, but more true to life, a guy in his late thirties, a guy struggling to just plain survive, incongruous to the well-bred students. He could have passed for somebody working janitorial services or boiler maintenance, a guy doing a crossword puzzle between shifts, not someone reading poetry.

Throughout the almost two years since Pendleton's attempted suicide, Wright had inculcated himself in both Adi's and Pendleton's lives, or, more exactly, Pendleton's life, stopping at the house to sit silently alongside him. This had disturbed Adi at first, but as Wright had persisted long after faculty had stopped, she had come to see him in a different light, to see the compassion in him.

In fact, a revelatory aspect of her thesis had come one evening while she had been collating the series of expletive cutout ransomlike letters she had thought Pendleton had mailed to himself to prompt his writing of *Word Salad*. After leaving Pendleton, Wright had stopped by to say good night to Adi and, seeing her working on the mass of letters set out on the desk, candidly and eerily admitted that he had sent the letters to Pendleton, mimicking *Word Salad*. This had initially scared the hell out of her, given the psychotic nature of what they contained, but in the dull light that evening, Wright had gone on to explain in a slow and deliberate way how his life had been back then, how Pendleton had treated him.

A day later, Wright had given her the series of op ed pieces that had run in the newspaper, all of which Adi had ended up using to form a discreet section within her thesis, balancing the essential genius of Pendleton with his human foibles. That Wright had given her this measure of confidence had gone a long way to shoring up their differences, though they had never become actual friends, nor had he asked her out again after the evening he had given her the copy of *Carrie*.

Rather, what Wright had dedicated himself to, as he continued to visit Pendleton, was his bachelor of arts. He had told that to Adi one evening as he was leaving, and from then on out, Adi had never heard him shorten the degree title to "BA."

He was going to be the first of his family to earn a college degree. It had become his sole goal.

In deference to Wright's reformation, and because he had allowed Horowitz to submit the shot he had taken the night Pendleton attempted suicide, as the release of *Scream* was drawing near, Adi had given Wright an advanced review copy signed in Pendleton's scrawling signature, or, more exactly, Adi's hand, holding and guiding Pendleton's hand, because there had been no intent on Pendleton's part.

She had never seen such a genuine sense of emotion as Wright stared at the signature and then read the synopsis on the back of the book. She had whispered, "I discovered it hidden in the basement. It's being republished, Robert's opus."

The only thing Wright had said as he looked up and stared at her was, "The last time I got an autographed copy of anything was when I was eight years old and my father took me up to Wrigley Field."

It had been the last genuine sense of fraternity she had felt, the last true memory she recalled, during the horror of what unfolded less than a week later as she had discovered the connection between Pendleton and Amber Jewel.

It seemed strange that she had come to rely on Wright in the way she had, but as Adi stood up, she was glad of a face she knew. She said Wright's name, and he looked up from his reading.

Adi pointed at the book on the table. "How you liking Williams, Henry?"

Wright said directly, "I like the fact he kept his day job. That says a lot about him."

Adi smiled. "Well, that's the curse of poets . . ."

Wright finished the sentiment, "And *most* writers."

Adi smiled again. "Sure. . . . Poverty equates to greatness, or that's how we romantically envision the life of our great writers, except for your friend King, I suppose."

"Everybody starts somewhere. King had it hard originally. He ended up writing under two names, his own and the pseudonym Richard Bachman, just to improve his chances, not to get stuck with one reputation."

Adi said. "Really?" But then she changed the subject. "You haven't been out to visit the professor lately. I think what he might need now more than anything is a sense of continuity, a *friend.*"

Wright looked at her. "The thing is . . . I loaded up on credits this semester. I figure I don't have time on my side any longer. I want that bachelor of arts degree."

Adi answered quietly, "I know how you feel. Just don't go killing yourself, okay?" Then she rose into the cool fall day, into a Bannockburn of privilege and distinction, a student life pastiche that could have been culled from any upscale clothing catalog.

This was the essence of Bannockburn College, of modern education—a brand name, a lifestyle.

TWELVE

Pendleton was sitting alone in his office, drinking coffee that the home care nurse, Mrs. Annie Blaine, had brought up to him, when he heard Adi pull into the driveway. He had spilled the coffee over the front of his trousers. He was particularly agitated, though now he had lost exactly why he was in such a state. He wanted to speak with Adi. That's all he knew. He struggled to stand, leaning against his desk, and stared at Adi as she gathered her papers from the backseat of the car.

Something was bothering him.

Pendleton had recovered a sense of recognition over the past year, a slow semblance of a new order, a life reconstructed from the ruins of his old life. He had no recollection of his past, of a time before his recovery. He knew, as a matter of fact, that he had lived in the house before, but he didn't feel it. There was no memory of a former life, just this eternal present. Even the rabbit that sat on his lap all day long evoked no memory, though sweaters from the closet had rabbit hair on them. Yet the evidence of a former life was all around him, the gray electrical tape on the various cords where the rabbit had eaten through them, the books on the shelf in his office with his name on them, the reviews of his books in the gray hallway rising to the turret and widow's watch of his office.

In the living room, there was a picture of him and his mother the year she had her stroke and came to live with him briefly, but even that image stirred nothing within him. Curiously, the dented mailbox outside on the street was something he looked at from time to time, yet he could not say what it meant. He knew it was where the mail arrived each day. It was probably simply that fact, the first recognizable act of order, the arrival of the mailman each day.

For a long time, it punctuated the day for him, the arrival of the mail, before he learned to understand the representation of time on a watch, before the indeterminable hours between day and night took on any other meaning besides his need to eat and defecate.

It had been a slow process beset with illness, with colds and pneumonias. He had done something irrevocable to his body and soul, though of course that was not how he would have put it.

In the faces he had met over the year, he had been confronted by people who knew of his past, people expecting something of him he could not quite grasp. He felt strangely inadequate, even sad at times, for people looked at him with a sense of sadness. Why he elicited that reaction in people, he could not figure out. People who smiled seemed to stop smiling when they looked at him. That's what he observed, that simple fact. He understood he had been in a coma and that his recovery had been nothing short of miraculous, but why people stopped smiling at him, he could not understand. He thought the reaction should have been the opposite, though he wasn't sure.

Even through the initial glare of publicity over the publication of

Scream, people were curiously affected by him. They looked at him longer than he felt was necessary, their eyes locked on him. He thought it might have been simply the fact that he was unable to read his own work. He had initially lost the ability to read and write because of the stroke, though in recent months he had regained the ability to distinguish numbers from letters and had begun the slow process of reinhabiting the world of written words again.

On his desk were alphabet books with associated images, A (a) is for Apple, B (b) is for Bike . . . and other books about letters and numbers. His favorite was *Ten Little Monkeys Jumping on a Bed.*

Despite Adi's protests, eventually a number of photographers had come to the house, drawn by the publicity related to *Scream*. All had taken pictures of Pendleton's alphabet books alongside *Scream*, and even Pendleton had seemed to understand the irony of the situation, though "irony" was not a word he used anymore.

He had no recollection of *Scream*, no intuitive sense he was at the heart of the story, that it was his semiautobiography, though he knew factually that he was the author. At least, that was what he was told. He had learned to read his own name or, more exactly, point to the letters until the sum total of them became synonymous with his name, with who he was.

What Pendleton *knew* was that he had suffered a stroke, that his brain had been starved of oxygen. He felt that sense of lacking within himself, that sense of loss. It was hard defining a loss he could not fully comprehend. It was like that feeling of putting a seashell to one's ear, hearing a *whoosh*ing sound of some distant world. Not that Pendleton understood that metaphor, but Adi had tried to explain the loss in such terms and had put a seashell to his ear. It was, in fact, how Pendleton felt deep inside himself, the hush of a cosmic ocean of sound, the distant sound of waves breaking somewhere beyond conscious thought.

For a long time, when he looked away from an object or a face, it, or the person, simply vanished: a feeling akin to sitting facing forward in a train, everything passing by ceasing to exist even in the moment of comprehending it. He was confronted by a series of images and situations that had no context, that simply presented themselves to him.

Pendleton's true history was incomplete to him.

He did not know that he had attempted suicide. During his initial recovery, as caretaker for Pendleton, Adi, along with the doctors, had decided not to tell him that he had tried to commit suicide. He was told that he had suffered a massive stroke. It was agreed that if he were to recover emotionally, to live out whatever cognitive life he might regain, it was best he do it under the illusion that he had survived a medical tragedy, not a psychological breakdown and attempted suicide.

It was a guarded secret Adi had insisted be kept from Pendleton throughout the publication of *Scream*.

THIRTEEN

A DI GATHERED A BUNDLE of mail from the hallway, maintained the façade of dutiful assistant. There was nothing she could do, really. She looked exhausted but hid it in a quick scan of the mail, as Pendleton's nurse, Mrs. Blaine, sat watching TV in the living room. They didn't even exchange words, Adi just passing through the hallway and out back to the carriage house, where she now lived and worked, sorting through the mail as she walked. There was so much of it these days, reviews and requests for interviews. Horowitz had hired a clipping service and had insisted on forwarding the reviews even before the publisher did.

Adi sat at her own small desk and scanned the reviews. They were almost all inspired by Horowitz's initial article, many referencing his association with Pendleton, the brief and sad circumstances of how Horowitz had come to discover the Lost Novel.

All reviewers seemed to follow Horowitz's lead. All lauded Pendleton's "close to the bone" perverse treatment of the biblical story of Abraham and Isaac. In one review, Adi saw where Horowitz had underlined a quote and written in the margin, "potential paperback quote": "Pendleton takes one of the most brutal and megalomaniacal stories of the Old Testament and shows the pathologic sickness of the Almighty."

Looking up, Adi thought of the piles of rejection letters Pendleton had received that she had found in another box in the basement. Written on the box was a simple descriptor: "Humiliation." How come nobody had seen the genius before he had gone insane?

Adi shivered. She needed a fix. Still, she waited, wanted the moment to pass, stalled, looked outside. The day was going on as usual, nothing out of the ordinary. She set aside the incident of the man at the library. She went and stood near the window.

There was nobody around except for Porterfield chopping wood next door, dressed in a flannel shirt. And despite what she knew about him, his having jerked off to her, and maybe *because* of it, it made everything more poignant, normalized the secret life everybody inhabited at some level.

In the smallness of the toilet, Adi locked the door and held out her arm, pulling a rubber band over her wrist to above her elbow as she tapped her veins. It took a while until a vein plumped slightly, a pinhead of blood showed as she eased the needle into her vein, her tongue pressed between her lips in anticipation, a tremulous breathlessness, at the edge of a rush. Her hand became a tight fist as she slowly felt a pinprick tincture of sickness injecting the drug into her vein.

For almost two months, she had been writing prescriptions on a stolen doctor's pad, trawling the various pharmacies throughout the county to avoid detection. It had been prescriptions for pills initially, but during one of Pendleton's episodes, she had watched Mrs. Blaine administer an injection and saw how quickly the drug worked. She had moved to injecting herself in the evening not long after, replacing vials intended for Pendleton with distilled water.

The pills never had the same rush she had come to need.

Adi put on her best face and beamed at Pendleton when she reached the top of the stairs. She said in a fawning way, "How is my favorite professor this morning?" She did not, however, look at him, literally looking beyond him when possible.

It took Pendleton a moment to process things said to him, a slight neurological delay before he reacted. Under stress, the delay was longer. Adi had already turned her back to him and was setting down the mail when he said, "Am . . . Ammer?"

Adi didn't understand him at first, and then her body froze, but she kept her back turned and said matter-of-factly, "What?" and began opening a letter.

Her eyes shifted sideways.

Pendleton displayed an urgency he had not exhibited since coming out of the coma. He said again, "Ammer . . . Ammer Jewaul." He trembled and got out of his chair.

Adi turned, holding a letter opener in her left hand, its blade cutting the yellow midmorning light. "What are you saying?"

The strain of emotion made Pendleton tremble slightly as he struggled to find the words, his hands becoming fists as he tried to concentrate and speak.

Adi set down the knife, took his hand, and rubbed it, a stimulus that overrode everything else in his head, something she had learned over the past year to control him, to calm him, whispering, "Will you relax? My God, you are sweating! It is not good for you to be this upset. Do you want to get an aneurysm?" She spoke the way one would to a child.

Pendleton's face eased, or went lax was more exact. His eyes drifted away toward the world outside with a flagging sense of distress as he swallowed and breathed more easily, taking longer breaths. His tongue showed between his lips, giving his face a curiously vacant and yet perplexed look, as Adi kept rubbing his hand, making a *shoo* sound.

He had lost his train of thought, had that bewildered look of an older person being led somewhere, slightly against his own volition but unequal to the task of objecting. He shuffled in his slippers as Adi eased him into his high-backed chair, as she kept making a *shoo* sound.

On his desk, Adi saw a copy of *The Berenstain Bears*, a book Mrs. Blaine must have brought up to the room. It was too advanced for him, though, disconcertingly, she saw the book was turned to the latter pages.

The infiltration was coming slowly. The memory of what he had done, surfacing.

Adi poured a glass of water from a jug and helped Pendleton swallow two pills, wiping his mouth. He looked at her, his eyes blinking. His mouth opened and closed, and Adi began rubbing his hand again. After a while, she opened the alphabet book she had been reading to him for months and began, "C (c) is for Cat," and pointed at a picture of a cat and went, "Meow." She moved his hand over the letter, and he let her move his hand, letting her hold him by the forearm, his index finger half pointed, tracing the letter C. She said, "Meow," again, and Pendleton said, "Meow," felt his elbow touch her breast as she held his arm and turned the page. Then she said, "D (d) is for Dog," and went, "Woof," and Pendleton said, "Woof."

It was a simple incantation, Pendleton following along with her, letting her lead, her face coming ever so close to his as she formed the words, though by the time they got to L (l) is for Lion and Adi made a growling sound, Pendleton was asleep, his head lolled to one side.

The pills had pulled him under.

Adi left the room quietly and stood in the small landing. She could hear Mrs. Blaine vacuuming downstairs. In the window of the stairwell, a halo of light showed against the wall. She stopped and steadied herself, waiting to see if he stayed asleep, waiting in the dim rise of the hallway with his reviews framed and nailed to the wall.

It seemed like another lifetime ago.

In the quiet of her own room, she swallowed two of Pendleton's pills, lay flat out on her bed, and tried to will herself to sleep, but she couldn't. She listened to Mrs. Blaine rise up the creaking staircase, followed in her mind's eye the routine that had been so established for almost a year, Mrs. Blaine running a bath and washing Pendleton like a child, his pajamas laid out on the ribs of the old heater.

There was a roughness about her care, the way she handled Pendleton, something Adi had objected to at first, but then how many people could suffer caring for the aged? Mrs. Blaine had been the third caregiver that first year, the one who stayed, who had brought her own routine and ways into the life of E. Robert Pendleton.

What Adi had done was simply tolerate her presence, always with an eye to hiring someone more caring—until, that was, she had discovered the lax way Mrs. Blaine managed Pendleton's medication.

PART 2

THE INVESTIGATION

FOURTEEN

APRIL 8 HAD SEEN the last of winter 1977, as the temperature rose above freezing for the seventh consecutive day and a silting runoff of a spring thaw sent a brown, scudding water gushing down the overflowing riverbanks, depositing minerals and nutrients as nature had done for millennia. The fertile ooze would yield corn in the baking summer scorch of July and August, as part of the cycle that had brought Sam Henderson's ancestors to the middle of America.

The previous fall, Sam Henderson had lost his wife, Emily, the two of them sequestered in the solitude that had so defined their lives. Emily Henderson had died in her armchair, slipped away from this life doing what she had always done in her own quiet way, praising the Lord, her hands still holding a cross-stitching of the Lord's Prayer she was planning to send to one of her abundance of relatives.

Jon Ryder listened quietly. It was what good cold case cops did, let a person run out on their own, then catch up and reconcile their story with the facts.

Sam Henderson spoke of the land and his wife in the same slow way, a voice tinctured with a loneliness of one given to days, if not weeks, alone, a farmer's solitude. He looked as though he could have been one of the cast of *Petticoat Junction*.

What Sam Henderson liked to talk about was weather. He had done it all his life, or so he said. He had never trusted in weather-forecasting reports out of places like Chicago and Detroit, TV stations he picked up on occasion, and didn't trust either the easy, fat affability of those weatherman types in their suits and ties who stuck suns or rain clouds on a map, as if the weather were a child's game and not the measure by which men planned their day, if not their entire life.

No, what he had done was record the morning temperature from a small thermometer outside the kitchen window, something he had done for seventy-two of his eighty-one years alive, something he had taken to doing with his father, whose father had done it with his father, in over a century of recorded Henderson history in America, in Wade County, all of it set down for the family almanac, farmers reckoning with their particular homestead amid the various fronts, against the changing seasons.

So it was not so unusual for Sam Henderson to put his discovery of Amber Jewel in the context of seasons, in the attenuated detail of so many days of thaw.

Jon Ryder let Henderson continue to talk, the two of them standing in the late fall light, the wind picking up from the north in a cool mist. Ryder liked the reprieve, liked just standing in the cold, always amazed at the varied sense of his life, how as a cop he entered so many varying situations and lives, though his own "rain cloud"—to use a Sam Henderson metaphor—hung over him this morning, personal issues.

It had been a long morning's drive up from Evansville, up past what Ryder had always felt was the world's all-time surreal place name, French Lick, Indiana, a name that for him had always hinted at the underlying weirdness and complexity of the so-called simple country folk.

Throughout the drive, he had listened over and over again on his small tape player to a copy of a cassette that had been mailed anonymously to a newspaper in Muncie, Indiana. The postmark on the envelope had indicated the tape had been mailed from New York City. The tape methodically drew graphic and striking parallels between the unsolved 1976 murder of a young Indiana girl, Amber Jewel, and the gruesome killing of a so-called fictional victim in a 1977 novel called *Scream*.

The voice on the tape asked at the end, simply, how the author had gotten the parallels so precisely between the two victims, given that *Scream* had been *originally* published *before* the April 1977 discovery of the true-life victim's body.

According to the voice, the two victims were the same person. Adding to the eeriness of the tape had been the voice, computer generated, merely concatenating isolated monosyllabic sounds into words and sentences in a voice pattern made famous by the physicist Stephen Hawking.

As yet, the information on the tape had not been released to the public, the journalist in Muncie having had the decorum to wait, given the nature of the case, something that was becoming less and less the norm. But the journalist had been old school and not given to *breaking* news. He had contacted the police, who in turn had contacted Ryder's Cold Case Division.

The arrival of the tape had been the first break in almost a decade in a case that had stalled, turning on its head what investigators had long theorized, that the prime suspects in the murder had been the victim's own older sister, Kim Jewel, and Kim's lowlife boyfriend, Gary Scholl, a guy who had been in and out of jail for years.

Amber Jewel, her sister, Kim, and Gary Scholl had been involved in a bizarre love triangle, with Gary Scholl having sexual relations with the victim while her sister was pregnant with his child. The proximity of where Amber's dismembered body had been discovered five months later, less than two miles from her home, had further underscored that the perpetrator(s) had been local, again leading investigators to suspect Kim Jewel and Gary Scholl.

Initially, the anonymous tape had been regarded as a cheap and felonious attempt at publicity, to catapult *Scream* into the public consciousness and to the top of the best-seller lists.

Under close investigative scrutiny, no supporting records could confirm the allegations outlined on the tape that the original version of *Scream* had been printed *prior* to the discovery of Amber Jewel's body. The press that had printed the book, Jacobs & Sons, had been bought out in 1984 by a conglomerate that in integrating records had archived J&S accounts going back only five years. All that could be verified was a general time frame in which the novel had been printed. A typeset anomaly was recognized in multiple works produced by J&S. A *t* missing its tail appeared in various print runs between approximately September 1976 through July 1978.

What had unfolded thereafter, as Ryder had sought to establish the original print-run date, had been a first glimpse into the gallows of despair that permeated the academic world. Quickly, things took on a labyrinthine dimension as he investigated the defunct Matavia Press: A Publishing Concern, a small company cofounded by three struggling poets, Peter S. North, L. Malcolm Hintz, and Marcia A. Regina, and the novelist E. Robert

Pendleton. Ryder unearthed the only founder not dead or institutionalized, the accountant for Matavia, a vagabond beat poet, L. Malcolm Hintz, residing at a studio apartment in Milwaukee, Wisconsin.

Hintz had given Ryder a long-winded story akin to some illicit black market trade as to why all Matavia transactions had been cash only, all members of the board having taken care of their own works, paid out of their own pockets in a rat's ship of clawing despair in which none of the cofounders had been actual friends. Hintz had called them "the confederacy of the doomed."

There had been no general accounts, no purchase orders, and no accounts payable or receivable in the Matavia charade. According to Hintz, if Pendleton's novel had been printed by J&S, then it was something undertaken by Pendleton alone, with a business card and a wad of cash. What Hintz did as accountant was merely file a bogus company tax return, which according to Hintz was, in its own right, "Matavia's greatest work of fiction."

It got more absurd when Ryder had asked Hintz about his blurb for *Scream*, Hintz simply stating that Pendleton must have made up the quote, that it had been their agreed policy to make up quotes from one another, thus relieving any of them from having to read one another's works.

The investigation was ongoing. A data entry firm had been employed by the conglomerate to enter data from handwritten J&S ledgers. The data entry clerks had worked from home, so the records potentially still existed in a box in someone's house, though three of the women entering the data had died.

In following this protracted line of investigation, Ryder had come to believe the original version of *Scream* had most likely been published *after* the discovery of the victim's body, that the anonymous tape was a hoax to drum up publicity, rather than the solution to the decade-old cold case file on Amber Jewel.

Oddly, for Ryder, the fact that Pendleton was likely not the murderer didn't fundamentally change things, for there was a murdered victim at the heart of the investigation, the case no different from all the other cold case files he investigated. On his way north, Ryder had followed his standard MO, stopped for coffee while reading through the original case file, specifically, in this case, the account of a farmer, Sam Henderson, who had found the victim's body.

Ryder had caught the tugging subtext of an old world loneliness in the Henderson statement, and his interest piqued because he knew a farmer watched his land.

In Henderson, Ryder saw a witness with the potential latent memory of that time, a memory Ryder wanted to tap into as he listened to Henderson casting back to the day he found the body of Amber Jewel.

Ryder noted the way Henderson used almost the same words he had spoken a decade earlier in his statement, how he made reference again to the pockmarked field of melted snow, gave the exact temperature that morning, thirty-nine degrees Fahrenheit.

Henderson stated that he had thought originally that the dark sack at the far end of his property was a stash of bank robbery loot, because that was the kind of thing that was wont to happen in movies back in his day—Prohibition and Bonnie and Clyde–type gangsters stashing heist money in fields. Even now he was following the same line of a story he had internalized over all these years.

And so the story proceeded by degree, Henderson talking in the way of someone passing stories from generation to generation as Ryder listened. He had a stopwatch running as he walked alongside Henderson and, checking it surreptitiously, saw five minutes had already elapsed as they had crossed the field.

Henderson conceded, after the quip about Bonnie and Clyde, to thinking almost immediately that the bags were just garbage dumped by the sub-population of new poor who had taken to driving out of town to throw their garbage from car windows into fields; then he changed his story again, or not exactly changed his story but went through the sifting sense of what he felt he had observed back then, of how things had unfolded in his head that day, for who naturally assumes they will uncover a human corpse?

Stopping close to where the body of Amber Jewel had been discovered, Henderson looked at Ryder and said, "I knew something was wrong, that this wasn't a drive-by garbage dump. You just get that feeling sometimes. The bags . . . they were too far off the county road. . . ."

Ryder betrayed no emotion, though he had stopped the stopwatch, his hand in his trademark long black coat as Henderson's eyes met his, the soft pouch of skin under each of Henderson's eyes a bruised bluish black. He was wearing overalls on the thin skeleton of his frame, his hands deep in his pockets. Maybe they were the same overalls he had worn back then. Time pooled so much out in the country.

Henderson turned back toward the road, his house visible through the decaying cornstalks as he went on to describe how, against a cold drizzle of foggy rain that morning, he had climbed down from his tractor, the memory of his wife still recent, that aloneness wrapped around him, knowing what he was going to discover.

He talked in a slow, deliberate way, spoke of using his walking stick like a feeler, opening one of the bags, seeing the teeming swarm of vermin move over what turned out to be a torso, the dismembered legs hacked off at the knees, the right arm cut at the elbow, then turning over the torso and seeing, eerily preserved in the cold permafrost, the marble death mask of a face he knew, the daughter of one of his neighbors, a girl who had been missing some five months, the face of thirteen-year-old Amber Jewel.

FIFTEEN

ADI EXITED on the eighth floor of the library with a sense of trepidation, walking out into the checked shadow of the book aisles, slats of early morning light cutting the gray bulk of cataloged books. There was nobody about.

Paranoia had taken hold of her since she had seen the stranger in the aisle, and as she opened her office door, a note fluttered in the sudden draft of air. Instinctively, she swung around. There was nobody there, and she locked her office door.

The note was typewritten:

> It is difficult
> to get the news from poems
> yet men die miserably every day
> for lack
> of what is found there.
> (William Carlos Williams)

P.S. Why does nobody teach this Williams poem?
Is it too plainly obvious, too direct?

Adi looked up, her heart still pounding, though she had calmed somewhat, felt relieved as she uttered under her breath, "That son of a bitch. . . ." It had been the arrogant biology student who had left the note as a rebuttal to her challenging him, making him do his assignment over.

Adi looked up, took another deep breath, and, looking into the deserted aisles outside her office, tried to focus on her lecture; her class started in forty minutes. The more she tried to concentrate, the more the note kept nagging at her. The biology student was a C– student. Would he have taken the time to find such a quote?

She read the note again. Then the phone rang, making her jump at the first ring.

It was Allen Horowitz. He said, "Greetings from the Big Apple!"

"Oh, Allen, it's you."

Horowitz's voice was loud. "That's the most lackluster greeting I've ever gotten from somebody whom I'm trying desperately to make famous! We slipped out of the top hundred last week. I know it's a drop-off, but listen to this. I called in a huge favor at the *New Yorker*. Here's the tagline we're running with for the piece: 'If a tree falls in the woods, and there's nobody there to hear it, does it still make a noise? What if *Scream* had never been heard? Would it still be great art?' Tell me that's not genius!"

Adi stood up. The note was still on the desk. It was hard for her to focus on what Horowitz was saying. He was on speakerphone, a hollow voice coming across the line.

Horowitz kept talking. "Look, I think we can get both the populists and the academics on our side. We're *so* nearly there. Bob is already the patron saint of the struggling artist, of small academic publishing houses. The houses here in New York are starting to see the potential. I had lunch with my agent, and confidentially, people are tripping over themselves to find the next great lost masterpiece! Can you believe this? We're so close to a breakout, Adi, I know we are. That's why you should be up here with me, both of you should. People want to see Bob . . . and *you*."

Horowitz stopped abruptly. His voice took on a sudden intimacy. He was off speakerphone. "*Can* I see you?" He let the question hang for a moment. "Aren't you going to answer me?"

The overbearing pressure of the past twenty-four hours had gotten to Adi. There were tears in her eyes. She took a deep breath, tried to regain her composure, and said coldly, "Look, you handle it, Allen. That's what we agreed . . . I've got to get ready for my class."

"Screw class! This is the biggest break of your life, don't you get it?"

Adi leaned into the phone, her hair falling over her face. She had her eyes closed. "Is this in Robert's best interest? He understands nothing of what's going on."

"You telling me you have cold feet now, after everything we did to get this far? Don't put this over on me. This is about *you*."

Adi tried to measure her response. "It isn't about me. I'm *nothing*. Don't you get it? I don't have anything here." She looked up and pushed her hair off her face. "I'm living at Robert's house, and what the hell am I to him? He can barely function. I'm a caretaker!" Her eyes watered. "Now look what you made me do! I'm crying. . . ."

"I think you've changed the subject here. What do you *want*?"

Adi looked out on Bannockburn's campus, the ivy quads impeccably manicured, the statue of the college's founder catching the morning light. This was what she wanted more than anything else, to be accepted as an equal, to find a job, to do what had escaped her parents. She said as much. "What I want is my doctorate."

"You're going to get it."

"I also don't want Robert to be made a freak. . . . That's what he has— what both of us have—become. I don't want that sort of fleeting fame, to be a spectacle like that. I'm just a simple person at heart. Maybe it's time to let things just pass now." She hesitated. "Look, I've got to go."

Horowitz shouted, "Don't hang up, Adi Wiltshire. Don't! You know I got involved in all of this for *you*, not Bob. I took your calls. What did you expect?"

"I don't know . . . but this is bigger than any of us imagined. This is about Robert's life, not mine or yours."

Horowitz's voice eased. "What are you afraid of?"

Adi said coldly, "You know, the fact is, you met me in person once, just *once*. Do you really know who I am?"

"I think I do. . . . Let me ask you something. Do you believe in love at first sight?"

"Yes."

"Let me put my cards on the table. I wouldn't even have you sign a prenuptial. You could take me for half of everything I'm worth. That's how much I'm willing to gamble on *us*."

Adi said abruptly, "What would you say if I told you my goal in life was to be an independent woman?"

Horowitz let out a theatrical moan. "Give me anything but a feminist. In fact, let me give you a little advice about independence. I met this famous vanguard feminist a while back at a literary conference, and I said to her, 'So you're still not wearing a bra, even all these years later?' And she looked at me dead seriously and said, 'Yes, but not for the same reasons. Now I don't wear a bra because my breasts pull the wrinkles off my face.' There's a lesson there somewhere. Think about it!"

Adi turned and faced the campus. "I didn't know feminism and independence were inextricably coupled."

"Hey, I'm a victim of my generation. I don't pretend to be anything other than what I am. I just speak the facts. The truth is, there is no book *The Joy of Menopause*."

Adi said, "I think you're talking me out of liking you. What are you saying—life is over at forty for women?"

"Well, let me ask you this: What age was your mother when she left your father?"

"Who says my parents are divorced?"

"Are they?"

"Yes."

"So what age was your mother when she left your father?"

"Thirty-eight."

"See where I'm going here? I bet she had another child?"

"She miscarried four times."

"Okay, then she and her new husband have a miniature schnauzer or a Mexican hairless they take everywhere with them?"

"Not quite. It's a teacup poodle named Trixie."

"Damn, I should have gotten that one, the teacup poodle . . . with the weeping black eyes."

Adi looked into the book aisles. They were still deserted. Maybe it had just been a pervert the previous day. It seemed strange to think a pervert could be the better of two alternatives. She said quietly, "Is this what you do all day long, Allen, psychoanalyze people?"

"You say that in a pejorative way, but let me let you in on a little secret. The essence of fiction is *empirical* observation, the scientific method applied to human interaction. Fiction requires a more rigorous discipline than all other art."

"How?"

"Jesus, for starters, the stakes are so much higher, the audience is that much more intimate with language than any other medium of expression. You must get things just right. There have been child prodigies in music and mathematics, because there are elemental laws of accord and discord, but where are the child protégés of literature? Are there any? That's a question."

"I can't think of any."

"That's because there are none! Fiction is an accumulation of the observed born of years of living. Fiction is essentially representative and therefore, alas, may be the most intellectually conservative of all the art forms. We writers live in the ghetto of the familiar, in the literary tropes of the perceived temporal life of the masses, with a beginning, middle, and end. Do you know how screwed up that convention is in the face of Einstein and relativity, in relation to string theory? Fiction writers are the flat earth artists—"

Adi cut him off. "Who are you, really?"

"I'm just a guy who now writes coffee table books."

"Are you?"

"It's what I chose in the end."

"Do you like yourself?"

There was a moment's silence.

"You want a confession? Okay, well, here goes. You tell me if I like myself. When Bob showed me *A Hole Without a Middle*, with the twenty-one and a half blank pages a third of the way through the novel, I nearly shit myself at the audacity of what he was trying to do creatively, and there he was, a guy taking me as his equal. We weren't friends, but we had mutual respect, at least Bob did. We were going different ways in our work. I saw that. He was looking for guidance, maybe even an advocate for what he was trying to do. It was a gamble. His future was on the line, but he told me he didn't want to write the same book again. Art meant something more to him. . . . Shit, there's no short version of what happened. . . . This is one for your thesis . . . okay?

"We were sharing the same agent back then. I think what Bob wanted was for me to prep the agent. I was set to see her for lunch. It turned out Bob was right to be nervous. The agent thought the blank pages were a Xeroxing mistake when she got to them, or that's how she opened the story. An editor from a major house that was interested in my latest book was there at the lunch. I pretended I had not read the book. I let my agent go on. She was saying Bob had gone off the deep end. The agent ended up figuring out the twenty-one and a half blank pages weren't a Xeroxing mistake after all. I mean, you read it. Maybe Bob was crazy! Who the hell creates a protagonist who writes a goddamn ransom note to the reader, holding twenty-one and a half pages hostage? I mean, he was out of his mind, right?"

Horowitz paused momentarily, then started again. "I remember laughing with both of them at the time. The agent said she wasn't returning Bob's calls anymore, that he was a liability to her credibility as an agent, but here's the kicker. Just to close the door on Bob, I said, 'Hey, don't be so quick to knock this, Barbara. I got three hundred blank pages I'm willing to sell for a mere six figures!' That got the editor laughing her sides sick. . . . Good old crazy Bob. He ended up getting the book published by some academic midwest press, which I always suspected was just short of a vanity press. The book tanked. It was barely reviewed. It killed something deep inside him. That same year I hit the best-seller list for the first time."

Horowitz tailed off, "See . . . we all have sins we have to answer for. But what I did was survive. I played the safe hand."

Adi said quietly, "Look, I want to talk to you about something, but I have to get to class. Let me call you this afternoon, all right?"

SIXTEEN

THE NEON BLEED OF eateries flashed against the dark as Ryder unpacked his small suitcase at the Howard Johnson motel by the highway exit. The small clock radio dial flipped to 6:52 p.m. In the next room, a TV was on loud. He heard gunfire, then the dramatic music of the aftermath, a woman screaming in the melodramatic fashion of old-style westerns.

The dispassionate voice pattern on the tape had added a surreal quality to the specter of the black earth field where Amber Jewel's dismembered remains had been discovered so many years before, a sound track that had made the universe cold and arbitrary, godless, and somehow it had affected Ryder more deeply than he wanted to admit.

In an odd way, it was the same feeling he had experienced as he read *Scream*, the deep, pathologically spiritual loss that had pervaded the book.

It had been a long day for Ryder, the undercurrent of his own melancholy there still. The unsettling fact was that the crime scene hadn't come together, seemingly fitting more with the original suspects, Kim Jewel and Gary Scholl.

What he needed was a definite date for the original print run to establish whether the leak about the novel was a hoax, to see how he should proceed in the investigation.

In reviewing the original murder investigation file after he had left

Henderson's, he had also come across the fact that Kim Jewel had called in a missing persons report on her sister less than two hours after she was due home, something suspicious in its own right.

Why would Kim Jewel have jumped to such a conclusion? It again gave credence to what investigators had long presumed, that she was involved in the murder, that she had overcompensated, miscalculated just how much time she should have waited after her sister's murder to call the police and how much concern she needed to show.

Given the window of just two hours before Kim Jewel called the police, as Ryder read further through the detailed report regarding how the victim had been dismembered, he came to understand that the dismemberment and disposal of the victim most probably occurred at a later date.

Ryder was somewhat baffled that investigators had not pursued the possibility that Amber Jewel had been first abducted, then murdered and set out at Henderson's property at a later date, and as he continued to review the file, looking at the crime scene photographs, it troubled him how Jewel's face had been so well preserved, so much so that he called his home office to run a report on the exact temperatures from the date of the victim's disappearance on November 6 through December 31 of 1976.

An hour later, he was informed via fax that the fall of 1976 had been particularly warm. A stretch of nine days from November 6 through November 14 had seen the median daytime temperature hover at forty-seven degrees. Was it possible that her face could have been so well preserved through the whole winter given the early run of warm days?

It was the sort of question one referred to FBI forensic scientists, who ran a human decay research farm, quantifying the rate of decay of the human body under varying weather conditions and circumstances, bodies in lakes or car trunks, bodies left exposed in summer heat or winter freeze. Insects had become key indicators for time of death, various insects interested in the body at different stages of decomposition. Where a particular insect was in its life cycle often helped indicate how long the insect had been present in the corpse.

Of course, no such extensive analysis had been carried out on Amber Jewel's corpse. Her body had been recovered in the relative dark ages of forensic pathology. Maybe the FBI could still give an educated assessment based on the photographs regarding the possibility that the victim might not have been immediately murdered and dumped in the field.

That the victim's body had been dumped at a later date was just a working hypothesis, part of the provisional process of reengaging with the facts, of reassessing evidence with a sense of distance and perspective. Having the victim removed from the locale and buried at a later date at least opened up the possibility that someone like Pendleton could theoretically have kidnapped the victim, then returned to the area and buried her remains close to her own house.

It was a stretch, but then Ryder, in reading *Scream*, had glimpsed into the psychotic mind of the author, and he felt that the murderer, in setting the victim's body back close to where she had gone missing, added a surreal dimension to the crime. It was not something Kim Jewel or Gary Scholl would have done, casting suspicion so close to themselves.

Again, Ryder had to stop and just gather his thoughts, align the facts first and foremost. Without the definitive print-run date, he already felt he was becoming mired in lines of speculation that went beyond what he ordinarily processed early in his investigation, and it was clear that what he had been sent to investigate—namely, the allegedly random murder of a young girl by a disaffected college professor—was already becoming shaded with unsettling questions. This was not the sort of case he needed now.

It was the forty-second winter of Jon Ryder's life, the forty-second trip around the sun. He had lived a life punctuated by the good and the bad, remarried now to a woman who had given him two boys whose portraits he kept in his wallet along with his wedding photograph.

Ryder put his socks in a small top drawer along with his underwear, which his wife had ironed and lightly starched for him the night before. He had watched her in the family den in her housecoat and bare feet a few nights previous. It made him stop and think about their relationship, catching himself unawares as he looked up and saw himself in a large backlit mirror. He saw the crow's-feet of middle age spreading from his tired eyes, his face darkened by a five o'clock shadow.

He looked worn and told himself he should be glad that he had found a place in this world, that he had a wife and children to take him through the rest of his years. It was that faith that had saved him the past few years, alone as he was so many nights in nondescript motels like this, that faith in his children and their future that had staved off the vengeance or blackness that had afflicted so many others in his profession, that kept him doing what he did for a living: staring into the souls of people who did desperate and terrible things to one another.

This was the narrative Ryder wanted to believe, the story he told himself against the loneliness of these evenings.

At 7:00 p.m. Ryder rang his wife, Gail. She answered on the second ring. She was in the bathroom with their sons, Tommy and Frankie. They were in the bathtub.

Gail held the phone out, and Ryder heard the quack of a rubber duck and the slosh of bathwater as his two kids said in unison, "We love you, Daddy!"

Gail moved away from the kids. "How are you holding up?" There was no prelude, just the flat question. The fight of the previous night still lingered.

Ryder said, "Okay."

Gail persisted. She was not letting things go. "You sound down."

"Do I? I don't mean to. . . ." Ryder yawned. "I'm tired." He said quietly, "I miss you."

Gail didn't respond, the tension still there between them, and Ryder had run out of things to say, except for what was really on his mind: whether his daughter, Taylor, had called home.

Taylor was Ryder's daughter from his first marriage to Tori Adams, his true one-and-only, a marriage Ryder considered, even still, his *real* marriage, for in 1976—eerily, the same year as the cold case he was now investigating—Tori had disappeared without a trace, leaving him and Taylor alone. The disturbing facts in the case, the rocky relationship between Ryder and Tori, had led investigators to suspect Ryder of foul play, something that had tainted his career and existence ever since.

The shadow of accusation had again surfaced as Taylor had grown into adolescence, alienated from Ryder's new wife and the twins, and as she had turned sixteen and come of legal age to leave, she had begun blatantly to accuse Ryder of having killed Tori, staying away for a week or more at a time, living on-again, off-again with her boyfriend, a twenty-three-year-old loser with a rap sheet.

In the initial days of reopening the Jewel case, Ryder's relationship with Taylor had neared a flashpoint as she had been gone the longest period yet from home, fifteen days and counting; and Ryder, in a desperate attempt to connect again with her, had spoken to her at school with the intervention of a counselor.

He had tried to explain that in the course of his duty, he had put away numerous people who had sworn to get revenge on him, hoping the counselor would side with him. Taylor had countered with what she had learned from her grandmother, Tori's mother: that Ryder had been physically and emotionally abusive to Tori, that her disappearance had come during a time when Tori was separated from Ryder, when Tori had a restraining order against him.

Even Ryder had seen the look in the counselor's eyes, the prejudice against the menacing figure he cut, though in the wake of Taylor having screamed and then cried herself out, Ryder had gotten the better of her and promised to get her a car as part of a deal if she came home. It was something Taylor had reluctantly agreed to do as the counselor pressed for additional off-site professional intervention, but then Ryder had reneged on the offer after Gail had kicked up a fight about finances.

The fight the previous night had been particularly heated, Ryder accusing Gail of having never taken to Taylor, blaming her for the emotional distance that had developed between him and his daughter.

Gail continued to wait silently on the phone, resolute she was in the right; and Ryder, closing his eyes, conceded to her, saying, "I don't want to fight again like last night."

Gail still didn't answer, making Ryder work at an apology. He said, by way of appeasing her, "She set me up to fail her a long time ago . . . I know that now."

Gail said sharply, "Don't put everything in the context of you failing her or her failing you. This is a stage girls go through. Adolescent girls use whatever they can, indiscriminately, to get what they want."

"That's why I wanted her back, Gail. I know if I had a chance with her, I could make things right."

Gail didn't let up. "I'm not going to let you bankrupt us. I'm not. What would she do, anyway, take the car out, get drugged up, and end up crashing it? You know the crowd she hangs with. That's what would happen, Jon. If you want the honest truth, that's just as much behind me not letting you do this. You want to go identify the corpse of your own daughter, do you?"

Ryder put the receiver to his other ear. "You're right. Look, I'm sorry I dragged you into this."

"Dragged me into what? What I'm looking at right now are two beautiful boys in a bathtub who have your eyes."

Despite himself, Ryder's voice flared, starting up the fight again as he said, "Don't!"

Gail's voice got hot. "Don't what?"

"You know! Why do I feel like I'm always being made to choose between them or Taylor? . . ."

Gail hit back, her voice on the verge of a shout. "I never asked you to choose, and—"

"I'm talking about Taylor! She did, a long time ago, when Tori left, and I failed her. I looked elsewhere for something *I* needed." He let out a long breath. "You know, sometimes I find myself wishing she'd never been born."

"Jesus Christ, don't ever say that, Jon! Do you know how that sounds?"

Ryder sat at the edge of the queen-size bed, looking down at the commercial-grade orange shag carpet burned here and there from cigarettes, this the cheap sort of motel the Cold Case Division budgeted for as he worked these cases. Shaking his head, he said more to himself than to Gail, "What kind of cop am I, out finding other people's bodies and not my wife's body? . . ." He trailed off.

Gail said nothing.

Ryder took a shallow breath. "Maybe I'm losing it. I don't know, the coincidence of that girl disappearing the same year as Tori, everything happening now with Taylor . . . Somehow, going out today to where she was found felt like that feeling of seeing the movie after having read the book. I don't know what I expected. It was exactly like it was described in the book, the house in the background, the combine harvester with the scarecrow on it, the grove of trees and the river, all there. It was as though I were experiencing everything again, like I'd lived it before. I had this sense of clairvoyance, something spiritual, as though I were going to understand everything when I got there. I thought this girl was going to come to me in some revelation, tell me everything, about her and about Tori, about every missing person that ever vanished. Her and Tori's souls went to the same purgatory that year. I thought, in what was happening with Taylor, in losing her, that a mother's love could somehow transcend . . . that Tori could help me." Ryder had his hand to his face. "It had a feeling of destiny driving up here this morning, like I'd come to a place I needed to find all my life, but the longer I was there, all I saw was a field in front of me, nothing else. Nothing else revealed itself."

Gail answered stiffly, "I don't know what you want from me anymore! Look, I've got to get the kids out of that bath. They're turning into prunes."

Realizing she was hanging up, Ryder said, "Wait, put the phone up to my kids!" And he shouted into the small round mesh of the receiver, "I love you guys!" trying to imagine them in the bath as he heard them shout back, "We love you!"

Then Gail hung up without another word to him, and he felt the sudden loneliness that only a highway motel can elicit.

SEVENTEEN

THE BIOLOGY STUDENT SKIPPED the 8:00 a.m. Intro to Poetry class, and Adi's fear dissipated, for now she knew he had typed up the note. This was all part of the weirdness of private college life, the nuances between those *giving* grades and those *paying for* grades. There was no such thing as impartiality here. Money tainted everything. With inflationary grades, every second student was a straight A student. Were there that many natural geniuses walking around campuses?

It was a cynicism Adi was willing to wallow in, anything to keep her mind at ease, to stop thinking about Pendleton and *Scream*. She had decided to forestall Horowitz's efforts. She was set on that. She was going to call him and obstinately refuse to go to New York.

Adi closed her eyes, let that argument she would inevitably have with Horowitz play itself out in her head. What she had to focus on was that she had survived so far, had not broken down, and she *would* survive the next few weeks.

The nightmare would pass. It *was* passing, *Scream* already in its precipitous descent out of the top hundred, heading for the chasm of the top five hundred. Beyond that, how many books did it take even to stay in the top thousand? Was there even such a list?

Throughout her class, her mind had thankfully been preoccupied with Wright, who had asked her for permission to take shots of her students, or more precisely to take a pastiche of close-up shots of body parts, an ankle, a knee, an earlobe, an eye, a hand, a smile, a composition he announced to the class as provisionally titled *The Student Body*.

Adi lingered in the cool morning autumn light as the last of her students left, somewhat relaxed now that she had come to her decision regarding Horowitz. Even the tug of her addiction had abated somewhat. Could she hold out for the rest of the morning, and then the afternoon, and then a day, and then another and another after that?

Life was about incremental change.

Wright was still there with her in the classroom, setting up his tripod for an autumnal shot of the quad for the yearbook. The grounds staff had been advised to work the quad that morning, and all of them were out in full force with their leaf blowers, making piles of leaves.

In the sums of money being spent at Bannockburn, nothing was left to chance, every image, every event, captured for posterity. Even the mass burning of the autumnal leaves involved a macabre, nonsanctioned, student tradition. On an appointed starry night after all the leaves were gathered, the Lucy Bannockburns, or simply the Lucys, in period costume, ran a gambit of flaming leaf stacks out back of the college, while scarecrow figures of bearded Iosifs ran wailing after them.

These cultist bonding rituals defined Bannockburn, harkening back to the occult secret societies of eighteenth- and nineteenth-century England, and for Adi it all had the tempered quality of something she coveted most—family. But then her mind settled on Pendleton, as it always did these days. It was hard to imagine this campus as a nightmare, that it could have driven him crazy, driven him to murder, but it seemingly had.

It was as Adi was leaving the classroom that she heard the rapid-fire click of the automatic shutter. It stopped her midstride, and, turning in a fearful moment filled with memories of the night Pendleton attempted suicide, she shouted, "Don't! Goddamn you, stop!"

Wright looked up from his box camera, and almost immediately Adi tried to apologize. "I'm sorry . . . I just . . ." She didn't finish her thought. Did she really need to explain things? Wasn't it obvious?

Wright just stood there, looking at her as she left the room.

She had overreacted, of course, and she understood this as soon as she had exited onto the quad, which was now empty of students. Classes had begun again. This was, after all, Wright's job, ironically secured because of the fallout of his tumultuous fights with Pendleton years before, a job given to him by the college to dissuade him from pursuing legal options, an ex-marine just trying to make life-altering choices, wanting a purpose in life, not a *handout*, not some *gag money*, some *settlement*, or so he had told her the night he had admitted to sending Pendleton the death threats. What he had wanted was a *career*, a *future*.

Adi kept walking under the eye of the humanities building clock tower, conscious of Wright's presence. Was he staring at her? She had let him down, ripped apart whatever fraternity they had established. There were, she knew, few people as forthright as Wright, few people willing to take the hits, to keep on trying against the odds. Would anyone at the college have envisioned that almost a decade after he had been thrown the bone of this so-called project, he would have made it his own, made it a legitimate enterprise, so that he, the outsider, had become the eyes through which Bannockburn would be remembered?

Walking across the quad, Adi swept her hair off her shoulder and, turning her head surreptitiously, looked back to see Wright standing at the classroom window, watching after her.

EIGHTEEN

IN THE GLASSHOUSE EFFECT of morning light streaming through the Howard Johnson diner, Jon Ryder smelled of Brut aftershave, a gift set Taylor had gotten him perennially for Christmas since she was nine years old. It was a scent that marked him as a father, a raw, bracing smell, close to alcohol, an aftershave meant to be patted between the palms of the hands and slapped against the cheeks and neck.

There had been a commercial for the aftershave years ago that had somehow defined how he had envisioned life once upon a time, a guy with a bear's chest of hair standing before a bathroom mirror, a towel wrapped around his waist, and a woman in a housecoat holding his arm.

So much for wishful thinking and a past that had simply vanished.

Taylor had, of course, been on Ryder's mind all night long. He was tired. The late night movie had taken him through the night, with its Craftmatic Adjustable Bed and term life insurance commercials.

A middle-aged, saddlebagged waitress with ham-hock legs came and poured him coffee, taking out creamers from her apron and setting them down like a bet. Her tag read, "Dorothy—16 Years Serving You." She smelled of menthol cigarettes, her fingers stained a jaundiced yellow.

The special was a short stack of blueberry pancakes with a side order of bacon, sausage, and egg and a bottomless drip coffee. He went with the special.

For his part, he looked no better off than the woman serving him, maybe worse. He looked every part a bail bondsman, or a repo man out collecting a debt, or maybe a PI, undoubtedly someone who lived within the criminal element of society, an enforcer, big and heavyset in that behemoth midwest stock of Polish and Irish immigrants who had built cities like Chicago. Everything about him was intimidating, from his potato face to his hard, piercing blue eyes, to his short-cropped black hair combed back off his forehead with hair cream, to his ill-fitting jacket that showed its age and bulged with a shoulder holster, to his trademark long black trench coat draped over the vinyl seat.

Ryder looked at the clock over the diner's cash register, a fifties Elvis with swaying pendulum hips, Elvis's outstretched hands telling the time, Ryder waiting as events unfolded around him, for all was *never* as it seemed.

That was the simple lesson Ryder had taken from life. He was suspicious of everything and everyone, a reality affirmed each day. For the better part of his adult life, he had lived amid murder in all its permutations, crimes of passion and hate, some spontaneous, others cold and calculated. In the end, the cases that chilled him most were those that displayed the clinical pathology of calculated murder.

He was aware of the vast, complex psychological machinery that held guilt in abeyance; alter egos so distinct and separate that it was tempting to believe, as the medical profession did, in multiple personalities, to accept the notion that there were parallel consciousnesses within the same person, or, on a more profoundly spiritual level, to believe in the supernatural forces of darkness, to believe, as in scripture, in the incarnation of incubus, or, dare ever admit it openly, to believe in possession.

It seemed strange that he had drifted back in his own psyche to the fire-and-brimstone indoctrination of his parochial Catholic schooling on the West Side of Chicago, but then he had lived through his own nightmare of his wife's vanishing, believing in his heart that all disappearances were part of a cosmic battle between heaven and hell, between good and evil.

It had been a strange abandonment of logical deduction for what had once been a rational man, though he had borne witness to horrific and ritualistic murders in Chicago, before he left for Evansville. How did one cope with what he had witnessed, from grainy home videotapes, snuff murders of hooded victims, their imploring cries begging God for help, undocumented cases of missing persons, prostitutes, and runaways, to looping video surveillance of children being led out of malls by strangers?

How did one go about investigating such crimes when the leads dead-ended? Where was God? It had been the question at the heart of *Scream*, something Ryder had identified with, although he had asked the questions not the way Pendleton or philosophers asked such questions, but at a personal, visceral level. He wanted answers for inconsolable families.

In the end, he had sought alternative ways of seeing into the souls of these victims, tarot card readers and clairvoyants with crystal balls who always spoke in cosmic terms, struggles between light and dark, good and evil. It made sense at some deep level. It figured with what Ryder had seen as the years had passed, a world recoiling from faith and compassion, a world grown hard with fear and alienation, a world of automatic car door locks and home security systems, of tamperproof labeling and closed-circuit TV surveillance, and yet the numbers of missing had increased exponentially.

There was something preternatural about it, this mystery of the vanishing. Where did these souls go? In a more ancient time, it would have augured ritual and penitence, but not anymore. There was a saying, "If you stare into the abyss, the abyss stares into you," something he had understood and managed to conceal from the police psychological review board when questioned regarding his potential involvement in his wife's disappearance. When he had closed his eyes at night, he, too, had begun to dream in that grainy surveillance mode, the infinite loop of an abduction, video without sound, he alone a mere witness to events, watching them unfold on a black-and-white TV monitor, knowing in his heart the real events were happening just out of view, in a room down a hallway, and he could do nothing to stop it. It was beyond his power to alter the chain of events.

He had spent four months under psychiatric evaluation as his wife's case went cold, afraid to pursue it himself for fear that being overzealous in wanting to find her would hint at his involvement in her disappearance. Nobody at that time had used the word "murder," not around him. As he went back to work, he felt alienated from his fellow investigators. The sordid facts of his tumultuous relationship with Tori had come out again, the restraining order, the fact that Tori was dating again. If anybody knew how to cover his tracks, wouldn't it have been someone like Ryder? There was no getting away from the shadow of suspicion.

Two months back on the job, the strain had finally showed as Ryder investigated the missing persons case of a ten-year-old girl, the same age as Taylor at the time. Ryder had beaten a confession out of a suspect. He had dressed in a long dark coat and ski mask, a sort of superhero vigilante getup, but it had worked.

The suspect had confessed, and the ten-year-old girl had been recovered, in a storage unit along the Calumet River, hog-tied. Tragically, she had suffocated to death. She had been raped and sodomized.

Soon Ryder was having recurring dreams of a school yard game of tag he had played during recess at his Catholic elementary school, a game based on the mysterious black-shrouded figures of the Brethren of the Misericordia, who had carried the sick to hospitals and buried the dead during times of plague, a society so secret that its members hid their identities even from one another. He began to see himself as one of those shrouded, spectral figures of the Brethren, moving through a fallen world, gathering the dead.

One night he dreamed he was back in grade school, in the shadowy corridors, with its statues of saints, the Virgin Mary crushing the head of a snake with her bare alabaster foot, and beyond, the yard filled with the dead. He was one of the Brethren again, and he stared into the dark, smiling eyes of Venetia Goretti, his first true crush. She secretly touched his hand, though she was supposed to be one of the dead, as he picked her up in the school yard with his fellow Brethren.

What he had seen at that moment in his dream was his true mission in life, to find the bodies of the dead and deliver them to consecrated ground.

His dream occurred during the time he was under suspicion of having been involved in his wife's disappearance. In the ensuing weeks, he found he could not inhabit the house, or even the city, he had shared with her. It was why he'd put in an application when the job came up with the Cold Case Division in Evansville, Indiana, so removed from the streets of Chicago, from what he had known all his life. But that was the point. He wanted a place with no personal history for him, a white canvas upon which to paint a new existence.

* * *

Through the years, Ryder had not given up the notion of the Brethren when warranted. With the stalemate with his daughter hurting at a deep level, and so, too, his fight with Gail, Ryder knew he was facing the dissolution of everything he held close to his heart if he did not get home soon. As the convoluted turns in the Pendleton case evolved, Ryder felt himself pushed to a heightened anxiety, the choice set squarely before him—his family or the case.

It had all gone a long way to Ryder taking on the mantle of the Brethren again at Bannockburn library. In the most unorthodox of investigative procedures, dressed in his long coat, a quasi-religious spiritualist wacko, he had set himself in the book aisles and stared dead-on at Adi Wiltshire, simply to see what she would do.

He had wanted to intimidate her by his sheer presence. Someone with nothing to hide would have called the campus police when he appeared in such a haunting and menacing way, but she hadn't, and Ryder felt sure she knew about the connection between Amber Jewel and *Scream*.

In his case file, it had been noted that Wiltshire was doing her thesis on Pendleton and that prior to working on Pendleton's material, she had struggled to find a thesis subject and had been close to losing her academic stipend. He had seen, also, Wiltshire's financial statements, knowing that she had received over $120,000 from Allen Horowitz since Pendleton's attempted suicide.

Ryder felt that between the two of them, they had masterminded the rerelease of *Scream* and were responsible for sending the cassette. Ryder knew that only someone with an intimate knowledge of Pendleton's book could have drawn such concise parallels.

NINETEEN

JUST PAST 9:30 a.m. central standard time, on that same brilliant morning of cold blue sky, as Adi walked across campus and Ryder ate his breakfast, a mobile TV satellite van snaked into the long incline of the historic neighborhood lined with skeletal old-growth trees.

A half hour had passed since the New York City press release announcing *Scream*'s nomination for the National Book Award.

Pendleton was, as usual, in his turreted home office in his striped blue pajamas and robe. A half-eaten breakfast sat off to the side, a soft-boiled egg, toast, and Earl Grey tea served on a wicker tray, along with a freshly cut pink carnation, as per Adi's instructions, Pendleton pampered with a nod to some preconceived notion she had of what a tempered English aristocratic life might have been at the turn of the century.

Pendleton was merely a life-size doll in this construct.

He pressed an interactive farm animal book, and a green frog in a pond popped up just as he looked up and saw the flurry of activity out on the street. It registered at a surface level, as something vaguely different from what he usually saw outside his window. His morning pills to control his tremors clouded his senses and had the effect of making his right eye droop.

He went back to the book, pressed a picture of a dog that said, "Woof, Woof," a sound that made his white rabbit nervously nose the air and hop onto his lap.

When the doorbell rang moments later, he looked up again with a sort of turtle slowness, the stalk of his neck holding his stubbly, tonsured head. He had already forgotten he had seen the mill of people outside on the street. He could focus on only one thing at a time under the drowsily narcotic effects of the medication.

He turned away again, returning to the familiarity of the picture book, pressed down with his index finger on a picture that went, "Cluck, Cluck!" He said the word "chicken" without emotion.

Then he looked up and watched the people outside.

Pendleton did not associate the fuss with anything to do with him. Only the rote processes of life within the house had assumed any lasting substance, those and his reliance on Adi, and Pendleton called her name in his monotone voice, blinking as he watched the van parked across from his house.

Another van arrived, and a woman in a dress suit got out, along with a cameraman.

Stroking his rabbit slowly, Pendleton felt the softness of the undercoat. The rabbit kneaded against his legs, and Pendleton wet himself in a spreading stain that roused him slightly.

He took hold of the rabbit and used his other hand to balance as he stood up slowly. His pajama pants bunched in a V. He shuffled toward the door leading onto the widow's walk, opened it, and, balancing against the door-knob, took a step onto the walk and heard a din of sound as someone shouted, "Professor! Professor!"

Already the urine had turned cold against his crotch.

What was caught next, in a ten-second video clip, would come to de-fine the rest of his life, capturing him in a frailty characteristic of military junta dictators in the failing stages of health at some secluded medical fa-cility, the sort of video shown on the evening news to a world left to con-template the enigmatic incongruity of these stooped figures against the rumored killing fields of their legacies.

Pendleton stood just so, at the cusp of his new life, on his balcony, in his soiled pajama pants, his rabbit under his arm, not yet murder suspect, still eccentric author for *just* a few more minutes; for even as the video was beamed live to a relay studio, reporters at ABC's New York newsroom were working frantically to break the news that a TV reporter at a station affiliate in Muncie had received from a local newspaper reporter the anony-mous recorded message concerning the connection between Amber Jewel's murder and Pendleton's *Scream*.

Ryder tapped a Sweet'N Low into his coffee, alone in the moments be-fore the story broke live, feeling strangely omniscient. He had once read of an analogy describing God as a clock maker, the universe a vast mechanical machine set in motion according to a law of cause and ef-fect. He liked the notion of causality and, ergo, the predictability of such a system.

Events were unfolding as he had planned, a coordinated plan in which the newspaper and the local TV affiliate, owned by the same media group, got a national scoop, breaking the details of the anonymous tip on the morning of *Scream*'s nomination for the National Book Award. Sitting in the background, Ryder watched as the short-order cook shouted out to the waitress to turn up the volume as ABC interrupted its regular broad-cast of *All My Children*.

The media went live with the story, first from Muncie, then to footage less than half an hour old from New York, where Pendleton's nomination had been unceremoniously announced on C-Span to a few nonplussed reporters, and finally to Pendleton's lawn, where for the first time the public heard the eerie snippets of the computer-generated voice against a backdrop of archival footage, a home video of thirteen-year-old Amber Jewel in her yard the summer before her murder, and on through to the grim discovery of her body by Sam Henderson the following spring.

Meanwhile, less than a mile farther up the road along the commercial strip, Amber Jewel's sister, Kim, cashier at Rite Aid, watching images on the TV, broke down in the arms of store manager Whitey Whitmore. Minutes later, her 1982 Firebird raced by the diner, as Ryder had expected, and he paid his bill simply by leaving the money on the table.

When Ryder pulled up at Pendleton's house, the glare of lights made everything flat and two-dimensional, like a film set.

Still wearing her Rite Aid white cashier's shirt with her name tag, Kim Jewel was fighting against two cops holding her back, a wildness in her eyes, screaming, "He killed my sister . . . he killed my sister!"

Ryder waited, watching Jewel's reaction, her long legs flailing in high-top sneakers, writhing against the grip of the two cops holding her.

Thirty-something years old, Kim Jewel still had the body of a teenager, was still beautiful, and in a momentary sense of déjà vu, Ryder was struck that she shared the same body type as his first wife, Tori. It took him a moment to understand it had been something he had been thinking about since he had first entered Rite Aid and seen her the previous afternoon, that it had been her image that had caused the melancholy of his phone call with Gail.

Ryder took a deep breath, realigned why he was here, concentrating on the facts. Kim Jewel and her boyfriend were still prime suspects in Amber's murder. It had taken her four minutes and nine seconds to pass the diner. He had timed it from the moment the story broke, knowing she would be watching TV when it did. She was a habitual watcher of *All My Children.* It was why the story had been leaked to ABC, a series of seemingly random events that had been anything but random. Even her work schedule had been rearranged, through the reluctant store manager, at the last minute, to coincide with the news bulletin.

But looking at her now, as she continued to shout, Ryder could not make up his mind if a certain delusional self-denial might not be at the back of Kim's reaction. Her tumultuous arrival did not prove that she or her boyfriend hadn't killed Amber.

Adi Wiltshire arrived minutes later in her small new red Civic. Like Kim Jewel, she seemed frantic, though she was starkly different in appearance, beautiful in her own right, though not his type, a pleated skirt hanging off her hourglass figure, black cotton tights, and practical black shoes.

Ryder took it all in as he watched Adi struggle against the throng of media. She looked stunned, and strands of her hair had come undone from a tight bun at the crown of her head.

She stumbled and regained her balance, and as she fumbled with her front door key, a reporter shouted, "Miss Wiltshire, were *you* aware of the real-life events in *Scream*?"

Kim Jewel broke free of the police hold just as the front door swung wide open, and running toward Adi, she screamed, "What's it like sleeping with a murderer, you fuckin' whore? I'm going to get you both!"

In a sudden moment of surreal quiet, in the yawning grayness of the hallway stood the shadowy figure of Pendleton. His voice was weak.

He was saying Adi's name over and over again.

TWENTY

BY LATE AFTERNOON the weather changed, a cold wind from the north bringing a steely bank of clouds threatening a downpour. It grew unnaturally dark. The faux candelabra streetlights in the historic district glowed in lambent yellowish halos.

The caravan of media, back in their vans after the initial flurry of activity, awaited further developments, technicians occupying the dead time, reviewing, splicing, and spooling tape, while the starlets of the local affiliates interviewed kids at Bannockburn filing to and from the dining hall.

An official police statement issued by authorities simply confirmed police were investigating the similarity between the actual location where Amber Jewel's body was recovered and the location where the protagonist in *Scream* described discarding his victim.

Behind the scenes, it had been agreed between Ryder and the county investigators that neither Pendleton nor Adi would be formally approached for at least twenty-four hours, though their phone line had been tapped. It was part of a strategy to let time pass before approaching either of them, to let time eat away at whatever complicit and mutual resolve there might be between them.

In the small confines of the town's police headquarters, in a cramped offshoot storage room with a small window at street level, Ryder stood between two old-fashioned projectors and reviewed the day's events on tape against a spliced two-hour-long tape of police and TV footage related to when Amber Jewel first went missing.

Ryder refocused on Pendleton as the potential prime suspect for now, and in reviewing the tape, he looked to identify Pendleton in any of the footage.

In Ryder's experience, murderers often participated in the full drama of their crimes, showing up to help search for the missing and showing up again years later at the funerals of recovered bodies, some psychotic allure drawing them to view grieving family members. It was a power rush.

It was a tedious process that, after two hours, hadn't yielded breakthrough images of Pendleton's presence, another subtle indication he was not the murderer.

A second pot of drip coffee percolated on a small metal table.

Ryder stopped, yawned, and drank the coffee black. He began again, worked another hour as numerous matches materialized in the various dated clips, though it was not unusual, given the rural locale. Ryder noted the appearance of Sam Henderson in the background in the various slices of footage.

A check of associated files related to the case listed those who had volunteered in the initial massive search effort. Such lists had regrettably become, as a matter of course, one of the first starting points investigators reviewed when establishing potential suspects. Henderson had volunteered to search for Amber Jewel when she had first gone missing, given he had lived so close to her house.

In the outer office, a smell of Chinese takeout food filled the air. A uniformed cop knocked on the door, and Ryder went out and ate his meal in an unadorned rectangle of a room with large-paned windows looking onto the main street.

The uniformed cop was seated again, pecking out a report on an old-style typewriter while two county investigators who were engaged in a passive-aggressive territorial standoff with Ryder conveniently went outside to smoke.

It was something Ryder had grown accustomed to in such situations. In fact, he sympathized with them. He was perceived as coming to uncover the mishandling and mistakes in old investigations, and most times that's how it turned out.

Ryder ate in silence. The office was an old building that had originally served as a Grange in the early years of the town's settlement, the official title of the Grange done in a stylized script above a slate blackboard: "Order of Patrons of Husbandry." Its motto proclaimed, "In Essentials, Unity—In Non-Essentials, Liberty—In All Things, Charity."

As he ate his fried rice, he stared at the motto, a worldview so fundamentally different from the ghettoized collective of his Polish Catholic Chicago West Side upbringing. He kept looking at it. In its terse succinctness, its sentiments were true to the constitutionality of American life as set down by the founding fathers, a severe Protestantism of self-reliance and self-destiny, almost a frontiersman's suspicion of community. He felt that divide between city and rural life, sitting there in the small police office. Maybe, more so than with any other people, out here beyond the precinct of cities, in these midwestern states lay a genetic fanaticism that had compelled generations of religious zealots to sail toward the unknown new world, to seek out isolation, to live alone. Even now, beyond the town was still a dominion of loosely connected isolationists, a vast constellation of farms sprinkled across the plains. He had been particularly aware of this as he had driven out to the remote property line where the body of Amber Jewel had been disposed of, and he had felt it in the aloneness Sam Henderson exuded.

Ryder set aside the plastic fork and wiped his mouth with the back of his hand. In the starkness of the light, he waited a few more moments before going back into the small room. What faced him there were the files on three missing persons, all young girls. It was going to be a long night. He knew he should have called Gail to check on Taylor, but he didn't, knowing she would have contacted him if Taylor had come home. Ryder had nothing to say to Gail, not here, anyway.

Ryder used the toilet and came back out slowly.

Two cops in uniform had come into the station. He recognized them as the same cops who had subdued Kim Jewel earlier at Pendleton's. One of them, the more slightly built of the two, seemed to have known Kim well. There had been an altercation as Kim had cursed and kicked at the cop. She had called him by his first name, Trent.

Ryder watched them, they, unaware of his presence in the narrow hallway.

The fatter cop looked like an ex-linebacker, jovial in the way only fat people could pull off. He seemed to be the lead partner, upbeat, charged up even, laughing inappropriately given the circumstances, but then again this was overtime, money in his pocket, and he was privy to the heart of a national mystery. He said to one of the investigators who had come back into the station, "You see that priss, Madame Librarian . . . what a number, huh?" His belly hung over his polyester pants, riding high up his crotch.

The thinner cop, Trent, said moronically, "College women," as if they were the greatest mystery in the world, and as he shook his head, his eyes met Ryder's. He looked away quickly, but as he turned, Ryder saw the shadow of a younger face, a profile he had seen in the archival footage, the cop over a decade younger in uniform during the initial days of Amber Jewel's disappearance.

*   *   *

Back in the snug claustrophobia of the small office, Ryder began sifting through the three separate missing persons files.

The three cases seemed to fit the same MO. All three girls had ridden home on a school bus, all had lived along rural stretches of outlying farms set far back off county roads, and all three had gone missing while Pendleton had been at Bannockburn.

The girls were Cassie DuMont (fifteen), missing since 1975, and Elizabeth Witter (sixteen), missing since 1979. Amber Jewel's disquieting disappearance was set between the two cases, in the fall of 1976.

Of the three, only Amber Jewel's body had ever been recovered. The other two had stayed in a limbo world of the missing. No coordinated effort had ever been undertaken to see if there was a connection between the cases. Individual investigators in all three cases had been quick to point toward family involvement in each case.

There was no indication of a connection between the cases, and none had ever been made. The files given to Ryder had simply been amassed in response to his request to have a report compiled on missing teenagers in the surrounding area going back a decade.

Ryder read the brief synopsis on each disappearance. The case of Elizabeth Witter was the most compelling for family involvement. Elizabeth had been adopted by a severe religious couple, Enoch and Ruth Witter, and had endured what seemed to have been a long history of habitual psychological and physical abuse, or *discipline*, as Enoch Witter had stridently argued.

On the grounds of the family farm, during the investigation, police found a dark tornado bunker dotted with clumps of human feces, small candles, and a Bible, where Elizabeth Witter had been repeatedly locked in for days, with just bread and water, to do penance. Upon questioning, both Enoch and Ruth Witter had openly admitted to confining the girl.

A single incident stood out in the weeks prior to the girl's disappearance. She had a secret boyfriend whom she had asked to a Sadie Hawkins dance. Enoch and Ruth Witter, suspecting as much, had gone and spied on her. She had been dragged home before an assembly of stunned teachers and volunteer parent chaperones. Later, she had confided to friends that she had been subjected to nights in the bunker, though nobody in authority had been informed.

The girl liked her school, liked her friends. She was thankful for being adopted, she told them: Her life could have been otherwise, alone, a ward of the state. In her heart, it seemed she had the religion of her adopted parents. Or perhaps she wanted to honor them for what they had given her.

Vouching as each other's alibis, neither Enoch nor Ruth ever changed their stories. They said they were both working the land when Elizabeth got off the school bus. They had seen the bus stop and had waited for her to come out into the fields. She hadn't. They elaborated no further and were at all times laconic in their statements.

A pair of blood- and semen-stained, torn, old-fashioned panties, recovered during a search of Elizabeth Witter's room, suggested a more ominous ending to her life. The panties were hidden behind a chest of drawers. At the time, forensics had not been advanced enough to compare the semen stain with Enoch Witter's DNA, though he outright refused to give a blood sample when requested. He didn't believe in what he called "devil science."

That same evening he was detained for questioning, in an act of moral cowardice, Enoch Witter hanged himself in a holding cell.

Ruth Witter, despite her religion and her fear of the wrath of God, never did testify to what all suspected Enoch Witter had done to his adopted daughter.

Ryder shook his head and put the file back in its box, instinctively aware that Elizabeth Witter would never be found.

Both of the other two missing girls had come from broken homes and had lived through acrimonious family divorces. Both of their fathers lived out of state. In both separate reports, these two factors had been underlined, as though the investigators had taken the same criminology course on missing persons.

As Ryder scanned the files, he sensed behind them the inherent denial that anything had happened to the girls other than they had simply run away. Investigators had been prejudiced against the victims from the outset of the investigations.

Ryder came across disparaging remarks about DuMont and Jewel almost immediately. Cassie DuMont had been busted at a party involving alcohol, along with her loser senior boyfriend, Willard Riggs, a serial juvenile offender out on bail for possession of marijuana with intent to distribute. According to the report, police had been working with Cassie to testify against her boyfriend, though no deal had been struck. Willard Riggs, however, had an airtight alibi. He had been in woodshop class, in an after-school detention program, when Cassie got off the bus.

A search of the area where Cassie DuMont had gone missing had yielded no material evidence of foul play.

Leads in the case had centered on Cassie's volatile relationship with her mother. Her mother's live-in boyfriend figured in the picture, a guy named Scott Brandt with a rap sheet for petty theft and aggravated assault on a previous girlfriend. A search of his home revealed a penchant for pornography featuring lactating women, all of it legal.

Brandt never established an alibi covering the hours of Cassie DuMont's disappearance. He said he was home alone, and he cooperated with numerous interviews and submitted to a lie detector test.

The final figure in the milieu of the investigation had been Cassie's father, Jared DuMont, whom she had idolized. Phone records at the time detailed a series of collect calls to the DuMont residence from a motel outside Baton Rouge, Louisiana, Jared DuMont's last known address. Jared DuMont's whereabouts had not been established during the time of Cassie's disappearance or thereafter. He had left the motel without paying. At that time, he was wanted for child support in arrears. He owed a total of $6,240, the sort of money that would have bought two new cars in 1975.

It was the kind of family dysfunction investigators hated to waste manpower on, and hadn't.

Ryder wrote a note to run a search against incarcerated inmates on both Cassie DuMont's father and her former boyfriend. In the past, he had often found that criminals gave themselves away, boasters, especially in jail, a machismo against the fear of being raped in the showers.

Amber Jewel's file was the last one Ryder picked up. He had done so on purpose. Already he had scanned a provisional history on her at his office in Evansville, part of the standard procedure when he was first contacted to review such cases.

The Amber Jewel file was another textbook case of family dysfunction. Amber's mother, Connie, had a trucker boyfriend, Kurt Kinder, whom she had been accompanying on long-haul trips since Amber was eight, leaving Amber and her older sister, Kim, alone for stretches of up to two weeks.

Undiagnosed with learning difficulties until the fifth grade, Amber had struggled through elementary school. A counselor noted she exhibited antisocial tendencies, a function of her personal frustration at having failed a grade and the fact that she was more advanced physically than her class-mates.

She had a feathered Farrah Fawcett hairstyle, used Lee press-on nails, and wore a halter top that had gotten her suspended for violation of the school dress code. Her mother had been out on the road with her boyfriend during the incident.

A letter on file at the principal's office outlined a series of psychological tests and interviews Amber had been mandated to take under the terms of her return to school. Her ambition in life as of sixth grade spoke volumes for her precociousness. She had stated that she wanted to be "*stinking* rich."

Facts known about her came from her own diary, recovered at her home. They had all been gathered during the investigation into her disappear-ance. Her case, more than the others, had sparked a sense of curiosity, given her reputation.

She had first menstruated in the spring of her fifth grade. Within a year, she "hated the taste of cum" and wondered if that made her a les-bian. It was a concern that haunted months of her writing until she got used to "swalowing without tasting."

There was a litany of prosecutable names in her diary, guys from the JV football team who had seemingly lined up to be with her.

At eleven, she got a tattoo of a butterfly on her thigh.

She bragged in another entry that she chugged a twelve-ounce beer in four seconds flat at a party and that she was sure it was a world record, for her age, at least.

That same year, the year she was murdered, she had a D cup, which was her proudest achievement in her short life.

She said as much, including a diagram of her bust as compared with that of her sister. It was a comparison that hinted at the beginning of a rivalry that would explode later that year, when she reported losing her "anal cherry" to Gary Scholl, boyfriend to Kim, a guy who she said had made her feel "special" and "wanted."

She lamented in her diary, in a moment of true candor and regret, that all she could offer Gary was her asshole. She was just thirteen years old.

Ryder stopped and thought of Taylor. He closed his eyes and thought of his boys in the bathtub, but when he reached toward them they were gone. What he saw was Taylor's submerged body, floating facedown.

Ryder took a drink of water from a jug on the table. He was overly tired, cold to the bone, shivering, and yawning so his eyes watered. In the outer office, he was aware of voices. He started reading.

It was the first series of run-ins between the two sisters over a long summer and fall, a rivalry that had festered for years: Amber, the younger sister who had lived in the afterglow of her older sister, consigned to Kim's hand-me-downs, a cheap imitation of her sister, even down to Kim's feathered hairstyle.

The escalation of violence was all documented by Amber, an innocent chronicler of her own last year.

She described Gary's getting out of the penitentiary in August, his interest in her, Kim dragging her through the house, threatening to kill her, pulling bloody clumps of hair out of her head.

In mid-August, she wrote that she had been stabbed in the hand during a fight with Kim.

In another entry, she revealed that Kim was pregnant but that Gary was still having sex with her at that time. One of her last entries read:

> I told Kim today I didn't got my period I told her I was carring Gary's baby. I said Kim we are both going to be mothers but alls Kim did is lock herself in her room for a long time but she had a BIG fight with Gary when he got here. She jumped on his back and he threw her off him getin all crasy like he dose. Kim hit the ground good and she was holding her belly and all upset, cryin and stuff. Then Gary cals me a slut and said he would die for Kim. He twissted my arm real hard behind

my back and said for me to take it back or he was going to kill me. He made me say I fucked lots of guys caus he is jelluss and I did but not for him but just to make Kim stop cryin, but Kim is a BITCH and isn't spekin to me now. I HATE HER!!!! Then our mother called from Tala-hase and she was drunk good and all and I could tell even though I didnt see her. She breathes hard like shes out of breath when shes drunk. Kurt wasnt talking to her neither and it seems all of us Jewels have man-trouble or thats how it seems. That's what my mother calls it man-trouble like its something you catch. I didnt tell her I was pregnat cause she knows Kim is pregnat and what she said to Kim before she left was Kim needed to start thinkin with her head and not with what was between her legs which made Kim go crasy and say that she wants to be burried in a Y shaped coffin

After he looked up from the file, it took Ryder a moment to realign that the girl he had been reading about was the alleged victim in Pendleton's *Scream*, for here was a life untold in *Scream*, a parallel story that somehow had converged November 6, just another fall school day in 1976.

The strain was already showing on Ryder's face, the protracted survey of potential other victims, adding to the magnitude of what lay before him, and he knew he should set aside the other cases. They were, as the investi-gators before him had somehow intuited, unrelated.

Ryder looked toward the telephone on the desk. Why not call Gail, make up? Why the stubbornness, the passive-aggressiveness, as it was called these days? But he didn't; instead he remained obstinate, set against her.

His dissatisfaction with her went deeper than he wanted to examine, and in his mind something else impinged, like a reel of tape playing in a corner bedroom. Closing his eyes for a moment, he saw the flaying legs of Kim Jewel earlier that day, still wearing her high-top sneakers. The disquieting similarity to Tori had unsettled him, and then Ryder just blanked the im-age from his head, yawning so that his jaw made a snapping sound.

He had the recorded copy of the anonymous message in his small cas-sette player. He hit "play" and listened to the eerie, computer-concatenated words, strung together in a slow accumulation of details, and as the tape ended, a thunderclap rumbled through the small police station, the lights in the office flickering in a dull brownout.

Outside, rain fell in a torrent. Looking up, Ryder saw the window, a milky cataract against the streaked headlights of a passing car, while across town, in the downpour, a single shot from a high-caliber rifle flared and echoed.

On the floor of Pendleton's turreted office lay a bleeding corpse with a hole in its head.

TWENTY-ONE

ALLEN HOROWITZ SAT IN SEAT 2A, with a Scotch and soda, his fourth so far, the glass sweating. He cupped his hand to the cold window, staring at the moon. There seemed to be no world beneath.

Despite the turbulence, the plane's fuselage was awash in a bluish quicksilver in a vast night sky above cloud level.

Horowitz finished his drink, swirling the ice, making it chink. An uneaten steak-and-asparagus-tips dinner had been set aside, along with a cheese plate. He wasn't hungry. He sat alone in first class, save for a guy across the aisle in a golf shirt, snoring.

The flight attendant pouring drinks was middle-aged, wearing flats, engrossed in a *People* magazine. The world had become, for Horowitz, a sequestered nightmare of the privileged and the aging. He got the flight attendant's attention by coughing, and with a sense of disdain, the attendant stared at him as he held up his drink. All the drinking did was pass the time, a distraction against the indeterminacy of what lay ahead. His commuter flight out of Chicago to Bannockburn had been canceled because of the weather. A two-hour car trip in driving rain awaited him at the end of the flight.

The hours had passed infinitely slowly throughout the day, four excruciating hours during which he had been unable to contact Adi. From a small office cubicle in the first-class waiting lounge, he had sent off a hasty handwritten note, faxed to Pendleton's home office, trying to contact her.

In a way, this was a defining moment in his life. *Scream* had brought him back to prominence among the subpopulation—academics and critics—he had despised years ago, but, dare he admit it, he was looking toward posterity. Pendleton's words had come back to haunt him: "How will *you* be remembered in a hundred years?"

Throughout the early part of the day, he had fielded interview requests twice over, first while at his house, in the flurry of excitement at the announcement of *Scream*'s nomination for the National Book Award, then again in the harried rush to the airport by limousine as the media trumpeted the story of Pendleton's involvement in the murder of Amber Jewel.

Horowitz checked his watch. There was a half hour of flying time left.

In all the requests for interviews throughout the day, the strangest had been from a *New York Times* arts reporter who had posed an abstract question to him at the airport: "Does the inclusion of an actual life event within a novel necessarily disqualify it as a work of fiction?" It was a question Horowitz had already anticipated in his continued involvement in the coming crisis—namely, a philosophical debate over the nature of what constituted fiction, central to how *Scream* should be read. In fact, that was the sort of esoteric crap that he could milk on a college lecture circuit.

No, this kind of publicity wasn't a bad thing at all, but what Horowitz needed was for Adi to maintain she had known nothing about a connection with the real-life murder of Amber Jewel, something he felt she must have discovered while researching her thesis. He was, of course, peeved at what Adi had done to him, but after the money he had spent financing *Scream*, with the headway he had made with her over almost two years, he was not about to blow his chances challenging her overtly.

What he felt was that if they stuck together, they could as yet rally around the genius of the work. There was a potential book simply surrounding their involvement with Pendleton and *Scream* if they played their cards right.

Sitting in his first-class seat, Horowitz worked this new angle, defender of genius, reverting to the literary sensibilities that had initially guided him years ago.

He posed his own questions: "Does a painter's self-portrait discredit the piece as art; does it denigrate it to mere representation? What constitutes art? What distinguishes fiction from nonfiction?"

What he wanted now was not fame, but a way back to credibility, a way back from coffee table books, from Rotary Club addresses to blue-rinse octogenarians in the gilded cages of gated communities. He wanted to be with young people again, ironically wanted what Pendleton had despised all his life. He wanted anonymity at some college campus . . . well, not anonymity, but at least someone like Adi Wiltshire to see him through his failing years.

Through the rainy window, Horowitz watched Chicago emerge again; a city he had not been to in two years. He knew he was heading back to the nightmare of E. Robert Pendleton's legacy, but he could handle all that, for so, too, was he heading back into the life of Adi Wiltshire.

He watched the plane bank, the Chicago skyline smoking in low clouds, the John Hancock with its radio antenna a hypodermic syringe sucking down the night. A huge Ferris wheel at the end of Navy Pier turned in a circle of flashing light, as though the city were moving like a great floating riverboat.

He kept staring out the window into the rain-sodden city below. It was how people experienced new cities, through the portal of such windows, confronting the macrocosm of place, not the individual lives of its inhabitants.

What he saw below him had all the hallmarks of a great coffee table book, photographs of cities taken through a portal window thousands of feet aboveground, cropped just so.

He would work out the particulars with his editor. The possibilities abounded for a guy like Allen Horowitz.

Halfway toward Bannockburn, he had to stop his rental car at a rest area because of the pelting rain, other cars and trucks marooned in the dark. After turning on the small grotto of interior light, he took out his pen.

He was still thinking about the coffee table book.

He wrote down the word "Visitors"; it would be an ambiguous title, suggesting something extraterrestrial, perhaps, or simply something slightly alienating, distant, the shots a sort of photographic montage, maybe, reportage or surveillance, some in black and white, some out of focus, their origin unknown, simply the city and its population written in script beneath each shot or, yet again, enigmatically, just the population count, no city name.

The fewer words the better. And then he slept with the doors locked.

TWENTY-TWO

AGAINST THE BACKGROUND ROAR of a downpour and the distant echo of what seemed like a thunderclap, Adi did not rush up the stairs, though she thought she heard the thud of something. Adi had sent Mrs. Blaine upstairs in the stalemate of night to retrieve Pendleton's tray from earlier that morning.

Another clap of thunder rumbled and a fork of lightning split the night, an image of life outside burning in a moment of brilliance, the vans lined up along the street.

Then darkness settled again.

It was past 9:00 p.m., and the downpour punctuated a siege that had been played out by the police, who had not contacted her directly as yet. The phone had been unplugged for most of the evening, though the police could have knocked on her door.

They hadn't. Nor had Adi contacted them. Whatever would unfold for Pendleton would happen under the light of day.

Adi stood up and went toward the stairwell, heard the pull of wind in the trees, the drum of hard rain on the corrugated car porch roof at the side of the house. Earlier that evening, she had seen Amber Jewel on a home video on the TV, in cutoff shorts and a halter top on a summer's day.

Despite having looked at photographs of Amber on the microfiche, Adi realized she was not exactly as she had imagined. Amber was rougher, but also sadder in her own right, more pathetic, a girl just short of ever being pretty, thirteen and yet already haggard, the severe part of her feathered hairdo accentuating the fact that her eyes were too far apart, giving her an atavistic stare, an expression that would have hardened with the years, if she had lived.

It was obvious Amber Jewel, even at that age, had seen her best years pass her by. It had sent a chill through Adi, staring at the grainy TV, holding up the rabbit ears to stop the fizzle of the reception. It was as though the images had channeled through her body, a dark history pouring in from the ionosphere, from some netherworld of the disappeared.

Standing alone in the hallway, Adi felt disoriented, light-headed, her addiction screaming inside her.

More thunder clapped, skeletal trees swaying and creaking in a downdraft of wind that made the fire glow.

Adi turned and looked at Pendleton in his wheelchair, sedated.

It was hard to believe it was happening, the thing she had most feared, and so quickly, after such a brief flare of fame, and on the book's decline. How could it have happened, something that had taken her almost two years to discover, uncovered in such a strange and calculating way, anonymously?

Adi processed it all without emotion, or that was not exactly right. Clinically, she was in the initial stages of shock. On the way to the toilet, she called out Mrs. Blaine's name.

There was no answer.

In the stark brightness of the bathroom, she suddenly caught herself off guard in the medicine cabinet mirror, as if she had walked in on a stranger as she watched herself shoot up. She dabbed the small dot of blood, and her stomach lost its butterflies, the fitfulness of her breath becoming regular, the anticipation of the drug already working at some psychological level, bringing her back to a baseline existence.

In the gray dark hallway, Adi emerged, the sky again flickering. She counted off the seconds before the concussive rumble of thunder shook the house.

Pendleton stirred in the far corner of the room.

Adi went over to the window. The vans were still there. It was all real. She let the curtain fall again and, turning, caught Pendleton looking at her, his eyes catching the errant light from a streetlamp. His head came forward as he strained to speak. "Adi . . . ," he said, struggling to keep his focus. His chest rose in a wheeze of labored breath. "Help me die. . . ."

Adi's arms came up in goose bumps, the drug coursing through her. She stared at him. "You *understand*?"

Pendleton looked at her, extending his bony hand toward her, said again, "Help me die."

Adi formed her words slowly. "How long have you been hiding?"

Pendleton lowered his head.

"You *know* what's going on out there, do you?" Adi's voice was shrill. "Answer me!"

Pendleton whispered in a plaintive way, "Please . . . help me die."

Adi hugged herself, her body shaking fitfully. "No!" She pointed toward the window, said in a hard way, "Isn't this what you wanted all your life, fame for your work, for people to read you? You have it!"

Pendleton said nothing.

"Was it worth it, what you did to that girl?"

Pendleton answered with a single word, "No . . . ," staring at Adi, who felt her eyes tear with his admission.

"My God," she whispered.

Pendleton reached for her hand, his arm sticklike.

Adi drew back. "Why didn't you tell me you could understand, *why*?" She wiped her eyes with the back of her hand.

Pendleton looked at her. "I'm sorry. . . ."

"They won't believe I didn't know."

The outside light caught the gloss in Pendleton's sunken eyes.

Adi shook her head fitfully, pushed the hair off her face. "I'm not part of this! You *tell* them!" There was noise out on the street.

Adi jumped, put her hand to her mouth. "Goddamn you . . . look what you did to me. I'm a junkie. What's going to happen to me now?"

Pendleton looked up again. "Help me die."

In the eerie silence of the house, Adi went to the bathroom, put on a pair of latex gloves, and got a syringe, trembling as she filled it, staring across the gray dark at Pendleton in his chair. She listened for Mrs. Blaine, heard nothing, hesitating one last moment before she went toward Pendleton again. She could taste the salt from her tears at the back of her throat as she leaned into him, putting the syringe into his hand, directing it over his leg, then helping him jab deep so he hit bone.

Pendleton opened his mouth in a weak moan, his fingers closing around Adi's hand. Moments later, his body slackened, and Adi felt the full weight of him on her, his breath against her neck.

She set him back in his seat and filled the syringe again, each time placing his hand around it, helping him inject a second and then a third time, and finally a fourth time, until there was nothing left in the bottle.

Pendleton stared at her, but in a distant way that she knew meant he was fading. His failing last words were ones of denial: "It wasn't me. . . ." It was a last struggling effort to redeem himself, to put into context what he was, an artist struggling against what he had done, against how he would be remembered.

His grip tightened one last time, then eased.

Adi set the syringe with the small bottle on Pendleton's lap and stood up. She turned again toward the glow of lights, feeling a sudden release within herself.

Things were truly ending with his death. There would be no trial. She would simply fade into obscurity with his passing.

In a slightly frayed voice, Adi called Mrs. Blaine as she rose and went up the vaulted space of the staircase, calling out again with a disguised sense of aggravation, but her heart was racing the higher she ascended into the dark.

Images of the man at the library flitted inside her head, an unhinged fear that something supernatural was happening around her as she ascended the spire of the staircase. She turned and looked back at Pendleton. Was any of this really happening?

On the landing, she saw the eyes of Pendleton's rabbit by a seam of light glowing under the door. It hopped silently into another room.

Adi called out Mrs. Blaine's name yet again.

She found her lying on the floor, facedown, a small entry wound at the base of her skull obscured by a bun of jet black dyed hair tied up like Adi's; and for a moment, Adi could have been forgiven for thinking Mrs. Blaine had just passed out against the strain of what had unfolded through the day, that she had simply faltered under the burden of the tray.

But then Adi heard the tapping of a branch at the window, felt the pull of wind, aware of a broken pane of glass in the ruins of the breakfast. Turning, she saw the splattered gore of Mrs. Blaine's brain matter against the wall opposite the window.

TWENTY-THREE

THE NIGHT GLOWED in the phosphorescent pink of police flares as a ribbon of plastic crime scene tape cordoned off Pendleton's house. The camera crews had been pushed back to the road, the movie-set backdrop of their stark lights illuminating reporters hunched under crow black umbrellas.

The rain had not abated. It came down in long silver scratches across camera lenses filming tight shots of faces speaking with a strained intimacy of breaking news, while unbeknownst to the media, an unmarked police car pulled to a halt in the dark of the unpaved alley at the back of Pendleton's house.

Over CB static in the car, the driver told the cop inside to wait for Ryder to help bring Pendleton out.

Ryder listened to the sluice of the window wipers rocking back and forth.

A hazy halo of weak light glowed over the back door of the house. Then something else caught Ryder's eyes, the figure of a man in the alley, and he cursed. They had been discovered.

Immediately, Ryder exited the car into the pouring rain, ran by a slatted garage into an overgrown yard.

Pendleton, in pajamas and a robe, was near comatose, his head lolling back on his neck as he was held up in a sort of fireman's lift by a cop at the back door who said to Ryder, "We found a syringe in his lap." The syringe was in a plastic evidence bag.

Ryder quickly took hold of Pendleton's other arm, edging forward into the night, getting him to the rear of the car.

Ryder handed the cop the syringe and shouted, "Tell them he took this!"

The cop took the syringe and, pointing, said, "What about her?"

When Ryder turned, he met Adi's eyes.

The recognition was immediate, as Adi, soaked in the drumming downpour, blurted, "*You!*" And even before Ryder could respond, she hit him across the face with a stinging slap, while suddenly the night lit up in a series of incandescent flashes and the photographer who had infiltrated the alley materialized out of the dark, capturing the exchange before Adi was shoved into the car.

In the smear of the car's taillights, Adi stared back at the image of Wright struggling against Ryder.

The solitary shot that killed Mrs. Blaine had come from a high-caliber hunting rifle fired from the other side of the river in driving rain and darkness. It had been carried out by an expert huntsman, or so was the opinion of Trent Bauer, the leaner of the two cops Ryder had talked to earlier at the station.

Pointing off toward the far bank of the river, Bauer seemed intent on imparting the logistical complexity of the shot, sure the shot had come from over there. He also figured he knew the type of bullet fired: a triple-effect flat-nose, popular with game hunters, characterized by its narrow entry wound, its secondary charge making the bullet expand in a catastrophic mushroom effect to inflict as much internal damage as possible inside big game.

Standing by the broken window, in a confluence of heat wafting up from a squat radiator as a wind-driven rain blew through the broken window, Ryder felt the pain in his collarbone from having struggled with the photographer. In the sudden aftermath of intense activity, the pain throbbed now with the ebb of an adrenaline rush as Ryder stared across the chasm of the river to a dark embankment of trees, though what he processed was not as much what Bauer was saying as simply the fact that Bauer was out of uniform, his face red and his hair damp.

Bauer had obviously rushed to the scene from his home.

Matter-of-factly, Ryder turned, despite the pain, and said, "You got here in a rush."

He let the statement hang, then said, "Seems like you expected something like this, almost. So who do you think did this?"

Bauer answered, "Gary . . . Gary Scholl. . . ."

It was the immediacy of the response that struck Ryder. "Retribution could trump vindication for a guy like Gary, is that what you're telling me?"

Bauer shrugged. "You could put it that way."

"So, you got any qualms about an innocent woman getting murdered?"

Bauer lowered his eyes. "I didn't say I knew for certain it was Gary. It's just when I heard it on the news . . ."

"So, you know if Gary has any experience with firearms, if he's capable of pulling off a shot like this?"

"He's an ex-marine . . . avid hunter, too. . . . He could make a shot like this easy."

Ryder muttered, "Shit. . . ."

In the hallway, there was the bustle of noise as the coroner arrived. Bauer stopped and looked at Ryder, who said to the coroner, "We were just leaving, Doc," as he set his hand on Bauer's back and led him out of the room onto the landing.

The medics had left a collapsible gurney off to the side in the narrow hallway leading to a series of bedrooms, and as Bauer attempted to navigate around the gurney and head downstairs, Ryder said, "Let's go in here a minute, Trent."

Ryder found a wall switch, and a solitary bulb hanging from the ceiling suddenly gave the bedroom a yellowish, low-wattage glow. The bedroom was stone cold, with an ancient fireplace and an unadorned single bed and dresser with a porcelain washbasin, all vintage, last-century decor, the bed tiny in the way beds were way back when people were smaller. It was obvious it hadn't been used in years.

Ryder gave Bauer a moment, then again directed the conversation back to the murder. "You sure Gary did this?"

Bauer hunched his shoulders. "Look, I don't want to talk out of turn. I got to make my life here. All I can say is, there's the law, and then there's another law. Gary Scholl was that other law. I just knew he would do something crazy. . . . I think we were all afraid he would go after us, get back at us, since we'd all believed he'd killed Amber. . . ."

"Maybe he did."

Bauer's forehead wrinkled. "What? I don't . . ." He didn't finish the thought.

Ryder didn't answer the question. "Let me ask you, what evidence was there leading you to believe Gary was guilty?"

Bauer hesitated. "None . . . I mean, not material evidence. I guess you don't know Gary well. . . . When he was like twelve or something, he used to steal his old man's car and go out and run over dogs, not kill them outright, just upend them, then drive off leaving them to die. That was his idea of a good time before he discovered women. That's the sort of evidence we went on. I figure Gary mistook that woman in the room for Wiltshire. If Gary could hamstring you, that's what he would do. He wanted to make the professor suffer, take what was close to the professor away from him. It has all the psychotic trademarks of Gary's reasoning."

Ryder appeared vaguely conciliatory. "Seems like you know Gary inside out, huh?"

"It's a small town . . . everybody runs across one another."

"Right. . . . That answers my next question. I couldn't help seeing earlier how Kim Jewel reacted to you. It seemed heated. What was that about?"

Bauer's face reddened slightly. "Nothing. . . ." His body language said otherwise.

"She called you by your first name. You know her?"

"We go back a ways, back to when we were kids. We grew up near each other—" Bauer broke off abruptly.

"So what was she mad about?"

Bauer touched his index finger to his nose.

Ryder waited, a simple question having unraveled into something else.

Bauer finally spoke. "Look, this is no big deal . . ."

"You're making it a big deal, Trent. I'm just asking a question is all, okay?"

Bauer acquiesced. "It goes back to when Amber was abducted. . . . I was new on the force when it happened. I mean, it hit us real hard, something like that. I had ridden the same bus for ten years with Kim, the same bus route where Amber got abducted." He shrugged.

Ryder waited. "And?"

Bauer put his hand to his forehead so it lined with worry. "I tried to help as best I could. I knew the area, knew people, places . . . hiding places mostly, root cellars we had drunk in, abandoned tornado shelters. Everyone assumed someone local had taken her. You can't really go round here unnoticed. It seemed premeditated, her being met off the bus like she went willingly. I mean, everything pretty much pointed to Gary from the start, Kim calling in the disappearance so quick. It just didn't seem right—"

Ryder cut in. "So what did Kim have against you in all this?"

Bauer seemed more agitated than he should have been. "There was this one incident Kim didn't want to bring up that I thought needed investigating, something I knew about from her past—"

The bedroom door was slightly ajar, and Bauer broke off again, diverted his attention to the coroner, who had come out into the hallway.

Ryder simply shut the door and said, "You were saying?"

Bauer turned. "Look, this is just water under the bridge. It went nowhere. That professor killed Amber."

Ryder noted Bauer's left hand closed into a fist. "I want to get a history of what went on here, okay, Trent?"

Bauer looked at Ryder. "Okay, see, junior year we set up this biology teacher out at the high school, Ed Kline . . . or Kim set him up. The guy was this thirty-something pervert who had been brushing up against girls during frog and fetal pig dissection labs. You know, typical scumbag high school biology teacher who wasn't good enough to become a doctor or a real scientist. You expect shit like that in high school, I guess. So one evening me, Kim, and a few other guys were smoking, talking about Kline. He had done something to a freshman when Kim decided he needed 'getting rid of.' She had that kind of streak in her, caring about other people, even though she had a reputation."

"What sort of reputation?"

"Dating older guys. . . . She drifted between this older crowd and us, but then she would redeem herself, just sit down at lunch or something, and it was like she was just one of us again. . . . I think everybody was in love with Kim at one stage."

Bauer trailed off as though there were something bittersweet just remembering.

"So this guy, Kline?"

Bauer looked up. "We got a guy who could take pictures. Kline took the bait, and he and Kim got it on out at Skeeter Lake. They were all over each other. Kim's nipple was in Kline's mouth in this one shot. . . . It was like Kim had gone all the way with setting him up. It was weird as hell, her doing that, you know? After we sent Kline the photograph, he skipped town."

Again Bauer stopped and looked right at Ryder. "Look, I'm just giving you what you want here, the details."

Ryder tipped his head. "This is what I want, Trent. You're doing a hell of a job."

Bauer started talking again. "That all happened years before Amber disappeared, but something like that doesn't go away. When things stalled, I brought up Kline, but she didn't want it brought up. She made me swear I wouldn't. I promised her . . . but this wasn't some game, so I went back on my word, went behind her back, or that's how she took it. When she got questioned, she denied anything had happened, but the guy who took the pictures still had the negatives. Kim was pissed that I went and got it. That's all she fixated on . . . the fact the picture still existed."

Bauer rolled his eyes. "People change, I guess. . . . I felt sorry for doing that to her, for bringing up what she'd done out of kindness. I didn't want her demeaned or nothing, but then the shit really hit the fan with Gary, when he heard about the shot. He wanted to get me and the guy who had taken the shot. I mean, he went insane, started calling Kim a whore and everything . . . knocking her around. I guess she knew him better than anybody, knew what he would do. The thing of it was, in the end, it was a wild goose chase. It took almost a month before Kline was tracked down, living in Santa Fe, teaching high school again, using an alias, but he had an alibi for the week Amber went missing."

Bauer stopped. "Like I said, it was a dead end." It seemed as though he had run out of things to say, but then he said, "So you going to put out an APB on Gary?"

Ryder said, "Why don't you take care of it?"

Bauer said reluctantly, "Sure. . . ." He turned to leave, then stopped. "This doesn't mean a hill of beans, but, you know, the weird thing is, if one sister was going to kill the other, then I would have said it would have been Amber trying to kill Kim, not the other way around. I know that isn't something that should be said about the dead, but it's the truth."

TWENTY-FOUR

IT TOOK ALMOST ANOTHER two hours before the coroner removed Blaine's corpse from the crow's nest of Pendleton's office. All that remained was the chalk outline.

Ryder was again conscious of the pain in his collarbone as a cop calling from the hospital advised him that the photographer, an employee of Bannockburn College, was being treated for a broken nose. All it had done was add a further complication to Ryder's life, though, thankfully, the other news had been somewhat better. Pendleton was not dead.

Ryder put his thumb and index finger to the bridge of his nose and squeezed the tension. Had Scholl acted out of revenge for being falsely accused? Though it didn't necessarily follow, simply because Scholl had tried to kill Pendleton, that Pendleton had been the murderer. It took a moment for this realization to settle.

Ryder knew he should have taken Wiltshire and Pendleton in for questioning. It was a clear failing, a bad decision that had led to the murder of Pendleton's nurse, and Ryder felt that, if pushed, he would defend himself, calling Bauer before any disciplinary hearing, because in a way, the local police should have been proactive given what they knew Scholl was capable of doing.

Ryder now tried to go through the investigative process as he would in other cases. He took in the small dimension of the rounded room, a writer's perch encased in leaded glass above an old neighborhood, tried to feel the intimate space in which Pendleton had ascended each day and penned *Scream*, where he may have conceived of his plan to arbitrarily take the life of an innocent. An underlying despair permeated the small office. He surveyed the pathological orderliness within the office, the essential stalling and struggle Pendleton must have endured, rising into the office each day to stare at blank paper. It was there, too, in the leather back of Pendleton's swivel chair, like the maw of some giant Venus flytrap.

Ryder let his fingers trail along the rolltop desk with its brassy studded inlay of burgundy leather paneling, an inkwell and fountain pen set off beside a neat pile of writing paper embossed with the letterhead of Bannockburn College, a silver letter opener like a dagger, the attenuated detail of a man fixated on a former genteel and mannered time, a time of letters, though the gravity and density of the room was sadly focused on what was supposed to be a workaday vintage black typewriter.

It was set in the dead center of Pendleton's desk, a minimalist contraption with an exposed fan of spokes, the key heads a cold polished pearl the color of blanched bone, a typewriter of noir reportage, of a staccato *rat-a-tat-tat* of correspondence, punctuated in the *ping* of each carriage return.

Ryder felt himself going deeper, leaving for a time the morass of how he had handled the case, his eyes drawn to a series of books on Pendleton's shelf, philosophy books, numerous titles containing the word "Superman," though the books weren't about the comic book hero; rather, they were the product of a German philosopher, Friedrich Nietzsche, whom Pendleton had chillingly quoted twice at the beginning of *Scream*:

"What if God were not exactly truth, and if this could be proved? And if he were instead the vanity, the desire for power, the ambitions, the fear, and the enraptured and terrified folly of mankind?

Superman has reached a state of being where he is no longer affected by 'pity, suffering, tolerance of the weak, the power of the soul over the body, the belief in an afterlife.' "

He had heard of Nietzsche, but that was all, one of those names bandied about by college kids, in the public domain of names one came across, something to do with anarchy, with some notion of God as dead, one of those philosopher category questions that came up on *Jeopardy!* occasionally, where the answer was always, invariably, one of the only names anybody ever knew: "Who is Plato, Aristotle, or Nietzsche?"

Ryder opened another book and flicked through the pages until he came across a highlighted section:

> One ought not to make "cause" and "effect" into material things, as natural scientists do (and those who, like them, naturalize in their thinking—), in accordance with the prevailing mechanistic stupidity which has the cause press and push until it "produces an effect"; one ought to employ "cause" and "effect" only as pure concepts, that is to say as conventional fictions for the purpose of designation, mutual understanding, not explanation. In the "in itself" there is nothing of "causal connection," of "necessity," of "psychological unfreedom"; there "the effect" does not follow the "cause," there no "law" rules. . . .

The passage continued, but Ryder stopped reading. It was like another language. He had not understood a word. The divide between the world of academia and his life was never more apparent than at that moment. He paged through the book again, came upon another underlined section.

> The existential predicament is grasped as the imminent risk of having one's belief in reason as a criterion of truth and reality exploded by the unintelligibility of flux and, as a consequence, having to stare into the presence of nihilism. The question *IS*, how can one live with a knowledge of the latter abyss?

It made more sense, a flickering glimpse into Pendleton's mind. Ryder understood "abyss."

As he set the book back on the shelf, his eye was drawn to another book, titled *The Crime of the Century: The Leopold and Loeb Case*, and something stirred in his memory, some distant case study he had read about years ago in the sad psychopathology of the criminal mind, something to do with two teenagers.

Yes, he remembered that much, some infamous murder. He didn't remember the particulars until he turned over the book and read the flap jacket, and then the connection to Nietzsche was apparent.

The first line of the flap jacket was ominous.

> The only crime a Superman can make is to make a mistake.
> —Nathan Leopold

Ryder kept scanning the flap jacket, read about the brutal and random murder of the duo's victim, and at that moment, for the first time in the investigation, he arrived at the sudden and chilling reality that Pendleton *had* carried out a copycat murder, that he had taken the statement of Nathan Leopold as a challenge and had gone about proving he was a Superman, taking the life of Amber Jewel.

Ryder kept looking at the books above Pendleton's desk, the chilling albeit circumstantial evidence there in plain sight, the books on Nietzsche and Leopold and Loeb offering the most profound insight into the psyche and methodology of Pendleton's pathological fixation with finding the most heinous act to challenge the existence of God, whom Pendleton's protagonist had railed against throughout *Scream*, before and after the murder of his victim, until his protagonist's eventual death in a whiteout, still not revealed as a murderer.

Ryder wanted this real-life case to end otherwise. He tagged the Leopold and Loeb book to be dusted for prints, to establish that Wiltshire had picked it up, that she had read it. If he could establish that simple fact, catch her lying and denying she had read it, from there he could work toward psychologically undermining her.

It was as he was leaving that Ryder heard a fax machine pick up. The machine was in a small closet on a wooden trolley. A spool of contiguous fax paper had curled in a scrolling tongue all the way to the floor.

Ryder picked up the long sheet and saw what had been a message repeatedly received through the course of the evening, the date and time stamp of each fax printed in a tiny monotype, the looping cursive of the scrawled message.

It read simply, "Admit nothing!" The same message had repeated over and over again for hours.

TWENTY-FIVE

As with so many nights of storm, the skies came up a cool pale blue, a smell of ozone in the air, a world washed clean, although in the small private room the morning was trimmed into drab ribbons of venetian blinds. It was still early, the hospital in deep silence at the edge of morning.

Ironically, what had eluded E. Robert Pendleton for so much of his life, both literary and commercial fame, came to pass against a nightmare of convulsive dry heaves and spiking fever that surely would have been seen as a pact made with the devil during a less enlightened age, as *Scream* vaulted, overnight, ahead of a cookbook and an aerobics book to secure the outright number one slot on the *New York Times* Best Seller List.

Adi awoke slowly in a steel chair beside a bed and, without raising her head, opened her eyes, let them blink, taking in the darkish solemnity of the room. An immense tiredness weighed on her, making it hard for her to move. She was disoriented, heavy-headed, though slowly she remembered now that she had been given a sedative when she arrived frantic and crying.

A trolley rattled outside the door, voices growing louder, then fading.

She waited, didn't move her head, and remained with her torso and head on the bed. It was only when she averted her eyes upward that she saw it was Pendleton.

He was still alive.

Adi closed her eyes. There were more voices in the hallway that came and went. She waited, then opened her eyes again. Still, she didn't raise her head, just stared at Pendleton propped up in the bed, his skull unnaturally big against the wasting of his lower body. He was wearing a hospital gown, a thin crepelike material that smelled of antiseptic. His right arm was connected to an IV drip, and wires were running from his chest to other monitoring devices.

Adi closed her eyes yet again and, in the blackness, thought of Mrs. Blaine and knew the shot had been meant for her. She felt her heart racing, the quickening of her pulse in the sudden rush of blood, until it was replaced eventually by a hollow feeling, the coldness of an addict in the first moments of a quiet longing that would grow more intense until it was satiated.

What was happening to her?

As yet, she didn't know if this wasn't just a dream. Her reality had become that skewed.

She was about to sit up when her eyes saw a head in shadows through the hospital room door, a face backlit by the fluorescent glare of the hospital corridor.

It was the cop she had hit across the face.

All Adi did was close her eyes, submerge again into darkness, and hide.

What Adi didn't know was that Ryder had seen her eyes open in the glint of light streaming around the edge of the venetian blinds. He knew she had seen him from the way her head moved slightly and how she had shut her eyes. She had betrayed herself.

Ryder felt a rush go through him. The side of his face had come up in a dull imprint of her hand, like a birthmark. The only other woman who had ever done that to him had been Tori. It was only a matter of time before Adi opened her eyes again, before the pulling tug of her secret addiction grew worse.

Yes, Ryder knew that much about her.

An intern on call who had administered a sedative to her had seen the telltale marks of what he felt might have been an addiction, a rash of pinprick dots along the inside of her arm. He had dutifully noted it in his report, and already, various pharmacies had been contacted in the area.

Even at this early hour, it had been established she had likely committed a felony.

A prescription Adi had presented less than a week ago at a pharmacy had been faxed to the hospital. The signature hadn't matched the doctor's signature on file. A second pharmacy's fax substantiated the fact that she had been trawling pharmacies for drugs.

Eerily, even the Rite Aid, where Kim Jewel worked, had filled a prescription within the past month.

Adi Wiltshire had been hiding from something. Ryder was now sure of it, and as he kept looking through the window of the door to Pendleton's room, waiting, he knew he had her trapped. When she came out into the hallway, when the desire for a fix overrode all sense of self-preservation, at the moment of greatest vulnerability, he would take her into custody. But for now Ryder wanted to see her suffer, watch her go cold with withdrawal.

Ryder rationalized that Pendleton's crime, if he had truly killed Amber Jewel, could have been mitigated by a growing insanity that had led to his eventual attempted suicide, but that Wiltshire's actions were colder, carried out by a rational mind. She had uncovered somehow that there had been no record of *Scream*'s original printing and, along with Horowitz, had participated in dredging up the body of a thirteen-year-old girl for the mere advancement of her career. She was a monster of a different order, more cunning and calculating.

In his pocket, Ryder fingered the scroll of fax from Pendleton's office, the damning words of Horowitz's complicity scrawled in a desperate attempt to reach Adi Wiltshire: "Admit nothing!"

Ryder drained the gritty remnants of his vending cup of coffee. Yes, time was on his side. There were two of them in on it. Horowitz had shown his hand, sending his desperate fax, and now he had gone missing. Undoubtedly he would show up somewhere, turn himself in to the authorities, giving his side of things, cut a deal. And after the disaster of the previous night, Ryder felt that maybe he was a day away from at least implicating Wiltshire in concealing facts related to the crime, along with the pending charges related to the prescription fraud; and maybe, born out of those charges, she would come up with the drafts of the novel, Pendleton's handwritten notes, some tangible, direct evidence of his guilt in murdering Amber Jewel—for there had to be notes, had to be some paper trail she was hiding.

No, he was not as bad off as he had imagined.

The previous night had been the worst of it, but things were on the up-swing. Coincidentally, as he had gone to the emergency room in the early morning to get something for his aching shoulder, he had run into the Bannockburn photographer, Henry James Wright, whose nose he had broken. Despite the puffs of cotton in his nose and the blackish swelling under his eyes, Wright had decided not to press charges.

In fact, Wright had been conciliatory, even sorry for having interfered in the investigation and simply explained how he had been working on the *Bannockburn Through the Ages* project, further explaining how it had been he who had taken the haunting suicide shot of Pendleton, having been sent out to the house along with Adi Wiltshire by the Chair of the English Department the night Horowitz had come to speak.

It had all gone a long way toward easing Ryder's mind, the down-to-earth affability of Wright, from impending disaster to impending resolution. He had liked Wright's blue-collar demeanor and the way Wright had extended his hand, as though a handshake were all that was needed to sort things out between grown men, which of course had appealed to Ryder's sense of how so many things should have been handled in life—pragmatically, eye to eye—so much so that Ryder had insisted on personally replacing Wright's camera.

Regrettably, the footage in the old camera had been ruined in the struggle, but Ryder had been accommodating in allowing Wright to photograph Pendleton, since Pendleton was a professor emeritus at the college and therefore technically in their employment.

Pendleton was Bannockburn's most noted faculty member, and whatever became of the case, Ryder agreed with Wright that it should be captured for posterity, and he had seen no reason not to help out a guy like Wright, just to set things straight between them, to show that they were two of a kind, outsiders in this college world of so much angst and madness.

Yes, Ryder felt that the measures he had taken in the case were coming together despite everything, and as he got ready to leave for an early appointment with the Chair of the English Department at Bannockburn, he said to the cop guarding the door, "Call me when she tries to leave. Hold her here no matter what!"

TWENTY-SIX

THE SLUR OF TRUCKS filled the early morning as Horowitz awoke from a fetal curl, his driver's seat leaned all the way back. He was cold and had the urge to urinate. Getting out of the car, he felt the cool air. He had parked under a crescent of trees. They swayed in cold shadows of filtering light, the brown needles of ferns carpeting a mossy pavement of blacktop.

The ground gave off a dank fragrance, though there was something invigorating about it.

Horowitz filled his lungs in deep breaths before he went into a gray cement stall and shuddered with an aching sense of relief as a haze of gnats hovered around the pale glow of a light.

It was the first time he had ever slept in a car overnight. He was a consummate New Yorker, raised on New York's Upper East Side, and had not even learned to drive until his mid-twenties, but here he was, in the middle of his life, experiencing something new, a night at a rest stop.

In a way, he felt vaguely like a criminal on the run as he went and stood before a warped steel mirror that threw back an almost unrecognizable, distorted, house-of-mirrors reflection.

His breath showed in the dim light coming through a frosted wire mesh utility glass. He felt the concrete press around him, a sort of interment, like the cold sarcophagus of a root cellar. Spiders clung to wood support beams fixed in a crisscross pattern.

This was the bone-chilling, raw coldness of nature he had only read about from the comfort of his New York life, and somehow the urgency to rush to Adi had abated.

The new idea for a coffee table book had crystallized into a legitimate enterprise, a notion of estrangement or, equally, omniscience, tangentially captured in windows high above the world.

What he was experiencing was a strangely liberating feeling, free of the bonds of his beachfront house on the Florida coast and his apartment in New York, an existence honed down to the basics.

So often in American literature, white aging males had turned to the contemplation of nature for solace, reckoning with their fading lives, men like Thoreau and Emerson, drifting back to an American existentialism grounded in a quasi-religious aloneness.

Was that what he was feeling now, tapping into that tradition?

Maybe, but it was a change he had desperately needed, the vastness of nature spread out around him outside, a seasonal change that until then he had not ever really contemplated, never really faced, a change that demanded more than a mere exchanging of one's parking space on the road for an enclosed, heated garage.

A skinny guy with a small potbelly in a rhinestone-studded shirt and cowboy boots came into the toilet with a spit cup and pressed a wad of tobacco behind his lower lip. He had the look of a denizen of a Merle Haggard song, of hard living and heartache.

The guy went in the toilet in a splattering way, his guts ruined from cheap eats and caffeine. His cowboy boot held the door closed. The latch was broken.

Outside, at a pay phone, Horowitz stood facing an island of shade, the small oasis of the rest area set back from the highway, the land undulating, spread out in fallow fields. Fronds of mist lay in pockets where the land dipped.

He called Pendleton's home office. He had a sense of well-being, wrapped in the euphoria of denial.

The phone never picked up. It rang a long time before the answering machine came on, and then he lost that good feeling.

It was 7:15 in the morning.

Where was Adi?

As he went to his car, he saw the skinny trucker's wife, a huge woman of Mama Cass proportions, sitting at a picnic table, her legs set apart. They were both smoking and drinking coffee. Behind them was the most beautiful sunrise imaginable.

It would take a half hour more in the car before Horowitz heard the news of the murder at Pendleton's house on the AM car radio.

TWENTY-SEVEN

ADI OPENED HER EYES in a squint again. Her head was still on Pendleton's bed. She heard the suck of monitor sounds. How much time had passed she couldn't tell, though the day was brilliant in the slash of the blinds.

A nurse stood over Pendleton, monitoring some machine, holding a chart, writing something down.

Adi stared at the heavyset midline of the nurse, the shift of the rump as the nurse leaned forward and adjusted something.

She sat up slowly, pushing her hair off her face. She felt hot.

The nurse turned. "Oh, you're awake. . . ."

It was hard for Adi to speak; her throat was dry and raspy.

The nurse poured a glass of water from a teardrop-shaped decanter, and Adi gulped down the water, which the nurse dutifully filled again.

On the nurse's round-faced pocket watch, clipped to her breast lapel, Adi saw the time: 9:15 a.m.

She took another long drink and was aware of a sharp pain between her shoulder blades from having lain in one position for too long. She wiped her mouth with the back of her hand, her lips chapped.

"Dry heat," the nurse said, pointing toward the old-fashioned squat metal radiators.

Adi looked but was conscious of being watched by the nurse. She looked at Pendleton, and then to the nurse, who set the decanter on a speckled Formica roll-away table. "If you want ice, I can have some brought to you."

Adi shook her head. "I'm okay," she said, and shivered. Her arms came up in goose bumps. She said tentatively, "How is he?"

The nurse looked at Pendleton. "It'll take a day or so to see how he recovers."

Adi nodded and smiled in a weak manner, her hair, which she curled behind her ear, falling over her face.

She was suddenly aware of the exposed marks in the softness where her elbow folded and felt her addiction, crouching, waiting for her.

As the nurse went to leave, she said, "I'm going to tell the doctor you are awake, then."

Adi stared at the door, waiting for a face to emerge, fearing the cop was waiting for her. On the wall, the second hand of an institutional clock turned in a fluid, silent sweep, and Adi counted off two whole minutes before she looked away.

There were more voices in the hallway.

Adi shivered and waited again, watched where a seam of light showed under the door as she slowly looked around for her coat.

It was draped over the back of her chair.

She resisted the urge to check it immediately, instead looked at Pendleton.

How had he survived? She had injected him with what she had thought should have killed him, a dosage ten times what he should have received. His body had built up a tolerance to the drug. He was invincible, trapped in an indeterminate limbo, as though God had indeed shown His silent and cunning wrath. Adi shuddered and thought of the shadowy figure of the cop in his long black coat, standing, looking at her in the aisles of the library.

There was something sinister and unreal about him, about everything that was happening, and against that fear, Adi surreptitiously slipped her hand into the torn lining of her coat, her eyes watching the door as she felt the small vial hidden in the recess of hemmed stitching, then felt the capped syringe.

Before a porcelain washbasin, she rolled up her sleeve and made a fist, alternatively looking between the door and her arm.

It was as she was injecting herself that she looked up and into the mirror over the basin. In glossy red lipstick was a scrawled script, a question written backward, so it took Adi a moment to try to decipher what it said, then she whispered the words:

Why did William Carlos Williams write such short poems?

With the needle still in her arm, she kept looking at the question, felt as though she had stepped out of herself, went numb all over, and a sort of vertigo overcame her as she passed out.

TWENTY-EIGHT

THE SKY STILL HAD a predawn of blue and charcoal light as Ryder drove onto campus. He couldn't help but feel he was entering a country club of the privileged. He felt diminished somehow, the incongruity of this life set against his own existence and the existence awaiting his own daughter, or sons, for that matter.

The sooner he got the hell away from this place, the better.

Ryder parked and began walking toward the desolate quad set against the flatness of the surrounding landscape. He stared at the columned buildings, not sure of the architecture, Greek or Romanesque, unsure of even the language of the scrolled names signifying the various colleges, so much so that it took him a while to figure out which building housed the English Department. It was on the second floor of a two-story building adorned with gargoyle heads.

He scanned a directory list for the Chair's name, then climbed a stairway into a long corridor of offices, walked by cardboard boxes with professors' names and student papers piled high.

The Chair was not in yet, though his secretary, Alice Parker, was a lean beanpole woman with a high forehead and good cheekbones, wearing a turtleneck and tweed skirt. She greeted him with the gentility one associated with New England manners.

Ryder could tell immediately she was not some ordinary secretary, but one of the many wives of faculty who had entrenched themselves within the college. There were only so many jobs to go around, so many circles of like-minded to associate within, given the hinterland beyond Bannockburn.

A drip coffeemaker percolated and gave off a pungent and bitter odor, and a tin of homemade cookies had been set out next to it. The campus was awakening slowly, light coming up over the world.

The secretary led Ryder into the Chair's office to a seat across from a palatial desk of shining mahogany, a desk littered with papers. It was an office done in an Old English drawing room motif, complete with dark black wood shelving inlaid with brass-tipped studded leather, giving everything a clean smell of saddle leather.

The crisscross old world windows looked out on a central quad, the Chair making a play at overlord, as guardian of all set before him. The seal of Bannockburn College was embossed on the back of his chair, and just taking it all in, Ryder knew great lengths had been taken by the administration to create such a commanding façade of power, the administration's constant struggle to gain a sense of dignity and authority, to maintain that hedge against the arrogance of a student body accustomed to a privileged and pampered life.

Time passed as droves of students headed for the dining hall. The Chair was obviously late. The secretary said as much through the open door, and Ryder sat for a time, quietly, like some schlock awaiting detention.

Ryder looked around, trying not to seem put out, until eventually his eyes set on a montage of pictures on the Chair's desk. Looking closely, he saw the Chair, with his handlebar mustache, in leather chaps and a leather biker vest, standing next to an older man, both beside a sign that read, WRIGLEY FIELD. The older man was obviously the Chair's father. They shared the same facial structure, though the father was in a vinyl jacket with stitched lettering for a pipe fitters' union. He was carrying a baseball glove and a ball.

The difference was so dramatic and sad. Ryder leaned forward, saw the father thin in a sickly way, as though he didn't have long to live, his horsey dentures showing and his pants pulled way too high so his black socks showed. In a way, it put the latter part of the century into perspective, and if Ryder had been inclined toward thinking in terms of metaphor, this might have been the image that defined either the horror or the beauty of the age, depending on one's perspective, an aging father beside his gay middle-aged son in leather chaps.

Ryder kept looking at the image, transfixed at the brashness of the shot set there on the desk in open view for everyone to see. He knew the area from his time in Chicago working vice years ago, Halsted Street, the first gay enclave, the first urban renewal of dilapidated neighborhoods. He had worked a beat there through the initial influx of homosexuals from the suburbs and beyond, from Wisconsin and Indiana and out even to Minnesota, off farms and small towns.

They had all come in search of anonymity, drawn to the bigness of Chicago, to the heavy resonance of velvet-curtained clubs like the Man Hole and Berlin, the strangely erotic Third Reich flesh pit cabaret of sadomasochism.

In his time he had seen it all, before it became mainstream, the nipple and cock rings on display, the leather masks with the rubber mouthpieces to bite down on while being flogged, the huge ass-ripping dildos in window displays, the XXX stores and clubs set under the rumbling el train, under the old world industrialism that had so defined Chicago, a city of big shoulders and Midway bombers.

He had even questioned and harassed guys like the Chair and his sort during the early years of underground gay liberation, knowing most had jobs they couldn't afford to lose. They had paid up mostly, before things changed, before Gay Pride. It's how cops had survived back then.

Suddenly there was a commotion in the secretary's office, and when Ryder looked up, he saw Wright weighted down with camera equipment.

The secretary let out a little shriek when she saw the state of Wright's nose, which had swollen so that it had made his eyes mere slits, then Wright turned and, seeing Ryder in the Chair's office, said with feigned fear, "Oh, shit. . . . Alice, answer any of his questions! This guy is trouble!" To which

Ryder just grinned and rose and went out into the secretary's office, his hand extended toward Wright, who likewise had extended his hand.

His grip was strong. So few people invested in handshakes anymore.

Wright said, "Confidentially, between you and me, Dectective, the Chair isn't getting in on time, I *know*."

The Chair's secretary said, "Henrrry . . ."

He winked and said, "Hey, there's no flies on me." And brushing off his shoulder, he said to Ryder, "You want to get a cup of coffee, Detective?"

"Jon, call me Jon."

The secretary said, "You go on, Detective. The Chair's doing admin work all morning, so you can come back whenever."

Wright chimed in, "Just tell him the detective was here on time, okay?" Wright pointed at his watch, and the secretary rolled her eyes in the way one did with the overly familiar, the truly unfunny or annoying, or the dangerous.

Wright lit a cigarette and opened a can of Dr Pepper that fizzed so much, he had to bring it to his mouth to stop it from overflowing, although it still dribbled down his chin and stained his shirt.

"Crap. . . . You would think science could do something about that, wouldn't you? What is the soda industry, like the second biggest industry in the world? I bet they're in league with the dry-cleaning business."

Ryder measured his response. "You a conspiracy theorist, Henry?"

Wright smiled. "Are you?"

Ryder said, "I don't know what I believe anymore."

It was an overture toward the case, but all Wright said was, "I think that's a function of age . . . Jon . . . I do."

Ryder nodded. "Maybe."

Wright leaned forward. "So, you married?"

Ryder nodded again.

"Kids?"

"A girl . . . senior in high school."

Wright smiled. "You should think about sending her here."

Ryder made a face. "I don't think I'm in that league."

"Shit . . . this is a democracy, Jon. That's the sort of cynicism that ruined this country . . . union-minded thinking." Wright raised his hands. "Don't take me wrong, I just believe the future is there to be invented by each and every one of us."

He said it with such frankness that Ryder understood he meant it, though he was getting a better sense of Wright, of his essential manic quality.

Wright kept talking with a pressured speech. "You know, I'm enrolled at the college. They're good that way. You just have to put up with the political correctness crap. That's the price of admission into modern life . . . keep your opinions to yourself." The slits of Wright's eyes opened wider, the whites threaded with broken blood vessels as he leaned forward and put his hand to his mouth, like someone who was about to tell a secret, which he was. "I could tell you, Jon, the Chair is at home taking it up the ass from a first-year grad student, but I won't, okay?"

Ryder said, straight-faced, "Okay, but I don't like being stood up for another man."

Wright hit the table so hard, the salt shaker fell over. "That's stand-up comedy material, Jon. So help me, I'm going to use that when you're not around. I'm going to steal that line, 'stood up by another man.'"

Ryder felt now that he wanted to get away from Wright. They both looked out of place in the cafeteria, and even someone as forceful as Ryder didn't like being the spectacle, being stared at, which was what the students were doing.

It was just a matter of getting away from Wright, but then, suddenly, Bauer's story about nailing the biology teacher struck Ryder as he stared at Wright's elaborate camera equipment. How many photographers could there be in the town?

Ryder said, "You been doing photography long?"

"This . . . yeah . . . all my life. My father worked as a professional photographer for trade magazines with Studebaker before they went belly up. I tagged along with him on jobs. He had a darkroom set up in the house. . . . I got to know all the stuff, then I left for Vietnam, thought that was all behind me. When I came back I made a go of it in Chicago. Came back home when my old man died, inherited the equipment, picked up where he left off. He'd worked part-time for the paper before he died. I got his job. Life is like that, haphazard, you know?"

Wright's eyes grew big as he shrugged and, leaning back, smiled. "That's pretty much my life story in a nutshell."

Ryder nodded. "Hey, you do what you gotta do." He measured his time before he said, "Let me ask you something, Henry. I heard through the grapevine about Kim Jewel setting up a teacher out at the high school. The guy got sent a compromising photograph. Any chance you were the photographer?"

Wright answered, "All the chance in the world. Let me guess, bigmouth Trent Bauer told you."

"I'm not going to say he didn't, but word has it Gary was real sore about it, that he pretty much laid into Kim."

Wright rolled his eyes. "Look, Trent came by my place asking me to help. I told him to stay out of it, but he kept pressing for the negative. I said I didn't have it. I didn't want to get involved. This was something I didn't think needed bringing up, or at least he didn't need to produce a photograph. But there was no talking to Trent, so I kept telling him I didn't have it. Then, lo and behold, Trent comes round and tells me he has a copy of the photograph. He wanted me to pretend I'd kept it."

"And did you?"

"Yeah . . . in the end."

"Why?"

"You know, for the kid's sake, for Amber's . . . in case it might have helped. I produced the negative after Trent told me he'd been seeing Kim that summer before Gary got out of prison. He'd been trying to make a go of it with her, that's what he told me. Admitting he'd kept that photograph of her was . . . well . . . He thought that was going to ruin it for him in Kim's eyes. But if I produced it, that would be different. I guess in the end, I didn't want that getting in the way of maybe catching Kline if he was behind everything."

Wright let out a long breath, raising his hands in characteristic fashion. "There are no simple stories, are there, Jon."

Ryder answered, "I guess not. . . ." Waiting.

Wright leaned forward. "I better finish it, then . . . I mean, everything sort of backfired in the end."

"How's that?"

"The whole uncovering of Amber's body the following spring turned everything on its head. Everybody felt Amber's body had been hidden somewhere and then dumped after the investigation had gone cold. That never made it into the papers or anything, but it was a general consensus round the place. We'd checked Henderson's field. The body wasn't there. . . . I guess people were asking themselves, why would the murderer put Amber's body so close to where she had been abducted? It didn't make sense, unless the real murderer had some interest in being in on the discovery, if he wanted to participate in the ongoing case—"

Ryder interjected, "Real murderer? You saying Trent did it?"

"I don't know what I thought back then, but it's what people were saying. It didn't make sense. If Gary killed Amber, he'd have dumped the body somewhere else, right? I mean, that's what you'd think."

Wright rolled his eyes. "Shit I don't know what I thought, Jon. See, Trent had fixated on Kim since they were in second grade. You hear Trent tell it, they played doctor together when they were eight or something. It was destiny in Trent's eyes, them living close like that, riding the bus all those years together. He had a thing for her real bad. I was at Trent's eighth-grade graduation dance, helping out my father, who was there taking pictures. Trent had this dance with Kim, and he comes over to his friends afterward, says, 'Smell my fingers!' He was sniffing his own fingers, holding them up like the fuckin' president getting sworn in. He said he finger-fucked Kim, so it got around, and some girlfriend of Kim's tells her what Trent said, and Kim starts talking it up and says, 'That's right, me and Trent are going steady, isn't that right, Trent?' and Trent just about shit himself."

Wright shrugged. "Good old Trent. Shit! Kim didn't make a fight of it or nothing, but everybody knew it never happened. Turns out Trent had finger-fucked his fat girlfriend, Dawn, who ended up crying in the corner all night long. She had this pumpkin head that took up the entire dimension of her yearbook shot. She's fat, as in the roll-her-in-flour-and-find-the-wet-spot sort of fat, right? Though now the shoe is on the other foot, because Trent ended up with Dawn. She's got him by the balls. Trent got the job with the police through her father's connections with politicians."

Ryder said again. "That all sounds like you're saying Trent did it."

Wright shook his head. "Yeah and no. . . . You know, Jon, I guess I could never really believe Trent could do something like that, or want to believe it in my heart. God knows, Gary was a *sick* fuck . . . I mean, sometimes there's no understanding the human mind, accounting for why people do things. I'd helped Trent out so maybe I didn't want to believe he had anything to do with Amber going missing. I figured Gary set Amber there, maybe to get back at Trent. Kim was into confessions, into admitting her mistakes. Chances are Gary knew about what went on with Trent and Kim that summer while he was in prison. He wouldn't let that slide, something to his dignity, his manhood. That's the sick mind you are dealing with. Gary would make you pay somehow, some way. . . . You know, Gary was fuckin' Amber, just to get back at Kim. It was like the sickest shit between them all."

Wright trailed off and drummed his fingers on the table before looking up. "Anyway, we were wrong on all accounts, right? That professor killed Amber."

Ryder didn't answer. He found himself wrapped in the convoluted turn in the series of relationships Wright had set forth, his mind drifting to Kim Jewel, believing a guy like Gary Scholl might have killed because of her.

Wright said, "Jon, you in there? This has got your head spinning, I can see it. Think about law enforcement back then, betwixt and between, chasing their tails."

Ryder recovered. Nodding with due solemnity, he said, "Look, I appreciate you helping me out here."

Wright sat back. "Hey, no problem. . . . You know, I always envied a job like you got. I solved the Rubik's Cube when it came out, you know that? I'm not bragging or nothing, but I got a knack for what they called spatial relationships, or that's how I tested back in school. I think, if I had more guidance growing up, I might have made more of myself, but I don't dwell on things. School wasn't ever a priority. We never looked to the future when I was growing up. My father had his paycheck, came home, and divvied it up for various things, allotting what he could for himself, for booze and cigarettes, for gas. You know, I miss that simplicity."

Wright smiled, and Ryder was again aware of what he'd done to Wright's nose. It made Wright's candor all the more genuine. There weren't enough hardworking stiffs like him around anymore, the backbone of a people who just went on with life. He thought of Wright's father losing his job at the Studebaker plant, the untold story of what it must have done to Wright's life.

Ryder broached the subject tangentially. "You served one tour in 'Nam?"

Wright held up two fingers. "Two. Call me crazy, Jon, but I was one of those rare few who believed in what Nixon was doing over there. I guess, in all the antiwar movement, in all the love-ins, people never realized the American way of life was under threat. I think something like that was worth fighting for."

Wright mock laughed. "You know what was a more impeachable matter in my mind, Jon, more of an affront to the office of the presidency? Jimmy Carter jogging is what. I mean, why wouldn't the Iranians take us hostage, after seeing a guy out in shorts, jogging, like he had time to exercise, like the world wasn't going to hell in a handbasket? That was the turning point in American politics for me!"

Ryder just smiled, recognized the honesty but also the diplomacy in Wright not asking him whether he had served, which he had not, simply because his number had never been called.

Ryder sat again waiting for the Chair in his office and watched a rich kid using his scrolled-up term paper as a telescope, staring at the secretary and then at Ryder, before the kid thought better of it and went back to staring at the secretary.

The Chair arrived eventually, saw Ryder, and so dealt with the kid in the outer office in the commanding way Ryder felt only a gay could pull off, laying right into the kid.

Ryder just waited and understood that the Chair's power came from the fact that any confrontation with him could eventually be characterized as "flaming" or "gay bashing," so the Chair ended up exercising a greater sense of control than the so-called normal faculty. At a deep level, this sickened Ryder, the politics of sex, or liberation, of all things that had eventually marginalized him, that had all conspired to make him a man out of sync with the times.

And then the Chair came in and flopped down with an exasperated expression, then launched into what he personally thought about the Pendleton case, tacitly acknowledging Pendleton was guilty of murder, and on through what he thought of Wiltshire, whom he maintained had to have had prior knowledge of what Pendleton had done before the rerelease of the novel. As the Chair put it, "She was doing a doctorate on him, for Christ's sake! How wouldn't she have discovered something?"

The Chair had literary precedent backing him up. Wiltshire's work, according to him, was steeped in "a literature of virtue and deception, a literature concerned with the beguiling ways in which women had survived throughout history," what he said went under the heading "gender studies." A scan of her doctorate course load would, he said, give anyone a sense of her predilection for melodrama.

It was all unsolicited stuff, derogatory remarks that the Chair just offered up as he went through the volumes of work on Wiltshire's reading list for her modest MA thesis on George Eliot, titled *Madame Ovary*, a pun lost on Ryder, though the Chair's disdain for Wiltshire was not.

It was a rapid-fire attack, the Chair cataloging what he had called Wiltshire's abiding interest in a pulp fiction of bodice rippers—the psyche of virtuous medieval feminine heroines given to throwing themselves into flowing rivers for love's sake, to tales of knightly chivalry and damsels in chastity belts confined to ivory towers, to Wiltshire's recent interest in the staid literary tradition of undying female loyalty exemplified in Penelope, Odysseus's wife, who sat weaving and unweaving at the loom for years to stave off suitors.

In the Chair's estimation, Wiltshire's marked retreat from her early protofeminist work was proof of her deep, underlying, psychological need for a father figure. He even went so far as to tell Ryder about Adi's reputation, about the rumors regarding her having tit-fucked the two Pulitzer Prize winners.

Exactly what the philosophical differences between the Chair and

Wiltshire were, Ryder hadn't been able to discern completely, though the Chair had gotten one thing right when the call came regarding Wiltshire's collapse out at the hospital, interrupting their meeting.

The Chair said, "Don't be fooled, Detective. Adi Wiltshire is acting in character. She's passed out with the dramatic flutter that would do a corseted Victorian proud. Watch her!"

It only affirmed Ryder's gut instinct. He was already watching her.

TWENTY-NINE

ALMOST AN HOUR had passed in a commotion of activity, first with the discovery of Adi, unconscious, with the needle in her arm, then to her being roused with smelling salts, and finally to her sudden and frantic screaming as she again faced the question scrawled on the mirror.

She had clawed against an orderly and nurse, struggling to get away from the mirror in what could only have been described as a person who had gone insane.

She had screamed, "Who did this?" over and over again in a hysterical voice, trying to turn toward the writing on the mirror.

In the hospital room, Ryder stood quietly. He stared at the scrawled red lipstick script. He felt an eerie sense of the supernatural in the block lettering written backward, something akin to "ЯƎ⅁ЯUM" on the mirror in *The Shining*. It had been one of the more profound movies he had ever watched, the shifting reality of the ordinary and the supernatural, Jack Nicholson talking with the dead in the splendid solitude of a writer's oasis, going slowly mad, typing over and over again, "All work and no play makes Jack a dull boy."

Ryder sensed he was being laughed at, ridiculed by Wiltshire, for what was *The Shining* but an everyman's glimpse into the life of a writer, into the apparent madness of writer's block and lack of inspiration? Was that the coded message here, her grim message to him?

And as he stood there, trying to decide how to take what had happened, as he kept looking at the words written on the mirror, he thought of a quintessential image in the movie, Nicholson throwing a handball against the vast quiet of the mothballed mountain lodge as he slowly went insane, while his son, on his big wheel, had roamed the corridors of the grand hotel, confronting the spirit ghosts of two murdered girls awash in a torrent of blood, chopped up by their consummate stuck-up English butler father.

It was while Ryder was still standing by the mirror that he felt the presence of someone behind him. In fact, he had felt the presence longer than one would necessarily have expected a person to wait out of mere politeness.

Ryder realized he was being watched. When he looked into the mirror again, he recognized the figure immediately as the author Allen Horowitz, who was disconcertingly taking notes.

Gone was the tropical beachcomber look of Horowitz's autobiographical photo. Instead, he was dressed with the measured disheveled quality of a guy just coming from a lake cottage retreat. He had on a creased white cotton shirt, a gray V-neck sweater with worn elbows, and khaki pants that stopped short of reaching his ankles. He wore penny loafers without socks. His cologne gave off a warm, subtle blend of leather, wood, and tobacco.

When Ryder turned, Horowitz was tapping his pen against his chin and saying in a sort of exasperated way, "Please, Detective, just hold still. I like this a lot, pensive detective stares at enigmatic question on mirror. The art of writing is voyeuristic. When people know they are being watched, they don't act like themselves, but I suppose you know that already, Detective, right?"

Horowitz smiled with a deep, satisfying nod of his head, and Ryder took note of Horowitz's day-old growth of beard and the sweep of ill-combed hair, even as Horowitz advanced and said, "I see in you a man I could learn from, Detective. . . . I insist you take me on as apprentice. We can go eighty-twenty on our first novel together. Tell me you drink heavily, or did once upon a time. We'll need a lonely hearts middle-aged woman with whom you find solace, though maybe we should complicate matters with erectile dysfunction. I'm open to your views on that. Maybe you were an orphan, the quintessential outsider, alone, without apparent lineage. That's a surefire literary trope. But, first things first, I haven't even *introduced* myself."

Horowitz extended his hand. "Allen Horowitz. Call me Allen."

Ryder went with the overfamiliar tone Horowitz affected and, turning toward the mirror, said, "You're the very man I need, a literary critic. Do you happen to know the answer to the question on the mirror?"

Horowitz looked at the mirror and smiled. "Call this beginner's luck, but I do. William Carlos Williams . . . Ah, one of the usual suspects in all English 101 poetry anthologies. The story goes that Williams, a doctor, wrote many of his poems out in rural areas while waiting for women in labor. All he had to write on were small prescription sheets, hence the brevity of so much of his poetry. Maybe you might have heard of this one, Detective, it's his most famous and important poem, called 'The Red Wheelbarrow.' Let me see now . . ." And Horowitz quoted the poem:

so much depends
upon

a red wheel
barrow

glazed with rain
water

beside the white
chickens.

Ryder pulled a contemplative face, furrowing his eyebrows. "In *your* considered opinion, what exactly does the poem mean?"

Horowitz kept up the charade. "Well, according to *reliable* sources, Williams unapologetically presents a concatenation of images in his poetry, not symbols. His purpose is not to point a moral or teach a lesson. Rather, Williams is content to rest with the assumption that the reader can duplicate Williams's own sense of the importance of the red wheelbarrow."

Ryder said dryly, "Maybe red wheelbarrows figured more prominently back then?"

"You got it, that's a point of logical debate and argument. You're contextualizing your inability to interpret the signifier, the red wheelbarrow, as culturally significant, given your relative historical perspective, a denizen of the late twentieth century. There's been a paradigm shift from an agrarian collective—i.e., the red wheelbarrow—to a more individual and democratic post-industrial age. You see where I'm going here? Any student worth his salt should be able to crank out a ten-page paper minimum on this poem."

Ryder let the game go on a moment longer. "Ten pages . . . You're joking?"

Horowitz shook his head gravely. "Lamentably, Detective, I'm not. That's what passes for a so-called liberal education these days at most colleges!"

Under different circumstances, Ryder might have liked Horowitz, who had a beguiling charm and ease about him. In fact, it was hard not to let Horowitz wield a certain power. It wasn't just that he was one of the nation's top writers, but he had street smarts coupled with a wry, humorous intellect, something Ryder associated with a certain type of Jewish humor. Ryder understood why people bought Horowitz's books. He didn't seem beyond people; rather, he just said the things people might have felt but never fully recognized until it was pointed out to them.

But then Ryder knew other things about Horowitz, so he ended the façade. Turning the tables, he reached into his pocket, took out the scrolled fax he had retrieved from Pendleton's house, and said quietly, "Maybe we could start by interpreting something less ethereal, Allen? What do you think 'Admit nothing!' means?"

THIRTY

TWO HOURS INTO THE meeting between Ryder and Horowitz, the fringes of the day had crossed over into long shadows, although it was not yet two o'clock. The interview had stalled and been misdirected by Horowitz, who had insisted on taking notes, maintaining his previous bravado of wanting to understand Ryder's work, wanting to know the arc of the interview process. Horowitz wanted to know when he should be aggravated, when he should be exasperated, surly, or contrite, when he should request his lawyer. He wanted to *feel* the interview.

Ryder had gone along with Horowitz's antics as he tried to see through Horowitz. Only when the interview seemed to be coming to a natural end did Ryder bring up Nietzsche, saying without pause or preamble, "How would you characterize Pendleton's interpretation of Nietzsche's concept of the Superman?"

Horowitz's assurance faltered, but then he smiled. "A Nietzsche man! Well, well, that *is* something for our novel, Detective. We might as yet find our way! But, point of fact, in academic circles they use the word 'Übermensch,' or 'Overman.' If you are going to talk the talk, say it with a German accent. It sounds more authentic."

Ryder said, "Übermensch," with the accent of Sergeant Schultz from *Hogan's Heroes.*

Horowitz rolled his eyes. "God, the leveling effects of sitcom TV. I want a true authentic German voice, Detective! Listen!"

Ryder said, "Übermensch," again.

Horowitz clapped his hands. "Much better, now you're giving Nietzsche the trenchant intellectualism he demands, though lamentably we've lost Nietzsche's Superman, linguistically anyway, to comic books, to a vision of a man in tights. One of the greatest concepts of modern philosophical thought subsumed by a comic book. . . ."

He shook his head. "Appalling, really . . . though I think the irony, or the genius, of American culture has always been its intellectual bias toward mediocrity, to dumbing things down. Nietzsche said, 'God is dead!' and I think, in the American psyche, that was understood, if only at a deeply subconscious level. Nietzsche could not be denied. There was T. S. Eliot telling us we were living in a wasteland, but maybe, more so than with Eliot or Pound, D.C.'s Superman more subtly acknowledged the existential nihilism of modernity. Without the pontification of intellectuals in a poetics of the bygone era, or Pound swinging from his cage in the *Cantos*, D.C. Comics, in a cartoon splash of color, quietly debunked traditional Christianity."

Ryder just stared at Horowitz, who stopped abruptly, took out a pen, and began writing.

"When I'm on a roll, I like to get things down on paper. In fact, I would submit that the subtle demise of our Judeo-Christian God could have been pulled off only in a comic book, in a nonthreatening genre, a genre of child's play and fantasy—existentialism sold on the back of cereal boxes with decoder rings."

Horowitz set down the pen and smiled. "I hope I've answered your question. I think you've given me something to go on here. We work well together, you and I. You've given me something *big* here!"

Ryder made a cathedral of his hands in a sort of contemplative gesture, cracked his knuckles as if he were getting down to business, and said in a tempered voice, "Now, how about I give you Nietzsche's definition of the Superman? I have it here."

He reached into his long coat and took out a copy of *Scream.* "Pendleton quotes Nietzsche in the preface to *Scream*":

> Superman has reached a state of being where he is no longer affected by "*pity,* suffering, tolerance of the weak, the power of the soul over the body, the belief in an afterlife. . . ."

Horowitz said, "Chilling, brilliant stuff . . . an iconoclast in a priest-ridden age of saints. I suppose you haven't read Nietzsche in German? . . ." He raised his hand. "No, of course you wouldn't have. . . . But go on, please."

Ryder did. "What I find troubling in Nietzsche is this intolerance of the weak."

Horowitz raised his index finger, seemingly enjoying engaging Ryder in a discipline he knew Ryder knew nothing about. "Actually, I'm not sure that is necessarily what Nietzsche was saying, Jon. I'm afraid that might be simply the translation. Nietzsche is probably the most misunderstood of all philosophers. You see, men of ideas are not necessarily poets, and sometimes they are arcane not just for the sake of being arcane, but because the subject matter of the metaphysical is complicated."

Ryder went toe to toe with Horowitz, countering, "That is interesting . . . the notion of misinterpretation. Maybe you could give me an assessment of Leopold and Loeb's interpretation of Nietzsche?"

Horowitz waited.

"Let me jog your memory. Two Jewish teenage geniuses from Chicago committed a murder, similar to Pendleton's alleged crime, back in 1924, an indiscriminate, cold-blooded murder, for what they called 'philosophical reasons.'"

Horowitz shrugged in a noncommittal way. "Yes, well, 1924 . . . that was a long time ago, before I was even born."

"We recovered a book about Leopold and Loeb above Pendleton's desk containing not only Pendleton's but also Wiltshire's prints throughout the book."

Horowitz rolled his eyes. "Please, not fingerprints, not *that* old standby. Frankly, between you and me, Jon, advances in DNA forensics evidence is where the future of crime fiction lies. Let's not solve something on the banality of plain old fingerprints. It wouldn't wash with a reading public, believe me. I'm all about reader expectations!"

Ryder said, "Okay, let's set the fingerprints aside, then, but this brings me to a more *fundamental* and interesting question: the nature of your relationship with Wiltshire."

He set a stack of paper on the desk. "I've bank receipts here from Wiltshire's account totaling over a hundred and twenty thousand dollars sent to her in the last year alone."

Horowitz answered, "On Pendleton's behalf! It was easier to wire Adi the money than to try to have her gain power of attorney and manage the money." But he had lost his smug affability. "My involvement, my decision to help Bob, had nothing to do with Wiltshire. She was merely an intermediary. Bob and I go back a long way. That was the point of connection, our past."

Horowitz stopped abruptly. His mood had changed.

"I suppose you are aware that Bob attempted suicide the night I arrived at Bannockburn? There's your answer to why I gave him the money . . . atonement, or whatever you want to call it. I saw something very sad in Bob's eyes that night, regret, failure."

Horowitz cast his eyes downward, shaking his head slowly. "I had to come to terms with the fact that, on that night, just my mere presence had pushed Bob over the edge."

He looked up again. "Adi contacted me months later. She had taken over his literary estate, such as it was. Bob had written a suicide note to that effect, bequeathing everything to her. Wiltshire was in the midst of doing a doctorate on Bob's work. She wanted me to read something of Bob's. What could I say? I felt guilty. Bob Pendleton was lying in a coma at that time, pushed aside by society, and he had written probably the greatest book I had ever read. Where was the justice in that?"

Horowitz's voice eased as though he had come to the end of what he had to say.

"Adi Wiltshire had seen that genius, too. That *is* where our sensibilities lay—our mutual regard for Bob's work."

"Maybe, but it doesn't answer the question why Wiltshire kept a source from you, does it?"

"Maybe you missed the point. Our sensibilities lay with helping Bob. If you want an answer, why don't you ask her?"

"Oh, I will."

"What are you after, Jon?"

"The truth!" Ryder placed the fax Horowitz had sent on the table. "I want to know what this means." He pointed at the scrawled handwritten script. "What was Wiltshire to 'admit nothing' about?"

"That! Is that what this is about, something written in haste? Just a bad choice of words. 'Say nothing,' 'Admit nothing,' I think they convey the same meaning. Adi was distraught and in shock with the revelation linking Pendleton to the murder. One has the constitutional right to take the Fifth. That's all I wanted to remind her."

Ryder pressed, "So she had something to hide?"

"No."

Horowitz made a motion as if he were about to rise, but Ryder tacitly set his hand on Horowitz's hand. "How come you never referenced the Leopold and Loeb case when you wrote your *New York Times* piece about the novel? I bet if I got a search warrant for your home—"

"Homes," Horowitz interjected. "I own more than *one* home, Jon, just for clarification purposes."

"Okay, *homes*. I bet if we get a search warrant for your homes, we'll discover you have a book on the Leopold and Loeb case."

"I'll tell you what. I'll save you the time. I have a copy."

"Why did you deny knowing about the case?"

"I didn't deny knowing about the case. I simply said it was a long time ago. I think if you go back and check on the tape, you'll find my exact words."

"Let me ask you again, did Wiltshire tell you about the book?"

Horowitz shrugged. "I can't remember offhand."

"She didn't, right?"

"I'm afraid, Jon, I'm still drawing a blank. I'll have to get back to you on that."

Ryder folded his arms. "For what's it worth, I think you were used by her."

"Is that a prosecutable offense?"

"It depends if you were in this together or not. See, I think that the first time you read the book, you knew at some gut level that Pendleton had murdered the victim in his novel."

"Really?"

"You were infatuated with Wiltshire, so you agreed to help get the book published, but at the same time you had your eyes on ruining Pendleton. I checked up on you, Allen, and the consensus is most were shocked that you were to the fore in pushing the book. It's generally agreed that both you and Pendleton hated each other."

"We reconciled with age, Jon, but go on. I hope I can be as brilliant and conniving as you make me out to be."

"Are you telling me the graphic, detailed nature of the crime didn't stand out at all, the particularities? I'm no expert, but it's a different style."

"Inventive license is the essence of the art of fiction! For God's sake, do you hold that every murder novel is written by the murderer? Please!"

"So you never did any background check to see if there had been any murders committed in the general area of Bannockburn similar to the one described in *Scream*?"

"No."

"I know you didn't care about Pendleton, but Wiltshire had given you the book, and you weren't sure if she was setting you up or not, so you decided to give her time. You placed the book with a publisher, subsidized her and Pendleton, made it seem that you were on her side. The book was autobiographical in every sense, and with Wiltshire doing her thesis on Pendleton, at a certain point you felt there was no conceivable way she would not have at least researched local murders. So you waited, expected her to take you into her confidence. There was time to remain outside the fray of foreknowledge, to have Wiltshire come up with the revelation. It kept you innocent. She was the researcher, not you. You felt there was time to break the story before the book's publication, a sort of chilling find that would have shot the book to the top of the best-seller lists. That was the plan, anyway. You had invested a hundred and twenty thousand dollars to expose and ruin an old rival."

Ryder's voice grew more animated. "But Wiltshire never did confide in you, and the longer she held out, the more upset you became. You didn't want to implicate her, but you knew she had the facts somewhere. You knew she was using you."

Horowitz smiled. "Go on, Jon, please!"

Ryder leaned forward. "Too close to the truth, Allen? I know Wiltshire refused interviews. The Publicity Department at the publishing house has corroborated that Wiltshire was resistant to helping promote the book. She let you front the publicity, let you put your neck out. I think, in a way, that was the last straw. It proved she knew. She had her perfect pawn, *you*."

Ryder looked directly at Horowitz. "Somehow I don't think that sat well with you, right? But the problem was you never could admit what you discovered. There would have been too many questions as to when you made the discovery, and anyway, Wiltshire would have seen through you, understood your motivations all along. Maybe she even knew that you knew. I wouldn't put it past her. I think her motivation all along had been to get the book published at all costs. She had no real interest in you at all. She was seven years at the school and going nowhere. This was her ticket out. Pendleton, as far as she was concerned, was already a prisoner. Any revelation meant nothing, really. He was beyond the law, locked away within. . . .

"In the end, even a guy as levelheaded as you couldn't stop yourself from wanting revenge. Unrequited love can skew a person's sense of reason.

You had been used—you, the world-famous writer, upended by a grad student!

"As publication came, you wanted spectacle, you wanted scandal and revenge, so you made the tape and then mailed it to the newspaper in Muncie. We know it was mailed from New York.

"I assume you did that on purpose, as a sort of not so subtle dig intended for Wiltshire, so that when the facts about where the tape had come from were revealed, she would know it had been you who'd revealed the connection to the Jewel case . . . but then, after the fact, as the story broke, you felt a sense of remorse. You didn't want to lose the woman you had fallen in love with, so you hastily sent her the fax as you rushed to get to her to hide whatever evidence she had already amassed that would implicate her of foreknowledge of what Pendleton had done."

Ryder stopped for a moment. "Look, I'd prefer to get her, Allen, okay? I've my own reasons. She used you. I know what that feels like. Let's talk man to man here, cut the crap. Listen to me, Allen, I see the compassion in you, deep down, the sense of *regret.*"

Horowitz said nothing until he realized Ryder had stopped, and then he reached across the table and set his hand on Ryder's. "Bravo, Jon! Brilliant hard-boiled stuff, tried and tested. There are no fag crime fighters, Jon, and you nailed it, stayed within the confines of the genre but laced it with enough of *you* to make it real. I sensed the compassion and touch of truth, so that I knew you, in talking about the sense of hurt, were talking about yourself at some deep level, but it's what artists do. I knew it was coming, the trite conjecture and so much expository horseshit. Sometimes those lines are the hardest to deliver with conviction, but you came through. Cliché, I must admit, and that's not a criticism, because things need to get said. We need to see your thoughts. I think throwing in the tangled web of unrequited love at the heart of the matter, well, that did it for me. It brought the foibles of humanity into perspective. Everyone wants a love story! You know, that's something you can't teach, that nascent regard for story. I loved it, Jon! Two big thumbs-up."

Horowitz patted Ryder's hand, then looked at his watch. "This has been a learning experience." Then he took on a more serious tone.

"You know, I wonder, and I'm not being critical here, Jon, but exactly what are your motivations? Why are you harassing Adi, or me, for that matter? I think the particulars of *if* or *when* certain discoveries concerning Pendleton were made, and the hesitation by some or all the parties to revealing that information, don't amount to criminal intent, do they?"

Horowitz let the question hang for a moment. "Didn't putting the book out into the public domain bring the case to light again? The central question, I'd submit, Jon, is, aren't you supposedly here to investigate if Pendleton did, in fact, murder Amber Jewel?"

"Oh, I am, Allen. This conversation between us is what we call in the business 'a parallel line of inquiry.'"

"Ah. . . ." Horowitz nodded. "I'll keep that in mind."

Horowitz had turned to leave when Ryder said, "Before you go, you never did answer why you didn't reference the Leopold and Loeb case in your *New York Times* articles. I think, given the kind of book and people you all are, and I mean that in a good way, wouldn't literary precedence only have bolstered what you call Pendleton's genius?"

"You keep coming back to the book. . . ."

"It's just the initial denial, Allen. It has me confused."

Horowitz looked exhausted, his eyes glazed, although he held his own against Ryder. "I'd refer you to my exact words, Jon, but no matter. I see this is something that is keeping you from what you should really be investigating."

Horowitz stalled, took a drink; the water caught in the growth of stubble, so he wiped his mouth with the back of his hand, then looked at Ryder. "You see, in my considered opinion, there is a fundamental philosophical difference between Leopold and Loeb and Pendleton's protagonist. I made a conscious decision not to include the reference because what Pendleton's protagonist felt was the *lack* of God, *not* the *freedom* of there being *no* God, as with Leopold and Loeb. Those juveniles had been inspired by a sense of megalomania, by their own self-centeredness. It was a puerile act, without any deeply philosophical underpinning. Bob's work would have been diminished in merely referencing those two. They merely committed an act of murder; Pendleton created a masterpiece. He took the philosophical questioning of what is Superman and created an existential nightmare that will stand the test of time. Regardless of what you think, Jon, the book is up for the National Book Award, its genius has been validated, is being validated as we speak, and that was both my and Wiltshire's guiding principle, the philosophical genius of the work. The murder was incidental from our perspective, and I don't say that callously. Rather, murder has been a literary trope used to explore existential ideas.

"In context, the murder at the heart of *Scream* seems a literary device. I assume you haven't read Camus' *The Stranger*, but a murder along a stretch of beach figures at the heart of that novel, and I've never heard of anybody researching to see if, indeed, a man was murdered along a beach. Furthermore, and this is important, Jon, I think, if you read *Scream* as it was meant to be read, as spiritual crisis, as God quest, then murder would have been the ultimate sin. The novel was a search for redemption. In committing such a random murder, Pendleton's protagonist would have been denying his soul eternal salvation."

Ryder said bluntly, "But Pendleton did kill Amber Jewel."

Horowitz shook his head slowly. "You interchange the two, Detective, the writer and the protagonist. I don't. I can only talk about the novel, about Pendleton's protagonist."

"They're one and the same."

"Okay, prove it! You're the cop!"

THIRTY-ONE

HOROWITZ FELT SHAKY and cold as he walked down the hallway of the old hospital into a big room that had once been a solarium for polio patients and now served as a makeshift social room.

He was coming down from a surge of adrenaline he had maintained while speaking with Ryder. He considered whether he needed a lawyer, whether it was now time to extricate himself from any association with Adi, though he wasn't willing to give her up, not yet. Had he been used by her?

Horowitz tried to put a spin on events, tried to rationalize. How often did a guy like him get to meet and confront, with such intimacy of suspicion, a guy like Ryder? He was a mere character study. In fiction, he would make him an antihero, make him uglier, more profoundly pathetic.

Ryder was getting erectile dysfunction. That was a definite. Horowitz nodded his head. Leopold and Loeb were right! The profound nature of superiority lay in total control, in unequivocal self-belief.

At a fifties cafeteria-style vending area within the solarium, Horowitz got a cup of coffee. The cafeteria smelled of meat loaf and fried onions overlaid with a hot smelled of menthol, arthritic rubbing ointment, the carpet a green Astroturf of a miniature golf course, threadbare but with its own utilitarian quality. The solarium's roof could be opened with a giant contraption of pulleys.

Horowitz took a sip; the coffee was bitter and tepid. He was taken aback by Ryder's accusation that he had sent the anonymous tape from New York.

He closed and opened his eyes, feeling them water, the strain apparent again on his face. He trawled for some logical explanation.

Had some fact-checking zealot in the publishing house's Production Department correlated the facts in the Jewel murder with the murder in *Scream* and then produced the tape to drum up publicity? It didn't seem like the sort of stunt a reputable publishing house would orchestrate.

Had the tape really been mailed from New York?

It bothered Horowitz, though. Finally he settled on the notion that Ryder had to have been lying. He remembered something he had heard and all but forgotten. A crime writer had once told him, during an awards ceremony at the New York Public Library, that cops had the right to *lie* to suspects during interviews, and they did as a matter of course.

Horowitz put his hand to his forehead, the tiredness closing around him. He was struck by the sense of being older than he had ever acknowledged—a growing sense of fatigue at the end of days, but also at the tenacity and insight of Ryder, who was more accomplished than he felt most cops were.

Ryder had been right. Unrequited love had, of course, been fundamental to his motivation in helping to get *Scream* published. Something had rung true in Ryder's sentiment regarding betrayal. Horowitz fixed on that. He would find out who and what he was dealing with, find Ryder's vulnerability. People didn't speak to Allen Horowitz as Ryder had and get away with it.

At the back of it all, though, Horowitz knew what was really bothering him—Adi Wiltshire's betrayal, her not telling him what Pendleton had done. It hurt with a heartache he had always scoffed at, the stuff of bad poetry, but what he was feeling was *true* pain. Looking up, Horowitz stared at those sitting around him as though they had been set before him as metaphor, spouses sitting silently together in habitual routine.

He watched an old woman sitting across from her sleeping husband, saw her knitting in a rote way, the feelerlike needles moving with the agitated click of a praying mantis feeding on the innards of some other living thing.

This was the endgame of even the most stable and loving of relationships, of life's sacrifice of fidelity, everybody living in solemn obligation to someone. Was love worth it?

In the end, he just looked away, not answering his own question, looked toward the big window, where in the distance the horizon met the land in strata of cerulean and charcoal.

Adi lay in the hospital bed, her face waxy with a warm sweat of withdrawal. A crescent of darkness had formed beneath her eyes, betraying Italian heritage, a darkness that would settle in the lax softening of aging.

Horowitz took a cloth, wet and wrung it in a kidney-shaped metal bowl, and dabbed at small cracks on either side of Adi's mouth. Her eyes moved under her eyelids in a rapid movement of dreams, her face twitching from time to time.

There was something even more beautiful about her than he had remembered. He kept wiping her forehead, tried to imagine her a decade or so on, the steely salt and pepper of her hair pulled back tight, revealing the growing shadowy darkness of her face, the hollowed-out eyes recessed with a certain wisdom characteristic of so many ethnic mothers he remembered from childhood. Here was a woman so different from the immodest, aerobic, spandex-wearing exoskeletons that inhabited so much of his life down in Florida.

He continued to dab her forehead and lips, looking for a glimmer of hope, for a way out from the pall Ryder had cast over him. It was hard trying to regain that sense of perspective, to extricate himself from what was going on around him. He now acknowledged the interrogative process, the sense of self-doubt it created. He had been a victim of that process. Clichéd as they were, confessions were born of this lack of perspective, this sense of entrapment, and, after all, Ryder was a professional. Ryder had wanted him to implicate Adi.

Squeezing and tightening the damp cloth, feeling the sinews of his forearms burn, Horowitz decided, there and then, that the interview had been a learning experience. That's all it had been.

Adi's face came into focus again. He touched her forehead.

In a way, things had worked in his favor. She had nothing and nowhere to go. This was fact. He had her exactly where he wanted her, her addiction an unforeseen complication that was now proving a leveling factor in connecting with her again.

She needed him.

Horowitz took another breath and felt at ease for the first time in a long while. He laced his hand through Adi's long fingers, took her hand, and kissed it, feeling the stubble of his beard against her hand.

So what if she had tried to use him?

Adi's chest rose and fell, her nipples a darkish color beneath her flimsy hospital gown, and he thought of the vigil of the old woman in the solarium. Leaning his head on the flat of Adi's stomach, he closed his eyes and whispered, "I want to grow old in your arms."

What he did not know was that as he rested his head against Adi's stomach, she had opened her eyes.

She had not been asleep at all.

THIRTY-TWO

GARY SCHOLL, WEARING a stained blue jumpsuit with his name embroidered in a stylized script that simply read "*Gary*," was in the twentieth hour of partying, slowly coming down from a hyped-up sense of his own innocence, when his girlfriend's dogs started barking out in their kennels. An hour earlier, his girlfriend had left the house, after they'd had an uproarious fight concerning his immediate and pressing need to speak with Kim Jewel.

Gary rose awkwardly, stoned, expecting her return. He was winding down a call to Kim that had been basically one-sided, his side, a diatribe that had run the gamut of emotions, from baleful commiseration at what life had thrown them to tearful regrets of what ifs to, finally, manic rage.

According to Gary, Kim had stopped believing in him, and that was her biggest crime and why she was "the world's biggest *cunt*!"

Kim listened, simply because much of what Gary said was true, but also because she, too, was drunk.

Pulling back a curtained window, Gary was taken by surprise. It wasn't his girlfriend returning, but the police arriving, and in a moment of hazy paranoia, he went for his hunting rifle and shouted with a sense of righteous justice that the cops had no goddamn right to come near him, since he had for so long been wrongfully suspected of murdering Amber Jewel. He said something to that effect to Kim, the phone still pressed against his ear and shoulder blade as he fired off a round to make sure the cops knew he meant business.

Kim was screaming at him to stop, not to die like this after all they had been through, but Gary wasn't listening anymore, almost hyperventilating with a renewed adrenaline rush.

In the aftermath of what had been a long-standing injustice done toward him, the cops were arriving to find him stoned. On his girlfriend's living room table was an elaborate bong, a bag of celebratory weed, lines of cocaine, a bottle of Jack Daniel's, and a two-liter bottle of Coke.

With previous drug violations, he wasn't going down for something like this. The instinct for self-preservation just kicked in. His last words to Kim were, "I'm sorry, Kimmie," a pet name he had not used since Amber Jewel's body had been discovered.

Counselors who dealt with the Kim Jewels of the world compartmentalized the lives of such women as follows: life as a series of Good Choices and Bad Choices. Their mantra was, "Make Good Choices!"

The stark summation of Kim's life's tally was, she had made more Bad Choices than Good Choices. She had given birth to the daughter of the man everybody believed had killed her sister. Bad Choice! Though it wasn't as bad as morbidly choosing to name the child Amber. That was off the chart of Bad Choices. In fact, it was plain crazy, but Kim was crazy in love with Gary back then, and it had been in both their natures to make such defiant statements of solidarity through the initial months of suspicion.

The fact was, the Kim Jewels and Gary Scholls of the world were of the kind who kept tattoo parlors in business with indelible statements of true love. When they hadn't had the money for tattoos, they had given each other savage territorial hickeys, and when they had, they'd sat through hours of excruciating pain, each getting identical hearts wrapped in the serpentine coils of embracing lovers. Gary also had a heart stabbed through with a dripping dagger tattooed onto his left pectoral that maybe got closest to his definition of love. The dripping daggered heart had a wavering banner that read, "Gary and Kim Forever."

Not to be outdone, surrounding Kim's navel was the word "Gary," though with childbirth and age the letters had begun to spiral into the dark of her navel like a collapsing stellar system.

If the ruination of their lives could have been confined to each other, well and good, but in an age of the new gothic of Jasons, Freddys, and Carries, the child was treated as spawn of the incubus, a freakishness that was reinforced as she grew up and developed a preternatural likeness to the first Amber Jewel.

Kim did nothing to hide the similarity. Lamentably, such had been her parental shortcomings, both past and present. The new Amber Jewel was on the cusp of further psychological damage as Kim left her house and ended up minutes later outside the property of Gary's girlfriend.

It was a situation counselors would have defined as another of Kim Jewel's Bad Choices.

Ryder arrived a half hour later as evening turned toward dark into the heat of what was emerging as a standoff. He saw Kim being restrained by cops. Dressed in a vinyl jacket, sweats, and high-tops, she was shouting out Gary's name, and he was shouting back through a curtained window that he loved her in the faltering voice of a guy who was not coming out alive. Her presence seemed to make matters worse.

Trent Bauer was off to the side, in the dull glow of a dome light in a cop car, another cop sitting sideways with his legs outside the car, talking on his CB in an animated way, when suddenly Gary emerged in a pair of boxer shorts and a netted tank top, drugged up.

Bauer shouted Gary's name, and Gary turned violently, his rifle aimed toward the cop car. Bauer reacted on a hair trigger, his gun drawn, returning a barrage of fire instantaneously, cutting Gary down in what seemed like slow-motion death.

Gary lurched forward, then halted abruptly, turning toward the wailing voice of Kim. She broke free of the cops restraining her and reached Gary as he stumbled and fell forward.

Ryder didn't have time to react, or more exactly, he had stood back and watched it all unfold, processing the instant flash of recognition and vengeance in Gary's eyes as he had picked out Bauer, Gary's gut reaction to shoot.

It was hard to tell who had fired first in the crack of gunfire.

Bauer emerged from behind the cop car, his gun still trained on Gary slumped in Kim's arms as she looked up and screamed hysterically at

Bauer, "Why?" over and over again until Bauer stopped and lowered his gun as other cops moved tentatively toward Gary, one of them kicking Gary's rifle away from the slumped body.

Life meant nothing in the scheme of things, not a life like Gary Scholl's, anyway, only the screams of Kim Jewel signifying a human being had died.

It was hard to believe that in an instant the long-standing suspect in the murder of Amber Jewel could be cut down like this, the prospect of interrogating Gary over.

Whatever had gone on over the years had played itself out in this final standoff, another humiliation for Ryder, another omen auguring that he should be elsewhere. Scholl's death was an inevitable end that could have not ended otherwise, or so Ryder told himself against his own failings in the case so far.

It was as Ryder turned and walked toward his car, facing that reality, that his eyes locked on the figure of a child standing in the background, dressed in a pink down coat with fake electric blue fur, a child with the face of Amber Jewel. It stopped him cold.

Ryder had known nothing of the likeness that Kim Jewel's daughter bore to the murdered Amber Jewel, and he didn't make the connection. For Ryder it was an apparition, a sign he had sought out at the place where Amber Jewel's body had been interred.

But here she was, watching over him now.

Ryder nodded solemnly, and the child blinked. He had not slept properly in days, and that may have contributed to the fact that he didn't say a word, just passed by slowly, that he even smiled softly toward her, but he was glad she had regained the likeness of her earlier years, for he knew this was her true essence, not the troubled thirteen-year-old whore she would become.

As Ryder started his car, the child remained off to the side, looking at him, and he nodded, felt again the weight of destiny that had been handed down to him in his dreams, remembering again the childhood school yard game of gathering souls, where he had dreamed of the dark, smiling eyes of a dead Venetia Goretti staring back at him.

THIRTY-THREE

A FAX WAS AWAITING Ryder on his desk when he arrived at the station, stating all persons related to the data entry of the Jacobs & Sons ledgers had been contacted and none had kept the original data. A handwritten addendum to the fax advised Ryder that investigators were now pursuing other avenues of inquiry, specifically whether any library had ever acquired an original copy of *Scream*, archiving its date of acquisition. The investigation was moving forward in this paper trail, in a search to find definitive proof needed for the district attorney to bring charges against the now comatose Pendleton.

The continued uncertainty surrounding the actual printing of the novel unsettled Ryder all the more in light of Trent gunning down Scholl.

Could Pendleton have feasibly moved unobserved through the rural back roads, not just one time, but twice? Circumstantial evidence now suggested that Jewel had been murdered elsewhere and then dumped in Henderson's field, long after search parties had given up looking for her. It was a troubling scenario, differing, too, from the novel, where the murder had taken place immediately, a gruesome sexual assault and dismemberment and interment out in what would prove to be Henderson's field.

Ryder stopped, felt his temples pounding with the pressure of circumstances both with the case and with his home life. He thought of calling Gail but didn't, just ran his hand through his hair, his thoughts settling back on what had happened earlier that evening.

Through the course of three cups of black coffee, Ryder tried to turn from thinking about Bauer, watched reels of surveillance and media tape of the Jewel investigation for over an hour, as he looked for *something*, he didn't know what, the sense of exhaustion there as he struggled to stay awake.

What emerged were numerous appearances of locals, the most notable

Sam Henderson, not only at the removal of Jewel's body, but even prior to that, back when Jewel first disappeared, Henderson in his characteristic overalls, a scarecrow figure in the offing at the local junior high school when the first of many search parties had been organized. Why, then, Henderson's protracted story of his discovery of Jewel's body months later, when surely he would have known or intuited what he had come upon that spring?

As evening waned, Ryder waded through the box of investigative material related to the Jewel case. There was no indication Henderson had ever been a suspect in the interview notes of various investigators, yet Ryder read through the detailed statement Henderson had given again, a statement almost verbatim with what Henderson had told him during the initial interview.

Ryder settled again on his first impression of Henderson, or more exactly Henderson's house, its austere religiosity, everything bare save the crocheted crosses Henderson's wife had perpetually stitched throughout her life, or so Henderson had told him, the crosses the sole adornment, nailed throughout the house, the windows without curtains, revealing all within or, conversely, revealing all on the outside. Wouldn't Henderson have been able to see something, some activity in the adjacent field across from his house?

What had been vaguely disturbing during his initial interview at the house, before going out into the field, had been the absence of pictures of children, no offspring, an unsettling fact Ryder now reconsidered. What sort of sublimated life had Henderson lived, a farmer without children to pass on his land? Had it been a decision based on religious grounds, or otherwise?

Sifting through the notes, Ryder came across a reference to Henderson's wife, who had died of cancer the fall Amber was murdered. He let the coincidence settle a moment, reflected on the grief a man left alone might have endured in a cruel, merciless world, a recent widower, his faith challenged, staring out at what passed each day by his door, a school bus carrying the likes of Amber Jewel, the iniquity of the Jewel family and their sordid life set against what he held sacred all his life.

Ryder looked upward. It could play so many ways, this sense of supposition, of what ifs, but in a way, at that moment it was easiest of all to imagine the likes of a Sam Henderson killing Jewel, more so than Bauer or Pendleton, to dwell on the surreal gothic of rural life embodied in cult movies like *Children of the Corn*.

Indeed, his own fascination with crime, with the psychopathology of serial murderers, went back to a place such as this, the epitome of the modern American horror film, Hitchcock's *Psycho*, inspired by the real-life horrors committed by Wisconsin farmer Ed Gein, the psychologically scarred son of a domineering religious zealot, who kept the corpse of his mother at his farm, which he had turned into a human abattoir of hanging female torsos, becoming cannibal and necromancer. Even *The Texas Chainsaw Massacre*'s Leatherface paid homage to Gein's hunger for human flesh.

Ryder poured himself more coffee and continued to look at the reel of film, the same faces materializing over and over as he kept reviewing the film, searching, hiding from the image of what he had seen earlier that night, the ghostly child image of Amber Jewel looking at him, beseeching him, or so he felt now in the dragging night.

Besides Henderson, Bauer emerged throughout the footage, as did Wright, there with his camera at the recovery of Jewel's body, working for the newspaper, scanning the crowd, the rapid click exposure of the lens eye blinking, capturing the sad spectacle of what one human could inflict on another human being—in this case, the dismemberment of a thirteen-year-old girl, a thought that so chilled Ryder, he simply shut off the projector as though that single act could erase the fact of what had happened so long ago.

In the outer office, Ryder found what he had been waiting for all night: Bauer. He was sitting at his desk, on the phone to someone. From the way he was shaking his head back and forth, the call seemed personal.

Bauer caught sight of Ryder and ended the call abruptly, and Ryder could tell Bauer had been waiting for him, saw the way he made eye contact with another cop before he stood up.

Under a cold, clear sky, on the steps of the police station, Ryder lit a cigarette and offered Bauer one, which he lit and inhaled in a long pull, holding the smoke in his lungs before exhaling two tusks through his nostrils.

Ryder decided to make a play at familiarity and solidarity. "Look, I don't give a shit about Gary, about what happened earlier, okay? As far as I'm concerned, you stopped Gary shooting up a hell of a lot of people . . . that's how I see it."

Bauer flicked a scab of ash off his cigarette. "I appreciate that . . . I saw something in his eyes . . . something desperate . . ."

Ryder bided his time, tapping his own cigarette, inhaling again, looking out toward the glow of light pollution over the town, pointed with the red scab of his cigarette. "You know, there are hundreds of billions of stars out there we can't see, but you drive out of town and you see the heavens filled with them, but that doesn't account for the billions that are still out there. I guess what I'm saying is, there's going to be stuff we know or feel, but can never see."

Bauer said, "Like gravity?"

Ryder held his cigarette. "Yeah, like gravity . . . right, or like the enigma of attractions . . . though, how come attraction doesn't always work like it does with gravity when it comes to human attraction?"

Bauer stared straight ahead, looking off toward the distant glow of light coming from the domed cap of Bannockburn College. He took another drag of his cigarette to hide his sense of agitation. It had gotten cold, so his breath showed. He stepped from one foot to another.

Ryder kept watching Bauer out of the corner of his eye. "I mean, if you believe what science tells us, we're something like ninety-eight percent water, with a dash of some neurotransmitter chemicals. Basically, we're signaling systems out there, trying to establish connections. So how come you were attracted to Kim, for instance, but somehow she never returned that feeling? I mean, from a scientific standpoint, it doesn't make sense, does it?"

Bauer swallowed. All he said was, "I guess it doesn't." He brought his cigarette to his lips so it pulsed in the dark, his face lit for a brief moment.

"What were you doing tonight, Trent?"

Bauer made a motion to turn, but Ryder raised his voice. "I mean, killing Gary . . . getting back at Kim for what she did to *you?*"

Bauer stiffened but didn't leave.

"I heard you were seeing Kim the year Amber was murdered. . . . Gary was off doing a stretch. He got out and Kim went back to him."

Bauer made a snorting, dismissive sound. "Who you been talking to?"

"You denying it?"

"You got it wrong . . . I was looking out for her is all."

"So you were involved with her?"

"I checked up on her! We knew each other all our lives."

"Right . . . all your lives. I heard all about the *junior high dance*!"

"Junior high school! That was like another lifetime ago. Is that what this is about, you trying to stick that on me, something like that?"

"I'm *not* sticking anything on you. I'm concerned about what people here were saying about you back then when Amber went missing."

Bauer turned. "People are going to say all sorts of things. It doesn't make it true! I followed up on a lead is what I did! You think I didn't know forcing Kim's hand about Kline was going to blow up in my face, all eyes on me getting involved like that . . . but I did it anyway. I did my job."

"Don't try to double-talk me, Trent. I know you kept that shot of Kim with Kline."

Bauer lowered his head. "Wright . . . you been speaking to him?"

"What was it, Trent, you wanted to show some earnest investigative work, cast suspicion far and wide . . . take investigators on a wild goose chase tracking down Kline . . . or were you really just trying to get back at Kim for rejecting you?"

Bauer looked up. "You got a real question, ask me. If not, stay the hell away!"

Then he turned, flicking his cigarette so it fell in an arch against the darkness, leaving Ryder standing alone, but not before Ryder shouted, "I know what I saw this evening, Trent! You gunned Gary down. Why?"

THIRTY-FOUR

Two DAYS INTO HER voluntary hospitalization, Adi Wiltshire had not been questioned yet regarding where she got her drugs or interviewed as to how Pendleton had injected himself with an overdose. The death of Gary Scholl had taken precedence, his last moments alive captured on TV, the tragic image of Kim Jewel caught running toward Gary Scholl's slumping body. Even Adi had seen it early that morning.

Since the ongoing investigation into trying to establish the actual print-run date of the original *Scream* had not been revealed to the public, for them the tragedy centered on how the lives of Gary Scholl and Kim Jewel had been ruined in the harrowing years of living under the suspicion of having murdered Amber Jewel.

It all made a set piece, a story with old footage that had the station anchor at the studio and the regional reporter on location, both almost a decade younger then, with vintage hairstyles and hopelessly dated clothes.

Dressed in a hospital nightgown, Adi stood outside Pendleton's hospital room, a portable IV drip at her side.

A cop guarded the door.

Adi was allowed only to look through the small round window into the room. Her breath made the glass fog. It was like staring into a looking glass, into something deep and far off, something very old.

The room was in the oldest quarter of the hospital, ironically endowed by the Russian émigré who had founded Bannockburn and where the burned survivors of the clothing factory fire had been brought over half a century before.

Behind her, Adi heard a voice. When she turned, Wright was watching her from the end of the long corridor slashed in intermittent bars of light and dark. It was still early morning.

Adi said his name in a whisper, almost relieved to see him, though as he approached slowly, she saw the swollen aspect of his broken nose and just stared at him.

Wright had a bouquet of white roses. He handed them to Adi and defused the emphasis on his own condition, saying softly, "How is the professor?"

In her hospital gown, Adi looked ghostlike. She simply shook her head. "I don't know. They won't tell me anything."

Wright set his hand on Adi's shoulder in a paternal way that made Adi meet his eyes and then look to the IV in her arm and then at him again. "I guess you never know somebody, really."

Wright avoided answering the question. "I came by now because word has it tonight they might be doing the fires up at the college. I got to get back out there. The board is going through the roof. They don't need this added spectacle with what's going on now, but you know students, the continuity of tradition. I guess what's happening now will be eclipsed in the greater sense of what Bannockburn means. They don't want to abandon tradition."

Adi nodded.

Wright had already turned, as though he were set on leaving, as if he had nothing else to say.

Adi returned the smile, walked alongside Wright toward the exit, then stopped and lowered her head.

Wright hesitated. "You okay?" he asked, staring at the neckline of Adi's hospital gown lying off her shoulder, revealing the hollow between her neck and collarbone.

Adi whispered, "I feel ashamed. . . ." She looked down the slatted light of the corridor. "It seems like another lifetime ago, you know, the college, Robert, everything. You get that feeling, or is it the . . . the drugs?"

"What is it they say in the Bible, 'This too shall pass'?"

"And then what?"

Wright didn't answer. They had reached the exit just as Allen Horowitz pulled abruptly into the gravel parking lot. Seeing Adi, Horowitz shouted her name, and Adi felt the trail of her fingers touching air where a moment earlier Wright had been, as though he had simply vanished, leaving her with a sad and curious longing deep inside her.

In the gray steeliness of the morning light, the old world cafeteria offered country-fried steak breakfasts with grits and scrambled eggs and sausage links served by a large-faced woman in a hairnet who would spend the better part of her life doing this job.

When he came back with his tray, Horowitz opened a small notebook and wrote something down, then looked up and said, "It is women like that over there that make me want to understand the big questions, 'Why are we here?' 'What is the nature of existence?'"

Adi forestalled saying anything of consequence. Horowitz was the last person she wanted to see, his overbearing personality coming to the fore again.

Horowitz continued to talk about the woman.

Adi felt cold and not up to speaking, though she looked toward the woman sloshing out breakfast to patients lined up with trays. She said, "Maybe that is why she exists, to spark questions like that in people like you, Allen. Not everybody can be *great*. . . ." She regretted having said anything even as she spoke.

Horowitz raised his hand and in his brash way said, "Hey, I'm not knocking her. I think, in psychological circles, they call them 'facilitators.'"

Steam rose from his breakfast, and a natural stalemate fell again. Adi thought she had escaped further conversation, but then Horowitz said, in a probing way, without looking up, "On which side do you fall?"

Adi answered despite herself. "I don't quite understand the question."

Looking over the rim of his coffee cup, Horowitz said, "Are you a facilitator or are you after greatness?"

"I think you know the answer. What *greatness* could I possess?"

She looked at Horowitz, then to the bouquet of flowers Wright had given her.

Horowitz seemed to pause as he took up a home-style biscuit and buttered it, looking between Adi and the flowers; but he said nothing about it, instead pointed the knife at Adi. "Maybe there are varying degrees of greatness. I think *recognizing* greatness in someone can be a form of greatness in and of itself. Greatness doesn't always know or understand itself. Greatness can be abhorrently self-centered. It can be monstrously cruel. Sometimes greatness needs an advocate, it needs to be interpreted. Sometimes greatness needs *a great facilitator*."

Adi felt Horowitz trawling tirelessly for a confession of her foreknowledge, even now. She didn't answer directly. She wanted to just walk away but didn't.

"Is that what I am, Allen, a facilitator?"

The flour on the biscuit Horowitz was eating had dusted the growth of his two-day-old beard, making him seem older than he was.

Adi reached across the table, the IV needle affixed with strips of gauze in an X to her hand, and, touching Horowitz's hand, made a play toward her avowed commitment to Pendleton. Her veins showed in an iodine discoloration as she squeezed Horowitz's hand.

"Tell me it *is* a great book, Allen. Tell me we weren't wrong." And she let her eyes go glossy as the morning light caught the slow drip of her IV meting out solitary teardrops.

Horowitz left Adi's hand on his. "*You* gave him more than he could ever have dreamed of."

Adi's throat tightened.

Horowitz said, "You should eat." He had lost a measure of control. He broke eye contact and poured a slow, viscous circle of syrup over his pancakes.

Almost a minute passed, and then, without looking up, he said, "Just tell me something."

Adi looked at him.

"When did you know Bob killed the girl?"

Adi retained her composure. "I didn't . . . not until everybody else found out."

"Look, I'm on your side. I just need to know where things stand. I'm not judging you, you hear that? I know you wanted this thesis more than anything else. I understand people do desperate things, make decisions that it's hard justifying, but I don't judge, I don't! I see the human condition as nothing more than survival of the fittest in the end. You apply moral reasoning to any situation, and chances are it's against your best interests. You know the moral precepts of our so-called modern age came from the ancients, from guys like Plato, who whiled away his years waxing poetic while ass-fucking his students."

Adi said abruptly, "Can't you stop, Allen, just for once, be yourself?"

"This *is* me."

Adi felt shaky, her addiction tugging at her.

"There had to be something in Bob's notes, some reference to what he did, some *evidence*. Writers don't write in a vacuum."

Adi looked at Horowitz. "There were *no* notes. There is nothing to find, there never *was* . . . or Robert destroyed everything long before he attempted suicide. It was Robert's last published book, a quasi vanity press publication, and it went nowhere. He was never published after that. Would you have wanted to be reminded of that failure? There are *no notes!*"

"I did everything for you, financed you, put my reputation on the line. I'm as much a part of this as you!"

Adi didn't raise her voice. She said softly, "I know you are. What we . . . no, what *you* did, Allen, with your money and your fame, was *facilitate* true greatness."

There was the slightest trace of contained contempt in her voice. "Be happy with that, Allen, that you will be remembered in the same breath as Bob."

She said it in a way that hurt more deeply than she felt she could ever have hoped to hurt him.

Horowitz stood up. "Why don't you trust me?"

"I could ask you the same thing." Her nose was raw and running.

"Look at you, junkie! Just tell me, where are you and he going to hide now, without your drugs?"

"In the same obscurity we all die in. Just look around you, Allen!" And as Adi looked around, she saw Ryder sitting at a table behind them.

Ryder rose quietly, not sure if he had been witness to a staged argument, and, looking straight at Adi, said, "You are under arrest for illegally obtaining prescription medications."

THIRTY-FIVE

DESPITE THE APPARENT STRAIN of withdrawal, Adi Wiltshire seemed to regard Ryder with contempt, staring back at him with increasing defiance through the early part of the interview, as Ryder asked her a series of procedural questions, asking her to state her name, age, and occupation for the record.

Then Ryder said flatly, "Do you think Pendleton killed Amber Jewel?"

Adi said stiffly, "At the present time, I would like to invoke my right to request legal counsel."

"I'm just asking your considered opinion as an expert on Pendleton. What do you think, he killed her or he didn't?"

Adi looked toward the mirrored window in the interrogation room and said calmly, "I want it made known that I now feel that my constitutional rights are being violated."

Ryder leaned forward across the metal table. "What I don't get is your belief Pendleton did this—not unless you have proof. Do you have proof?"

Adi said nothing.

"How about if I told you the microfiche roll for the local newspaper was stolen from the library? You know anything about that?"

Ryder leaned to his side and picked out of his bag a copy of the Leopold and Loeb book. "We recovered your prints all over this as well. You knew he'd committed a copycat murder."

Adi averted her eyes toward the mirrored window in the interrogation room and said calmly, "I want it made known that I now feel that my constitutional rights are being ignored."

"Everyone's a legal eagle these days, but before you invoke your constitutional rights, don't you want to know how we were able to recognize your fingerprints? You don't have a record, do you, Miss Wiltshire?"

Ryder pointed at a mug shot of Adi, meting out slowly what he had discovered from her past.

"Let me refresh your memory. Four years ago, you were convicted of shoplifting. I have here an affidavit given by department store security personnel, and I quote, 'White female suspect was seen acting suspiciously in the women's dress section. Security began tracking suspect, who took various clothing items into a fitting room, whereupon video surveillance began monitoring suspect's activity. Video surveillance recorded suspect removing tags and a security device from a dress, which suspect then stuffed into a large over-the-shoulder purse, along with various bracelets and jewelry that were eventually established as a cubic zirconia necklace and matching earrings.'"

Adi looked blankly past Ryder, who took out another sheet of paper embossed with Bannockburn College raised letterhead and with a flourish licked his thumb.

"I have here comments from a member of your thesis committee regarding your academic progress, and I quote, 'Doctoral candidate, Miss Adi Wiltshire, continues to flounder in an eternal limbo of research that has yet to coalesce into a reasonable line of academic inquiry. The long-term effect of such chronic academic malingering sets a bad precedence. Miss Wiltshire is entering her sixth year as a graduate student. I recommend that her request for continued academic assistance should be thoroughly reviewed and tied to definitive milestones.' End quote."

Ryder made a whistling sound. "That's a pretty damning assessment of your academic potential."

Adi waited, stone-faced.

"This is from a letter dated January fifth, 1984, the first year you took a graduate course in theory with Professor Pendleton. Was that the year you read his novel, the year you told him what you knew?"

Adi just looked at Ryder.

"I cross-checked, and Pendleton had a mental breakdown two months after you took his course. Did you try to blackmail him?"

Adi shook her head. "Why would he will *me* his literary estate?"

Ryder held up his hands. "Right. Good, now you're talking, at least. You got me! See, I can't answer that."

The sudden change unnerved Adi. She hesitated, took a drink of water, set it down, and looked toward the mirrored glass, but this time she didn't ask for her lawyer.

"We know Horowitz sent the tape from New York, that he revealed the connection. We traced the postmark. How does that make you feel?"

Adi didn't answer. Her neck flushed at Ryder's random questions; he was trying to keep her off-kilter, as if he didn't want to reveal any direct line of inquiry.

"The prescription fraud charges, they can be taken care of, you hear me? All I want is for you to level with me. You and Horowitz were in this together. Let's start there."

Ryder set the fax on the table, the words "Admit nothing!" scrawled all over it. "One of you is going to talk first."

Adi took a drink again, her hands cupping the glass, felt a slight pressure between her shoulder blades. Still she said nothing.

"Look, I know you don't trust me, that you *hate* me! That's it, right, what I did to you out at the library? But if you were the mother of a child, and that child was murdered, wouldn't you want somebody to do anything to find out what happened, to find out who did it? You *would*! See, all I was doing was my job, Adi."

Adi acquiesced at the reference to Amber Jewel, closed her eyes for a moment, then looked up. "I don't know what to tell you. What do you want?"

"Pendleton left something behind. Notes, early drafts of the book . . ."

Adi looked at Ryder. "You have the original book. You know he killed Jewel. What are you after? You heard me tell Horowitz at the cafeteria, there were *no* notes." Her voice was almost a whisper. "But nobody will believe me. . . ." She took another drink, her lower lip wet, trembling, the addiction waiting. "He'd left nothing behind. I think he erased the book from his mind, destroyed everything associated with it."

"But not the book?"

Adi's shoulders hunched slightly. "No. . . ."

"Why?"

"I think he knew there was something great in it."

"So why didn't he just remove the murder from the book, or change things and then republish it? It seems like not a single person ever read it."

Adi looked at Ryder. "You know how many books are published and nobody reads them? It wasn't a matter of being caught, of changing it. This was between him and God. Maybe sometimes one writes solely for oneself—"

Ryder interrupted. "Then you don't get it printed, if you're writing for yourself!"

"You keep asking me what he thought. I hardly knew him! All I can tell you is what I think after having read his other works. On the way to utter despair, maybe there can be one last scream. His career had been about trying to express the ineffable, a feeling. It didn't lend itself to plot, to the language of ordinary life." Adi stopped. "It's not the kind of stuff you want on a book jacket." She circled the rim of the glass with her index finger. "Sorry . . . I don't even remember your question."

"Why he kept the novel?"

"Just to know it *existed*. I think it was enough." She drank again and set the glass on the table.

Ryder scanned his teeth with his tongue. "Let's get back to the microfiche you removed and threw away. You knew about the connection to Amber Jewel."

Adi tensed, unsure if she had admitted to removing it. She looked at Ryder. "All I ever found were cuttings about Jewel's murder from the paper, clippings I thought Pendleton had used for another of his books, for *Word Salad*, a novel about the psychological breakdown of a college professor."

"There was a girl murdered in that book, too?"

"No . . . no . . . it was about someone stalking a professor who was getting death threats mailed to him."

"And?"

"And it seemed by the end of the book the professor had been mailing the letters to himself. Then in the hospital the letters just kept coming. He hadn't been sending them to himself at all."

"Or maybe he'd forwarded them to himself, had prearranged for them to be mailed?"

Adi furrowed her brow. "I guess you could interpret it that way." She looked up. "Maybe that is the whole mystery, everything is up to interpretation when you can't really know." She took a deep breath. "I don't know what more I can tell you."

"I don't get how the clippings relate to this *Word Salad*."

"I didn't say they did."

Ryder shook his head as though summoning all his patience. "You did!"

"No . . . I said the *letters* he got did, not the clippings."

"*What* letters?"

The whiteness of the room seemed to close around her. "The *letters*! Robert was stalked at one stage."

"This is in real life or in *Word Salad*?"

"In *real life*! Why are you making fun of me?"

"I'm not."

"Robert had an altercation with a student whom he'd demeaned in class."

"One of those prima donnas out there at Bannockburn?"

"No. A continuing ed student." Adi looked at Ryder. "You know him."

"I do?"

"The photographer guy, Henry James Wright, the guy whose nose you broke. Wright took a course with Pendleton, and they never hit it off."

Ryder's eyes narrowed. His shoes scraped the cold floor of the interrogation room. "How do you know it was Wright? He didn't sign them."

"No, they were anonymous. Wright just came right out and told me one evening, after Robert was back home. I was doing research on my thesis. Wright saw the letters spread out on my desk. He just came out and told me. He had reconciled what he'd been. It had been so long ago since it had happened. Wright was the only person still coming to see Robert. The faculty had stopped, so he just told me when he was leaving one evening. I think it was out of guilt."

"*Guilt?*"

"Wright took a shot of Robert and me at the house when Robert tried to commit suicide, the one Horowitz insisted get put in *Time* when *Scream* was rereleased. In the shot, Wright caught something of the despair Robert had lived with for so long. It was like he'd captured his soul." Adi shook her head. "I don't know how this all got so complicated. I found the book, saw something in it, got Horowitz to resubmit it, and that was all. This was supposed to be a gift to Robert, a testament to his genius, to what I'd found in the basement. I didn't find out what he'd done until I got the microfiche. I swear, only a few weeks before the general release of the book. It's how the addiction started. You can check the records of whatever you have against me writing the prescriptions. It happened when I was finishing my thesis. I got the microfiche to cull all the material related to the case to add on to my thesis—"

Ryder cut her off. "And how did Horowitz know?"

"I don't know what he knew. He never told me anything."

"But he thought you knew. He acted first. He exposed what Pendleton had done."

Adi bit her lower lip at the flush of accusation, at the fact that Horowitz had done this to her. She looked at Ryder. "Are you going to arrest me now?"

Ryder rose. "No, you can go . . . for now."

Adi hesitated and looked toward the mirrored glass.

Ryder waited, then said, "You know, what I don't get is you sending yourself the William Carlos Williams note to your office, then writing that quote on the mirror at the hospital. What were you trying to do, set the grounds for the beginning of a diminished mental faculty defense?"

Adi looked hard at Ryder. "Why are you doing this to me? I was honest with *you*. I told you what you wanted. You were out at the library. You stalked me. You wrote that stuff. It was *you*!"

"Me? What the hell do I know about poetry?"

THIRTY-SIX

STANDING ON THE STEPS of the county courthouse, Adi Wiltshire, dressed in gray sweatpants, an oversize Bannockburn sweatshirt of the same color, and high-tops, seemed to capture the shabbiness of modern existence. The outfit had come care of Henry James Wright, who had taken the liberty of buying her clothes and dropping them off at the station. The sweats still had the price tags attached.

The pale sun had reached its zenith in the noon hour, taking the temperature into the low forties, a typical November of crisp cold.

It was hard staring into the light.

Wright stood waiting under an old clock tower, cradling a cup of coffee, stepping from foot to foot, then he walked toward Adi. Somehow, despite the sweats having come from Wright, she had expected to see Horowitz waiting for her.

Adi just looked at Wright, who sensed as much.

Driving away from the courthouse, Wright did not pressure Adi, just drove toward Bannockburn and joined the procession of cars backed up, all returning from the beer run, with kegs and crates of grain alcohol, the blare of horns and music filling the early afternoon as they passed back across the moated bridge, waving at the security guards like toy soldiers, all readying for the fires later that evening.

Life simply went on, despite everything.

Wright looked at Adi. "I need to make sure everything is set for later, okay?" The presumption was that he was not dropping her off at the college, that she was going to stay with him.

Adi nodded. "Sure."

After crossing the bridge, Wright drove through the throng of students. Some were already dressed in period costume, the Lucys and the bearded Iosifs heading to the dining hall, drinking from giant plastic cups. Most were wasted or on their way to getting wasted. Unofficially, there would be no classes tomorrow, the campus wallowing in the torpor of hangovers.

Adi looked out the window as the car moved slowly around the perimeter. She saw the biology student from her poetry class, now being taught by the Chair in her absence, the guy atop a car pumping his chest and pointing at a gaggle of Lucys who all wore high heels and looked more like prostitutes than the Little Nell Lucy Bannockburn most probably had been.

It seemed so remote and alien to her with even this vague sense of distance, a place where she'd spent over seven years of her life and never fully settled on as real, a feeling she had heard expressed by faculty adrift of so-called normal life, sequestered at Bannockburn, former liberals who had quietly succumbed to the security of tenure. This was where the jobs were, and Adi's thoughts drifted toward Pendleton and *Scream* in that it had captured that awful, soul-killing sense of surrender.

How many times had he witnessed this spectacle? In a way, Adi thought it a wonder more faculty did not lose it eventually; and, of course, she thought of herself, of what had become of her.

She hadn't written the notes. She had to keep saying it to herself.

Wright took his equipment out of the trunk.

Adi waited, unsure why she was here or what she would do now, and simply looked at the workaday roughness of Wright in his denim jacket and T-shirt, the X of gauze over his broken nose. Was this the choice she was being offered after everything she'd gone through?

Still, Adi got out of the car.

* * *

It was a cold but clear afternoon, though snow was forecast in a day or so, hence the immediacy of the fires, this event preceding yet another Bannockburn tradition, the all-out snowball fight that defined winter's arrival at the college.

Adi followed Wright as he walked along the trail heading away from the college, along a spine of service railway track that brought the mountains of coal to Bannockburn's heating plant with its man-made cooling pool of steaming water. The heating plant had been purposely built on the ruins of the destroyed factory, a sort of unholy ground where the charred remains of eighteen women had been recovered, though all had been burned beyond recognition.

It was the sort of history the college did not want, and in the passage of seventy-plus years, the old center of what had been Zhvanetsky's moated empire had become part of a repressed history, the original site purposely lost to a wilderness of reeds and a bank of trees that had been allowed to grow, contrasting the manicured quads that defined the reincarnation of Bannockburn.

A simple, inauspicious plaque memorialized the tragic events of what happened there so long ago.

Adi stopped and looked at the plaque, bided her time. Wright had pushed on ahead, and she was glad of the reprieve.

How was she going to get away from him? It was something she did not want to admit to herself, but in the quiet moment of reflection, she knew something had been asked of her, and her answer now was no. But how to tell him? She dreaded the prospect of going out to his house, of being alone with him.

Adi started walking again toward Zhvanetsky's childhood home, a surreal vestige still preserved—his *actual* childhood home smuggled piecemeal out of Russia after the Communist revolution and rebuilt in America. It was something Zhvanetsky had insisted remain when he bequeathed the land and money for the founding of the college.

Adi stopped again, felt faint.

Less than forty-five minutes ago, she had been interrogated at a police station, the details of her failed life laid out before her as evidence of the personal failure she was. She felt the cold wrapping around her so that her teeth chattered.

Ahead of her, Zhvanetsky's house looked like the home of the Three Bears, absurdly set against the backdrop of the heating plant, though no less absurd than how Zhvanetsky had envisioned it originally when he had it dismantled piece by piece and smuggled out under the nose of the Communists, his personal homage to the American dream, his childhood set next to what he had achieved, his glorious moated empire, for there were men born peasants who had gone on to change the world.

In the grounds of the small house, too, were interred the supposed bones of his beloved parents, dug up and also smuggled out with the house, and somehow it all affected Adi more now than at any time before, the sad attempt at immortality.

Adi saw Wright in Zhvanetsky's small house, storing his equipment for later.

Inside was the infamous wax life-size image of the bearded, skeletal Zhvanetsky, the image students had taken to immortalizing in costume, Zhvanetsky seated at a desk, poring over a ledger of accounts, the wax figure that had gained a sort of national celebrity status in the early eighties when education had become a joke, when students had stolen Zhvanetsky and photographed him across America at places like the Hoover Dam, Niagara Falls, Rushmore, and on spring break in Daytona, at the Kentucky Derby, and the Indy 500. For those escapades, Bannockburn had made the rounds of the *Tonight* show and been voted one of the top party schools in America three years running.

There was no way of controlling one's destiny in the end, and standing there in the cold pull of wind, Adi looked at the effigy of Zhvanetsky, the grim irony of his immigrant, nostalgic pathos set against what he had been accused of doing in the postfire investigation, locking his *chatterbox* women employees into rooms for the sheer sake of efficiency, not letting them take toilet breaks.

That was the essential mania it took to succeed, the incongruity between egalitarian idealism and economic pragmatism, between how one thought and how one acted. Without really thinking, almost feeling the presence of Zhvanetsky's victims, Adi turned and started running as though her life depended on it, back toward the campus, where she ran right into the path of Horowitz, who had followed Wright's car.

All she said was his name before they drove off together, leaving Wright alone with his equipment.

THIRTY-SEVEN

NEITHER ADI NOR HOROWITZ spoke as he drove aimlessly before finally heading into the old historical district, winding his way along the black river, toward Pendleton's house.

Yellow police ribbon still fluttered between the two Romanesque posts of the entry to Pendleton's. An unmarked sedan was parked in the drive, standard law enforcement issue. In Pendleton's office, two shadows merged and then parted, undoubtedly forensics investigators. The house was still a crime scene.

Horowitz checked his watch.

The sun had dipped below the horizon in a salmon color, the antique lights on the street already beginning to show in yellowish halos. Across the divide of river, Bannockburn's gilded dome took on a burnished splendor, a solitary outpost against the vastness of the land beyond.

Horowitz spoke first. "If you want, I can call Ryder to see when you're getting the house back."

Adi shook her head and said quietly, "It's not my house. It never was."

Horowitz waited. "Do you want to go back to the hospital?"

"No . . . I checked myself out." Her mouth looked hard. "They gave me pills to cope with the withdrawal."

"Where exactly do you live?"

It took a moment before Adi answered, "Nowhere . . . I'm homeless." Then she broke down into deep sobs, her face in the flatness of her open palms.

Horowitz was about to pull away from the curb but stopped abruptly as a man shouted Adi's name from the house next to Pendleton's.

Adi looked up and saw it was Porterfield, dressed in his familiar Paul Bunyan flannel shirt and suspenders and holding an ax. She said frantically, "Keep going!" But Porterfield had crossed the road in front of the car. He set his big hand on the hood of the car, peered through the windshield, and shouted, "We have your rabbit. He escaped when the police went inside. We had a time catching him."

All Adi could do was try to hide the fact she had been crying.

Horowitz set the car in park, and in an instant, the aloneness he had so hoped to foster and capitalize on with Adi was vanquished.

The outside of Porterfield's house, a stylized colonial with a picket fence, belied the dark wood-paneled crypt of Porterfield's professional interest, the antebellum South, though his interest lay in civil wars in general, in the contempt and vengeance of familiarity, or so he said by way of introduction, leading Horowitz into a basement museum of vintage and modern firearms set against a billiard-table-green backing, to sepia images of slaughter across the ages, from revolutionary France to the American Civil War to the pogroms of Stalin to machete-wielding painted tribal Africans.

The center of the room was given to a mock battlefield.

Porterfield said, "Give them a few minutes alone. Women have a way of talking to one another. I'm sure she needs to talk to somebody." He seemed to be waiting for Horowitz to say something.

Horowitz just turned and looked at a Confederate flag and a uniform inside a museum-style cabinet. He checked his watch as Porterfield poured a measure of whiskey into a glass. He was anxious to get away.

Porterfield pointed at the Confederate uniform. "I led a Civil War reenactment weekend each spring on campus for a few years. It's amazing how many people want to be on the Confederate side. This is still a nation divided." Porterfield took a drink, nodding. Disconcertingly, he had the ax tucked under his arm. He pointed to a picture of Lincoln.

"Would you believe the so-called Great Liberator was the first military leader in history to place an order for the machine gun? He turned it on his own kind. More were killed in the Civil War than the War of Independence and all other wars we have fought since."

Horowitz arched his eyebrows. "I didn't know that . . . about the machine gun."

"Few do. . . . You know, out at the college our departmental budget has been slashed. Lamentably, the Civil War reenactment dissipated into a farce a few years ago and now revolves around mud pit wrestling and chariot races ever since our hooded KKK campus ride was banned. It's become a love-in up at the college. We don't want to recognize the historical realities of class and race. As a department we've been supplanted by a cop-out sickness of postmodern Freudian psychobabble, with its sublimation of our darkest fears and desires to the realm of sexual dysfunction, to whether we were breast-fed for too long or too short. Am I right?"

Porterfield seemed to search for Horowitz's name.

Horowitz obliged. "It's Allen, and I think you're on to something!"

Porterfield gave off a sweet odor of metabolized alcohol. "Being right means nothing anymore. Being right is like pissing against the wind up at the college. Do you think it a satisfactory answer that the Napoleonic Wars were simply a result of Napoleon having a small cock? That's the sort of thesis I'm asked to preside over these days. Interdisciplinary studies are all the rage. I'll tell you, Allen, if at one stage we were sexually repressed, the pendulum has swung the other way. We have run from a Marxist materialist conception of history. We don't recognize the burden of historical circumstance anymore. We don't see ourselves as a collective governed by economic forces. Do you know, there's not one mention of the word 'cock' in *The Communist Manifesto*? That's a fact."

Horowitz smiled despite himself, while Porterfield shook his head. From upstairs came the tortuous sounds of a cello as his son, Clement, continued to practice.

Porterfield piped up again, pointed at an image of potbellied pygmy headhunters holding up the severed heads of victims. "A so-called primitive people who located the soul in the head, not the heart . . . now there's a thesis!"

To the side of the shot was a rectangular basement window, the only source of outside light. Pendleton's house was visible. Porterfield gazed out the window. "You know, it's strange, I spoke to Bob through that very window for the first time ever in the fall of seventy-six."

Horowitz looked out the basement window. The day had almost succumbed to dark.

Porterfield kept talking. "Simone was finishing her master's, back east. We had provisionally separated that fall. She wanted to raise Clement in France. I had come here, defiantly, alone, knew nobody. Bob befriended me."

Porterfield turned and pointed to the mock battlefield set up in the center of the room. "What I liked to do back then was position opposing armies, to get the sense of scope, to understand the perspective of battles, to see with the eyes of generals. I used to read from battle accounts, drink, and then read again. That summer, I had toured the South, recorded reenactment battles, drum corps and bugle charges, from the thunder of cannon fire to the roar of hundreds rushing into battle, to the plaintive cries of the dying. Bob had been raking leaves or something. He thought all hell was breaking loose."

Porterfield smiled, remembering the details. "He stopped and just appeared at the window, like a giant, peering into the smallness of the battlefield."

Porterfield's eyes opened wide as he stared over the rim of his glass, inhaled the vapors. Before draining his drink, he said, "You know, it's how I've come to see Bob, staring with a weird omniscience, outside and within simultaneously. *Scream*, it reads that way, or that's how I read it, curiously detached, a sort of autobiographical reportage."

Horowitz looked at Porterfield. "You read it when it came out the first time?"

"The truth, ashamedly, no, I didn't! I've a signed copy of the book, but I never read it, not until . . . well, until everything came out. I remember one day Bob coming over here and taking it off the shelf. He got all mad that I had not read it. I told him I was waiting for the paperback edition, that I kept my first editions pristine. I tried to keep things light between us."

Porterfield turned and poured another measure of whiskey from a crystal decanter. "I guess the problem with books is, you got to read them, right?" He shrugged. "You knew Bob back in college, right? Was he always so intense?"

Horowitz nodded and saw Adi's feet on the steps leading into the basement.

Porterfield swirled the liquid in the glass before he took a drink and made a smacking sound with his lips.

"Look, I fully admit I never really understood Bob, not intellectually, what he was trying to do. You know, he gave me a signed copy of *A Hole Without a Middle* as well, told me it was something like an anti-Euclidean work arguing against the axiomatic notion of proofs, against the knowable. Another evening he came to the house and wanted to know what I thought about Heisenberg's uncertainty principle and what it meant at a humanist level for objective truth to not exist. He spoke to me like I should under-stand what all that meant, or more importantly, care. I mean, what the hell do you say to that sort of stuff? We were colleagues and neighbors and friends, but we might as well have been from parallel universes. . . ."

Horowitz smiled. "That was vintage Bob."

"You know, we used to go at it. I wasn't going to take Bob lying down. When he'd start up with his Heisenberg crap, I'd say, 'I'm an old world socialist, Bob. I'm simple. I divide things between the haves and the have-nots!' I'd say, 'You know the minimum wage hasn't gone up in six years? Do you know that unions are on the decline, that we are all just a job away from welfare no matter what the Dow Jones says?'

"Bob, of course, hated economics. I guess our last point of mutual in-terest lay somewhere in the nineteenth century with Dostoevsky, but not for the same reasons. Like I said to Bob back then, you want a proletarian revolution, then give the world a destitute student like Raskolnikov, a withered pawnbroker hag like Alyona Ivanovna, introduce an ax, and bingo, you got something of historical importance. That's a blueprint for revolution, a tacit portrayal of grinding poverty!"

"That why you carry the ax, Lee?"

Porterfield's face shone with the effect of alcohol. He didn't respond to the joke.

"I think in an age of such easy credit, where you're allowed to get up to your ass in debt just to survive, *where* can you turn when things go to hell eventually, when you can't go find and kill the pawnbroker hag, when all you're left confronting is some faceless bureaucracy?"

Horowitz said to appease Porterfield: "Kafka."

"Kafka!" Porterfield looked up. "Opt for the *surreal*, wake up as a cockroach in your room. You see, that's the historical leap I wish we didn't take, jumping right over realism into the surreal and absurd. I was thinking more in practical and real terms of what people do when they find themselves broke these days, like killing themselves and maybe killing their family into the bargain, though maybe it amounts to the same thing as Kafka's cockroach analogy in the end: aloneness, alienation. You're the writer, Allen, that's essence of Kafka anyway, right, estrangement? I don't think that bodes well for revolution, that sort of inwardness, that sort of disassociation from the masses."

"You're expecting this revolution to happen here in Indiana, Lee?"

"Yeah! I'm one step from the madhouse." Porterfield looked toward the basement window. Night had settled.

Porterfield's wife, Simone, came to the edge of the stairs and said with an incredulous scorn that only the French could pull off, "Oh, this is where you are hiding? Drinking, *but* of course."

Adi moved into the basement as Simone continued down the stairs. She had the delicate birdlike thinness of a Parisian woman, though she had a presence and a shape made for Chanel rather than the faded jeans she wore.

Porterfield winked at Horowitz as he turned toward Simone. "You see, dear, I was telling Allen here that I was having a hard time stopping you from cooking the rabbit, that it was a day away from being eaten."

Simone shot back, "He is, of course, lying. I prefer horsemeat, rare horsemeat."

Horowitz smiled, trying to negotiate what was a land mine of marital acrimony. "We were just talking about Bob, actually, Bob from next door."

"Ah, yes, this crazy Bob! I say to Lee, maybe it is possible he drinks with Bob the evening he killed the girl, no? They were fellow commiserates that year."

Porterfield rolled his eyes. "I think you exaggerate the extent of our friendship, especially since you weren't here that year!"

*   *   *

As Horowitz and Adi crossed the street to his car, they heard the sudden rev of an engine from a car parked behind them. The car's lights flicked on to high beam, the flare of light intense, momentarily blinding both Horowitz and Adi, so much so that Horowitz shouted to the driver.

Then the sound of music started playing from the car, the Big Bopper's "Chantilly Lace."

The car revved again, and in the sudden burnout of tires, it pulled out and drove straight at them, then swerved at the last moment. And in a smear of recognition, Adi saw what she already knew, the face of Wright behind the wheel, living out some Stephen King gothic revenge.

THIRTY-EIGHT

KIM JEWEL AND SANDI Kellogg were a strange pair, united in common love for a man most of humanity considered scum, as evidenced by the pitifully few mourners at Scholl's funeral—straggler relatives with long-drawn shovel faces like Gary Scholl's.

It was a freezing cold morning. A hoary frost gleamed on the short grass between the graves, while overhead, long wispy ribbons of cloud drifted high in the sky, the moon still visible, a faint husk against the wintry pale blue of morning.

The graveyard was set on a sloping moraine facing east, a legacy of pioneer tradition, the dead looking toward Jerusalem, to the resurrection of life.

Gary Scholl's great-great-grandfather was buried at the cemetery. There was a Scholl Road, named for the family when, at their apex in 1860, they had a five-hundred-acre holding and the commercial sagacity to start a co-op of farming interests, all before the onset of the Civil War, before four of Chester Scholl's six sons died fighting the Confederate army. A hundred years on, and the remaining anemic Scholl descendants had married badly for the better part of a century, corrupting their own founding seed and falling victim to calamity, natural and otherwise—the influenza epidemic of 1917 and the slaughter of two world wars—so that by the time Gary was born, there was no Scholl landholding. There was no one who could remember how to can tomatoes or pickle beets and onions, to knead and roll and bake bread, nobody to remember how to slaughter and hang and age meat in cellars, to cure ham, or even to darn and sew—nobody with the compensatory skills of self-sufficiency. Gary Scholl was the first descendant of the American Scholls to be born in a rented apartment, an apartment above Lloyd Picket's gas station.

Ryder stayed back from the actual funeral, on a dirt service road, scanning the hill again in a surveillance that revealed nothing, pointless, the gathering simply family members, no one else, save a cop from the county covering the investigation concerning Gary Scholl and Wright, who acknowledged him briefly as he stood in the background, zooming in for whatever shot was going to define the passing of Gary Scholl.

Though inevitably, Ryder's eyes found Gary Scholl's women, or Kim Jewel, really, though he wouldn't let himself acknowledge that.

Gary Scholl's women were opposites, physically: Kim was thin, Sandi hourglass shaped and doughy. Kim wore an unzipped ski jacket over a white shirt and black work slacks; Sandi was in a high school varsity jacket, with the same-style black slacks and moon boots. Both women were scheduled to work that afternoon for the hourly minimum wage, Kim at Rite Aid, Sandi as a hostess at Ponderosa Steak House.

The minister, a solemn scarecrow specter, continued to deliver his eulogy, his vestments fluttering, a mound of black dirt piled to the side of the grave, the remains of Gary Scholl in a simple coffin, and whatever he said was lost to the wind, to the coldness of the morning.

Trent Bauer arrived during the service in plain clothes, in an ill-fitting suit. He looked like the gangly Eb from *Green Acres*, contrite in an old-fashioned way. All he was missing was a hat.

Horowitz materialized minutes later near the mossy gravestone heads, moving slowly between graves. From time to time he looked toward Ryder, who briefly acknowledged his presence.

Ryder kept his hands deep in his pockets, his collar turned up, concealing his mouth. He watched Bauer and saw Kim Jewel look up and see Bauer, then turn away toward the minister, and he knew something had passed between them; but then Horowitz impinged on the moment, approached Ryder and took out a small notebook. He spoke in a subdued way.

"I would like to apologize for the way I spoke to you the other day."

Ryder ignored him, kept looking toward the mound of piled dirt.

"It's been hard coming to terms with knowing I was wrong. I knew Bob Pendleton for the greater part of my adult life. I didn't know what he was capable of doing. I screwed up. I've been rereading Nietzsche, Jon, trying to understand the sense of despair Bob must have experienced, how his mind had turned in on itself. I thought this appropriate for the occasion, Nietzsche's eulogy, not for a man, but for a religion." Horowitz opened a small book and began reading.

When we hear the ancient bells growling on a Sunday morning we ask ourselves: Is it really possible! This, for a Jew, crucified two thousand years ago, who said he was God's son? The proof of such a claim is lacking. Certainly the Christian religion is an antiquity projected into our times from remote prehistory; and the fact that the claim is believed— whereas one is otherwise so strict in examining pretensions—is perhaps the most ancient piece of this heritage. A god who begets children with a mortal woman; a sage who bids men work no more, have no more courts, but look for the signs of the impending end of the world; a justice that accepts the innocent as a vicarious sacrifice; someone who orders his disciples to drink his blood; prayers for miraculous interventions; sins perpetrated against a god, atoned for by a god; fear of a beyond to which death is the portal; the form of the cross as a symbol in a time that no longer knows the function and ignominy of the cross—how ghoulishly all this touches us, as if from the tomb of a primeval past! Can one believe that such things are still believed?

Horowitz looked up. "What Nietzsche saw was the crisis of modernity, a world where the old order of spiritual authority would no longer control humanity. What he feared most was the coming crisis of doubt. The Superman was supposed to overcome that doubt, debunk that remote prehistory of Christianity, and live in the temporal world according to laws laid down through rational discourse, not superstition."

Ryder kept his focus on the small group of mourners. He said quietly, "Leave."

"I'll tell you honestly, Jon, I'm dismayed. I thought of you as someone through whom I could project a sense of hope and integrity, a bulwark against the chaos of life. I thought the crime genre might hold forth certain undeniable truths. I wanted you to be my protagonist, but it wouldn't work, and that's not a slight against you. You are, invariably, an obsolete and pathetic figure, the stuff of pulp fiction. If you represent anything, it is the human frailty of the law, its ineffectuality. . . ."

Ryder dipped his chin below the collar on his jacket, intent on saying nothing. In the distance, he saw Wright out of the corner of his eye, the focus of the lens on both him and Horowitz, as Wright captured, in rapid sequence on film, the entire exchange.

Oblivious to everything else, Horowitz kept talking. "I can see you are taking this personally, Jon. Let me try another approach. What was the real significance of the Jack the Ripper case? Think about it! I think the case represented the reality of the metropolis, modernity, a mathematical phenomenon of exponential possible suspects whose whereabouts could not be feasibly correlated. Those murders represented a mathematical fault line, a game of probability, and Jack the Ripper won."

Horowitz got closer still to Ryder. "You see, this is what Nietzsche feared, the breakdown of Christianity, of good and evil. In the old days, society was *closed*. There were only so many potential culprits. A woman sat at her window each day, and she noticed somebody going by. She knew the exact time because she was having her tea at three, just before her children got out of school. The postman verified the sighting, passing along the same lane. He got a closer look. And so it went. You see where I'm going here?"

Ryder ignored him.

"This is significant for all of us. What we have lost is a past where true omniscience ruled, a world knowable, definable, deductible, and therefore *just*, affirming the law, affirming faith and, therefore, God's omniscience.

This is how I wanted to use you, Jon, as that divining principle, as the *law*. But this is not a closed world. What Nietzsche feared was this loss of the *law*, the ambiguity of crime *without* punishment, when the perpetrator no longer fears capture! What Nietzsche anticipated was the psychopathology of modern crime as spiritual quest, its perpetrators disillusioned, Don Quixotes attacking windmills. . . ."

Ryder looked directly at Horowitz. "I want you to leave."

Horowitz raised his hand. "Just hear me out, Jon! Tell me, are we not living in the most debased of times? What we need is for forensic science to advance, for the mathematics of probability to turn in favor of the pursuers, to bring back that omniscience, that fear of being caught, the fear of punishment. I've been giving this a lot of thought. I see cloning as giving back real meaning to the notion of eternal punishment and damnation. Think about cloning a person over and over again, across millennia, the horror of a perpetual death and resurrection within a prison cell, anticipating one's execution with each rebirth. I think only then will the specter of omniscience, the true prospect of eternal damnation, once again rule with the power of bygone ages."

Wright was feet away from Ryder before Horowitz saw him. "Ah, the resident stalker! I think I'd like to file a charge of reckless vehicular endangerment, Jon. This man tried to run Adi and me over last night!"

Ryder turned to find Wright looking hard at Horowitz.

Wright said, "I don't know what she sees in you."

Horowitz smiled. "Go figure. . . . Let me see, six best-sellers, five honorary doctorates, a New York penthouse apartment, a beach house in Miami and Maui, and a partridge in a pear tree. . . . How long did you think she was going to slum it, Henry? Let's face it, you're a born loser, but just to make it up to you, do you do weddings? I might be making a big announcement soon."

Ryder stepped between Wright and Horowitz. "Leave him, Henry! He's not worth it. He's a piece of shit."

A small group of mourners had broken up, and Wright just stepped back and reverted to his profession. Putting his camera to his eye, he started shooting again, walking crablike, taking in a shot of Kim Jewel as she headed down through the rows of headstones, right until she made her way to Ryder as though she were going to confront him.

Ryder hesitated.

Kim Jewel was shivering. Her cleavage showed. A small gold cross caught the soft late fall light. And then she did a strange thing. She reached out, touched Ryder on the arm, and said softly, "It's not your fault. Long before you ever came along, I gave up on Gary. I believed he killed my sister. . . ." Then she wiped her nose with the palm of her hand, sniffled, and walked toward the cemetery gate at the end of the long decline, where the store manager from Rite Aid, wearing a pharmacy smock under his coat, was waiting for her.

Ryder recognized him, Whitey Whitmore, a middle-aged guy he had worked with to set up Kim Jewel. Whitmore hugged Kim. She collapsed against him. Her cries carried on the wind, and Ryder lowered his eyes.

Sandi Kellogg stood behind Ryder. She said quietly, "I want to tell you something, Detective."

Ryder didn't turn around, though he looked up toward the pale eye of the sun.

"Detective?"

Ryder averted his eyes but didn't turn. Kim Jewel was still in the arms of the store manager.

"Gary . . . he didn't *kill* that woman!"

Ryder turned. There was a squint of skepticism in his eyes.

"I have *proof*."

"What proof?"

"A *tape*."

Ryder focused his attention. "Where is this tape?"

Sandi hesitated. "It's . . . it's at my house."

"Why are you telling me now? Why didn't you give it to the police?"

Sandi lowered her head. "When you see what's on it, you'll understand. I wanted Gary buried first. I wanted him to have some dignity."

THIRTY-NINE

IN THE MORNING PAPER, the official sunset was 5:02 p.m., though darkness had settled even earlier, and it seemed a long time since Gary Scholl had been buried, not just earlier that morning, as Ryder exited the confines of his makeshift office in the small police station. He had the disconcerting feeling one got when going into a theater in light and coming out into darkness, a hollow, cold, empty feeling, as though life weren't real.

For most of the afternoon, he had pored over the tape Sandi Kellogg dropped off at the station. He understood her hesitancy to reveal her proof. The tape was a camcorder recording of her and Gary Scholl's escapades the night Mrs. Blaine was murdered.

The video showed Gary snorting lines of cocaine, an ongoing frenzy of drugs and sex, Gary waving his cock at the camera, Sandi on all fours, rutting after his cock. All the while, a telltale digital clock in the upper-right-hand corner of the tape recorded the time, putting Gary Scholl firmly between the legs of Sandi Kellogg when the Blaine murder had occurred.

The likelihood of Sandi Kellogg doctoring the tape seemed remote, and as further evidence to the legitimacy of the time, there was a radio station playing in the background, a playlist of songs to cross-reference with the station, to firmly establish the time line. Seemingly, Gary Scholl had not fired the shot that killed Mrs. Blaine.

Scholl's record was on the table. Ryder picked it up, flicked through it, tried to reconcile how someone like Scholl just let himself be shot like that, given he had an alibi. He had done two four-year stints at the state pen, and even if he was in violation of his parole in getting wasted on drugs, extenuating circumstances would have prevailed if he got the right lawyer, if the particulars of that day were set forth, a day when he was finally vindicated of having murdered Amber Jewel.

As Ryder looked at the file, he saw that Scholl was not even on parole anymore. His last stint in prison had ended over a decade ago, on August 12, 1976, the year Amber was murdered and the time when Bauer had infiltrated himself into Kim's life.

Ryder rummaged through more pages, the typed transcripts of Scholl's interrogation by police totaling twelve separate interviews, a handwritten note scrawled at the top of the transcript from interview nine, dated March 12: "Suspect deeply affected by birth of daughter."

The phone rang minutes later. It was Gail. She spoke abruptly, maintaining the coldness from their previous call. "I spoke with your boss's wife, June. She told me the case is on hold, that you're coming home."

Ryder hesitated, deep into his own thoughts. "Look, Gail, I got loose ends to clear up here. It'll be a few days."

"What loose ends? June told me that the professor did it."

Ryder looked up and felt the pain in his shoulder again. "Are you telling me how to do my goddamn job? There are three people dead out of this . . . a child's memory defiled."

Gail snapped, "That's not part of your investigation."

"You telling me my job, Gail? Seems like you are the expert!"

"I'm telling you what Ken said to June. Ken doesn't want to drop any more money into this investigation. He said he called and you didn't return his calls."

"He called once."

"So what are you doing there now?"

"Pendleton's assistant *knew*."

"His assistant, you mean that *woman* they have plastered all over the TV? Please. You're pathetic, you know that? Why are you doing this?"

"Doing what, Gail? Don't give me the third degree here. Do you realize I work for a living, that this is my job? If you got an insecurity complex, don't blame it on me."

Gail said flatly, "I don't care about you. I called just to tell you Taylor's home."

Ryder closed his eyes and put his hand to his head. "Jesus, why didn't you just come out and tell me?"

"I'm telling you now. I got a call from the school today. Taylor was in a meeting with a counselor. I went down and met her. She agreed to come back. I told her you were coming."

Ryder said sharply, "Where is she?"

"At the kitchen table doing her homework." Gail leaned into the phone. "Something happened."

Ryder raised his voice. "Is she hurt?"

"No, not like that. It's just a look. I think she learned something. Women have to get hurt once."

Ryder said abruptly, "Put her on."

He heard Gail talking and Taylor answering in the background, then the noise of a chair against the floor, the spoon against the bowl, Gail saying softly, "I'll get that, you just go on now."

Gail gave a running, hushed commentary. "She's going to take the call in her bedroom."

Ryder said nothing.

In his mind, he saw the Pepto-Bismol pink of her room, the ruffled lace canopy princess bed, the dresser drawer lined with rainbow-colored ponies with synthetic manes, alongside the sentinel wide-eyed dolls he had bought for her over the years. He had, of course, overcompensated, tried to reclaim a childhood for her, and she had kept her dolls in their boxes, fastidious and meticulous in guarding from her half-brothers what was hers, the dolls somehow horrific, each locked behind a sheath of plastic.

The line clicked. Taylor picked up.

Ryder heard her bed squeeze down under her own weight.

Taylor broke the silence. "You want to know what she does while you're away?"

Ryder knew Gail had not hung up.

"Taylor . . . listen to me."

"She makes a pot of strong coffee, gets a magazine, then sits at the kitchen table, pulls her knees up, parts her toes with pieces of toilet paper, and paints her nails. She can do that for hours and hours. She's like one of those cold-blooded reptiles that come out to sun themselves in the desert."

Ryder could feel Gail's presence. She breathed a sigh of dissatisfaction that Taylor heard. He wanted to shout for her to get off the line but didn't.

"You okay, Taylor?"

"I'm thinking about an out-of-state college. I think that's a distinct option for me. I discussed it with a counselor today. Of course, it's going to cost an arm and a leg until I get residency, but maybe it would be worth it just to start over again."

Ryder said in a magnanimous way, "Don't you worry about the money. Money is no object. Look, you just stay put until I get back. I think you hit the nail on the head, an out-of-state college. I like that idea a lot."

Ryder waited until Taylor hung up.

The line was still live.

Gail's voice was tight. "Don't make promises you can't keep, Jon, don't. You got other kids to think about, you hear me?"

She said it as if it were a threat, before hanging up.

FORTY

Ryder looked to where Trent Bauer usually sat. His desk was empty. When he turned to go, another cop said, "He called in sick this morning."

Ryder left the police station, started the car, breathed in a freezing air that smelled of ethanol from the local refinery, and exited onto a slick surface of ice. He hadn't called his boss or the lead county investigator yet. Scholl's alibi was going to change the focus to Kim Jewel or someone close to her. The motivation: revenge.

Ryder passed a snowplow sprinkling salt along the strip of eateries off the highway and thought of just heading home. He could have been there in less than four hours, but instead he pulled into his motel room, showered, and shaved, subconsciously knowing he had done so simply because he was going out to see Kim Jewel. He had the feeling of butterflies on a first date, which he tried to sublimate and associate with his fear for his daughter, but somehow he knew deep inside why he had not gone home.

Gail was right, though she had gotten the woman wrong.

In the parking lot, Ryder walked toward his car, and in the cold light of the diner he saw Wright and Wiltshire seated at a table, Wiltshire's face pale and drawn.

Ryder went into the diner and ordered a coffee, simply to make his presence felt.

It was obvious Wright was making a last play for Wiltshire. Ryder couldn't help but feel sorry for Wright, that he was on the losing end to Horowitz. Anybody else looking on wouldn't have needed to be a psychologist to know it was never going to work out, but then who ever thought rationally in a relationship?

Ryder turned toward the mirrored display of pies and waited for his coffee; sitting there alone, he thought of the times he had sat in diners like this with Tori, through the early part of their rocky courtship. Over the years Tori had gone behind his back with other guys, the serial denial, then the confession and the making up. Just waiting he thought of the way she'd liked to go down on him in the car, remembering with a shudder how the center of his existence would mushroom in the darkness of her mouth, the way she gagged, his hand at the base of her neck, keeping her there, all of it set against the personal anguish of a broken relationship, Ryder always hoping for better times. And in his nightmares after she was gone, when he dreamed of the car, when he looked into the rearview mirror, at the moment of ejaculation, he saw, not his face, but the face of a stranger Tori was blowing.

The cashier set down the coffee, and Ryder snapped back to reality, to the cold light of the diner, the woman the same saddlebagged woman who had served him breakfast days before.

In the parking lot, Ryder felt an intense cold and shivered. He went toward his car. On the second floor of the motel walkway, he saw the throbbing pulse of a cigarette scab and intuitively knew it was Horowitz, then saw Horowitz's rental car pulled into the space. He got into his own car and waited until Horowitz went back into his room.

Ryder turned up the volume on the radio, blanking out everything else. He felt lost in a way that he had not felt for a long time.

The evening scores from the weekend football games came across a static AM reception. He listened simply to blank out everything, the cluster of powerhouse running-back teams grinding out workmanlike, smashmouth, safe, running yards, the Bears, Lions, Vikings, and Packers all coming into their own with home field advantages in the dark days of latter fall, in freezing blizzard conditions, waiting to crush the aerial games of the suntanned Montana and Marino. In sports bars, giant TVs flickered, and Ryder felt that if he opened his window, he would hear the faint roar of fans, hear the fierce loyalty this provincialism and isolation wrought. He had fought all his life for the underdogs.

Ryder hit another button on an array of preprogrammed radio buttons, moving from station to station to coincide with the various stations' taglines, traffic and weather on the eights or tens, sports on the quarter hour, Ryder repeating the scores over and over again in a sort of prophetic mantra. It was something he had done for years, a quirk that had bestowed a weird mystique on him in his early career, not long after the mysterious circumstances regarding his wife's disappearance.

One Sunday evening, while interviewing an informant in his car, he had just stopped and started giving the scores. It was an episode that had become lore among both criminals and law enforcement, one of the curious incidents of self-deception that had led to Ryder's remembrance of the childhood school yard game of gathering souls, to his spiritual rebirth as one of the Brethren, to the time when he began to wear his trademark black trench coat, before he eventually transferred off the street after brutalizing the suspect in the rape and murder of a ten-year-old girl.

A half hour later, going out toward Sam Henderson's, Ryder passed a mall and then constellations of new houses in gated communities with names like the Berkshires, the Commons, and English Turn, communities boasting man-made lakes and walk-on golf courses, the demographics of rural America changing in what had become euphemistically called "white flight." A recoiling strain of wealthy fundamentalist Protestantism had taken hold literally in cornfields in the wake of an urban decay with its jive-talking niggers and disco, and he thought how different this all was from the world in which Amber Jewel had lived and died a decade earlier.

Who would ever have thought this was where America would have re-treated to, and again it served only to marginalize Ryder, to have come of age in the dying breaths of blue-collar life. He would never own one of these homes, and it made him bitter.

Sam Henderson's house was beyond the pale of this new development, and in the darkness more so than in the light of day, the contrast was starker, the solitary light on at Henderson's house.

But all Ryder did was pass the property, stop the car, and stare into the blackness of a field where Amber Jewel had been discovered, as though, waiting there, he could conjure up her spirit.

Staring into the blackness, he whispered, "What happened to you, Amber?"

It was, when it hit, as though she had answered, a detail that had been nagging him all night long.

Ryder pulled into the Rite Aid parking lot. Kim was stocking cartons of cigarettes behind the counter when he came into the store. She instinc-tively looked up but went back to work. She had not seen him, though Ryder was picked up on a grainy surveillance, on a closed-circuit camera system that looped through various cameras set up throughout the store.

Ryder stood before a cardboard cutout of a cheery snowman set up within a display of aluminum snow shovels and bags of rock salt, along with pyramid displays of cold medicine and hot chocolate mix. Across the aisle was a competing vision of life, an NFL display of two buxom cheer-leaders in Santa suits and fur-lined boots drinking peppermint schnapps before a charcoal grill with fake red tinfoil coals and streaming ribbons of supposed smoke.

The pharmacy section was closed. He stood outside the caged-off area. This was where Adi Wiltshire had come on occasion to fill her prescriptions. There was a chance she had bought something else here, paid up front, taken change from Kim Jewel's hand. Their hands may have even touched for a moment in the simple exchange.

In the convexity of a security mirror, Ryder looked up and saw a distorted image of Kim Jewel continuing to stock cigarettes behind the counter.

He stalled and went into another aisle. His eyes focused. He found himself standing before a shelf of hemorrhoid suppositories and anal itch creams. In fact, there was no good aisle, one that didn't somehow speak of the frailty of the human body, from wart ointments to foot odor powders, from yeast infections to halitosis to dandruff.

It was as he was leaving that the store manager came out of his office and called him by name. It was Whitey Whitmore. He had been in the walk-in cooler, stocking bottles. He came over and took off a mitt and shook Ryder's hand, then put his hand on Ryder's back, steered him toward his office, and shut the door.

"She insisted on working." Whitmore crossed his heart. "What's that they say, '*Denial* isn't just a river in Egypt'?"

A bell sounded in Whitmore's office.

On a small TV security monitor on his desk, Whitmore turned and looked at Kim checking an ID on a kid who was trying to buy a case of beer. The kid left without the beer, and Kim looked toward the camera to show that everything was okay.

Whitmore turned from the monitor. "Some people come into their own later in life. Kim is one of those people. I told her she had to grow into who she really was—up here." He pointed to the side of his head. "She's on her way to being a store manager. All she needs is some community college behind her."

On the wall of the small office was a chart with monthly goals affixed with stars and employee names, the desk littered with invoices for goods received.

Ryder said, "I didn't know you two were together. You didn't mention it back when I met with you."

Whitmore shrugged. In his white shirt and tie, he looked like the guy in the game Operation. "Hey, I'm like an old ballplayer in the outfield. I don't chase balls anymore, but if one is thrown my way, I'll catch it."

Ryder smiled obligingly at the joke but noted the denial in Whitmore not answering the question. He said, "Maybe you two should get away for a while when this is all over. Some lodge away from everybody up north, take in a little fishing and gaming."

He looked right at Whitmore. "You hunt, right?"

Whitmore lost his smile. "We through here?"

A phone buzzed in the sudden stalemate.

It was Kim. She was looking up into the security camera.

"You got that detective up there with you, Whitey? How about I take a five-minute smoke break?"

She spoke loud enough so that Ryder heard her through the receiver.

Under the sanguine light of the Rite Aid sign, Kim Jewel cupped her hands around a flickering flame, lit a cigarette, and inhaled deeply before she started talking.

"I should hate you . . . you know that? Whitey, he told me what you did, setting me up, but I guess that's your job, so I don't hold it against you. I just hope I didn't look like somebody who could have done something that terrible, someone who could have lived with a secret like that."

Kim ran her hand through her hair. "Look, I'm sorry. You don't have to answer that!" She looked up. She was wearing her blue smock under her coat with a button-down white work shirt.

"If you're here to tell me Gary didn't kill that woman out at the professor's house, I know already. Sandi, she called me, told me why she waited. She's a good person. You just keep that in mind before the whole world has to know about what's on that tape with her and Gary, okay?"

Ryder's breath showed under the glow of the Rite Aid sign. "Sure."

Kim stepped from foot to foot, took a hit of her cigarette. She was petite, but in her flats she was even smaller, more compact. "So are you here to ask me where I was that night?"

"Do I need to?"

Kim set a hand inside the apron of her smock. It was freezing. "Would you believe me if I told you I'm way past revenge? This has been going on most of my adult life. I've come to live with it . . . or, no, that's not it. The truth is, I became somebody else inside."

Ryder tried to forestall Kim from leading him somewhere else. He said abruptly, "We suspect the Blaine woman was mistakenly taken for Pendleton's assistant, that she was the target."

Kim said nothing.

"You got any idea who might have done it?"

Kim bit her lower lip, her head turning slowly. "No. . . ." Then she moved her hand and touched her heart, her hand becoming a fist, determined to lead Ryder away from asking her anything specific, or so Ryder felt as she said in an intimate and searching way, "My life . . . it stopped a long time ago, is how I see it. . . ."

Ryder waited.

"You know, for the longest time I figured Gary killed Amber, since she'd gone around telling people what he was doing to her, shooting her mouth off and writing everything in her journal, but I couldn't make myself believe it. I stayed with him for a year, had the child, and believed in my heart on one day he had killed her, and the next, didn't believe he could do that. All I could do was write letters to her, tell her I was sorry. I just set them in the mail, addressed nowhere. I had to put down what I was feeling. There was nobody to talk to, nobody to care."

Kim held her cigarette down by her thigh. "They got all this help for people coping with things these days. It was different back then. I know writing is part of the grieving process. That's what they say now, anyway, but I discovered it by myself. . . . You know, things had been so bad between me and Amber for a long time. People figured, since I kept the baby, it was because I was in love with Gary, and maybe I was, in the beginning, but I couldn't kill the baby inside me, not with Amber missing like that. I just wanted everything back like it was before, so I had the baby. Then I got hard in my heart, hard against her. I believed she ran away. Gary kept telling me so. He denied killing her. He swore he didn't. He got crazy at being accused. One day he took this knife and cut his wrist, deep, and he said, 'You want me to cut the other one, Kim? Because I will, if you stop lovin' me!' I wanted to believe him, because life didn't stand looking at otherwise. I was holding his baby in my arms, and he was bleeding from his wrist, screaming at me, and the baby was screaming, and I was screaming, and for a moment I thought we were a heartbeat away from all dying."

Kim drew her shoulders forward. "God, Gary was so wild inside himself, screaming I didn't love him. He was retching like he was going to vomit. Now I know *why*." She closed her eyes. "He didn't do it." She kept talking. "Gary had cut himself deep. It hadn't been just for show. He had tried to show me he was innocent, and for a while I truly believed he was. Amber was wild and crazy, and running away was something I wouldn't have put past her, so my heart hardened toward her. That's what made it the hardest, knowing that she had the capacity to do something like that to hurt me, to make me fear the worst. But then they found her. It was the end for me and Gary."

Kim took out another cigarette and lit it, a small bowl of light illuminating her face. "Jesus, it's cold."

Ryder stared at her, saw where her upper lip had the small vertical lines of a smoker. In years to come, she was going to be one of those women men looked at, but it would be apparent, the incongruity, the face against the body. That was a decidedly sad thing to live with, especially for a woman who had known another look.

Kim blew smoke into the darkness of the sky. She had run out of things to say. Her eyes opened wide, but she didn't cry. She cleared her throat, flicked the head of smoldering ash, saving the remainder of the cigarette.

It was something Ryder hadn't seen a person do in a long time.

Kim said, "I get ten-minute breaks is all."

Ryder took a step forward. "There's just one thing I wanted to ask you."

"What?"

"Gary's rage . . . what you were just telling me, was that all because Gary knew the baby wasn't his?"

Kim just looked through Ryder, said nothing, set her cigarette back into the pack.

"Gary got out of jail in August 1976, Kim, and you had the baby eight months later."

Kim looked hard at Ryder. "Gary *was* her father! What the hell do you want? You think I didn't see you look at me that first time you came in here, like some pervert stalking the aisles, and tonight. I know the look in your eyes!"

Ryder said quietly, "Maybe we'll do this down at the station."

"*No!* I can't . . . I can't afford to lose a night's pay! You try living on minimum wage."

A car pulled abruptly into the parking lot, the night reverberating with a concussive thumping bass that suddenly flared into music as a car door opened.

"I have to get that. Don't make this worse on me."

"I'm not trying to make this worse for you. I want to figure out what I'm up against here. Trent gunned down Gary. You saw what he *did*!"

Kim shook her head. "No . . . that's not what happened. . . ."

"Come on! You and I know what happened out there. This goes way back. How did Trent react to you breaking up with him when Gary got out of jail?"

Kim pulled away. "What do you want to go into my private life for? None of this is going to bring Amber back."

"If you weren't involved in what happened to Blaine, and Gary wasn't, then who the hell had motive, Kim? Blaine's murder was a setup to shift suspicion toward Gary. Someone knew how crazy Gary would react merely being a suspect in the murder."

"Leave me alone . . . I can't help you. I lost everything I ever loved in this world. I got nothing except Whitey. I got to hold on to that. Don't ruin it on me!"

Under the brilliant fluorescence, Ryder watched Kim go back into the store and proof a kid and deny him a case of beer he had set beside the register.

The kid was arguing, visibly drunk. He wanted his ID back and reached across the counter to try to take it from Kim, who had one hand on the case of beer and was holding the kid's ID in the other.

Whitey Whitmore came into the picture.

The kid left, went out into the parking lot, and pointed back toward the store, shouting to his friends, "Check it out! It's Kim, Kim Jewel."

The kid made a fist and started moving it back and forth toward his open mouth, making a choking sound, his tongue making his cheek swell each time he moved his fist.

At another time in his life, Ryder would have taken the kid and put the barrel of a gun down his throat, but not anymore. He was through making mistakes like that. This was the world Kim Jewel would inhabit for the greater part of her remaining life, aging trainee manager, ID checker, guardian against adolescence, her fate and her past sealed in town lore, except now she had one more secret that people didn't know about, at least not yet.

FORTY-ONE

IT WAS PAST MIDNIGHT, and almost an hour had passed since Wright had left the diner and Horowitz had seen Ryder come back and go into his motel room. It seemed Adi had stubbornly decided to await daylight in the diner, that she had no intention of going over to Horowitz, so in the end he had to cross the frosted parking lot where the first sprinkling of snow was beginning to fall.

Adi looked up and said flatly, "I'm taking a Greyhound back to my father in Ohio."

Horowitz sat and waited until a waitress came and poured him coffee in a perfunctory manner, without even asking. He added creamer to his coffee and stirred it slowly, staring at Adi.

"Look, I want to get beyond whatever you knew. You said nothing to Ryder, and that's it. Bob is at the center of everything, not you. I want to start again, if you'll let me. Whatever you learned, and when you learned it, you were trapped. That's how I see it. The fact is, Bob went consciously insane at a certain point in his life. He murdered a thirteen-year-old child, for what, for *art*?"

Adi said nothing.

"I think Bob had that potential to kill in him all his life, a megalomaniacal sense of self. He created his own world, marginalized himself, fed off a sense of growing desperation and alienation. You think he was driven insane. That's the popular conceit of artists, but Bob drove himself insane. I knew him from the beginning, back in college. It was a conscious choice, performance art. He wasn't up to the task of conventional genre when it came right down to it. He wasn't as great as he thought, so what did he do but try to create this aura of difference, tap into a postmodern style out of a sheer sense of escape. He didn't do it with any true artistic sensibility."

Horowitz squeezed his cup. "Look, I can tell you don't want to hear this, but those are the facts. I know you hate what I write, but I fought my own ground, worked within the system. Don't slight commercial success so easily. It's not so easy to *sell out*—that's the pejorative popular term, right? What I want to know is, how come people like you are so seduced by the notion of an artistic relativism that elevates a lack of rigor and so-called open-endedness to an art form? Is artistic obtuseness so seductive because everything becomes relative? Is its appeal its relative mediocrity?"

Horowitz waited. "Have you ever considered this might be the first epoch where there are no geniuses, that all modern art is a sham? Can one truly compare Andy Warhol's Campbell soup cans to the ceiling of the Sistine chapel, and if so, why not elevate the Manson family murders to pop art, to the level of an Andy Warhol, or vice versa?"

Adi took her time before answering. "Why do you twist things around? I'm not a so-called relativist. I'm the opposite. Are you telling me you saw nothing in *Scream*, is that what you're saying?"

"What I'm saying is, without me there would be no book, not in the sense that *Scream* exists as it does now. I created that! How many people do you think are merely talking about what they heard said about the book? How many will ever really read it?"

"Why are you saying all this, to get yourself off the hook, to make me like you, or even understand you?"

Horowitz shifted in his seat. "If you hate me, you should hate Bob just as much. Maybe that is all I can hope for. The reality is, Bob invited me to campus just so he could commit suicide, just so he could get you to make me read his book."

"You're wrong! It wasn't planned! I was sent along at the last moment in the greeting party. It was the Chair's idea, not mine or Robert's. I ended up bringing a copy of Robert's first work with me. It was the first time I'd ever read anything of his. The discussion of his life and work was precipitated by *me*, not him. I told him he was infinitely a greater writer than you. That's how this started."

Horowitz's face flushed.

"You want the so-called facts, well, there they are, Allen. After all those years at the college, someone had simply validated what he'd been all along. I saw it in his face, the sudden flicker of dignity. That's why he tried to kill himself, to stave off the next day and the day after that. It had nothing to do with you or me. His intention was to simply die, nothing else. What he gave me was his *published* works, not what he'd hidden in the basement."

Adi looked at the diner window. It held the transparent reflection of her face, though the outside world still showed in halos of light, in the passing of cars out on the road.

Horowitz said quietly, "Just tell me, why you are willing to overlook the fact that Bob murdered a thirteen-year-old, and you can't see something in me?"

It was a question Adi didn't answer.

In the 2:00 a.m. hour, the phone rang in Ryder's room. It took him time to reach through the ruffle of sheets. He dragged the receiver to his ear as a muffled voice whispered, "Put me in consecrated ground. Will you do that for me, please?"

Ryder sat bolt upright in the dark. "Who is this?"

The voice was barely audible, hoarse. "I'm your wife. . . ."

Then the line went dead, leaving Ryder holding the receiver in the dark. He turned on the bedside lamp, sitting on the nightstand next to several upturned bottles of beer and a fifth of whiskey he had swigged down in the melancholy aftermath of having talked with Kim Jewel.

An unopened takeout Chinese meal seeped through its carton, making the room reek, though the fortune cookies had been broken open, the paper strip fortunes set out in a row.

Despite the hour, unsure whether he had just dreamed the phone had rung, Ryder called reception and woke the guy from a sound sleep, wanting to know if the guy had put a call through to his room.

The guy hadn't.

FORTY-TWO

IN THE SILENCE OF the small office, Ryder rubbed his eyes and yawned and tried to put aside the dream that had not felt like a dream at the motel, while on the wall of his office a home video played of Amber and Kim on a trampoline going head over heels in bikini tops and terry-cloth shorts on a hot summer day, the accompanying sound a static-filled commentary by Gary Scholl.

At one point, Gary featured in the video, a self-shot piece where he flicked his tongue between the V of his fingers as the surreal bodies of Amber and Kim sailed through the air.

Ryder's legs felt shaky as he stood up and went down the hall to the toilet, then came back to the office. He put the tape in again of Gary and Sandi Kellogg, looked at Gary snorting a line of cocaine, a table littered with beer cans and a bottle of whiskey, and again he looked at the date stamp and time in the lower-right corner of the tape.

He set aside the file, knowing Blaine's murder investigation would center on the initial interviews of Kim Jewel and Whitey Whitmore, the two of them the obvious suspects, the footage of Kim's rage captured on tape by local TV stations. Hadn't he seen the look of consternation on Whitmore's face when he had asked him if he hunted?

Ryder changed tapes again, looked to the reel of film of Kim Jewel smiling at the camera in a halter top. Her nipples showed, and he thought of the way she had accused him of stalking her, the way she clung to her own sense of self-preservation, not helping him, setting up Gary as she'd done. He felt his lips forming the words "worthless bitch," the rage deep within him that she had spoken to him like that, a woman who had fucked scum like Gary and then cast him aside.

Those kids had intuited right, Kim Jewel, the blow-job queen in her flats and smock, getting old, getting so nobody was going to want her.

Ryder had to get away. He knew that. He had become mired in speculation, in dogging Bauer for something that didn't necessarily relate to Jewel's murder. So what if Kim's kid was Bauer's? That wasn't part of the cold case he was here to solve.

Pendleton's case was stymied. Ryder faced that simple fact. Whatever Pendleton had done or hadn't done, he was in a coma now. He was no threat. The parallel investigation related to the print-run date would eventually yield a definitive answer, establish if Pendleton had prior knowledge of where Amber had been buried, his apparent guilt, or if Wiltshire and Horowitz were behind an elaborate hoax in sending the tape.

It was matter of time. Something would surface.

Ryder checked his watch, looked out into the dead world. It was still dark, snow falling. He turned again, faced the silent footage of Kim and Amber Jewel playing. It was time to let go; the obsession with Kim had hemorrhaged into a part of his past he didn't want to revisit. He still felt shaken about the dream.

All he needed to do now was write the briefest of reports, citing what he had uncovered—the Leopold and Loeb book above Pendleton's desk, circumstantial evidence suggesting Pendleton had become bent on challenging the notion of God. If it was established that Pendleton had murdered Jewel, here was the perverse justification.

Why not leave it at that, retreat from the case?

For a while Ryder put his head on the table, exhausted, coming to terms with the fact that his involvement in the investigation was on hold, finding a solace in sleep before surfacing into the nightmare of what he had dreamed hours before: the phone ringing again.

He awoke and felt outside himself, cold in a way he hadn't felt in a long time. The phone was still ringing. Eventually he picked it up, feeling himself still inside the nightmare.

A silence prevailed for a moment, Ryder waiting, before a voice spoke. "Is someone there?"

Ryder hesitated. "What do you want?"

"I'm looking for Detective Jon Ryder?"

"You are?"

"Ed Kline."

Ryder gripped the receiver. "Who *is* this?"

"Is this a joke? I'm returning a call from a Detective Jon Ryder—"

Ryder sensed the voice was about to hang up. "Wait! Give me your number. He'll call you back." He took down the number, then, unfamiliar with the area code, he pulled open a phone book, scanned the area code listing—Santa Fe—and dialed the number.

The caller picked up. "Yes . . ."

It was the same voice.

Ryder held the phone between his ear and shoulder, thumbing through the file related to Jewel's murder. Kline's interview with police was listed alphabetically, a file he had not reviewed. He saw Kline's address listed as Santa Fe. Still unsure what was going on, he said by way of stalling, "What are you working at these days, Ed?"

"Teaching. . . ." Kline hesitated. "Look, I don't want any trouble. What do you want?"

"What do you *think* I want?"

Kline said, "I called back out of courtesy . . . I don't have to do this."

"Right, I bet you got a parole officer breathing down your neck. . . . So why am I calling, Ed?"

"The case . . . Amber's case. I read about what happened with that professor."

"Right! So are you surprised with the turn of events?"

"I don't know the facts in the case."

"Well, given the facts back then . . ."

"I was gone when Amber disappeared. I don't know what the facts were other than I was living down here, that I had an alibi."

"*Alibi!* You're talking like every guilty guy I ever ran across, Ed."

"Try being on the other side of the law."

Ryder kept scanning the file. "I see you changed your name, or I should say were using an alias when you were tracked down. That sounds like a guy hiding from something?"

"I made a mistake in judgment."

"What mistake?"

"Kim."

"What about her?"

"I cared . . . *we* cared for each other. It wasn't some passing thing. I planned on getting divorced and us moving away."

Ryder kept paging through the interview transcript. "I don't see any of that in your statement to police . . . a *relationship* with Kim."

Kline answered abruptly, "It's not there."

"Why?"

"Back then I thought I could be extradited for having been with her. I didn't know what the statutes of limitations were, so I said nothing incriminating."

"You said nothing incriminating! Give me a break, Ed . . . I'm staring at a copy of the photograph of you with Kim here in your file. I know the real story!"

"Which is?"

"That you're a pervert, Ed. You did something to some freshman, and Kim and her friends decided to get rid of you. Kim came on to you, and you took the bait. It was a once-off date, a setup to catch you. That's why you ran."

Kline let out a long breath. "I thought you had the murderer up there?"

"What do you mean?"

"I mean, what do you want from me? What do I have to do with anything now?"

"I'm cleaning up all loose ends, Ed, just like in the movies. So back to you. Why did you run if you were involved with Kim, if it wasn't a setup?"

Kline put his hand on the receiver and spoke to someone, then got on the line again. "Look, you got the story wrong. Kim was lied to about me. There was no incident with any freshman. They made that up."

"They?"

"Trent . . . Trent Bauer."

Ryder felt his face flush, sending a chill through him. "How do you know it was Trent?"

"I *just* know."

"That's not good enough, Ed."

Kline waited. "Okay . . . Kim . . . she told me it was Trent who sent the photograph. I called her once after I left. I wanted to know why everything had gone to hell between us."

"And?"

"Kim told me what Trent had told her I supposedly did. . . . She said she felt betrayed by me, that she did it to get back at me."

"That's what you get dating high school girls, right, that kind of passion?"

"I guess. . . . Look, I'm telling you what happened here . . . I learned my lesson, okay? Every high school teacher goes through infatuations to some degree if they look any way reasonable. It just happens. I'm not making excuses, but this went beyond just me. It wasn't really about me! Trent was fixated on Kim."

"How so?"

"The guy had a screw loose. . . . Kim told me earlier in the year before we started seeing each other that Trent had gotten a car for his sixteenth birthday, that he'd started coming up to her stop all proud, wanting her to ride with him. The thing of it was, Amber got in, but Kim wouldn't . . . so Kim was left standing in the cold while Amber went off with Trent. It wasn't like he could kick Amber out. That went on for a time, Trent following the bus, Amber sitting up front with Trent. He'd follow the bus on its route. It was the beginning of Amber's animosity toward Kim. In the end, Trent started taking the bus again. It ticked Amber off big-time. That's all Kim talked about when we got together, her fear of Trent finding out."

"She was afraid of him?"

"I don't know, afraid, scared . . . I never figured it out. She had this on-again, off-again sense of endearment about him that I never got. He gave her presents, kept everything right at that point where he was sweeter than he was . . . *psychotic*. Anyway, she stopped taking the bus home eventually after we were together a while. Then Amber got nosy and stopped taking the bus as well, following Kim, and next thing you know, Trent began staying back at school, too . . . so Kim started taking the bus home again, then leaving to see me after she got home. It got complicated . . . but I hung in for her . . . then this one time Trent saw us together. He was waiting out in his car with Amber up by the road where we used to meet. It freaked the hell out of me. I wanted to end it."

"What happened?"

"Kim . . . she wasn't willing to let go, though Trent made a big push to get her then, asked her to a dance. It was like the final straw for Kim . . . but she agreed to go to the dance, then it went on from there, Trent being around her, basically blackmailing her in as many words. In the end, she came up with a plan to end it—a drive-in-movie."

Kline cleared his throat. "Trent . . . he had this problem with premature ejaculation. I guess girls talk about guys in high school. It was a big issue with Trent, something everybody knew about. For all his psychosis, when he went out with Kim all he ever wanted to do was hold hands. But at the drive-in Kim hit on him. The next thing, he lost it. He was totally humiliated, and Kim pretended to freak . . . started into how she cared about him, but how she didn't think he could give her what she needed.

"It stopped Trent dead in his tracks, though. Kim got out of the car, walked out of the drive-in. I was there, parked near them. For a time it worked, until Trent started watching her again, saw us together, until he set his sights on getting back at her."

"Getting back at *you*?"

"*Me* . . . no, it wasn't about me. It was about him and her. That's the real reason I said nothing about us being together when the police called when Amber was missing. I didn't know what the hell was going on, if I could trust Kim anymore. I just followed their lead, and nobody ever asked about us having a relationship. . . ." Kline's voice trailed off.

Ryder put his fingers to the bridge of his nose. "So why are you telling me now?"

"I don't know . . . I guess that part of my life is so long in the past now that I can admit things."

"Did Kim tell you to call me?"

Kline raised his voice. "What? No . . . you contacted me. You gave my wife your number! That's how I called you."

"However you want to play it, Ed, I can play along, okay?"

Kline didn't answer.

"Listen, did anybody else ever know about what you told me about Trent, about why you left?"

"I don't know. Ask Kim. All I did was run when I got the photograph."

Ryder said, "I appreciate you calling."

Kline seemed to have lost confidence in talking, Ryder's denial of having originally called him rattling him. "I hope to God I can trust you, that you're who you say you are, and that we don't have to speak again. I got an okay life down here, teaching at a private school. I'm not the same person I was back then. I just want you to know that."

Kline hung up, and Ryder set the phone down, slowly.

It had become light outside the window.

FORTY-THREE

THE MORNING SEEMED FIXED and motionless in the 6:00 a.m. silence as Horowitz dropped Adi off at the hospital, leaving her alone with Pendleton. Then he drove back along the same river he had traveled with Adi and Pendleton two years earlier and felt the weight of time, of what had passed between them all.

Against that melancholy quiet, Horowitz turned on the radio, catching the news at the top of the hour. A list of school closings was being announced, a storm forecast for midmorning. There was the briefest mention of the Pendleton case, a reference to the burial of Gary Scholl.

Horowitz kneaded the back of his neck. The sinister details of what Pendleton had done to Amber Jewel had finally settled deep within him. There was no finessing the brutality of Jewel's murder. It was no longer a game, and driving in the quiet of the morning, Horowitz regretted having called Ryder in the middle of the night, of having added his own petty sense of revenge to everything else.

The thrill was gone. He should not have gotten his agent in New York to hire a PI, to investigate Ryder, but it was what he had done in the aftermath of being accused by Ryder of having mailed the tape from New

York. As Horowitz had expected, intuited during the interview, Ryder's reference to lost loves, about betrayal, had a basis in fact. The PI had come back in a matter of hours with Ryder's domestic battery charges. Court-appointed marital counseling had been ordered. Ryder had not complied. A restraining order had been issued against him, his wife having gained sole custody of their daughter just two months before she went missing.

Horowitz knew he should have let all that stuff go, avoided Ryder, yet he hadn't, dogged by what Ryder had done to him. His own pride had not let him just ignore anything.

It was what had defined him as a writer, a sublimated sense of revenge behind everything he wrote, despite the veneer of easy prose.

He and Bob were not that unalike after all. He had always been hawkish in his pursuit of fame and revenge. His childhood had centered around being physically unassuming—or no, worse, a *weakling*, a New York Jew who had inherited the genetic paleness and thinness of his race. He had been late into puberty, his consciousness defined against the indignity of being a straggler in sports, facing the nightmare roll call of junior high gym team selection, *the shirts* and *the skins*, standing there with the *ectomorphs* and the *endomorphs*, against the prowess and ripped physique of the Italian and black *mesomorphs*, running the gauntlet of gym class and the showers, everything defined against the physicality of the body.

He remembered one instance, being grabbed naked in the shower and having his head stuck down a toilet, struggling, holding his breath, his head pulled out at the moment of drowning, the semihard erections of his captors inches from his gasping, open mouth.

Horowitz shivered. None of that had made it to the autobiography, to *The Big Lie*, as he had come to call it.

At Bannockburn College, Horowitz slowed as a retiree-age security guard, standing inside a small portable booth like a toy soldier, waved his advance. Horowitz stopped, got a temporary on-campus parking pass, and crossed the rumbling conceit of the wooden drawbridge onto the island campus.

Horowitz was still preoccupied with Ryder. What he had seen out at the funeral was Ryder look at Kim Jewel not as a cop, but as someone deeply affected, a look Horowitz knew all too well—the desire of an older man for a younger woman.

Pulling into a parking lot, Horowitz took a deep breath. It was nearly over, this, the last morning here. Stopping, he looked around at the salmon pink of the sunrise just breaking in the east, the campus still asleep, the easy existence of life here, the air still scented with a charcoal smell of burnt leaves and wood from the fires.

There was, after all, something to be said for being rich, and Horowitz took a moment in the floodlit lot of Bannockburn, filled with expensive cars, undoubtedly student cars left here for weeks at a time, to reflect as such. There was nothing like the hubris of the rich, this life removed from ordinary society, and he tried to dispel the momentary melancholy he experienced.

He had made it. It was what he needed to focus on, the positive, of how different this life was from the urban slum of his upbringing. He had achieved it by himself. That was the essential truth, despite everything, that was why people were buying his books, to understand, to maybe learn from him, though the strange thing was, he was not sure at that moment, if he lived life again, that he could have duplicated what he had achieved.

Horowitz shivered again and moved against the bite of early morning coldness. A scarf of mist had settled over the long expanse of the desolate quad, the weak yellow of lights on at the dining hall. He was now entrenched in this collegiate reading circuit, keynote speaker at commencements, commanding a king's ransom for a mere night's engagement, recipient of no fewer than five honoree doctorates, and paid administrator of cash-rich grant-in-aid scholarships, almost always disquietingly named after the dead, or near dead, insufferable socialite wives of the rich, from the L. Myrtle Schwartz Foundation for the Arts and the Kathryn S. Breedlove Grant to the Amaryllis Grubb Endowment, named for Amaryllis Grubb, a hard-of-hearing octogenarian heiress he had been forced to coddle for funds over numerous dinners, a woman who had lost the ability to fart silently.

The reality was, some of these very schools had rejected him when he had applied for open teaching vacancies when he was ending grad school. In fact, Bannockburn had been one of the many institutions that had not offered him a position, the selective memory of senior faculty evident the night he had come to speak at the college, the night he had come to blithely take their money, the night Pendleton tried to kill himself.

The indignities had run deep, the history of personal affronts if Pendleton had cared to stick around to see, the true history of Allen Horowitz, the unreferenced parts of his life, expunged from his upbeat, irreverent autobiography.

The irony was, he had escaped the madness of E. Robert Pendleton simply because he had been rejected from even trying it.

The wind picked up, a cold that portended snow, as Horowitz entered the earth sciences atrium, a legacy building and shortcut connected to the new library. The atrium had a cathedral vaulted ceiling, the floor an emerald swirl of cold marble, the centerpiece a statue of a muscled Hercules holding on his shoulders a huge bronze globe, the contrast so strikingly different from the desolate quad outside that it caught even one as sardonic and jaded as Horowitz off guard.

He had read somewhere that the flying buttressed colossal excess of medieval cathedrals had been created for the sheer effect of such contrast between peasant existence and the gilded mansion of heavenly eternal reward, though this building was different, of an earthly concern, a secular shrine to learning, the walls painted with various natural phenomena: images of erupting volcanoes, flowing magma, earthquake fissures, continental shelves, deep cave stalagmites, landscape images of a rain forest canopy, an ice sheet, a desert dune, a cross section of the earth with a molten ball at the core, a giant periodic table of the elements, all done in an art deco coloring of yellow and olive and tonal oranges, the drawings reminiscent of those in the *World Book Encyclopedia Yearbook* Horowitz's immigrant father had given him as a kid each year.

That sudden memory of his family's apartment in Queens set a lump in Horowitz's throat: him, as a child, watching his immigrant father in work clothes at the kitchen table, reading to him from the encyclopedia.

He looked upward, and above him a constellation of the nine planets of the solar system rotated in an elaborate mobile around the sun.

As Horowitz left the atrium, he saw a small statue, a humble figure that turned out to be the founder, not an Englishman at all, as the name suggested, but a fellow Russian émigré. On the block base of the statue was a quote: "Success Through Industry Is a Peasant Ideal."

The library lobby was less impressive, given to a new age, concerned conceptually and spiritually with space and openness in all its forms. A solitary obsidian statue of a suitably bemused *Thinker* occupied the lobby's center and seemed the only permanent fixture.

A makeshift exhibition of modernist student art was on display, from randomly placed Styrofoam blocks representing *Entropy*, or that's what the composition was titled, anyway, to another exhibit under wraps in black garbage bags, titled *Possibilities*, seemingly meant never to be unwrapped, though in staring at it, Horowitz could not help but think of the mutilated body of Amber Jewel in such garbage bags.

Against that melancholy thought and the memory of a father and a life he had systematically exorcised from his autobiography, Horowitz rode the elevator to the sixth floor and got off, went through the fire escape door into the exposed gray concrete of the stairwell, and walked two floors for the mere sake of making sure he had not been followed.

On the eighth floor, as per Adi's instruction, he found the disk containing her thesis, where she'd said it would be, tucked into a monastic text of works transcribed in the Dark Ages, the book's cover stylized in labyrinthine weaves and Celtic crosses, a time when the history of Western civilization had retreated to the windswept shores of Ireland, to what the foreword called "the Land of Saints and Scholars."

FORTY-FOUR

BAUER ARRIVED BEFORE SUNUP in a down jacket over his uniform, carrying a brown paper sack and an apple. Ryder called his name from the door of his office, the videotape rolling against the wall again, Amber and Kim going end over end on the trampoline.

Ryder looked between the video and Bauer. "How does it make you feel?"

Bauer didn't answer or approach. He turned toward his desk.

Ryder came forward and stood in the line of the projector, raised his voice. There were two other cops in the office. "I mean, getting close to Kim and then losing her again to Gary like that. Did that make you mad?"

Bauer's eyes shifted to Ryder. He shored up the distance in a matter of seconds, forcing his way into Ryder's office. "You're crazy."

Ryder looked beyond Bauer's shoulders to the open door. "You intent on keeping this a secret, Trent?"

"I'm saving you from making a fool of yourself."

"Shit, you're magnanimous, Trent, I'll give you that, caring about what happens to me."

Bauer shut the door behind him. "What do you want?"

"I had a talk with Ed Kline. You remember photogenic Ed Kline?"

Bauer stared back, shaking his head with disdain. "Ed Kline the molester! You're way off on this one. You run a check out at the high school on what Kline was up to. Go ahead. If you won't, I will!" He made as if to pick up the phone, but Ryder raised his hand.

"I will, in time, Trent. I guess what I'm getting is a sense of who you are, really."

"Who I am?"

Ryder turned and picked up a file. "Who *are* you? For starters, you're the father of Kim's daughter."

Bauer shook his head.

"Hear me out, Trent. Kim was pregnant at the time Gary got out of the penitentiary. I checked the date Gary got out. He couldn't have gotten her pregnant. I don't want to get into the biology of it, but trust me." Ryder looked up, tapping the file. "Just tell me, how did it make you feel, Gary coming back into Kim's life when you and she were together?"

"People get pregnant all the time."

"That an admission?"

"You know the reputation Kim had, who she was with over the years?"

"That's pretty disparaging, Trent. . . . But let's stick to the facts. Here was the love of your life, pregnant with your baby, something you'd dreamed about all your life. Jesus! That would make me crazy if anything got in the way of that."

Bauer shot back, "I had a wife! Like I said, you're way off."

He turned to walk away, but Ryder shouted, "I'm not finished here, Trent. This is a formal line of inquiry. You got that? I get to ask the goddamn questions here, got it?" He held up another manila file. "I have a file here pulled from Amber's school records. In October she was caught smoking dope out back of the school. The police were called. *You* answered the call. It's all documented here by the school principal, your coming to the school, questioning her. The thing is, no charges were filed against her. Why?"

"Everybody smokes dope."

"That's a good attitude, Trent. I think the high school would love to hear how you come down on that issue. . . . What happened between you and Amber?"

"Nothing . . . I told her to stay away from drugs."

"Sure you did. She was your confidante, Trent, just like she told you about Kline. I heard all about the drives you used to take together, stalking Kim."

"Not stalking her . . . *keeping* her from getting hurt. That a crime in your book? Whatever I did, it was to get Kim away from Kline."

"You know, for a dumb shit, you got it all covered."

"That all you got, insults, Ryder?"

Ryder ignored the question. "Did Amber tell you about her and Gary?"

"She didn't have to. Whatever Gary was doing to her, she considered it bragging rights. It was something she used against Kim. It was common knowledge what was going on out there with all of them. Amber was a . . ."

"A what? Go on, say it!"

"Fuck you, Ryder!"

Ryder raised his hands. "This isn't the mild-mannered Trent I know and love. . . . I think Amber regretted saying anything about Gary, started denying it, trying to go back on what she'd said, but you weren't going to let it go. See, I know how a scumbag like you thinks, Trent. Amber was a minor. Gary was out on parole. All you had to do was get her to admit what Gary was doing to her, and he was going to be put away again."

Bauer eased, a smile forming on his thin lips. "You talk such shit, you know that?"

Ryder kept talking. "You followed Amber home one day, met her coming off the bus. That was your MO, right . . . following people in your car, just like back in high school, the way you harassed Kim. That's how it started, following Amber. But she wouldn't go along with you!"

Bauer pushed against Ryder. "I'm through listening!"

Ryder grabbed Bauer's arm so that they turned in a sort of awkward waltz. "I got the whole story, Trent, complete with your premature ejaculation problems . . . what happened out at the drive-in. You're a sick fuck, you hear me? You pegged Kline as a suspect when Amber disappeared, then got so you could show the world that photograph of Kim with Kline. Two birds with one stone. That's how you wanted to pay Kim back . . . ruin her reputation, getting Gary into a frenzy over it."

There was a crazed look in Bauer's eyes. "You say one thing about me . . . about anything . . . about Kim's kid being mine, or anything, and I'm going to sue you, so help me God. You try to get Kim to admit anything about her kid anyway . . . she won't!"

"She already has!"

"You're lying! I know her. She's got that Whitmore guy she's clinging to. Whatever serves her best interests is how it works with her. What are you really after here?"

"The truth."

Bauer shook his head. "It's like everybody's been saying round here. There's something wrong with you. Everybody knows you killed your wife, and now you got a thing for Kim Jewel. That's the real reason you're still here."

FORTY-FIVE

THE BOXLIKE HOSPITAL ROOM was filled with the soft *sssss* sound of a whisper. A two-pronged oxygen feed pressed against Pendleton's nasal passages, making his chest rise and fall slowly. He was propped at an angle, still unconscious.

Adi stood by the hospital window. Snow fell now in thick flakes, coating the world in a winterland of imperial white. She was wearing the same gray Bannockburn sweatshirt Wright had bought for her. She had retrieved nothing from Pendleton's house.

Across the way, the island domain of Bannockburn was fixed against the landscape. Against the backdrop of snow, Bannockburn seemed but a vague charcoal sketch, insubstantial.

Down at the hospital parking lot, Horowitz was back from the college, waiting in the rental car. Adi had not wanted him to come up with her. This was her last good-bye to Pendleton, though she hadn't told that to anybody.

Her disappearance was to end a relationship that had endured for over two years.

Adi saw Horowitz check his watch and look up at her. She shook her head to signify Ryder was not there, and Horowitz nodded likewise. He tapped his watch again, as if to indicate she should get going. He was holding up the disk that contained all her work, the simple proof of what she had written for over a year.

Adi had asked him to retrieve it in case the time came that she would be called again by Ryder; she regretted having acknowledged that she'd taken the microfiche, having given in to him so easily.

Adi turned from the window. For now, anyway, she would escape, or so it seemed, without confrontation.

A cop sat across from Pendleton, the cop's head craned toward a small TV mounted from the ceiling.

The rules were that Adi could not touch Pendleton. He was a murder suspect.

Adi was conscious that her leaving would pass in a sullen silence, as so much of her life with Pendleton had passed. It was anticlimactic, staring at him, the long journey they had shared from his initial suicide through the publication of *Scream* to this final encounter.

Scream was still number one on the *New York Times* Best Seller List, but Pendleton's reputation was forever on the wane, as the novel was interpreted now as a literal, vicious, cold-blooded act of murder, an open letter of a psychopath. The rallying academic interests in forwarding the existential genius of Pendleton were now silent, the National Book Award Committee mum on their response to the burgeoning crisis of Pendleton's presumed guilt.

The *New York Times Book Review* had finally raised the issue of whether a novel based on a true incident could necessarily be labeled fiction. The article asked, at its essence, wasn't *Scream* an autobiography?

It seemed all too evident that *Scream* would eventually be disqualified on those grounds.

Public opinion had also turned sour; anecdotal stories from pissed-off former business, engineering, and pre-med majors filled the late night talk radio airwaves as they lashed out at the insufferable crap they had endured under the term "well-rounded."

As one late night caller complained, "How the hell do you get an A in organic chemistry and a C minus in neoclassical romantic poetry? My GPA *Tanked*! I didn't get into med school because of *The Rape of the Locke*! You explain that!"

If there had not been a cop there, Adi might have said something, tried to communicate with Pendleton, but as she stood there in those parting moments, Pendleton's enigmatic denial came back to her, troubled her, his last words, "It wasn't me. . . ."

Had he meant it figuratively? It was what she wanted to believe.

She repeated Pendleton's denial again, "It wasn't me," her thoughts drifting to Porterfield. He had seemed so manic, his rant about sex and politics so unnerving, that now in the settling last minutes alone with Pendleton, she wondered if Porterfield had simply chanced to be at the window that one time or if he had been serially watching her.

And what was she to make of the fact that Porterfield and Pendleton had befriended each other the year Amber Jewel was murdered, the year Pendleton was in the midst of both a professional and personal crisis, a year, too, when Porterfield had admitted to going through a marital crisis, when both had whiled away the summer evenings in the sequestered solitude of each other's company, drinking against a carnage of war games, speaking undoubtedly of lost love, of betrayals?

Adi felt a chill pass through her. There were no answers, not really.

She looked at Pendleton one last time, the X of the bandage strips holding a tracheostomy tube in the hollow of his neck, the strands of gray hair showing under the faded, washed-out cotton print of his pajamas, though what struck her most were Pendleton's hands set on his insubstantial lap, the large-boned hands somehow monstrously big despite the wasting of the rest of his body. From those hands, everything had emanated, the concatenation of words strung together, conduits between the interiority of thought and words on the page.

She would never know for certain what Pendleton's involvement had been or how he had known the facts of where Amber Jewel's corpse was buried. That sank in at a certain level, and lowering her eyes, she felt it was time to do as Horowitz had for so long hoped, for them to vanish and start life over elsewhere. As Adi turned from Pendleton, she became aware of the TV laugh track, just audible, brooking the deadening early morning silence, UHF-TV out of Chicago, and the cop smiling faintly.

On the TV, Samantha from *Bewitched* was pleading with her mercurial carrot-topped mother to turn Darren back from a goat to a human. Darren had eaten the stuffing out of the arm on the sofa. Samantha had him by the horns. She was wearing a short miniskirt and midcalf boots of the sort Nancy Sinatra had made famous for walking all over men.

The crisis of the show was that Darren's boss, Larry, was arriving with a client to hear a pitch for a new soup commercial.

Adi stopped, taken back to childhood, to the flux of her parents' volatile relationship, the show somehow tapping into a certain feminist perspective on the desperate absurdity and egocentricity of the male world, where husbands spent all their time trying to stop their wives from using their powers. It was the genius of sitcom TV, of metaphor and humor, an era where a nation watched as a genie struggled to serve her master but also get out of her bottle.

Adi left without even looking at Pendleton again.

Through the greater part of the evening, Horowitz headed east on I-80 toward Ohio, across a flatness of two states, where the late autumn snow fell in a front that stretched into Pennsylvania, until he arrived the following afternoon to the vast complex of the state college where Adi Wiltshire had been born and had come of age, years ago, in a Vietnam era of free love and pacifist protest, the child of two idealist grad students who once upon a time had wanted to change the world and make it a better place, and failed.

PART 3

INDETERMINACY

FORTY-SIX

THE INEVITABLE CALL CAME through to Ryder's office at 9:00 a.m. from his boss, Ken Orton, a longtime friend and lifetime smoker with the wheezing whistle of an asthmatic and a set of yellowing dentures that looked like old-style clothes pegs. There was at least solace in speaking with Ken.

His secretary came on the line. Ken would be there in a minute.

Ryder waited.

Few people could trace their demise to a single source, but Ken Orton could; his wife, June, was already lining up in a class-action tobacco suit, while Ken obligingly kept on smoking and speaking candidly, from time to time, to an eight-millimeter home videocamera about his addiction, per his lawyer's advice, to make his demise all the more powerful and poignant in a court of law.

What he said to Ryder once was, "I should have gone into robbing banks. That's where I went wrong in life. I've got all my hopes pinned now on terminal lung cancer."

Ken was short and matter-of-fact with Ryder, knowing the particulars of Ryder's family dynamic as much as Ryder knew Ken's life story. June and Gail were talkers.

The case was on hold, pending a change in Pendleton's medical status.

Ken said, "I can't afford to pay for you to hide out there any longer, Jon."

"They come up with anything on the print-run date?"

Ken coughed and cleared his throat. His voice sank almost to a whisper. "We might have something. . . ."

There was a silence on the line.

"You just saying that to bring me in, Ken?"

"Listen, Jon, I don't know how much longer I can cover for you. A complaint was lodged against you."

"Bauer, right?"

"He's threatening to sue if you keep claiming he's the father of Jewel's kid. What's that about?"

"It's a long story, Ken. Let's just say there's something else going on here. Pendleton *didn't* kill Jewel."

"You can *prove* that?"

"I'm working on it."

"Look, things have come up. . . ."

Ryder raised his voice. "I got information Gary Scholl didn't murder that Blaine woman. I got a tape from his girlfriend giving him an airtight alibi. He didn't do it! But you know who showed up right after the murder? Bauer! He has a history with Kim Jewel like you wouldn't believe!"

"How long have you been sitting on that evidence?"

"About Bauer?"

"No . . . the tape. Goddamn it, Jon! You're not there investigating Gary Scholl, you hear me?"

Ryder leaned into the phone. "Gary was a legitimate suspect in Jewel's murder. What do you mean he's not central to finding out what happened to Jewel?"

"This isn't the time to play the lone wolf."

"What if I told you the police are in on this . . . at least Bauer is. He cut Gary down in cold blood. I was there."

"In a *shoot-out.* Jesus Christ, what's got into you? You can't make flagrant allegations like that. Scholl came out with a gun drawn. I got the report here, eyewitness testimony that he fired off rounds, that he was an *imminent threat.*"

"I know what I saw. . . . It's part of a cover-up. You know there are all sorts of anomalies about how Jewel's body wasn't discovered during the original search, questions about how her face could have remained preserved during weeks of temperate weather before winter hit. Jewel was set out in that field after she was long dead."

"So?"

"So it doesn't gel with what was in Pendleton's novel, killing the victim and burying her immediately. That's not what happened in Jewel's case."

"Any of these anomalies cited in the coroner's report?"

"Shit . . . The investigation was mishandled. That's what the hell we do, Ken, uncover anomalies. What am I doing here but my job? I don't think proper measures were taken to establish anything back when this happened."

"Look, I can't discuss this over the phone. You write it up, Jon, write it up and come back, and we'll review this with a sense of distance and perspective."

"Why now, Ken?"

"Because I'm telling you to."

"They want me taken out, right? They got to you."

"See . . . you're talking like someone on the edge."

"*See* . . . what does *see* mean? It substantiates someone has been talking about me. You as good as admitted it, Ken. Don't let them do this to us."

Ken coughed away from the phone.

Ryder waited, heard Ken drinking a glass of water, Ken's breath a strained wheeze. "Listen to me, Jon. I appreciate the strain you are under. I wouldn't want to face a home life like you got right now, but don't go looking for trouble elsewhere, making excuses for staying away."

Ryder didn't respond.

"Look, there's nobody taking you off the case. This isn't a reprimand. I'm trying to save you from making a fool of yourself with that . . . that Jewel woman."

Ryder closed his eyes.

"People have been talking."

"What people? Bauer? Why the hell wouldn't he talk? He wants me gone. Think about it! He was involved in Amber's murder, I know it!"

"Jon, listen to me good. The fact is, an investigator interviewed a former employee at the printing press who got rumor of what was being investigated. The woman came forward and says she remembers the book being printed on Valentine's Day, says she remembered that as a weird coincidence given the title of the book."

"That's convenient! Come on, Ken, people come forward with all sorts of stories, trying to steal the limelight, you know that."

"This isn't somebody off the street. It's someone who's worked there over twenty years. I call that a credible lead, that's what I call it."

"Okay . . . okay . . . Look, I got parallel leads going here. A few days more is all I want. You can swing it."

"I can't. We were premature in beginning our investigation. I want the print-run date established first and foremost now. It'll define the scope and direction of what we are dealing with here. I'm giving you a direct order, Jon. Give that tape over to Clevenger and get back here. As of now, you're on administrative leave."

"I'm off the case, is that it?"

"I want you to take a break, sort out things with your wife and kids, okay?"

Ryder didn't answer.

"That's an order, Jon, answer me, hand the tape over and go home."

Ryder cleared his voice. "I'll hand it over."

"Good . . . I want you out of there midmorning, got it?"

"Anything you say, Ken. Sure. . . ."

Ryder set down the phone, knowing his access to the case information would end in a matter of hours, that he would be off the case for good.

In a desperate last act, he called Kim Jewel at home, got an answering machine, but he didn't leave a message. He called Rite Aid next.

Whitmore answered.

Ryder said straight off, "I got the call from Kline."

Whitmore answered abruptly, "Kim isn't here."

Ryder put his hand to his face. He was sitting with his legs set apart. "Okay, fuck you, Whitey. I'm through using you as an intermediary. Let me speak to Kim now. I know she's there! This is between us, not you, anyway! You're a fuckin' life raft she's clinging to. That's the reality here, Whitey!"

Whitmore said in a straightforward manner, "I want to inform you, all incoming calls are recorded as a matter of course to the store. I'm going to hang up now, and if you call again, I'm going to the *real* police."

"I am the *real* police!"

There was a muffled sound, and then Kim got on the line.

Ryder could tell she had been crying.

"I can't help you any more than I have—" She broke off.

Ryder heard her saying Whitey's name and the sound of the phone being set aside. Her voice faded as she walked away. Ryder waited, heard footsteps recede, stop, then begin to grow loud again.

Kim's voice was pitched with hysteria as she picked up the phone. "You see what you did, calling like this, the trouble it's causing? You don't got the right to speak to Whitey like that. He doesn't take to being talked down to. He's *management.* You got that! He told me not to get involved. Now look what you went and done."

There was a click on the line as though someone had picked up.

Ryder stood up immediately and went to the door, opened it. The outer office was still empty. He stood in the doorway, looking around, and said quietly, "You got Whitey to pretend he was me and call Kline. Why?"

Kim didn't answer, a silent admission, and Ryder, sensing the opportunity, said, "I'm not out to get you, Kim. I think you know that by now."

Kim's voice eased. "I know. . . ."

"Why didn't you tell me about Kline yourself?"

"Why . . . You know I've had people looking at me like dirt all my life . . . I couldn't bring myself to say what went on with me and Mr. Kline. . . ."

Ryder let it register, the "Mr." in Kim addressing Kline. It went a long way to exposing the incongruities in her personality, the harshness but also the gullibility of her character.

A voice on the line said, "We don't want any mention of Trent being the father of Kim's baby." It was Whitmore. "Kim doesn't need to be hurt more than she has."

"I'm on your side, okay, Whitey? I want to apologize for what I said."

"That's not answering the question."

Before Ryder answered, Kim cut in with an obsequiousness Tori had sometimes used to shore up differences after a fight. "You're not mad at me anymore, Whitey, are you?"

"No. . . ."

Kim whispered, "You see what a gem I got here, Detective?" She swallowed and drew in a breath. "I just want the past to stop haunting me, for it to end."

Ryder closed the door and moved away from the doorway, sat at his desk again. "Maybe it will now. So why did you get Kline to call me?"

"I wanted you to know about Trent from somebody else. I think you *were* right."

"About what?"

"Trent . . . him killing Gary like you said out there at Sandi's place."

"So why did Trent do it?"

"Because of what went on with us, me having Trent's baby. He kept calling me, wanted me to leave Gary, to be with him, saying he never loved Dawn . . . saying it was over between them. When I told him I wasn't leaving Gary, he wanted me to have an abortion. That's when I just stopped answering the phone. He got Amber involved, harassing me."

Ryder felt his pulse quicken at the reference to Amber.

"Trent gave Amber money for me to have the abortion. He gave her money, too, said he could help her start again. When Amber never showed up at home that afternoon back then, I figured she had left with the money Trent gave her. I was afraid to say anything about Trent, about what was going on between us. Trent arrived into the investigation, and I didn't know how to take it, Trent rounding people up to search for Amber.

"I didn't think Amber was really gone, not for good. I thought Amber was getting back at me and Gary, that Trent was helping her hide out someplace so the focus on her disappearing was put on Gary. Trent knew I was never going to admit I was carrying his baby. He knew what Gary was capable of doing to me."

Kim's voice started coming in mounting sobs. "You didn't know Amber, what she could do to you. I kept thinking she was going to show up. I swear on it. I had that hope . . . or fear that she was going to show up and ruin everything for me and Gary. And then the days became weeks, and Kline was called, and I went numb inside, lost a sense of what was really going on around me."

Ryder said in a slow, deliberate way, "You think Trent killed Amber?"

Kim stopped dead at the directness of the question.

Ryder said her name softly.

Kim whispered, "I don't know . . . I swear to God I don't." Then her voice cut off. She hung up, the line clicking.

Whitmore said, "You still there, Ryder?"

"Yeah. . . ."

"What I fear most is her killing herself, just remember that. She doesn't want her child knowing Trent is her father, not if it turns out . . . if Trent killed Amber." He paused. "I know you can't make promises like that. I'd just as soon this ended after you'd talked with her outside the store, but she broke down last night. It all came back to her, the nightmare of that time. I got no delusions of what I am. Gary was her true love. That's what she's grieving. It's not for Amber, not really, if we're talking honestly. It was a mistake, me calling Kline, but I did it for her. I don't think there's anything honorable in a man who did something like that to Kim. I don't mean to dismiss the temporal law, what you're doing, but the way I see it, I think after a time, some secrets are better revealed in the afterlife."

FORTY-SEVEN

THE EFFECT OF THE Gary Scholl tape had long ago diminished for Ryder, and he remained duly solemn as a fellow investigator was actively engaged in taking down the names of the songs playing on the radio in the background to provisionally authenticate the time the video was shot, though given the graphic nature of tape and the fact that Sandi Kellogg had handed it over, all indications suggested it was authentic.

At the tape's end, the lead investigator into the Blaine murder, Tobias Clevenger, pulled up the blinds, and the sudden brilliance of day materialized, a world beyond the office, a redbrick downtown like a prop against the interiority of the office.

It was snowing in big flakes, and against the quiet, save for the click of a typewriter in the outer office, Clevenger said nothing for a time, merely loosened his tie and poured a glass of water.

His face shone like that of a guy about to have a heart attack. He said out loud, more to himself than to Ryder, "I can't wait to see what the media does with this," setting his glass of water firmly on the table and continuing to stare into the outer world, scratching at his hip with his left hand.

Ryder could see that Clevenger's mind had turned inward, toward his own survival, the implications devastating from a legal and public standpoint. Gary Scholl had been shot dead by police.

When Clevenger turned, Ryder said, "If you're going to start investigating anything, start by asking Trent Bauer why he killed Gary."

Clevenger answered, "Okay," but in a way Ryder knew he was lying.

Ryder persisted, "Or better yet, start off asking Bauer for his alibi the night Blaine was murdered!"

Clevenger turned to the cop managing the AV projector. "Jon thinks we're real hicks here. I think we better check our shoes." And he made as though he were checking his shoe for shit, then stopped. "Put Trent down for questioning," he said, and turned again toward Ryder. "We got it noted, Jon. Anything else we should know before you *leave* us?"

Ryder shook his head. "I'll file a report regarding my findings so far."

Clevenger picked up a fax beside his desk. "You might be interested in this. It was addressed to you from the FBI regarding a trace on Cassie DuMont. It says she was located in Amarillo, Texas, married with three children."

Clevenger handed the fax to Ryder, sitting across from the desk. "You want to make the call to the mother?"

Ryder rose and set the fax on the table. "You do it."

Clevenger turned to the window again. "You know, I coach a Little League team, Jon, and the number one thing I tell kids is you can't swing at everything. It's a game of patience and percentages. You got to know the count. What other walk of life can you bat two fifty and be a star? Baseball teaches something about expectations, about the true odds we face. We're going to get it wrong more than we ever get it right. How your life turns out is how you deal with that reality. You bat five hundred here, Jon. You're way ahead of the game."

Ryder stood a moment longer than he might have otherwise. Down at street level, snow had softened everything, and he could see in a five-and-dime, people moving in the false brilliance of fluorescent-lit aisles, as if it were just the beginning of another day, and farther off, the shunting noise of train cars forming by a grain silo, yellow light flashing on a signal post amid the snow, all of it in some way defining the mediocrity Clevenger pitched to any seven-year-old who ever picked up a bat in this town.

Ryder sat alone in his office, heard voices in the outer room. The Jewel case file was on the desk, the two other missing persons' files he had initially read set off to the side.

He picked up the DuMont case, looked into the face of a fifteen-year-old girl who had disappeared over a decade ago for unknown reasons, the gut instinct of cops working the case right in this instance, a runaway leaving behind three brothers and a sister, looking to erase a past, to begin again.

How did one preserve that silence, that bitterness, across birthdays and holidays, across the joy of giving birth? Of course, his mind turned to Tori, that there were people with that resolve who never wanted to be found again.

In a momentary reprieve against his true feelings for her, Ryder called Gail. Maybe he was the problem, not her. He got no reply, imagined her on coffee break, probably talking about him in the break room, Gail, purveyor of home bakes, of apple turnovers and brownies, enticing people over, the history of her life there for anybody she could get to listen.

He found it hard reconciling that he had ended up with her, and his mind drifted as it did so often now to Kim Jewel, to the thought that she had given in to someone like Whitey Whitmore, that the older you got, the fewer your options, the more desperation set over every action.

Ryder set down the DuMont case and opened the Witter file, lingering on the image of Elizabeth Witter, the simple beauty of an adopted child who had endured so much in her short life. He read again the details of her disappearance, the statements her adopted parents had given, to Enoch Witter's cowardly suicide in a jail cell.

Coming back to the case a second time, he felt he knew her, an intimacy he had not experienced in years, and just before 10:00 in the morning, with the snow falling hard, he circled a simple fact, the mention of a white car that had been noted following the school bus in the days prior to Witter's disappearance, a fact that now registered against what Kline and Kim had told him about Trent stalking Kim in his car.

Ryder sifted through Amber's case file, remembering something—and there it was, in a single interview, a witness making mention of a car following the bus in the days before Amber's disappearance, an off white car. It corroborated what Kim had told him about Trent trying to get to Amber.

Ryder circled the words "white" and "off white."

He felt his heart racing, couldn't help thinking back to what Wright had told him about what Trent had done at the junior high prom, finger-fucking Dawn, pretending it had been Kim, going around having people smell it. Could you truly attribute that to juvenile hormones run amuck? Did someone outgrow something that sick and twisted? Or was it how Bauer fucked Dawn, that behemoth, substituting her with an image of Kim, or *with* Kim?

Trent had been married when he got Kim pregnant. He had pursued her again and again. Did that infidelity, his opportunistic forcing his way into Kim's life in Gary's absence, hint at other sexual encounters, a need to find someone other than his wife?

Ryder stood up, thought of calling Kim again, asking her about Trent's other love interests, but he didn't. At a deep level, he was conscious that he was sublimating what Ken had told him, that a long-standing employee at the printing press had come forward to place the printing of Pendleton's work on Valentine's Day, over six weeks before the discovery of Amber's body.

Still, Ryder persisted, picked up a phone book, flipped through the pages, and came across the names Bauer, Trent and Dawn, saw the address. Trent lived at English Turn, the man-made lake community he had driven by heading toward Henderson's. He had managed to inculcate himself into that world, trapped, his living at English Turn on account of Dawn's family money. It all added a sense of desperation to Trent's life, the question: What price had it cost him to endure someone he had never loved?

Ryder put a call in to the DMV, asked for a search run against vehicles registered under *both* Trent's and Dawn's names, spanning the years Amber's and Elizabeth's murders occurred, including Dawn in case Trent had been using her car.

It was his last official act in what was not his office anymore.

In the police parking lot, it was freezing cold as Ryder started his car and let the engine warm. He wiped off the accumulation of fallen snow with his gloved hand, stomping from foot to foot, and when he finished, he turned and looked up into the silent veil of snow, saw, in the corner office on the third floor, Clevenger on the phone, standing at the window.

Clevenger's eyes locked on him for a moment, before Clevenger simply moved away from the window.

It added a certain ominous cast to what had gone on in the town, at least it had that feeling for Ryder, or simply it was a justification for what he would do next.

By late morning, in a cold, small room at the county courthouse, Ryder stood at a steel table, wearing gloves, reviewing the state's physical evidence in the Elizabeth Witter murder. His request to review the evidence hadn't been challenged. Whatever Clevenger's reach, it didn't extend to the county level.

The articles retrieved from Elizabeth included the pair of soiled underwear with the trace evidence of semen and blood. Ryder examined the underwear, old-fashioned bloomers, obviously hand-me-downs from Witter's mother, plausibly accounting for the type O blood lifted from the underwear, along with the type A that had matched both Elizabeth and Enoch.

In a scan of the report, Ryder saw that Enoch Witter's suicide had brought an abrupt end to the investigation. The file had not been updated since a week after Enoch's suicide. In the intervening years, the presumption that Enoch Witter had murdered his daughter had prevailed, and though forensics had advanced, without the advocacy of relatives demanding a definitive answer as to who had murdered Elizabeth, investigators hadn't clarified the loose ends in the case. It was again part of a sullen history of cold cases, where so many lives had been eclipsed and forgotten, case files set aside to make room for new victims.

In the outer office, Ryder filled out the appropriate paperwork initiating the forensics test, hoping the trace semen was still viable, that it could yield a genetic profile, traverse a passage of years, and establish if Enoch Witter had had sexual relations with his adopted daughter.

Before Ryder left, he made a call from a pay phone to Ruth Witter's home number. He had written it down from the police report. He wanted her side of the story, feeling that maybe the passage of years would have softened her resolve, some hint in her voice at least that she had reconciled herself with what her husband had done, or otherwise. It was a last rational effort on his part to try to forestall breaking Ken's orders to go home.

If he got a simple confession, he would have solved not the case he had come to investigate, but two cases nonetheless. Given what had gone on with his overt harassment of Bauer, he felt he needed to establish some investigative prowess, to prove he had not gone off the deep end.

A woman picked up, a voice younger than Ryder had expected. Ryder said abruptly, "Ruth Witter?"

"No . . . Ruth doesn't live here anymore."

"Do you happen to know where she moved to?"

There was a sudden suspicion in the woman's voice. "What's this about?"

"I'm a police investigator."

The woman said, "Oh . . . ," seemingly taken aback. She spoke away from the phone.

A man's voice answered with a hollow sound from somewhere in the house.

The woman said, "Irving, you hear me, you going to pick up? There's a policeman on the phone wanting to contact Ruth."

A click on the line signaled someone had picked up, presumably Irving. His voice was loud, as though he weren't used to talking on the phone. "What need you got trying to contact Ruth?"

"You *know* Ruth?"

"What's it to you?"

"You said her name like you knew her."

"Enoch was my cousin. What's this about you needing to contact her?"

"I'm not at liberty to say."

"Don't talk fancy to me. 'Not at liberty' is just another way of telling me to mind my own business! So, this about Elizabeth, is it?"

Ryder said again, "I'm not at liberty to say."

Irving made a huffing sound. "That sounds like an investigation to me, that's what that sounds like. Well, for what it's worth, Enoch didn't kill Elizabeth."

Ryder waited as a guy in a short-sleeved shirt and pocket protector passed along the corridor with a secretary who was talking in an animated way. "So why did Enoch commit suicide?"

There was a moment's hesitancy. Irving's voice got unsettled. "He failed his daughter is why. They got her to save as a baby, took her in, and they were doing as best they could with her, but she started getting away from them."

"That seems like a motivation to kill her . . . a misplaced sense of failure."

"If you think so, then why are you calling after all these years?"

"You know it's against the law to withhold evidence or knowledge in an ongoing investigation. So what are you saying, exactly?"

"I got more bad years than I got good ones left. I don't take kindly to being threatened. You want to know about things, go see Ruth. I'm not one for telling anything secondhand, or hearsay, that's the legal term for it in a court of law, right?"

At checkout, Ryder waited with his overnight bag stuffed with his clothes. His solitary call in the settling gloom of late afternoon had been to Taylor, though Gail had intercepted the message as he'd left it on the answering machine.

Gail had hung up abruptly when he'd told her he was not coming home for a few days.

He hadn't even tried to call back.

The guy at reception charged him another night. Ryder didn't protest, even though the parking lot was already under a foot of snow and virtually empty. A neon sign glowed, VACANCIES.

Ryder noted Horowitz's car was gone as the staccato sound of the dot matrix printer filled the silence. A black-and-white TV was on mute, a weatherman pointing at a weather map, placing an image of a snowflake on the map, and Ryder couldn't help thinking of Sam Henderson.

The whole lower lobe of Lake Michigan was under a weather front of swirling clouds pressing down from Canada. As Ryder was leaving, the guy said, "Oh, about the other night. You asked if someone had called."

Ryder turned.

"I checked the records. There was a call placed internally, room to room."

"Who?"

The guy looked at Ryder. "I guess, seeing as you are a cop and all, it's okay to tell you. Room twelve A, Allen Horowitz."

In driving snow and darkness, Ryder headed west toward Chicago, then north along the shoreline, past the Waukegan military base, where Scholl had done his training, through a wasteland of discount Wisconsin cheese outlets and pornography oases alongside I-94, confronting the strange incongruity of life past and present.

FORTY-EIGHT

THE ZOO WAS CLOSED at such an early hour, the round food kiosks winterized with corrugated shutters, the disconsolate outdoor exhibits mostly shut down, the metal trapdoors locked, the rock outcrops with deep moat trenches piled with snow. A lone wolf stitched a trail through its snowy domain, going to and fro silently, the black eyes of a pack mate watching, curled up in a hewn-out cave.

Horowitz stood to the side, bone weary, stepping from foot to foot, his new-growth beard frosted, watching as Adi, inside a prefab building, spoke on the phone to someone. They were both nomadic, simply wandering the highways in these days of indecision, though things were coming to an end.

Earlier that morning, he had awoken, left the motel, and gone out alone for coffee. He had called his agent and learned that later in the day, at their weekly meeting, the National Book Award committee was going to make a decision regarding the philosophical controversy surrounding whether *Scream*, given its apparent autobiographical nature, should even be eligible for the award.

When asked by his agent if he had wanted to prepare a statement, Horowitz had given two statements, one for each outcome, not knowing exactly how the committee would vote, though secretly he hoped and felt assured that the committee would end the protracted controversy and drop the book from the short list.

The prospect of obscurity loomed for Pendleton and so, too, for Horowitz as he now decided to bow out, his own career subtly tainted with a sense of melancholy retreat. But in a way, that was a good thing. His career would be truncated, his motivations shrouded in mystery. It was the best of all possible outcomes, or so he told himself.

His involvement with *Scream* had forestalled his further decline toward a decade-long string of coffee table books and spiraling self-loathing. At least now his enigmatic latter years could be committed to his memoirs in some shambling cottage in New Hampshire, at the edge of some real and metaphoric wildness. He would forever remain a nagging interest of doctoral candidates, answering letters and questions, teasing out a renewed interest in his life and his involvement with Pendleton. What he saw was a future where he would befriend, with a salt lick, a family of deer—he as a sage, introspective figure in diaphanous morning fog, shivering, while behind him, his enigmatic younger wife, son, and some visiting doctoral candidate would watch, at a reverent distance, his waning years.

Horowitz had not yet told Adi the news concerning what he thought would be *Scream*'s undoubted disqualification, aware that, at some deep level, despite what had gone on, she had clung to the validation of the award in establishing the enduring genius of Pendleton's work, that the tacit rejection of the book would, at some level, undermine her. Against that forlorn inevitability, against the long shadow of what lay ahead that day, Horowitz had just followed Adi's lead, let her thread her way back to her past.

She had wanted to come back here again.

Adi came up behind Horowitz and said, "She's here. We can go see her."

As they walked the crisscross of paths, under a pale yellow sun, wind-blown snow eddied and teemed with ephemeral color. More snow was expected later in the afternoon.

The entrance to the primate house was done in the motif of a tropical rain forest of trees, with hanging fronds of mossy vines concealing slow-turning fans, though the fans did little but stir the fetid hotness of animal waste.

Horowitz stared at a life-size drawing of hominid evolution, sketched in a series of hunched, bipedal, flat-nosed, sloping-forehead apes that walked through a timeline of five million years, each image altered slightly from the four-footed, big-boned apelike *Australopithecus anamensis*, to the tool-making, language-capable, fire-making, meat-eating *Homo erectus*, to the rigid-browed *Homo neanderthalensis*, to the arrival of *Homo sapiens*.

The tunnel-like entrance gave way to the hothouse enclosure of a primate habitat that reeked of a ripe smell of alfalfa, piss, and feces.

The most notable animal in the habitat was a solitary silverback western lowland gorilla who sat on his haunches with his arms folded. He looked profoundly bored, the way people who had lost their jobs did.

The gorilla took a deep breath and met Adi's eyes before summarily ignoring her.

Horowitz came level with Adi, watched as two juvenile gorillas swung in the languid pendulum sweep of an old car tire, the long curl of one of the gorilla's arms trailing, while, in a straw bedding, a mother sat watching her infant drink from an artificial stream filled with a flotsam of carrots and lettuce, a stream that was simply a spluttering hose bubbling beneath a cache of stones.

On the other side of the enclosure, Donald Simms, a rake thin man in overalls and rubber waders carrying a bucket of fruit, was as hairy as his simian keep. When he saw Adi, he smiled, set down the bucket, and went out the back of the enclosure through a small doorway.

Simms had been an associate of Adi's mother, one of her on-again, off-again love interests, though he had aged in the way most hippies aged, badly, his hair a frayed gray ponytail pulled tight to his worn face and watery eyes. A small pouch of distended belly showed. He had no appreciable ass.

There was a picture of him in his former youth, along with another man, with a woman identical to Adi between them.

Horowitz followed Adi's gaze, as did Simms, who smiled and said, "It's something to know that your parents were always your parents, right? So, you met up with your father yet?"

"We got in late."

Simms took the hint. "I'd give you the grand tour, but there's not much here. It's all hard science, white-coat technicians, blood draws, centrifuged samples, DNA mapping. Most of the behavioral research facilities at the college were shut down. They sent the animals here."

When Simms stopped talking, Adi said quietly, "You still sign with them?"

Simms shook his head, took a drink of coffee from his mug, and wiped his mouth with the back of his arm. "Paradigm shift. . . . All those government research grants dried up in the late seventies. Diane Fossey and Jane Goodall screwed us. The only legitimate research, field research. You can only get so many *Life* and *National Geographic* magazine covers on simian signing before the novelty wears off. Maybe that's all it was, a domesticated circus. I guess you live long enough, and everything you truly believed in, you come to understand was just a fad."

On a poster behind Simms was a question: "If man evolved from monkeys and apes, why do we still have monkeys and apes?"

Horowitz looked at the poster, and Simms acknowledged Horowitz for the first time. "What we need is an advocate like you on our side, someone who can really write."

It was the first tacit hint Simms gave that he knew about the controversy surrounding Adi's involvement with Pendleton.

"You've got to see the reams of archival data we have on Adi and

Phoebe, old reels of film and home video. They were both less than a month old when the experiment started, a project that ended up lasting almost five years, one of the most documented and rigorous interspecies socialization projects ever undertaken, total immersion interspecies socialization."

Horowitz deferred silently to Adi, whose brow seemed worried. She said, "I can't remember any of it, really."

Simms nodded. "Well, it's there if ever you reconsider things. So, you wanted to see her?"

Adi said softly, "Sure."

Simms turned to lead the way. "We've got her along with the others from the experimental days sectioned off in their own habitat. Their use of sign language ended up causing socialization problems when they were reintroduced. It was caught for a *Nova* documentary here that never got shown. It was horrific stuff, so-called noninterventional reportage on the resocialization of signing chimps with a nonsigning community, high-stress reintroduction techniques that drove the dominant male, Bobo, over the edge. He started banging his fists, beating his chest, making sounds he never made before, in a show of dominance. The crew loved it, kept the pressure of reintroduction going. Three days into the experiment and Bobo snapped, made a rush at Phoebe, snatched her baby, and beat it to death, dragged the body around for days before he abandoned it."

Adi lowered her head, and as Simms turned the key to the enclosure, she said, "You mind if I go alone?" though she took Horowitz's hand in hers.

Away from the general simian population, down a corridor of institutional beige tiling, in a gray cement enclosure, Phoebe was with three other chimpanzees on a rock plateau, the chimps grooming one another with simian attentiveness, the dexterity of their fingers working the bristled hair, the lips curling to reveal either anxiety or happiness. It was hard to tell.

Phoebe looked hideously old. Her slack mammary glands came to jelly bean–size black nipples. The hairless features of her face and hands and ass had turned a withered brown.

Horowitz said nothing, simply watched.

Adi leaned against the glass. She said, without turning, "My mother grew up in a time when everybody was confronting the dissolution of the nuclear family, the struggle between the sexes for autonomy. The question was, what did you do with unwanted children, or children you don't want to care for? I guess that was the subconscious moral crisis of my mother's life. She argued against inherent maternal instinct. She'd had three abortions before she had me. She had advocated Freud's drive reduction theory of attachment, arguing that love had its origin simply in an attachment to anyone who could satisfy the need for nourishment. It seemed to validate day care, or an arbitrary assigning of love based on who most served the child's need.

"Then she got pregnant again and couldn't go through another abortion. She had a come-to-Jesus revelation, a sort of fortuitous moment where she ended up validating her pregnancy with her interest in research. Sign language research with primates was just starting. My mother had taken it as an elective. She always had a knack for getting in on things at the right time. So she wrote a grant proposal to study and correlate the developmental milestones between chimpanzees and humans, heady populist stuff that administrators and magazines ate up. Phoebe was taken from her mother at birth and came to live with us a month after I was born. There are pictures of us in the same crib, video of our mutual feedings, my mother and father holding us in matching outfits."

Adi turned around. "Say it, Allen, sham science, animal behaviorist crap."

Horowitz's beard gleamed in tiny droplets. "I think you are too hard on everybody. You have to consider the context of the time, of what was trying to be achieved."

"Which was?"

"I don't know, exactly. Let's leave that to historians. What I do know is maybe social anthropology should out itself for what it is, liberal sexual politics, and not masquerade as science. I think that is a fundamental point all of us on the other side of science need to agree on. Let's distinguish ourselves as something other than science. Who was it that said, 'Never doubt that a small group of thoughtful, committed citizens can change the world,' Margaret Mead, right? If that doesn't smack of political rhetoric, then I don't know what does."

Adi stared at Horowitz. "You've read everything, haven't you."

"Everything except *Popular Mechanics*."

Adi looked directly at Horowitz for the first time in days. "How long are we going to go on talking like this?"

Horowitz said softly, "As long as it takes."

Adi turned again toward the glass. "You know, what I remember most about Phoebe was when she began to enter estrus. She started throwing fits at the house, reverting back to her animal instinct, flinging feces when she got angry, jumping people when they came into the house. She was still wearing children's dresses, carrying a lunchbox, riding in the car, but she stank of pheromones. She started pulling down her bloomers at day care, running around with her dress over her head. Her ass turned scarlet."

Adi swallowed. "It ended the experiment. After that, my parents just went through the motions of research, fell off the doctorate track. They waded through the archival footage, tried to discern some developmental milestones between humans and chimpanzees, but the blur of ceaseless documentary footage was too much. Everything sort of died. My mother wanted another life. She cleaned herself up, left behind the hippie counterculture of grad life. She ended up with a high-powered pharmaceutical salesman. My father always said she was the real social experiment."

"And you?"

"Me?"

A moment of quiet passed.

Phoebe seemed to recognize Adi, moved across the floor, her body swinging through the cradle of her long arms, but all she did was cup her hand and drink from the pooling flow of water, the rounded bowl of her chin like a half coconut shell as she considered Adi.

Adi signed.

Phoebe's gums showed in a moment of perplexed contemplation. She scratched the underside of her chin, then went toward the glass and touched it.

Adi did likewise, both staring across the distance of so many years.

Phoebe took her hand off the glass and signed with the withered mocha of her liver-spotted, darkened fingers. Her small recessed eyes had a far-off look as she did so, and Adi cried as she formed the letters in her head.

Horowitz said quietly, "What's she saying?"

Without turning around, Adi whispered, " 'Help!' "

FORTY-NINE

RUTH WITTER LIVED at a retirement home close to her birthplace outside Boscobel, Wisconsin, home to the Gideon Bible. The Gideon story was printed on the back of a menu at the town's diner, how on September 14, 1898, two traveling salesmen, when asked to share a room in a crowded hotel hosting a lumbermen's convention, discovering they were both devout Christians, prayed and read the Bible together before settling down for the night. The name Gideon, chosen from the Old Testament book of Judges, referred to a man who was willing to do whatever God asked of him.

Ryder felt he was such a man. He had not slept in two days, so to him it was beyond coincidence, a sign, something prophetic.

From time to time, he stared into his cup the way soothsayers of old read tea leaves, his face reflected in the rimmed dark circle. He felt he was being led deep into the heart of a mystery set against his own travails.

Horowitz's enigmatic call mimicking Tori had unnerved and set off something suicidal in him, reminding him that for years a prejudicial body of psychological evidence had been gathered against him. A file held the transcripts of his voluntary interviews from years ago, when Tori disappeared, his psychological analysis and submission to psychotherapy. Horowitz had accessed the file.

The cold facts were that everybody believed he had murdered his wife. It was something Ryder had sublimated, just as he had ignored the accusing and then cautious stares of colleagues, so that he could carry on. If there was one thing he knew deeply, it was the clawing, soul-killing indeterminacy of being the survivor of the missing, a feeling that had come to define his life and work.

In the half shadows of a narrow corridor leading to the toilets, Ryder called home again. There was no answer, had not been all night as he had called from various rest areas. No doubt Gail was at her mother's, the long-standing sanctuary against their up-and-down marital relationship.

There had been times over the years when Ryder had wished Taylor had never been born, not because he hated her, but because her presence had been a flashpoint for the disaffection he had always felt toward Gail. He had entered into the marriage to reclaim a sense of normalcy and had never taken to his boys; instead, he had thrown himself into his work before they arrived. They were Gail's boys, her *real* children. He would never openly admit this, but at the cusp of postadolescence, Taylor was less his responsibility, a soon-to-be woman of the world.

Relationships naturally deteriorated, replaced by new commitments, new loves.

Ryder yawned so that his eyes watered. He felt a coldness, or deadness, in his genitals, the first stages of his personal deterioration. An operation, or euphemistically a *procedure*, loomed, the prostate time bomb. He remembered his last checkup, kneeling doggie style on a table, the smell of lubricant in the air, as he had felt an index finger up his ass, worming around his insides, a premonition of how he might die. Prostate cancer ran in his family.

Ryder called Gail's mother's house, wanting a truce.

The phone went to the answering machine, and just standing there, Ryder recalled a passage he had heard at church during another uproarious time with Gail, when he had been involved in the cold case of a missing child. It was Matthew 4:19, the Lord saying to his future disciples, then despairing fishermen in the Sea of Galilee, "Follow me, and I will make you fishers of men."

What had always struck Ryder about the passage had been the implicit entreaty by the Lord for these disciples to abandon their families.

One could serve but one master.

Ryder sat again and took a black coffee refill, felt jittery with expectation and exhaustion. He had traveled so far north, against Ken Orton's direct instructions, following what he knew was a tenuous lead that Trent Bauer could potentially be a serial killer.

Ostensibly he had disappeared. In his heart, Ryder knew this case was his last stand.

The retirement home didn't accept visitors until after 10:00 a.m. It was just after 9:00 a.m., though the town, so far off the beaten track, had barely roused. Across the street at a hardware store, a guy in a fifties-style apron salted his sidewalk like someone feeding chickens.

Ryder watched and waited, though in the end he headed up the street toward the hotel where the two traveling salesmen who had founded the Gideons had knelt and prayed, the room on the National Register of Historic Places, or so it had said on the menu.

At the apex of the street, a rising morning sun was skewered on the bayonet of a young Union soldier atop a war memorial, the young soldier cast in bronze, looking south. In a sort of dream state, Ryder walked the perimeter of the marbled monument and, for all his so-called gift, did not intuit the deep significance the monument held in the heart of the woman he was here to see, Ruth Witter. Ryder did not know that one of her ancestors' names was engraved on the Revolutionary War plaque or that her beloved younger brother, Frank, had his name added to the fallen during a Memorial Day ceremony on a splendid day of sunshine in 1941.

All this was lost to him, this history; so, too, the fact that in that same fated year of 1941, prior to Ruth Witter learning her brother had been blown to pieces, she had come into her own, at the unlikely age of thirty-one, plucked from the obscurity of rural life to work at a munitions factory in Sauk Prairie, Wisconsin. For a time, she had earned her own paycheck, gone to city dances, had fake seams drawn up the backs of her legs with eyebrow pencil, all this before the news of her brother's death reached her, before she recoiled from the horror of war, before she fell in love with a devout, religious conscientious objector, Enoch Witter, a man a decade her junior, before she retreated with him into a chaste relationship, abiding by his avowed wishes never to bring another human being into this world, all this before Ruth Witter would grow old and plead with her husband, before he acquiesced to adopting a child.

How Ryder actually got to the nursing home, he didn't remember. He just found himself following a nurse along a polished corridor that gleamed with a shyness of half-open doors, the solitary figures of the infirm in bed. An eye-watering overlay of institutional pine disinfectant served as a sort of smelling salts that brought Ryder around.

Ruth Witter was in the solarium. Someone had gone to fetch her, or so said the nurse, a stout woman in a starched uniform and white shoes, as she walked along the corridor, stealing glances at Ryder. "She's one of those women I daresay knows how to make up her mind and keep it made up."

The statement was primed with a question, though Ryder didn't take the bait.

Evidently, everyone on staff knew Ruth Witter's story; the burning question was, why had someone come this far north to see her after all these years?

In the small confines of her room, a nightstand held a constellation of pictures that had constituted Ruth Witter's world.

Ryder avoided saying much to the nurse, who lingered in the room. He picked up a vintage oval-shaped picture of Ruth in her younger years. She had a wide nose that made her eyes seem too far apart. She had not been particularly attractive. That fact struck Ryder, the lack of the nostalgic sense of lost youth so often experienced when staring at old photos. In the photo, she wore a drab polka-dot dress cut from the same pattern as the background curtains, posing stiffly beside a white lattice tablecloth with a centerpiece of wooden painted fruit in the parlor. The smallness of her waist was apparent, though a Puritan aesthetic prevailed. More noticeable were her ruined hands, the unnaturally swollen knuckles. She was twenty-two in the photograph, the date scrawled in a blotted fountain pen ink blue, yet she looked purposely older in the way back then when movie stars were older, when maturity and security meant everything.

Ruth Witter appeared at the door to her room.

Ryder turned, faced an older, garish version of her earlier self gone heavy and flaccid, the girth of her legs and barrel breasts showing in the powder blue polyester pantsuit she wore. Her eyebrows had been penciled on clownlike. She was not the weak, church-fearing woman he had expected. There was something hard about her.

The nurse spoke in the loud way people spoke to the aged as Ruth sat in a chair. "This *nice* man has come to visit you, Ruth."

Ruth said nothing, though Ryder saw the immediate reluctance in her look. He said, "I'm a friend of Enoch's cousin Irving. He sends his best wishes."

"Irving, who bought our farm? He owes us money on that farm. Did you bring it?"

This time Ryder didn't answer.

The nurse waited until Ryder met her look, and she reluctantly took the hint.

Ryder watched her leave, turned toward the dresser again, set down the picture, though he didn't turn immediately. This was his sole chance. He said directly, "Look, I understand how hard this is. Nobody wants to relive old memories, but I need your help."

Again Ryder was met with silence.

"I'm here investigating the murder of a teenage girl. We think there might be a connection with Elizabeth's *disappearance*."

Ryder stopped and waited to see if Ruth's expression changed. It didn't. He proceeded slowly. "We're trying to establish if there's someone still out there . . . if this could happen *again*. That's why it's so important that you talk to me."

Ruth turned and stared out across a moraine of snow-covered fields. She shook her head and said quietly, "I can't help you."

The clipped coldness of her resistance was something Ryder hadn't anticipated. He put the question in a roundabout way. "Are you telling me the prevailing opinion of what happened *did* happen?"

Ruth didn't respond.

The streaming morning sunlight was like a presence in the room. It was getting warm in a hothouse effect. Ryder sweated under his coat. The charge of caffeine had dissipated, leaving him with a low-level exhaustion. He took up the photograph of Amber Jewel and held it before Ruth Witter.

"I'm not here after Enoch, or you. I just need you to help me out." He pointed to the picture of Amber. "This is one of the victims."

Ruth's breathing got slightly faster. She said, "You've come to the wrong place."

"What does that mean, 'the wrong place'? Are you telling me Enoch killed Elizabeth? You think you can reconcile in the hereafter, is that it, Ruth?"

Ruth swallowed, her hands becoming fists in her lap. A warbled announcement over the PA system announced the commencement of physical therapy at 11:00 a.m. It was 10:50, the sweeping black hand of an institutional clock turning in a fluid, ceaseless motion above Ruth Witter's door. Ruth said, "I have to go to therapy." She pressed a button, and an intercom on the wall sounded with the voice of a nurse.

Ryder turned again to the small grotto of images on the desk. Set behind the other shots was a faded Polaroid of Enoch standing proudly with Elizabeth, Enoch in overalls, Elizabeth in a marching band uniform with white-tasseled majorette boots, both standing by a table with a hand-painted sign that read, "Maple Oak Junior High Band Fund-Raiser!" The photograph had been taken at the entrance to the local mall. *Jaws* was playing at the theater. It was the year before Elizabeth Witter's murder.

Ryder lingered on the shot. This was his last chance. He said softly as he turned, "What instrument did she play?"

It was a single question that brooked the sadness of so many years, the sudden gloss in Ruth Witter's eyes betraying a secret she had carried with her for over a decade, though she didn't answer the question directly.

Her eyes met Ryder's. When she spoke, her voice had a distant quality. "She raised every penny for that uniform herself, baked her own cookies and Rice Krispies Treats. It was Enoch that drove her to the mall for three straight weekends, stood by her side. It was against your own peril if you didn't buy something from her. Enoch had a way of looking at people." Her breath came heavy through her nose.

"I always think of Elizabeth out there, grown up with her *own* family. She has four beautiful children, three girls and a boy. She loved playing grown-up, played with dolls for years, could play for hours alone."

The nurse who had taken him to the room showed at the door, but Ryder narrowed his eyes and she subtly backed away.

Ruth was talking again in a flood of memories, more to herself than to Ryder, simply talking aloud.

"Enoch built her a big dollhouse the second Christmas she came to us. She brought out optimism in him he had fought against all his life. I had never seen that side of him, that kindness of heart. You think you know somebody all your life, and you find out you didn't really know them. It was like that soon after she came home to live with us. She was eight that year."

A tear ran in a rivulet down the side of her face. She wiped it with the back of her hand.

Ryder said nothing, receded into the background. He let her talk, saw the gleam of pale sunlight in her eyes.

"She took so to Enoch, made him sit down to tea parties. She used to make him cut up pieces of paper with a scissors and help her hang snowflake doilies in the attic. He was a sight to see, sitting on a stool with dolls and bears, Elizabeth serving him imaginary tea from a pink tea set. Enoch was never one to sit idle, but he played along, called her 'Miss Elizabeth,' which always made Elizabeth beam with pride. She always wanted to be called by her full name, Elizabeth."

Morning light fell in a slant across the room. Ruth nodded to herself, but her voice changed and she trailed off with ominous portent as she said, "They were a pair for such a *long* time, but the thing is, you don't ever know what you got when it's not your own. You just don't know."

Ryder said, by way of leading her, "I read about the Sadie Hawkins dance."

Ruth hesitated, but she had begun, so she kept talking, years of emotion locked away. She looked at Ryder. "Enoch, he was protective in a way people didn't much understand. We were of a different, older generation, where people did things like drag their kids home. It was called being a parent, saving a person from themselves until they knew better."

"And locking her in the tornado bunker?"

"The older you get, the more scared you become, the more you know what is out there. Times had changed so. Elizabeth got fed and clothed and kept decent. All she was ever asked to do was reflect on life, and on the gifts she was given. The world had got so you couldn't hear yourself think, radio and TV on all the time, Saturday morning TV making little girls look like they were a decade older than they were, all done up in makeup."

Ruth stopped. "Do you have children?"

Ryder answered, "A girl."

"Maybe you can understand somewhat what we went through. Elizabeth also had to fight extra hard inside because of how she had come into the world. She was born in sin. All we did was guard her against that inclination, guard her against herself. Enoch prayed with her the nights she was out in the bunker, both of us did. She *was* loved. It wasn't anything other than us trying to keep her safe, trying to steer her on the right path."

Ryder's felt his shirt stick to his back under his heavy coat, sensing the inevitable turn in the story, Ruth Witter moving toward the long-standing truth of what everybody had known from the day they had gone out to the Witter farm, that Enoch Witter had killed his daughter. Regretfully, against his own conscience, he felt sorrier for himself than for the sixteen-year-old victim Elizabeth Witter as he said quietly, "Where is Elizabeth?"

Ruth bowed her head, and Ryder asked the question again, but Ruth Witter didn't answer. She had guarded this secret for a decade. She would die with it. Looking up, she said, "I want you to leave now!"

FIFTY

ADI'S FATHER LIVED in an older part of campus, in a low-rise, utilitarian, gray cinder block, motel-like complex characteristic of functional fifties architecture now given over to subsidized housing. It had the look of a fallout shelter, a reinforced bunker against a fatalism that the end of the world was at hand.

It pained Adi that this was what had become of her father, the contrast to her mother's life all the more dramatic.

Horowitz said nothing, just set his hand on her shoulder.

Adi's father lived on the second floor, accessed by a metal staircase that was decidedly unsafe and seemed to give as they climbed it. The struts had come loose from the crumbling wall. The hallway carpet was industrial orange, fireproof, and smelled of chemicals.

A hunched old lady, a neighbor, hiding behind a linked chain lock, peered through the gap and said, after Adi had knocked repeatedly on the door, "You can stop knocking. They're gone."

The "they" as much as the word "gone" struck Adi.

"I'm looking for Richard Wiltshire. I'm his daughter. Do you know when he's coming back?"

"He's not."

"Not what?"

"Not coming back. They moved last week to Reno."

"Reno?"

The woman nodded. "They were talking about it a long time, then Rae got a settlement from a spill she had last year, broke her wrist on city property. I didn't think they would go, but money has a way of giving you a freedom you don't necessarily know you have in you."

Adi stood in the cool pull of the dark hallway. "Do you know where in Reno?"

The old woman took off the latch. Her apartment smelled of hot garbage, the blinds drawn in a warren of semidarkness. There was a half-eaten can of wet cat food on the table, an undeniable reality of what lay on the other side of success.

It sent a shudder through Adi.

It was not two o'clock, yet the neon lights of the motel sign blinked to a human pulse, or so Adi felt, as another midafternoon of daytime soaps filled the gray vacuum behind the drawn curtains of her motel room. It was snowing again.

Horowitz showered for a long time in a bank of steam that made the room damp.

Wearing an oversize T-shirt and panties, her hair brushed out sleek, Adi sat akimbo on the queen-size bed, wearing black-rimmed glasses, her contacts soaking in solution, as she spoke to an answering machine at her father's apartment in Reno.

She said, "I'm glad you found somebody. You deserved better. I don't know if you've heard things on the news, but I'm okay. I want to see you soon." She ended by saying, "I love you for everything you did for me. I want you to know that."

Adi hung up before she felt herself wanting to cry.

Horowitz came out in his towel, said nothing, as though he had not overheard anything, and went about his own business. He let the towel around his waist fall to the ground with the familiarity of a couple long past lust, stood naked, and stepped into his underwear. The light from the bathroom caught him in an unflattering way.

Adi stared at him without registering any real emotion, save that Horowitz had got what he had wanted. He was here with her, this pursuer of love with his pigeon chest and flat ass. She watched as he rummaged through his case for a pair of socks.

When he turned and saw her looking, all he did was smile faintly and say, "You look more dignified somehow." He looked at her, then clicked his fingers. "The glasses, that's it. You look like a cross between that Greek singer Nana Mouskouri and Gloria Steinem. It's a good look for you."

Later that evening, after pizza and Coke in the motel room, after an evening of what Horowitz called "slumming it," as Adi was beginning to drift off to sleep on her bed, a news flash cut in on the regular broadcast, breaking live to Pendleton's house to a caravan of reporters and on to the disheveled property of Sandi Kellogg, who had gone public with Gary's alibi.

Sandi Kellogg spoke live at her house, crying, struggling to tell reporters she had given police a tape of her and Gary's activities around the time the murder had taken place.

By the time Adi sat up, Horowitz had upped the volume with the remote.

A lead investigator appeared and confirmed that Gary Scholl was no longer a suspect in the Blaine murder. Despite a barrage of questions, the investigator refused to give further details, other than to say new leads were being pursued.

A reporter shouted, "It's been leaked that investigators have failed to establish the print-run date for the original *Scream* . . . but that a long-standing employee who worked for Jacobs and Sons has since come forward and remembers Pendleton's original novel being printed on Valentine's Day 1977, months before the victim's body was discovered. . . ."

The lead investigator said in a clipped voice, "As a matter of course, we don't respond to speculation or rumor. The investigation is ongoing."

A summary recap by a local news anchor ended, the telecast breaking to a commercial for carpeting with free padding and installation that somehow warranted a festoon of balloons and confetti and an American flag.

Horowitz hit the mute button and set down the remote.

Adi went toward the window and whispered, "It makes sense now. . . ."

"What?"

"Why Ryder wanted Robert's notes. He was trying to establish Robert had written about the disposal of Amber's body before she was discovered."

In the weak light, Horowitz looked at the subtleness of Adi's long bare legs showing just below her panties in the oversize T-shirt, struck by that image, feeling everything he had achieved with her on the verge of dissipating if he betrayed what he felt inside, but he said it anyway. "I don't get it. The Williams note . . . the stuff out at the hospital on the mirror . . . what was it all for?"

"I *didn't* do it!"

Horowitz's voice flared despite himself. "You were teaching the *goddamn* Williams course, Adi! Who the hell else was out there at the hospital writing that stuff on the mirror?"

He waited. "I've done everything for you, Adi. I know you tried to shift the blame to me for sending the tape. I know you got it posted from New York."

"How?"

"I've never given it enough thought. . . . I've made allowances for you, Adi."

Adi turned. "Why would I do something like that, ruin everything for myself? You sent the tape."

"Did I? Here are the facts, Adi. You said the box of books in the basement was unopened, that's what you told me. . . . I remember you telling me that.

Boxes come with invoices . . . that's just a standard operating procedure."

Adi flinched.

Horowitz looked at her. "You can't deny it. You found and destroyed the invoice. Why?"

Adi turned, her eyes squinting, adjusting to the gray of the room. On the small dresser table, the numerals on the clock glowed. She stepped toward the center of the room.

Horowitz moved toward the door. "Jesus Christ! Stop! Do you think I give a shit about Bob or any of this really now? We're alone in a motel in Ohio with nothing ahead of us. I'm making the sacrifice here, being with you. It's not the other way around. I want you to acknowledge that, give in a little. . . ."

"Give in . . . how?"

Adi's hair was flat against her head, damp. She could see herself standing in the bedside dresser mirror. She said in a simple way, more a statement of fact than anything else, "You don't know anything about me, who I really am." She touched her hand to her chest, her body trembling slightly. "I want to get my own room. I don't want to hold you back, Allen, do anything to your reputation."

Horowitz stood staring at her, tried to diffuse the sudden ultimatum. "Look, let's drop this. I'm sorry."

In the ensuing silence, with snow falling thick against the neon wink of lights racing around the motel sign, Adi said quietly, "I just want to stop running. I want to go back and get what's mine from Robert's house and begin again somewhere else."

FIFTY-ONE

RYDER STOOD FOR a time in the cool shadow of the back hallway of the assisted living facility, listening to the filtering clinking sound of dishes being washed, the drift of a radio station coming from a kitchen. He was shaking his head with a sense of denial, kept thinking back to what Irving had said with such forthrightness, that Enoch hadn't killed Elizabeth.

It didn't sit right, a conscientious objector raping and murdering his own daughter.

Ryder put his hands to his face, felt the tiredness and sense of exhaustion overtake him, felt that everything was just beyond his comprehension. He yawned, his eyes watering. He had to get away. This wasn't his investigation! He felt the words forming on his lips, telling himself that over and over again. How had he drifted so far in the space of this investigation, to find himself so far north, alone, with a desperate sense that this was the end for him?

What he had to do was call Ken. Nobody had to know exactly where he was. He nodded as he whispered the words. He could say he was stuck at a motel because of the snow, leave it that simple.

Ken was discreet. All he needed was to call, to check in, pretend everything was okay. Ken would cover for him. It could as yet be handled. If he started driving now, he could be home in seven, eight hours.

This time tomorrow, it would be as if he had never come.

He just had one call to make, to clear up at least the mystery of what Enoch Witter had done.

The provisional analysis of Enoch's semen was still under way, a centrifugal procedure that a technician started to explain to Ryder over the phone.

Ryder cut off the technician. "How much longer will it take?"

"A while."

Ryder was hanging up when the technician said, "Hang on, my boss wants to talk to you."

Disconcertingly, the voice belonged to a woman. Ryder had expected a man.

"I hear you were checking on the status of the sample analysis you submitted."

Ryder waited.

"There was a sort of administrative screwup with the file. Don't worry, the sample is intact, it isn't that! It's an administrative error. Inadvertently, the subject's name and medical records were sent along with the sample. Technically, for confidentiality reasons, we should send the material back and have it processed by another lab. We can do that, though in this instance maybe I can save you some time."

"How?"

"The medical records indicate the suspect had a radical prostate removal in 1972. After radical prostatectomy, semen ejaculation is retrograde, meaning semen is discharged into the bladder instead of coming through the penis. In layman's terms, the condition is a 'dry orgasm.'"

Ryder leaned against the wall, his fingers to the bridge of his nose. "What are you saying?"

"That your subject couldn't have produced the semen sample recovered from the underwear."

Ruth and several other residents were in a hothouse gazebo with fogged windows, all staring at the TV, which was tuned to a cartoon of the sight-impaired, senile octogenarian Mr. Magoo blithely driving his jalopy across a series of swinging girder beams on a skyscraper under construction. The volume was turned low, so all one heard was the backdrop of a laugh track.

The midmorning quiet in the room had settled into a somnambulant lethargy long associated with the deplorable overmedication of the elderly. These were, after all, somebody's mothers and fathers. A smell of menthol rub filled the air. A tray of Dixie cups with pills had been dispensed, along with cubed lime Jell-O.

Ruth looked up at Ryder. Something had changed in her face. He helped her out of her chair.

In the hallway, Ryder saw a grainy closed-circuit image of them walking slowly down the corridor, Ruth Witter using her cane. Another camera picked them up at a turn into another corridor, this one with a sloping ramp leading into a prefab annex of rooms where the carpeted floor gave back a bounce, as though gravity had been altered slightly.

When they got to the room, Ruth said enigmatically, "Am I under arrest?"

Ryder set his hand on her shoulder. "I want you to sit."

Ruth seemed at odds as to what to do, but she sat eventually. Her demeanor had changed, as if she knew Ryder had learned something.

Ryder began slowly. "I want to go over things again, about what happened to Elizabeth. I just got off the phone with some people. We know Elizabeth had either consensual intercourse or was raped."

Ruth Witter's hand closed over the crook of her walking stick.

"I'm telling you this because Elizabeth's underwear was kept all these years in the hopes that advances in science might answer where the semen came from. I got the results."

Ruth said her husband's name, whispered, "My God," looked off toward the moraine of snowy hills outside her window. Her voice had a far-off, pleading quality. "Please, I don't want people saying things about Elizabeth after all these years. I *don't*! Why do people have to know about *our* business? She's dead. We can't bring her back. It's set before the Lord to judge them."

The "them" struck Ryder. He was about to correct her, then didn't, realizing Ruth Witter was under the impression that the semen sample had come back a match for Enoch.

Ruth kept staring toward the hills, her body trembling, and Ryder tried to steer her again, trying to align that maybe something terrible had gone on out at the farm alongside what had eventually happened to Elizabeth.

Ryder kept his focus on her murder. "The day Elizabeth disappeared . . . tell me about it."

Ruth lowered her head, her eyes lost in the loose skin of her hooded eyelids. "We were out in the fields when we saw the bus stop up on the road. That's how we knew Elizabeth got off. The bus only stopped for her. It was one of the last stops. Elizabeth always went on into the house, got something to eat, and came out to us if we weren't there. It was harvest-time. We needed help out in the fields. That was the arrangement, how she got her allowance, helping us on the farm. She had her chores. I had made something for her that day. A half hour passed after the bus had stopped. Enoch was waiting. He regretted what had happened at the Sadie Hawkins dance."

Ruth looked at Ryder. "Enoch had got to a point, he said, 'where he could do nothing but hope.' We were at that stage with her. 'We were old parents,' is how Enoch explained it to Elizabeth. He said he was going to have to 'fight his own inclinations.' Enoch so wanted to make things up with her, so much that, in a way, I think he blamed me for not having children, for not insisting years before. We had come to a crossroads. He had turned toward Elizabeth, and she toward him."

Ruth's voice wavered. "So we gave her time and distance. I've lived for years wondering, what if I had just gone and got her sooner, if Enoch hadn't given in to her, given her that measure of freedom? An hour passed, and we worked, Enoch up on the tractor, looking to the house. It was getting so there wasn't going to be much daylight left. I saw the look in Enoch's eyes. He watched me crossing toward home. The last thing he said was, 'Just don't upset her,' said it like *I* was the division in the family, not her. . . .

"When I got to the house, I knew something was wrong. I knew she was home, or *had* been home. The screen door was knocking against the frame, something Enoch had warned her against. Elizabeth always had the radio turned up loud when we weren't in the house, but it was off. I called out to her. There was no response. The food hadn't been eaten on the table. I checked her room. She wasn't there."

Ruth stopped, leaned forward on her walking stick, so the knob of her knuckles showed.

"I say it against myself, that I hoped she had run off. She had come between us, between me and Enoch. I thought, Girls run away every day. Let it be her that runs away. That was the last feeling I remember, just before I saw her feet suspended in midair, when I got halfway up the stairs to the attic."

Ruth's whole body was rigid. "Time . . . it just stopped. I must have screamed for a long time, because all of a sudden Enoch was beside me. He set me in the kitchen. Then he went up to her. It had grown so dark outside, the house freezing cold."

Ruth shivered with the memory.

"I heard Enoch moving about up above, heard him vomiting into the toilet. That's when I knew it was all real, that it wasn't something I dreamed up. Enoch stayed upstairs a long time. I didn't dare go up. I knew Elizabeth was dead. I just kept seeing her legs in my mind. Enoch had gotten her new shoes after what happened at the Sadie Hawkins dance.

"When he came down, he didn't come near me. We were set against each other from that moment onward. Enoch didn't tell me anything. He wasn't crying or anything, but he had this presence like I'd never felt before, a coldness that never left. I guess it was what they call shock. He went back up and wrapped her in a sheet and came down with her in his arms. I tried to go to her, but he stopped me."

Ruth put her hand to her mouth. The garish lipstick had smeared.

"He left with her on his tractor. I just watched the light against the darkness. He went toward his cousin Irving's. He was gone awhile, came home before seven o'clock, went up to the attic, and worked for a time. Then he came down and said, 'She never came home from school. We were waiting on her, but she never came out to the field,' and that was all that was said between us. I knew he blamed me somehow for her committing suicide. Then he called the police. It all happened so quickly, the interviews, the accusations, the interrogation, the discovery of Elizabeth's underwear hidden behind a chest of drawers. Three days later, Enoch hanged himself."

Ruth stopped and traded silence for silence for a time before she said quietly, "I'm sorry. I told you, you came to the wrong place."

Ryder experienced a sort of vertigo as he tried to align what he knew as fact.

Somebody had raped Elizabeth Witter, and it hadn't been Enoch Witter. He clung to that incontrovertible fact. "Did you see anything, a car, a white car that afternoon? Somebody had to meet her! Think! Whatever happened to her, happened between her getting off the bus and walking the half mile to the house."

Ruth hesitated. "What do you mean, what happened to her? I told you!"

Ryder shook his head. "The semen analysis didn't come back a match for Enoch. Someone else had intercourse with Elizabeth."

It was a revelation that struck with such force that Ruth Witter just shut down, closed her eyes and said nothing for a long time, her head lowered, before she finally spoke again.

Her voice had somehow coalesced with a sense of anger. "He didn't speak to me ever after he found her . . . *nothing*, left me with nothing to hope for . . . with the darkest sin any human has ever had to bear."

Somehow, the fact that Elizabeth had been raped by someone else hadn't sunk in with her; instead, it was her own sense of what had been done to her for over a decade, a life truncated and ruined. Ruth spoke again. "*I* was never the religious one. *He* took my life away from me is what he did, left me behind. I could never say what I thought happened between them. What he wanted was for me to follow him over to the other side."

Ruth leaned forward. "That's what he wanted. I know it. He was never right in the head, always had a view of the hereafter, even when I met him. He had opinions all to himself, had his head stuck in a Bible."

Ruth looked up so the wattle of her throat quivered. "All my life with him I've lived in the shadow of knowing I meant nothing to him. He was always testing me. I couldn't commit that final act. It wasn't in me to kill myself. . . ."

It was as Ryder went to pick up the picture of Amber Jewel he had inadvertently left behind during the first interview that Ruth seemed finally to understand that she had been wrong about her husband all these years. A stranger had raped her daughter.

She said quietly, "I'm sorry I can't help you," then put out her hand and said, "Can I see it?"

The photograph was a portrait taken of Amber Jewel, done in a stylized way, with a doubling of the image in the upper-right-hand corner of the photograph.

Ruth's eyes watered. She sniffled and cleared her throat as she touched the image. "Elizabeth, she had photographs like that taken earlier in the fall. We got a whole set made up. She insisted on it, got me to pay, behind Enoch's back. He didn't believe in the vanity of photographs. It was something Elizabeth was so proud of. The photographer said she had 'a face that could sell magazines.' Girls fall for that kind of stuff. Elizabeth carried the photographs everywhere with her. She was beautiful. You hear people always say that about their own, how beautiful they are, but she was. She was saving up to have more pictures taken."

Ruth pointed toward her dresser drawer. "I got the pictures there. It's how she looked when she disappeared. I want you to see what she looked like, what was lost."

Ruth leaned forward on her walking stick, the pearly knuckles showing.

Ryder opened a dresser drawer and removed a page of proof images from under a pile of underwear and slips.

Ruth struggled against the memory.

"All I remember is police going through her school bag and coming across them, and it was like a ghost image, that double image like she had already taken leave of her body." Looking up at Ryder, Ruth shuddered and said quietly, "Do you believe in ghosts, Detective?"

But Ryder didn't answer. He was staring at the proofs.

FIFTY-TWO

A S HOROWITZ PASSED the mile exit signpost along the highway for Bannockburn, the name Pendleton surfaced again, the static of the local college station suddenly clearing. Adi was asleep, her mouth slightly ajar, leaning against the passenger-side window.

Horowitz turned up the volume slightly.

The college station was tied in to an NPR affiliate out of Chicago. It was 3:50 in the afternoon, but an hour later farther east, in New York, where after their long, extended weekly luncheon, the National Book Award committee had released a statement regarding their unanimous decision to keep *Scream* on its short list.

The recorded sound bite played against a backdrop of cheers and boos. At the end of the sound bite, the NPR host read a statement released by Horowitz's agent on behalf of Horowitz, regarding Horowitz's reaction to the committee's decision, as, quote, "a brave, unprecedented, spirited, and independent stance against the vagaries of popular sentiment, against the unwashed masses. This is a victory for art."

Horowitz felt it strange to hear himself quoted, how a grandiose sentiment he had formulated while unshaven and alone outside a diner two days ago had coalesced into a trenchant meaningful statement, how it had wound up on NPR.

Adi seemingly hadn't been asleep. She opened her eyes and said, "Did you really say that?"

"It's on the radio, so I must have."

Adi sat up, drew her knees to her breasts, and yawned so that her jaw made a snapping sound. "When?"

"Back in Ohio, at the motel, while you were asleep, I went out and called my agent. He had told me some official statement was forthcoming from the committee."

"How come you didn't tell me they were going to vote to keep the book on the short list?"

"I didn't know how it was going to go. I thought they *wouldn't* a few days ago. The other prepared statement went something like 'Today's vote is an unprecedented cowardly retreat, a caving in to the vagaries of popular sentiment, to the unwashed masses. This is a dark day for art.'"

Adi looked at the side profile of Horowitz's face, so he knew she was watching him. He said, "The worst thing to do in a situation like this is to say nothing, to appear like you've run away."

Adi said, "I thought this was all over."

"It is." Horowitz came to a rolling stop at the end of the ramp. "Look, there'll be an army of reporters on location up at the house over the Jewel revelation. We can't just go out there. We should give it a day for the news to settle before requesting we get your stuff out of the house."

Horowitz didn't wait for an answer, just turned onto the commercial strip of motels and eateries lined on either side with a dirty packed snow. Sensing the pall that had again set over Adi, he said, "Look, despite everything going on here, you know you should be proud. You found the book, saw the genius in it. This is something Bob talked about even back in grad school, wanting to win the National Book Award. Naïvely or not, he had no interest in making money. Novel writing was about something . . ."

Adi finished the thought. "Transcendent."

The host read a quote as a lead-in to a discussion surrounding the award committee's decision to keep Pendleton's book on its short list. "'You're a gentleman,' they used to say to him. 'You shouldn't have gone murdering people with a hatchet; that's no occupation for a gentleman.' First caller with author and title gets a copy of E. Robert Pendleton's *Scream*."

Horowitz said, "Dostoevsky! *Crime and Punishment*."

Adi looked at his profile and said softly, "I have to keep telling myself you are not what you seem, that you are hidden away inside, that deep down you are somebody different."

Horowitz kept driving slowly along the strip, a granular rock salt popping against the undercarriage of the car. There was ice in places the sun hadn't reached through the day, in the falling shadows of buildings and Dumpsters.

Already behind them, the sky in the east had given way to a setting darkness, near twilight, the waxy glow of headlights showing out along the highway, the sanguine aura of the commercial strip coming into its own.

The western skies out ahead of them had gone purple.

Horowitz had eased somewhat; the tacit compliment Adi had given him brought a new contentment for the time being. He leaned toward the windshield, looked out in the sky's vastness. "I think I'd like to live at no fixed address for a few years, maybe an RV would be nice, wake up at roadside areas, drifting from place to place. I think there's a virtue in that, in losing oneself for a time. I think there might be something out there for me."

The car passed Rite Aid.

Adi looked at a TV van in the lot, the glare of unnatural light as a reporter stood interviewing an employee in a blue smock. Undoubtedly, it had something to do with Kim Jewel being taken in for questioning, and all of a sudden, Adi felt the deep chill of having slept poorly.

She said in a searching way, "How come life feels so unreal, so meaningless? You know, somewhere along the way I think I lost something . . . lost the *reality* of reality, locked away with my books, all those years wasted, tearing things apart, dismantling things, debunking false power structures, sexual, economic, and otherwise, not out of some sense of nihilism, but believing that what one had to do was transcend the ordinary to arrive at the *profane*. There was something permanent and transcendent about the college . . . from its old ivy-covered buildings to its aging faculty."

Adi took a shallow breath, shivered again. "It existed outside of real life. It came to stand against the transitory nature and failure of everything I had lived through. But the thing is, now I don't know how to reconcile that life with this life out here. I have this superficial sense of self-consciousness. I see myself as nothing but a character passing by in a car. I see myself as *nothing*."

Horowitz slowed at an intersection. "I think you're talking like every inmate released on parole after a life sentence. You've got to ease back into society. Life on the outside is an acquired skill."

Adi went silent, turned, and looked back at the Rite Aid receding as Horowitz started driving again. "What I *want* is to feel sorry for Kim *here*." She touched her heart with her fist. "And I want to feel the absolute terror Amber felt. I think if I could *feel* that terror, it would be a kind of emotional breakthrough, get me past abstract metaphor. I want to come back to the *literal*. I want to feel at a visceral level the guts and the blood. I want the cheap terror of a B movie. I want to hear *that* sort of *scream*!"

Adi kept talking. "Jesus Christ, listen to me, I can't even put an emotional weight on what the hell I'm saying! It's just words. I can talk and talk, and it never changes."

Horowitz measured his words. "Maybe you're trying too hard. I don't think true life-altering changes happen at the conscious level. They happen somewhere deeper down. Give it time."

Adi shook her head fitfully. "I don't know if I believe people ever really change, or if we have the capacity to change. You know, ever since Simms told me about what Bobo did to Phoebe's baby, in my mind I keep seeing Bobo swinging Phoebe's baby, pounding on it with his fists. It's a rage like you see only in men who find themselves left behind the times. I see him ease and then go wild again, swinging the swath of black fur, bloodying it, trampling on it . . . hooting, defending! Defending, I don't know, the *primacy* of rage, the only life he knew, the efficacy of his hoots and grunts against the smug ASL signers."

Horowitz kept driving. "So you're siding with the Bobos of the world, with the *literalists*?"

Adi raised her voice again. "Don't! Don't make a joke of me, Allen, don't. Jesus Christ, I freely and openly admit I don't know what the hell I'm talking about anymore!"

"I'm not making fun of you. I think what you're pondering is the age-old question regarding intentionality and, at a grander level, meaning with a capital *M*! The Bobo episode reminds me of that theory regarding probability, that if you put enough chimps into a room together with enough typewriters, they'd eventually write Shakespeare, all of Shakespeare, but the question would remain: Would it be Shakespeare? Which begs another question: Who was Shakespeare, anyway, an ape with a quill pen? You see, I empathize with you and Bob, Adi, empathize with the circularity of such inane arguments that can consume and last a lifetime, and that can superficially seem to ask something profound. I can honestly believe academics have driven themselves to insanity and suicide over such matters. But I think your Bobo might have answered the dilemma."

"How?"

"Don't put the typewriters in with the apes!"

Two callers had missed the answer to the host's question as Horowitz pulled into the parking lot of a stylized fifties-era Big Boy beside the motel. He said, "Okay, let me get the room fixed up, and then we can eat. Just hang on."

Horowitz got out and booked the room, then came across the lot. "They got a honeymoon suite, if you can believe it. You know, one of the things that makes us great, as a nation, is our essential lack of irony."

Adi tried to smile but couldn't quite pull it off.

Horowitz was about to kill the engine when Adi said, "Don't! I want to wait for the answer."

"I told you the answer."

"Okay, I'm not ready yet. Let's just wait."

On the radio, a caller was addressing the historical precedence for the madness of genius, from van Gogh's self-mutilation to the ghoulish specter of Lord Byron, who purportedly drank bat's blood from a human skull when he wrote, to Swift's chilling satiric masterpiece "A Modest Proposal," detailing the economic merits and culinary possibilities for preparing and serving Irish babies.

The caller ended, "Tell me this guy didn't dream about eating Irish babies!"

Another caller raised a more ambiguous issue of art and artist, referring to the overt anti-Semitism of not only Eliot, but also Ezra Pound, the so-called father of modernism, asserting that Pound's inflammatory propagandizing during the war had contributed to the psychological climate and rationalization that led to the extermination of the Jews.

Horowitz said, "You know, I'm going to always think of this moment as a peculiarly existentialist Bob moment. Here we are in Middle America, sitting in the car outside Big Boy, listening to a discussion about Ezra Pound. I think this *is* the level Bob wanted everybody to talk at all the time. You know, at a deep level, I don't think Bob would be sorry for what he did, killing that girl. I honestly don't. After all, what's more interesting, the psychotic conviction of Abraham or the meekness of Isaac?"

FIFTY-THREE

FOUR HOURS DRIVING in blizzard conditions down through Wisconsin, Ryder outran the advancing front, arriving in the late end of the three o'clock hour into a world clear and studded with stars. He got out of the car at a rest area, gassed up, used the restroom, and got a coffee from a vending machine.

In the quiet, he stared at the stylized script initials in the lower-right-hand corner of Elizabeth Witter's photograph, the same scripted *HJW* embossed in gold lettering on Amber Jewel's photograph, his conviction waning that Wright had murdered either girl, the coincidence coming down to the fact that there were only so many photographers in the area.

What had he really fallen upon, the promiscuous secret of a victimized girl, an adopted child of troubled, religious zealots? Some kid at her high school had been having sex with her. She had a secret boyfriend, a natural coming of age, Enoch's and Ruth's fears realized. It had been why they had gone to the Sadie Hawkins dance, to catch her.

What the forensics lab was going to uncover in the DNA analysis was the remote and private history of a young girl and her boyfriend, a thought that sent a shudder through Ryder that something as intimate as that survived.

At a pay phone, Ryder called Ken Orton, got the answering machine, and said simply that he was having car trouble. It bought him a day, and as he started the car again and pulled onto the highway, he kept telling himself he would survive professionally, though he knew it was too late for his marriage, that it was irrevocably ruined. Gail had not picked up when he had called her.

The time had passed for reconciliation, or he wasn't willing to try, and he felt in the long silence of the drive something that had been settled between them a long time ago, an honesty and finality achieved now at a distance, something they could not otherwise have done face-to-face.

In the vastness between places, he looked out into the dark and felt it wasn't necessarily a bad thing, remembering the last physical intimacy of what had passed for lovemaking between them, passionlessly routine, after the twins' bath time, how he had been primed with four or five beers, furious, waiting, the lateness of the evening moving toward midnight, the *Tonight* show over, Gail folding laundry, setting out the brown bag lunches and the matching clothes for her boys, coming up on the soft pad of her feet with a chamomile tea and a *People* magazine, sitting alone in the halo of her vanity mirror, her face a green mask of face cream, paging through the lives of the stars.

It had gone that way for so long, Gail always waiting in her own tacit way for him to succumb to sleep, to leave her alone, and he doing so most nights, but not that time, his eyes slits, waiting for her to sink into the bed before he reached out and pulled her close so his front was against her back, as he lifted her nightshirt to the small of her back, and, without the deceit of kissing or talking, with his hand under the weight of her breast, feeling her heart beat fast, taken relief in the dark space of her insides, in the spreading warmth of his ejaculation as he groaned, as Gail waited and then simply pulled away in the end as she always did, like something unmoored from a dock, drifting away to her side of the bed.

There were, Ryder knew, crimes no court could legislate against: the passage to separation followed these long protracted rituals, the opposite of romance, if there was a name for that, and in the darkness of his descent, he dwelled on that past, simply because the future was unknowable.

In the end, Ryder did not go to a hotel as he turned off on the Bannockburn exit, but out to the hospital, to talk to the on-duty cop who had been there the night Pendleton had been brought in comatose, because at the back of everything, Ryder had not taken his mind off Wright.

Wright had gone into Pendleton's room unescorted the night Pendleton was brought in. Ryder had authorized his admittance after meeting Wright in the emergency room. It was a fact that had settled at a subconscious level somewhere out on the highway, that and the fact that Wright was taking Wiltshire's poetry class.

Standing outside Pendleton's room, Ryder stared through the small window in the door, staring at Pendleton's bed in relation to the toilet, to see how Adi Wiltshire, in a deep sleep and under the influence of her own drugs, could have remained asleep as Wright had gone into the room, removed her lipstick, and written the Williams question on the mirror.

Wearing a plum-colored Members Only jacket, black business work pants, and white shirt, Henry James Wright was a caricature of every midwest guy in strip mall retail trying to get by with a modicum of allotted dignity. Wright wasn't in a mall but in class at Bannockburn, in what had been Adi's Intro to Poetry, taught now by the Chair, who was reading aloud.

Wright was taking notes, his head down. He looked so much older and more earnest.

Ryder waited for the PA announcement requesting that Wright go to the English Department office, just to see the expression on Wright's face.

Wright looked up immediately at the mesh speaker above the blackboard, then to the door where Ryder was standing.

All Wright did was smile and step out into the hallway, rolling his eyes and saying with a feigned air of disgust, "Poetry first period in the morning. I think any poet worth his salt never got up before noon."

Ryder smiled likewise. "I see the Chair is teaching the course. He's not sticking to Wiltshire's stuff, is he?"

"Shit, you don't ever change the syllabus on a class, Jon, not at the price they charge for books at the bookstore. It's strictly a 'no refund' policy. No, all the Chair's doing is bringing a different critical approach to the same work."

Wright reached into the inner pocket of his jacket, took out a tin box of cigarettes, roll-your-owns, and lit one, his hand cupped to his mouth like someone playing the harmonica. He looked at Ryder. "You want one?"

Ryder shook his head. "So, you liking this college life?"

"Hey, I got no illusions as to what I am, but, you know, coming to things late in life can mean something more. What's that they say about youth, that it's wasted on the young? I don't think they *get* half of what's being taught in there. Right now we're onto the works of Sylvia Plath and Ted Hughes. You ever hear of them? They were like the Lucy and Desi of poetry, just not as funny. Same as all the greats, Plath offed herself, stuck her head in an oven, died in relative obscurity, deeply depressed, pretty much penniless. But the thing is, she ended up getting herself the Pulitzer, posthumously, twenty years after she stuck her head in the oven."

"You saying you got to be willing to die for art? Is that the message, Henry?"

Wright blew smoke out the corner of his mouth. "Hey, let's just say it sure as hell helps, Jon. It sure as hell helps."

"I guess that puts Pendleton ahead of the game, then, for this year's National Book Award. He's the only near dead guy on the list. He dies and he's a shoo-in, right?"

Wright's smile got wider. "Yeah, that's one way of looking at it! I like that." He pointed in the direction of the classroom. "The big push is on to rehabilitate Pendleton, to position his work. The Chair was in there today comparing Plath's despair with Pendleton's, you know, *the Chair*, who never went to a single Pendleton reading on campus! That's the new angle, though, the angst of the artist, the scream of the obscure. We just got done with Plath's 'Dark House.' I think it might speak to you, Jon, to something of what went on inside Pendleton's head. I memorized the first stanza.

This is a dark house, very big.
I made it myself,
Cell by cell from a quiet corner,
Chewing at the grey paper,
Oozing the glue drops,
Whistling, wiggling my ears,
Thinking of something else.

Ryder said flatly, "I can't say I fully get it. Let me just say, it's a long way from Stephen King. That's who you like?"

"King! Thing is, we move on. That's part of what a liberal education bestows on a soul, the ability to discriminate, to pass judgment. To be honest with you, I like a lot less things than I used to."

Ryder finally pressed. "Maybe. I guess what I'm driving at is, I don't know if that poem would fit on a *mirror* too well."

Wright's thin lips smiled. "You got a way about you."

"That's not an answer."

"Was there a question in there somewhere?"

"Okay, why did you write that stuff on the mirror out at the hospital?"

Wright shrugged. "I don't know exactly what we're talking about here, but I heard it said poetry is a way to a woman's heart. Does that work for you, at a general level?"

"You got an alibi for the night Blaine was murdered?"

"Hey, don't put more weight on this than necessary, Jon. I got seven alibis. I was in a study group all that evening. I left when the news broke about the shooting out at the house. My alibis are there in the class. You want to break up the class, get them to talk now, we can do it. Hey, I got an idea, why don't you interrogate the poetry class in iambic pentameter, make it interesting, at least?"

"You're talking more and more like a second-rate Horowitz, you know that? But I guess that's been the goal all along. I see that now."

Wright turned the cigarette between his index finger and thumb, the trail of smoke rising alongside his body. "You got anything else in particular you want to ask me, Jon, something substantive?"

"How about traveling to New York . . . You go there anytime recently? Is that *substantive* enough for you, Henry?"

Wright tipped a finger of ash with his thumb, trying to hide the sudden look on his face. He masked it with a smile. "Let me just say, I think everybody should see the Statue of Liberty before they die. I'm not getting any younger."

"You flew out of Chicago to LaGuardia, were back twenty-four hours later. They're the facts."

"I had school the next day. Just showing up here to class is worth like thirty percent of the grade. I got the syllabus in my bag inside, if you don't believe me. It's there in black and white, mandatory attendance."

"What did you do in New York?"

"*Do* . . . Let me see, last time I heard, New York was part of the *free world.* Maybe I'm missing something here, Jon. I went sightseeing."

Ryder stopped dead. "Come on, Henry, this isn't *us.* Humor isn't our strong suit. Level with me. We recovered your fingerprints on the tape. Why didn't you just come forward about the connection to Amber?"

"On the level . . ."

Ryder waited.

"This is going to sound pretty lame, Jon, but you saw what Wiltshire did to me out at the motel diner. You hit it right on the head. I got an inferiority complex. I wanted to be someone just like Horowitz, if that's what was going to get me someone like Adi. See, I figured I paid my dues to this country. I fought in the goddamn war when people ran into the goddamn National Guard, when they ran for the cover of a college education! I put my life on the line for this country, and what the hell did I get? I don't want to make the war *an excuse.* Too many people do. It's a cliché, I know, but a cliché is just another word for people experiencing something honest. You fall back on common feelings. That's what I am, Jon, a common man. I think maybe more people should bestow some sense of dignity on that, if you know what I mean."

Ryder looked at Wright, saw his eyes were not so hard, his jaw set not so tight. He was settling somewhere else. "You go out round where Amber was killed, and, shit, something happened around us, Jon. Me, Gary, Trent, and a shitload of others, all of us from the same high school. We never made it in our own town, in the place we were born. You want to go looking for the missing, Jon? Well, I got the high school class shots from sixty-eight through seventy-nine. You find us, what became of us!"

Wright broke off. His face was shining with sweat.

There were kids staring up from their desks. The Chair had walked down the far wall of the classroom and looked at Ryder, who just turned his back on him.

Wright spoke again, more softly. "Look, all I did was fight on Wiltshire's terms, in her language, that's all. I figure, she knew all along I sent her the Williams note. It was an overture toward showing her I could work at that level, and she just let it go. I guess she was preoccupied with other things."

Flecks of tobacco from the rolling paper had crumbled and come loose in Wright's mouth. He moved them with his tongue. "Look, anything other than that, and I don't know. I swear to God. I never knew her motivations in anything, what she knew the professor had done or hadn't done. She had just set the book down one day, the advanced copy, and so I read it. I saw the connection. I'd worked for the paper. I went out to Sam Henderson's, covering the story . . ." Wright pointed to his eyes with his index finger. "I got a gift for catching things just right, the subtlety of details. It's what makes a photographer."

He lowered his head, scanned his tongue across his teeth in an anxious way. "I don't know if I'm answering your question here. You know, I used to hear Adi out at the house talking with Horowitz up in New York. This was all a game to Horowitz to get to her. You can get so goddamn smart and not see something right before your eyes. Adi didn't see it. I guess I wanted to get two birds with one stone, let people know what *Pendleton* had done, but also make Wiltshire believe *Horowitz* had sent the tape, that he was doing it to ruin Pendleton. You know they hated each other, Pendleton and Horowitz, right? That's why Pendleton tried to kill himself, because of Horowitz demeaning him when he came to campus."

Ryder watched Wright's eyes look away, his head shaking ever so slightly. Ryder took his time. "So why do you still go out there to see Pendleton?"

"The truth? To watch him suffer for what he did."

The bluntness of the admission fell as the class inside started moving around. Wright dabbed out the remnants of his cigarette on his tin box and closed the lid as though things were done.

Ryder measured his final statement, watching Wright closely. "I think I need some rest. I was up the last two days visiting Ruth Witter at a retirement home."

Wright said nothing.

"You probably remember her daughter, Elizabeth, good-looking girl? She disappeared back in seventy-nine, around the time you photographed her. She had proofs you took of her in her school bag."

Wright's Adam's apple disappeared, then showed again. "I can't say I remember that."

"Remember what, the girl or the incident?"

Wright looked toward the classroom. "The *incident*! Look, I got to get the assignment from the Chair for next class. We got a quiz Thursday."

A bell rang as if at the end of a round in a prizefight.

Wright went back into the classroom.

Waiting out on the quad on a bench, Ryder saw Wright emerge from the humanities building, his backpack slung over his shoulder. He watched Wright head across the quad and up the steps of the business building.

Ryder had Wright's schedule: microeconomics until 11:30 a.m.

After watching the business building for a few minutes, Ryder rose, went to his car, and headed for Wright's house, an hour or so on his side.

FIFTY-FOUR

THE SCHOOLKIDS WERE OUT along the roadside, waiting for the school bus, in the predawn, and the memory of such mornings came back to Adi as Horowitz drove into the old world antiquity of Pendleton's neighborhood, the resplendent vintage homes encased in snow, some suffused with the glow of Tiffany stained glass.

Horowitz had arranged with the police for Adi to get her belongings from the house.

It hurt Adi at a deep level that this life, this time, had passed so quickly and ended so tragically.

Beyond the embankment of bare trees running along the bluff, the serpentine flow of river wound a dark ribbon round the moat of Bannockburn College, a principality unto itself in a rising smoky fog coming off the water.

Adi sat silently, took it all in, turned from Bannockburn to see a pajama-wearing woman, whom she knew by name, in moon boots and a puffy goose down coat, standing with a clutch of kids at a cross street. She was part of the weekly rotation of concerned women taking turns to chaperone, others there in the evening to account for and ensure kids reached their homes, acts noble enough for women to give up their careers or at least postpone career choices until later. When she had lived with Pendleton, she had received a neighborhood newsletter to that effect, asking her to volunteer for such duties, inviting her to be part of the disquieting morning coffee gatherings of women committed to family values and traditional life, the last holdouts.

The mothers' project that first fall had been the collection of neighborhood kid baby blankets, a project that entailed cutting up all the blankets into small squares and stitching the sundry parts from various quilts back together into a childhood pastiche of memories.

Of course, such lifestyle choices came with money, but in the early morning, it was amazing how such apparent gracious tenderness, such giving, could overlay the reality all guarded against, the bogeyman horror that had come to so characterize the American experience.

A flagging yellow police ribbon still cordoned off Pendleton's house, though the investigative work had seemingly been completed. The driveway, piled high with snow, made the house seem oddly abandoned, although a narrow path had been cleared up to the house.

When Horowitz and Wiltshire arrived, Trent Bauer was standing in boots and a heavy down coat. Bauer stubbed out his cigarette and went toward them with due civility.

At the overstuffed mailbox, Adi stopped and retrieved the mail, which

Horowitz took from her, but not before Adi noticed the large manila envelope embossed with the name Moore College, an exclusive interdisciplinary liberal arts college set within a small logging community in the rain shadow of the Olympic Mountains in Washington State.

Adi said nothing, but she felt her heart quicken. Large manila envelopes always boded well. Moore College had been her top teaching choice.

In the drifting-snowy alcove of the doorway, it took Bauer time to work the key in the frozen lock. The sky brightened overhead by degrees.

The alcove was littered with rolls of newspaper. The paperboy, a kid, had stubbornly continued to lob the daily newspaper into Pendleton's arched alcove, delivering a daily report to an unoccupied house. Adi remembered she had paid for three months in advance.

The faded quality of the paper hinted at the transitory nature of all news, of all things in general, and Adi's mind turned to the manila envelope, to Moore College, remembering the student-to-teacher ratio of ten to one and photos of the emerald green of manicured lawns, the mist coming off evergreen-covered mountains, trees that came down to the edge of campus, a temperate place where it hardly ever snowed. It was such a vastly different place from the plains. It was hard to believe that the possibility of a new beginning loomed as a reality. She was not as marginal as she had thought. There were people out there willing to hire her.

The house was a box of gray light, deathly silent, so cold that their breaths showed, the cold emanating from a massive brick fireplace from an era when it provided the sole heat for the house; though now no longer in use, and neglected, it was the source of a diamond dust of snow that hung in the air in daggers of advancing dawn.

The furnace had also cut off, contributing to the cold. Bauer said something to that effect, standing by the thermostat, tapping it.

Adi turned. "It does that in high wind. There's a downdraft and a broken window in the basement."

Bauer looked at Adi. "You want it restarted?"

Adi said without emotion, "It's not my house."

It was, for Horowitz, a revelatory and settling moment, a tacit alignment with the story Adi had told of how it had been while she had gone down to the basement, during a storm, to restart the furnace that she had discovered the hidden box of books under the stairwell.

Horowitz's eyes met Adi's stare, and she just looked away, then went out to the carriage house to get her belongings.

The lattice window beside Adi's old bed was full with morning light, a radiant heat adding to the fact that the carriage house was warm. It had its own gas furnace, its own kitchenette and claw-foot tub, a close-quarter homeliness.

The conversion of the garage to a carriage house was part of an ongoing saga Adi uncovered early on going through Pendleton's personal correspondence, in a series of letters to his mother she found in Pendleton's office, letters Pendleton had recovered among his mother's belongings after her passing.

Pendleton's mother lived out her remaining years at a care facility, and in many of the letters, Pendleton hinted at a lost opportunity in youth for reasonable relations. Ostensibly, he put off marriage during those years, or so Adi surmised, in what lamentably turned out to be an almost decade-long decline before his mother succumbed to some sort of cancer. Pendleton's relationship with his mother almost bankrupted him, from the conversion of the garage to a carriage house to accommodate her after a stroke to his continuing payments to the care facility she entered.

Adi had confided nothing of these facts to Horowitz. Her relationship with Pendleton had been brief, but somehow deeply complicated and personal, as his life had emerged in the early months after his attempted suicide as she went through his effects.

Pendleton had sacrificed a decade of his life to his mother's care, showed the capacity for compassion even as he had struggled through the nightmare of his own failure and fight for tenure. It was clear his mother's decline had dovetailed with, or precipitated, his academic and spiritual crisis. At some point, he had lost it. The reality was, the day he murdered Amber Jewel, he had written a brief note to his mother talking about the autumnal changing of the leaves, about the bite of early winter's cold.

How did one account for that sort of sociopathy?

What the letters did was tell a more complicated story, or at least add to the textual history of Pendleton's writing life, a parallel text written alongside *Scream*.

In all likelihood, the letters could form a series of publishable material, academic pay dirt, something Adi would need in a push toward tenure. She was, after all, the guardian of E. Robert Pendleton's legacy. What she needed to do now was embrace Pendleton in all his myriad possibilities, treat him as a subject, as artifact, let go of him as a living being.

In the main house, Horowitz was talking with Bauer on the porch, Bauer smoking and talking about Kim Jewel. Adi overheard him as she went toward the stairs. He was talking in a plaintive way, while Horowitz was nodding.

Adi went quietly up into the turreted crow's nest of Pendleton's office one last time. The chalk outline of Mrs. Blaine's body was still there, the dried blood seeped into the rug, and so, too, the bloody paw prints made by the rabbit.

The letters were tied with a silk, rose-scented ribbon, something Pendleton's mother had done.

When Adi came down, Horowitz was back in the living room. He had removed one of the old newspapers from its plastic wrap and set it out. Adi was packing the bundle of letters into her suitcase when Horowitz turned and stared at it. "Is that it?"

Adi stood upright and pushed her hair off her face. "Yes." She came toward the table. The newspaper lay open, brown with age and dampness, to a middle page, to the continuation of a story from page one. A faded color picture of Adi and Pendleton at the Bannockburn homecoming took up most of the upper half of the page, the defining shot of their relationship upon the publication of *Scream*, the stoic poise of Adi with her hand on Pendleton's shoulder. The caption under the picture read, "E. Robert Pendleton and His Assistant Enjoying Better Days," hinting, of course, at the not-so-good days that eventually followed.

Adi's eyes lingered on the shot, her life entwined forever with Pendleton's. It was the indelible image Adi would always associate with what she had wanted most in life, to be an advocate of genius and not the eerie image Wright had taken of her turned toward the camera over the slumped body of Pendleton the night of his attempted suicide.

She had uncovered a masterpiece. She kept telling herself that. Destiny presented itself so rarely, the vagabond existence of failure otherwise looming. Adi knew that now, had seen that in her own parents' lives and in the brief glimpse into the old woman's life at her father's apartment, an eater of cat food. Adi thought of her own previous existence, terminal grad student, tit-fucker of visiting writers, a one-night stand against the clawing humiliation of the modern writing life, against the infuriating dichotomy of glowing reviews set against the reality of an uninterested, nonreading public. And just the shuddering memory of those times made things all the more clear for Adi, the choice she was making.

It was as Adi turned to retrieve the mail set off to the side table that she saw the manila envelope was gone, Horowitz saying nothing, just standing, holding her case. All he did was smile vaguely and say, "We all set, then?"

It was the ultimate betrayal Horowitz could have committed against her, denying her a future, trying to hold on to her. Adi said nothing. She knew she was leaving him and, merely nodding, she walked out into the gathering front of low-slung clouds.

FIFTY-FIVE

HENRY JAMES WRIGHT'S HOUSE stood off in a snow-covered field, a half-acre lot abutting a raised moraine of interstate running toward Chicago. A utility access road ran parallel to the highway, a dirt road carrying giant electrical power lines making the air alive with crackling electricity. It was the most undesirable land in all the county.

Twenty-four hours a day, trucks traveled the interstate, huge eighteen-wheelers. Standing at Wright's kitchen window, looking across to the highway, Ryder felt the subterranean tremor of the trucks making the house tremble.

Ryder had wedged open the back door, breaking the lock on what seemed to be a door never used, though pools of meltwater from his snow-covered shoes had formed, telltale signs of an illegal entry.

It was colder inside the house than outside, a meat locker chill. The walls were cinder block, tacked with strips of yellowish insulation in the living room, a job started and abandoned. The only appreciable furnishings were a hutch, a sofa, and a La-Z-Boy set before a new TV hooked up to a VHS player with its clock blinking.

On the hutch was a series of glossy vintage Studebaker trade photographs from various eras of women in semisuggestive poses, beside gleaming new cars, from a woman in a tweed skirt and cat's-eye glasses leaning against the 1950 Studebaker Champion with its bullet-nose grill, to a bikini-clad woman beside the fintail sleekness of the 1957 Golden Hawk, to a girl in a sort of *Star Trek* outfit sitting on the hood of a futuristic space age 1963 Avanti the year Kennedy was assassinated.

All the photographs had been taken by Wright's father, the shots signed by the women to Dale Wright.

Dale Wright appeared in a sole shot, in a short-sleeved shirt and tie, a complex self-portrait caught in the reflective image of the company's showroom window the day Studebaker shut down, a shot that caught the essence of a guy who had lived behind the obscurity of the camera, a guy who had spent his life plying a cheap romantic fiction of cars and women. Here was a solitary shot of who he really was inside.

Ryder looked up, standing in this house gone to ruin, the house signifying the metaphoric and actual sense of decline of such people like the Wrights and their world. Ryder knew that he could number himself among that kind, that something terrible had happened to his kind, that there was something depraved in his lost generation. Or was it too easy to attribute everything to economic ruination?

Ryder checked his watch. The rush of adrenaline had not abated from having spoken to Wright. It had been Wright's unwillingness to admit to knowing Elizabeth Witter that had convinced him Wright was hiding something. Elizabeth Witter had been strikingly beautiful, incongruous in the old world clothes she had been made to wear by her parents.

Wright remembered her, Ryder was convinced of it. He looked at the

VHS clock blinking, cassette boxes strewn on the ground. On the side table, a fan of glossy brochures was spread out, along with a stack of business cards with raised black lettering and a sprinkling of raised stars done in gold and silver, all the essential trappings for the egos of such impressionable young girls looking to discover and define a sense of self. He picked up a trifold brochure from a modeling talent agency called L.A. Casting, Wright addressed as a so-called talent agent. The casting agency, Ryder could tell in just scanning the material, was a scam legitimizing lone photographers, giving them a "Hollywood connection."

The brochure unfolded to show the sample array of the shots needed to submit a portfolio, along with a detailed list of specs related to various head and full body shots needed for what was called, in the trade, "a composite card." The sample shots in the brochure were all of teenage girls, and Ryder thought of Elizabeth Witter, of her saving her money to have such shots taken.

Ryder pressed "play" on the VHS machine, and the mechanism clicked and caught; at first the screen was a blizzard of static, then, against the backdrop of a white sheet, a twelve- or thirteen-year-old girl sat on a stool, smiling at a stationary videocamera capturing the simple still white frame. As Wright gave instructions, the girl adopted a series of demure poses, smiling head-on at the videocamera, then off to the side, running her hand through her hair, tossing her head back, and laughing, all the while Wright's camera flashing and clicking in the background.

Wright went on then into a series of animated action shots where he used the videocamera, zoomed in as the girl pretended, per his instruction, first to eat a bowl of cereal and say, "I go cuckoo for Cocoa Puffs," then to sit on the floor, legs akimbo, combing the mane of an imaginary pony, then to a disconcerting scene where Wright said, "Now, ad-lib, Debbie. Tell me, what would you do for a Klondike Bar?" In the background, Ryder heard a woman's voice, and as the session was ending, the mother, an older version of the girl in stretch polyester stirrup pants and a T-shirt, came into view, toting a Samsonite vanity case.

The screen went to static again, then another session started against the same backdrop.

It was surreal, the rawness of the footage, the first girl obviously talentless, wasting money on this so-called screen test. It was as Ryder looked up that he noticed the hutch door ajar and opened it. The hutch was filled wall-to-wall with videotapes. Ryder reckoned literally hundreds of girls had posed for Wright on tape, Amber Jewel and Elizabeth Witter no doubt among them, their souls stolen, caught on one of the tapes.

The sullen fact was that there was nothing prosecutable on the tapes, nothing that he had seen so far, anyway: consenting girls, a legitimate enterprise, even if it was a rip-off. It proved nothing, nor would the DNA sample recovered from Elizabeth Witter's underwear, even if it was linked to Wright. Having sex with her didn't constitute a crime in a legal sense. She had been sixteen, of consenting age.

In driving out to Wright's house, Ryder had duly noted Sam Henderson's property less than two miles away. It had been enough of a coincidence for him. Wright had killed Amber Jewel, no matter that some woman at the printing press was contending Pendleton's book had been published prior to the discovery of Amber's body.

She was wrong.

What Ryder wanted to do was dispense with the ways of temporal law, go back to the Old Testament scripture of Moses, "fracture for fracture, eye for eye, tooth for tooth. As he has injured the other, so he is to be injured," a more brutal and honest way, a cosmic balance of pain for pain, scream for scream. He would make Wright talk for the sheer justice and sense of knowing the truth, of hearing him confess before he killed him.

Ryder felt a certain lightness settle, knowing what he was going to do. His instincts had served him. He felt good about himself; a certain euphoria, a spiritual high, filled him. He was in the mood for reconciliation. As yet, he would win Gail back. She could be handled, a weekend getaway on a riverboat cruise, something with flowers and champagne, a box of chocolates, roses, the stuff she fell for. The great thing about her, at the end of the day, was her simplicity. She wasn't a complicated animal.

Of course, Taylor was different, but Ryder had decided she would have to make her own way. She was not going to ruin his life. If he could help, he would, but a certain pragmatism and honesty was going to have to come to bear on their relationship. He was married with two boys now, a circumstance Taylor had used to divide him from Gail and get what she wanted.

It was going to end. He was going to be a *real* father to his boys when this was all done here.

A mottled-colored sky spread out toward a rim of charcoal horizon as Ryder went out of the house, parked his car out back of Wright's property behind a barn, and rummaged through his trunk. It was raining in a cold mist, tending toward sleet. Ryder stopped and stared at truck headlights fizzling out on the highway, the far-off slur carrying on the pull of wind. Then he looked along the county road one last time before heading back into the house with his equipment.

At the end of a long passageway, Ryder found Wright's darkroom, a converted bedroom. He plugged in the spectrum light and, waiting for it to warm up, went into the darkroom, leaving the door open.

An array of proof pages lay out on a cutting table, professional, stylized high school portraits of girls mostly, the bread-and-butter stuff of Wright's career, but there were also scenes from Bannockburn College, close-up shots of girls taken undoubtedly with a telescopic lens, the girls unaware of being photographed, girls astride with books, a series of shots where the camera zoned in on body parts in a rapid exposure of shots, on cleavage and ass mostly, entire sequences contained on a single proof sheet.

It had the chilling black-and-white aspect of surveillance.

The obsessive cataloging of tapes in the living room and inventory of photographs underscored Wright's need to reinhabit these moments vicariously, something that went a long way to explaining for Ryder why Wright had sent the tape from New York, his pathological need to resurrect and inhabit the mystery surrounding Amber Jewel's murder again, to feel that rush of pain and anguish of all those involved.

A buzzer sounded on the spectrum light apparatus as it waited on standby mode.

After donning a pair of rounded, light-filtering goggles, Ryder closed the door behind him and went into the darkroom. Everything went black, then he found the switch, turned on the intense blue-green spectrum light, adjusted the handheld dial on the light source wavelengths and bandwidths, until, out of the darkness, the room suddenly fluoresced in a sordid cumulus of desire, a history of ejaculatory emissions, a darkroom floor pasted with glowing semen, splat against walls and the legs of a workbench, on the seat of a chair, on the electrical cords under the workbench, the light probing the darkness. The copious amounts of spilled semen stunned even one as seasoned as Ryder.

For Ryder, each time he came to this part of an investigation, he always felt there was, ironically, something spiritually affirming in a scientific method that prided itself on facts, for this science of spectrum light seemed to prove a fundamental tenet of ancient religion, that our essence transcends time, that it survives in the places and people we meet. It was here in this blue-green spectrum, like shining a searchlight on the soul, revealing all the dark places of the inner psyche, or, at a more spiritual level, giving credence to the religious notion of original sin, that indelible stain that cannot be removed.

Ryder stepped back from the scene. He was standing in semen even then, the phantasmagoria of the small enclosure getting to him, sarcophaguslike, and so, too, the clinical smell of film-processing chemicals.

He imagined the ruby glow of the darkroom light reminiscent of the sanguine viscosity of blood in a horror movie, Wright in there alone, jerking off, panning with his other hand for images in a tray of chemicals, faces of girls emerging like dreams.

Ryder turned the dial, trying to focus the light source to fluoresce the signature wavelength for blood, but he found nothing.

He opened the darkroom door, stepped backward out of the darkroom into the long hallway, the fluorescent glow dimming in the pollution of hallway light. He was aware of sleet falling hard, pinging against the corrugated roof like lead shot.

He looked upward, unaware of Wright's presence behind him.

Wright, sensing the opportunity, grabbed him by the hair and cut a clean arc under Ryder's exposed throat.

Ryder pulled away as the hotness of the blade slid across his throat at an angle, slicing into his jugular vein.

Gargling unintelligibly, Ryder struggled, fell forward against the wall, the spectrum light falling end over end, casting a pale blue sheen in the long hallway.

Ryder looked almost alien, still wearing the filtered lens goggles, the blood erupting from his neck, so much so that Wright, for the briefest of seconds, hesitated in coming at Ryder again.

In that millisecond, in a last desperate gesture, Ryder reached into his shoulder harness for his gun, a forty-five, and, firing repeatedly at point-blank range in the narrow hallway, shot at Wright's face, mouth open in a scream Wright never vocalized as his face exploded, his body recoiling against the cinder blocks, the concussive impact of the gunshots ringing in Ryder's ears.

In the freezing air, Ryder made it to the snow-covered drive outside, scooped and pressed the snow against his throat, packed it into the deep, open cut. On his CB radio in his car, he tried to speak, pressed the V between his index and thumb against his voice box, struggling to say his name repeatedly before the dispatcher made out who he was and where he was.

Ryder slumped down again to wait in the freezing cold. He packed his throat with new snow, trying to stay alive. But a growing coldness over-took him, and he fell facedown into the snow, his breathing becoming ragged and then ceasing altogether, the death mask of his face reminis-cent of Amber Jewel's.

FIFTY-SIX

JON RYDER'S TROUBLED PERSONAL LIFE figured in the official in-quiry into his professional meltdown, released a month after his death, a damning report on the heels of the recovery of archival records estab-lishing that Pendleton's *Scream* had been printed on Valentine's Day 1977.

Ryder's daughter's long-standing grievance against her father and defi-ant exit from the family home was identified as the probable catalyst for Ryder's erratic behavior, exacerbating what psychologists described as his intense sense of personal failure as a father and resurrecting the latent memory of his first wife's mysterious disappearance that seemed to have troubled him throughout the investigation.

His second wife, Gail, spoke candidly of Ryder's melancholy discussion with her on the phone from his motel at the start of the case, relating how he had given an almost spiritual significance to the fact that Jewel's murder had taken place the same year Tori Ryder had disappeared, feeling Tori would somehow guide him to the *truth* from beyond the grave.

The report also explored Ryder's investigative lines of inquiry in the Pendleton case, information pieced together through interviews, since Ryder left no notes. What the report focused on was Ryder's tacit rejection from the start that Pendleton had murdered Amber Jewel, leading him to speculate that the republication of the book was part of an elaborate hoax and that consequently the real murderer was still at large.

One of the few paper trails Ryder did leave was a faxed copy of a weather report from the date Jewel disappeared, through to the first stretch of subzero weather, the anomaly of how Jewel's face could have remained preserved in six weeks of temperate weather a key factor in his assumption that the body had been dumped long after her dismemberment, something Ken Orton confirmed Ryder had been pursuing.

Also, in amassing files related to two other missing persons' cases in the area, in noting all had disappeared after riding home on school buses on rural roads, it seemed that early on Ryder had become convinced he was searching for a serial killer, someone local, able to blend inconspicuously into the rural outlying areas.

In short, it seemed Ryder had exhibited a certain investigative prowess in reassessing the perceived, established facts in the case, bringing an outsider's professional perspective. However, a darker, more maniacal side had also emerged as investigators probed Ryder's involvement in the case.

Adi Wiltshire, central to Ryder's investigation that the republication of *Scream* had been a literary hoax, related disconcerting details of being stalked by Ryder in a long black coat at her library office, of his having undermined her emotionally and psychologically, putting notes under her office door and writing a lipstick question on the hospital mirror, tactics he outright denied while interviewing her. Her cohort behind the rerelease of Pendleton's novel, Allen Horowitz, characterized Ryder's behavior toward Wiltshire as lurid and overtly sexually aggressive—and, for that matter, toward Kim Jewel, or so he had observed while attending Scholl's funeral service.

Ed Kline, contacted through a review of Ryder's phone records, spoke of Ryder's disavowal of having initially called him, of Ryder playing a game of cat and mouse with him, testimony further establishing a behavioral and investigative pattern consistent with Wiltshire's statements that Ryder had, according to state psychologists, displayed borderline sociopathic tendencies in the commission of his investigation.

Trent Bauer, the subject of Ryder's parallel and unrelenting investigation into establishing that Amber Jewel's murder was connected to other local disappearances, described harassment and intimidation tactics that included wild accusations and conjecture, uproarious shouting fits, and threats of bodily injury. Police department personnel testified to Ryder's constant haranguing of Bauer.

The DMV report Ryder had requested on Bauer and his wife was again one of the few paper trails left behind, substantiating that Ryder had been actively pursuing Bauer as a potential serial killer. In the Witter case, beside the mention of a white car following her bus in the days prior to her disappearance, Ryder had written in bold letters, "TRENT!"

The underlying motivation for Ryder's interest in Bauer was uncovered in the course of the follow-up investigation, locals revealing the sordid history of Bauer's relationship with Kim Jewel, from the infamous junior high fingering incident to Bauer's infidelity in fathering Kim Jewel's child the same year her sister, Amber, was murdered.

None of it was included in the official report because of the personal and potentially libelous nature of the information.

Ryder's investigation of Wright was, in a way, the most straightforward, established immediately with the recovery of the photographs of Amber Jewel and Elizabeth Witter on Ryder's car seat, both pictures taken by Wright.

Ruth Witter detailed her interview with Ryder, explaining he had told her he was investigating a potential serial killer, showing her a photograph of a victim, Amber Jewel. In the course of her discussion with Ryder, Witter stated she had produced the photograph of Elizabeth that had been recovered from Elizabeth's backpack the day she had disappeared, which Witter described as having had an unnerving effect on Ryder, radically shifting his focus.

In a way, it showed the manic sense of desperation Ryder had been experiencing at that time, first aggressively and fanatically pursuing Trent as a prime suspect, then turning 180 and fixating on Wright, not accounting for the likely probability that a local photographer could have taken both girls' photographs.

Investigators confirmed the alarming and spiraling sequence of events that unfolded in the coming hours after Ryder left upper Wisconsin, from his confronting, the following morning, a dumbfounded Wright, who had been called from class at Ryder's request, to his forced entry into Wright's house, discovered through fingerprints lifted from a broken lock on a side door, to his eventual and deadly encounter with Wright.

Investigators reconstructing the crime scene, the hallway blood patterns, the angle of the trajectory of Ryder's gunfire, and the fact that strands of Ryder's hair were found in Wright's hand, established that Wright had come upon an unsuspecting Ryder most probably backing out of the darkroom, grabbed him by the hair, and slit his throat.

Why Wright had taken such drastic action, murdering Ryder, was seriously investigated given the vast catalog of tapes Wright had amassed in his sideline business as a talent agent, though no improprieties or connections to missing persons were uncovered.

The investigation was abandoned when the DNA evidence in the Witter case, submitted by Ryder for forensic analysis, arrived via courier at his vacant desk two weeks later. The sample proved a negative match to Wright or Enoch Witter.

Prompted by the revelation of her husband's true innocence, Ruth Witter called the police, revealing the truth of her daughter's suicide.

Elizabeth Witter's body was exhumed that spring out in what had been the Witters' vast holding, the unmarked grave identified by a rash of perennial flowers that had bloomed each spring since her interment, flowers planted by Enoch Witter when he had buried his daughter.

Ryder's decision not to secure a search warrant and to exact personal vengeance on Wright aligned with a litany of allegations concerning Ryder's troubling vigilante tendencies documented first after his wife's disappearance. Many attributed an obsessive, latent religiosity that had reared within him to the pressure of having been the prime suspect in his wife's murder, a defense or coping mechanism, a life given to the commission of atonement.

In his locker, a picture of a secret European sect, the Brethren of the Misericordia, was discovered, a haunting image of robed and hooded figures mysteriously bearing a coffin between them, an image that seemingly had defined how Ryder had come to perceive his life.

Numerous suspects in cases in which Ryder had been involved had spoken of being stalked by a dark, spectral figure in a black coat. Most notable was the statement by a serial child rapist who eventually died from his injuries who had described his attacker as a figure clad in a *black coat*.

At a funeral service for Elizabeth Witter the following spring, in the same graveyard where Amber Jewel lay, someone showed up in the hooded garb of the Brethren of the Misericordia, a solitary, unknown figure presiding over the delivery of Elizabeth Witter into consecrated ground, establishing Ryder's troubled legacy as hero or renegade, depending on how one saw his actions, the final image that went national in the sad drama of Jon Ryder's involvement with the case of E. Robert Pendleton.

EPILOGUE

E. ROBERT PENDLETON SUCCUMBED to pneumonia one late fall afternoon of 1995, ending a Rip Van Winkle existence. He never woke up, slept through his novel garnering the National Book Award, right on through the historic collapse of the Berlin Wall and the infamous tank incident at Tiananmen Square, through the ethnic cleansing and mass graves in the former Yugoslavia, through the tribal machete genocide of eight hundred thousand Rwandans.

Pendleton's passing coincided with yet again another Bannockburn Homecoming Weekend and was marked by the AP wire, which led with the same jaded Bannockburn quip, describing the game as "Non-Believers vs. True-Believers, where tradition sees Bannockburn students hold up past scores while Carleton College students hold up numbered scripture references."

Adi got the news of Pendleton's passing while at her office, embroiled in her annual conferences with students struggling to interpret the deep significance of William Carlos Williams's "This Is Just to Say":

> *I have eaten*
> *the plums*
> *that were in*
> *the icebox*
>
> *and which*
> *you were probably*

saving
for breakfast

Forgive me
they were delicious
so sweet
and so cold

Adi canceled her conferences for the day, and as she gathered her coat and left the library, she couldn't help but look down the aisles of books. It sent a chill through her, but otherwise she did just fine.

The intervening years had been good to her, despite everything. Pendleton's National Book Award established his legacy and afforded Adi a life she knew she would never have achieved without him. Her thesis had become the seminal work on the moral paroxysm at the heart of Pendleton's work. She got tenure early in her third year at Moore College with the publication of Pendleton's letters and became the darling of what simply became known as Pendleton studies.

Pendleton was all the rage with fledgling doctoral candidates. He was *new* material. Even his lesser works experienced a renaissance with an emerging core of Pendleton scholars delving into the flawed experimentalism of what became known as Pendleton's middle period, exemplified by *A Hole Without a Middle* and *Word Salad*, leading to a general interest in a subgenre of late sixties postmodern experimentalism philosophically opposed to linearity, character-driven narratives, and the arbitrary, pandering simplicity of so-called closure, thus further resurrecting the work of discarded out-of-print writers who now found their writing at the center of doctoral research.

In essence, Pendleton studies gained its critical foothold as it became part of a self-sustaining machinery of critical analysis that Pendleton had, ironically, so railed against in *Scream*. But it was these diverse and varied critical approaches to his work that ultimately legitimized Pendleton studies and enabled Adi to secure a grant to have Yale Academic Press publish the *Pendleton Quarterly Review*, in tandem with releasing, in hardback, a 1,200-page annotated tome of all of Pendleton's writings.

Adi went back to supervise the death mask and hand casts Moore College had commissioned as a central part of the soon-to-be-unveiled Pendleton Collection.

The cremation service, a sad affair, was attended by a reluctant minister and some former colleagues from Bannockburn, most notably Pendleton's nemesis, the Chair of the English Department, a skeletal figure on sabbatical dying of AIDS. It put into perspective the letter Adi had received from Bannockburn advising her that the college was anticipating filling a faculty vacancy and considering instituting the Pendleton Chair, if agreeable terms could be reached to house the Pendleton Collection at the college.

It was the sort of irony Adi knew Pendleton would have choked on.

The end of the ceremony was filled with anticlimactic tension, a hesitant departure over lingering handshakes and god-awful reminiscences, with faculty hanging on in anticipation of a free meal or at least a drink at some predetermined location.

Adi was resolute in her defiance, though she was set to meet with the Chair to recover Pendleton's file regarding his so-called sabbaticals, wanting to submit a paper to a clinical psychological journal on pedagogy, correlating mental instability with classroom performance. She was going to use student teacher evaluations.

Horowitz showed up in the parking lot, standing alongside a young woman in a fur coat. He smiled at Adi, the girl waiting as he approached with his usual familiarity.

Adi stiffened as he hugged her. "I'll tell you, the Learjet 60 doesn't hold a candle to the stability and old world luxury of the Longhorn 29 series."

Horowitz was again atop the best-seller lists; his coffee table book series *Visitors* had taken on a life of its own, despite an initial scathing review in the *New York Times*, calling the book "a sort of 'Where's Waldo' for adults." Now a third installment in the series, *Visitors III: News from a*

Distant Galaxy, had shifted focus, the mysterious and omniscient Visitors staring down through their portal windows at a postapocalyptic landscape with images of slash-and-burn clear-cut deforestation, to the bleakness of a Chernobyl-like landscape, to African famine images and tanks, in what critics were defining now as "Horowitz's uncanny genius, shaping the new Gaia-centric politics in the wake of the Cold War vacuum," though it was hard to tell Horowitz's true intent.

Visitors III was a book without words.

Horowitz drew back from Adi, still holding her hand. "You look good."

Adi said, "So do you," tacitly taking Horowitz's hand off hers and looking beyond him to the Chair waiting in the offing. "I'm afraid I've a previous engagement, Allen."

Horowitz smiled. "I thought of you a year or so ago when I read that piece about Phoebe dying. You know, it's strange, but it's what I remember most of our time together. It said in the article that scientists were going to dissect her brain to see what neural pathways acquired signing may have spawned. You ever hear if they did it?"

Adi simply shook her head. As she began to walk away, Horowitz said, "Still the elitist snob, right, Adi? I'm still the intellectual lightweight. . . ."

Adi stopped and looked at him. "*Still?* You were never anything else. Why did you even show up, Allen?"

"I get it! Bob is all yours, Pendleton studies your creation? Well, what if I told you the forthcoming *Visitors Four: Future Days Gone By—Memories of a Time Traveler* borrows from and extends Bob's *A Hole Without a Middle*? I think philosophically, nonlinearity is an idea that has come of age, and not just literary postmodernist bunk. I'm thinking the middle section of *Visitors Four* is going to have twenty blank pages, or some resonance of the unknowable, a static galactic interference, some cosmic intercept, linearity turned inside out. I'm working it out with my editor. Its high-concept stuff, that blankness Bob wanted to express. I just got to figure out how to spell what that sounds like."

Bannockburn was awash in the fall reds of maples and sumac as Adi followed the Chair onto campus, the traditional Sunday brunch, in the wake of Saturday's homecoming game, served at makeshift stands outside dorms, the smell of pancakes and sausage and roasted apples wafting against the languid quiet of morning-after laughter.

Adi got out of her car and walked across campus, stared at the students, most in Bannockburn College sweats with the embroidered letter *B*. Seeing it anew, she thought it all appeared oddly allegorical, the embroidered *B*'s reminiscent of Hawthorne's *Scarlet Letter*; what they were essentially guilty of, she could not say.

Who could hate this spectacle, really, students tending the oil-drum fires in something akin to Pilgrim days, an easy, familial affair under a soft, golden sun, a time when lifelong friendships were forged, when the intangible sense of belonging to the Bannockburn family settled and defined one's identity against the vast anonymity of American life, against so-called democracy.

When Adi turned, the Chair was staring at her with the same lost look; this was his last year here. He looked wholly out of place, a lonely, sick, scarecrow figure, an urban animal of the Chicago gay scene with his handlebar mustache and stud earring, a guy who had spent his years interloping between two different worlds.

He was only fifty-one years old.

On the second floor of the English Department, the Chair requested Adi sign a release that she was acquiring Pendleton's material as part of Pendleton's literary estate and that no student names could appear in print. The Chair had not taken the time to have the student names blotted out.

Pendleton's files were contained in three boxes.

It rained as it always did in Washington, Moore College set amid a primordial forest of emerald spires rising into hillsides behind the campus, where luminous veils of fog were ever present through to midday, and where, in the dark hollows of ravines in the switchback of stairs leading to various dorms, the fog never lifted through the winter months.

From her office window, Adi, in an oversize fisherman's sweater, stood holding a mug of coffee as the rain fell steadily, as it had for four consecutive days, everything damp and smelling of mildew.

It was Thanksgiving, and the campus was deserted, Adi settling into a well-earned reprieve from teaching classes. It had taken her almost two months to get to Pendleton's work. She had gotten through just one of the three boxes, a laborious process for the sake of a frivolous publication that she was now considering abandoning.

She didn't need to push as hard anymore. A quietness had settled within her. A week earlier, she had received news that the Chair had succumbed to AIDS, the news coming along with the overture of her being offered a job at Bannockburn, an offer she had turned down.

Her life was here now, at the edge of the North American continent, in the rain-swept belt of a wilderness that set modernity on its head. People rode bikes or walked as much as possible. An ecoconsciousness had taken hold. People dressed down, wanting simplicity, organic, home-cooked meals and the proximity of small-town life. The biggest story that year in the area was a controversy over the hunting of a whale by coastal Native American tribes attempting to reclaim and define their heritage.

Adi, too, had taken to trying to redefine herself, getting ready to go away for the Thanksgiving weekend with an aging visiting professor she was dating, a rugged, self-reliant, bearded Renaissance man, an accomplished archer and fencer, Peter Holliman, an expatriate Englishman with a doctorate from Oxford, on sabbatical at Moore College. He was working on a book about the phantasmagoria of coastal Native American art, about totem poles and ceremonial masks, his thesis that the distorted carvings of indigenous art were the product of a consciousness defined by staring into the shifting image of oneself in the distorted chop of Pacific coastal waters.

Adi checked her watch. The rain was falling harder now, Thanksgiving here a vastly different experience from the Puritan aesthetic of the East Coast and the Midwest, with the seasonal harvest of corn, squash, and rutabaga, a holiday set against the discreet change of seasons, from the passage of baking summer heat to the approach of winter freeze.

Here the temperate climate afforded no such natural stock taking, and if there was something she missed, it was simply that natural sense of time passing, of seasonal change.

Adi turned from the rain and sat down again with the remaining boxes, giving herself the rest of the afternoon before leaving with Holliman. In her trawl of materials, by late afternoon, as the day gave itself to settling dark, as she felt she was nearly through, she came across the disciplinary hearing related to Pendleton's altercation with Wright while he had attended Pendleton's Art of the Novel in the fall of 1976. The hearing had taken place in mid-December, at the semester's end.

It sent a shiver through her, the mere mention of the name Wright.

Adi got up and turned on the waxy light in her office, a dull forty-watt bulb she had opted for to hide her fading looks as the years progressed, as she had become conscious of getting older. She wasn't beyond vanity or facing the fact that she probably would never have children, that she was, in a way, too selfish, though that was not the exact word.

She sat again at her desk, reading through Wright's grievance.

Pendleton's course that bicentennial year centered on theory, though it had been listed under the creative writing emphasis. That was part of Wright's chief complaint, that Pendleton had stuck to theory simply to avoid reading student work and that when Wright pushed to have his work critiqued, and Pendleton acquiesced, Pendleton had retaliated by summarily dismissing his work, describing it as vague, nonconstructive, and "lacking any academic rigor."

Adi paged through the formal complaint, the reams of paper generated in a bureaucratic nightmare that so defined academia.

At the end of the file was a stapled ten-page sample of Wright's work, an amateurishly rendered, hard-boiled murder mystery of a Vietnam vet turned cop who is dogged by demons of self-doubt over what he has done in Vietnam while investigating the mysterious disappearance of girls in his hometown.

Just reading the material, Adi felt a sort of vertigo overtake her, as if she were tumbling head over heels. Looking up from the white pages, she stared at the dark embankment of trees outside her window, the rain falling hard, remembering back again to Pendleton's last enigmatic denial as she injected him: "It wasn't me. . . ."

Adi rummaged through the boxes again, trying to find the folder related to class evaluations for The Art of the Novel in 1976, and came across another sampling of what Wright was writing at the time.

It was a personal statement by Wright for admission to audit the course, a ranting and yet honest two-page lamenting despair of his life then, a Vietnam vet working as a photographer for a local newspaper, covering high school sports and the crime blotter, an autobiographical statement coupled with a statement of intent, of wanting to be a *published* writer, positioning, unequivocally, Stephen King as the gothic writer he most wanted to emulate, to capture his life as he now lived it, what he called "a hemmorrhaging nightmare dreem life of living in two worlds, in two hemisphyres of the brain, flitting between two continents . . . with everything awash in blood."

Adi saw where Pendleton had circled the misspelled words and where he had also put question marks beside titles Wright admired, *Cujo* and *Christine*, along with mercilessly and unconscionably pointing out grammatical mistakes within a run-on sentence in which Wright had described in harrowing detail losing a comrade in a skirmish of fire in a Vietcong village.

The phone rang, making Adi jump. She picked it up. Holliman's English accent crackled on the line, sounding far off. He was buying arrowheads for his bow, a surreal thing for anybody in the late twentieth century to be discussing on a phone, but such was the social displacement, colonies of like-minded rationalizing loss into a lifestyle choice. They had mutually agreed, or Holliman had decided, that they were not buying a turkey; rather, he was going to hunt wild turkey, chance his luck, or they would resign themselves, if need be, to lentil soup, wild onions, cheese, unleavened bread, and sticky honeycombs.

Adi said softly that she was finishing up.

Sitting for a few more minutes alone after she set down the phone, she thought back to the dogged sense of vitriolic hatred Wright had initially expressed toward Pendleton, the hate mail he had sent mimicking Pendleton's *Word Salad*. She knew that buried within Wright's novel-in-progress were the details of what Wright had done to Amber Jewel, that Pendleton had unwittingly lifted the real-life facts surrounding Amber Jewel's murder.

As the full import sank in of what Adi felt must have happened, she knew that the moral dilemma Pendleton had faced, with the revelatory discovery of Amber Jewel's body, had been outweighed by his professional dilemma.

He was a *plagiarist*, a death knell for his career. It didn't matter that what he had plagiarized had been *mere fragments* and that his own work-in-progress had been vastly different intellectually.

Adi stood up, seeing the headlights of Holliman's Subaru coming up the long rise to the college. It was as she was turning out the lights to her office that she stopped again.

How could Pendleton have clung to a career he so despised that it had ultimately driven him to suicide? In keeping his silence, he had concealed evidence that Wright had murdered Amber Jewel, a fact that made the universe as cold and arbitrary as Pendleton had contended in *Scream*.

Adi shook her head and closed the door behind her. As she checked her mailbox, she tried not to think of the victims. When she closed her eyes, she saw instead Pendleton in that shot Wright had taken on the evening he attempted suicide.

At that moment, the two of them had been inextricably bound together.

Adi shivered again, realizing a deeper, underlying truth, that the turning point in *Scream* had been the murder of Amber Jewel, something she had experienced the first night she had read it.

The novel's true power had been born out of Pendleton inhabiting the harrowing authenticity of a child's murder. Everything had serendipitously coalesced in his mind by being forced to read Wright's novel-in-progress. The chaotic universe, in all its randomness, had come together; the spiritual and existential crisis that had dogged him for so long had finally found a stark realism in Wright's work, balancing the metaphoric nature of his own work, giving the novel the scream it needed.

As Adi left the mailroom with a bundle of interoffice correspondence and late papers from students, a question formed in her head. How did one define the sort of influence Wright had on Pendleton's *Scream*? It was a question that went to the heart of all storytelling, to the overlaying of narratives.

It was something Holliman had discussed with her with regard to his own research, the interweaving of tribal lore, of oral history, the reconstitution and transmutation of the real into artifact, into symbol, where the proprietorship of truth lay, once upon a time, *before* the printing press, with no one voice, but in the subtext of so many stories fashioned into saga, into the history of a people and an age.

Adi stopped again in the desolate hallway of the department. It was something Horowitz had admitted to her at the funeral with his characteristic smugness, co-opting and extending the vision of Pendleton's early work. Maybe that had been his particular genius all along.

Holliman beeped his horn impatiently, making Adi look up, and in those last moments as she walked the silent corridor of the English Department, she understood that, like so many storytellers before him, Pendleton, too, had instinctively tapped into the subtext of his culture, interpreting Wright's psychopathic crime as the defining metaphor for a godless age. She thought, What if he had been more like Horowitz, shared that audacity, that unflinching nerve? What if he had defended his apparent plagiarism, found a way to argue against the notion of the primacy of author as sole creator . . . anything but what he did, retreating within, sacrificing maybe not just Amber Jewel, but untold victims in his continued silence, burying along with them his own opus?

Special thanks to the following friends for their advice and support:

Benjamin Adams

Niko Aula

Steve Bamesberger

Gillian Blake

Christian and Dominique Bourgois

Sara Emerson

Rich and Teri Frantz

Helen Garnons-Williams

Carol Kennedy

Steven Kimball

Maggie McKernan

Jim and Karen Tyler

Mary Van Ness

A NOTE ON THE AUTHOR

Michael Collins is the author of six novels and two collections of short stories. His work has garnered numerous awards, including a Pushcart Award for Best American Short Stories and the Kerry Ingredients Irish Novel of the Year. His novel *The Keepers of Truth* was short-listed for the Booker Prize and the IMPAC Award. Collins is also an extreme athlete and won the Sahara Marathon and the North Pole Marathon in 2006.